The Bone Queen

ALISON CROGGON

WALKER
BOOKS

First published in Great Britain 2016 by Walker Books Ltd
87 Vauxhall Walk, London SE11 5HJ

2 4 6 8 10 9 7 5 3 1

Text © 2016 Alison Croggon
Cover illustration © 2016 Christopher Gibbs
Maps drawn by Niroot Puttapipat

This book has been typeset in Palatino and GoldenCockerel

Printed and bound in Great Britain by Clays Ltd, St Ives plc

British Library Cataloguing in Publication Data:
a catalogue record for this book is available from the British Library

ISBN 978-1-4063-6482-8

www.walker.co.uk

THE BONE QUEEN

Alison Croggon is the acclaimed author of the high fantasy series The Books of Pellinor, as well as *Black Spring*, a fantasy reworking of *Wuthering Heights*, and *The River and the Book*. Alison is an award-winning poet whose work has been published extensively in anthologies and magazines internationally. She has written widely for theatre, and her opera libretti have been produced all around Australia. Alison is also an editor and critic. She lives in Melbourne with her husband, the playright Daniel Keene.

For more information about Alison, visit:
www.alisoncroggon.com
or follow her on Twitter: @alisoncroggon

Other titles by this author

The Books of Pellinor

The Bone Queen

The Gift

The Riddle

The Crow

The Singing

Black Spring

The River and the Book

FOR MY COVEN SISTERS,
KATE ELLIOTT AND
COURTNEY SCHAFER,
WHO GOT ME THROUGH

A NOTE ON THE TEXT

IT is once again my pleasure to present to a wider general audience a classic of Annaren literature. As is the case with the *Naraudh Lar-Chanë* (*The Riddle of the Treesong*, originally published in my translation as the Pellinor quartet), *The Bone Queen* is mostly unknown outside the field of Edil-Amarandh studies, but I feel it has the capacity to delight far beyond the academic readership it now holds.

The trove of manuscripts, books and other cultural artefacts discovered in 1991, when an earthquake in the Atlas Mountains of Morocco opened up a hitherto unknown cave system, is one of the most significant archaeological finds of the twentieth century. This treasury of documents, which are in a remarkable state of preservation, has since (somewhat erroneously) become popularly known as the Annaren Scripts. They reveal the existence of a pre-modern civilization of unprecedented complexity and sophistication, occupying a continent that stretched from the polar ice fields to near the equator. To its various peoples, the continent was known as Edil-Amarandh.

It's now widely accepted that the Annaren Scripts comprise the collection that was held at the Library of Turbansk, which must have been conveyed there for preservation shortly before the catastrophe which finally destroyed this remarkable culture.

The *Naraudh Lar-Chanë* was one of the first of the Annaren Scripts to be translated in full. The story of Cadvan of Lirigon and Maerad of Pellinor's epic quest to find the Treesong in order to save their world from conquest by the Nameless One was clearly as appealing to its contemporary audience as it remains to the modern reader: since I began my own translation, laboured over between 1999 and 2008, no less than fourteen other copies have been discovered, written in Annaren, Suderain and the Speech.

As an introduction to the diverse peoples and landscapes of Edil-Amarandh, which stretched far beyond the central realm of Annar to include the highly individual cultures of the Seven Kingdoms, the nomadic collectives of the Pilanel in the north and the ancient Suderain civilization in the south, the *Naraudh Lar-Chanë* remains unparalleled. In contrast, *The Bone Queen* takes place entirely in Northern Annar, in the area bounded by the Schools of Lirigon and Pellinor, and the Osidh Elanor (the Mountains of the Dawn). The story concerns itself with an incident some fifty years before those recorded in the other four Books of Pellinor (but briefly referred to in *The Gift*), when Cadvan of Lirigon was a young man.

The Bone Queen was written in Annaren, but its original title, *Illarenen na Noroch* (*The Fading of the Light*), is in the Speech. It is a signature of Bardic-authored texts that, even if they are written in another language, they are titled in the Speech; but as with the *Naraudh Lar-Chanë*, no author is credited. This opens a rich field of speculation. Arguments have been made for Cadvan himself, Dernhil of Gent, Selmana of Lirigon or Nelac of Lirigon. My own research inclines me to the notion that it was written by Selmana, who later in life became a prominent Maker and is the confirmed author of several books (including an Annaren translation of Poryphia's *Aximidiaë*, as foreshadowed in this text). But in truth, unless further evidence comes to light, none of us can be sure.

The text, aside from its virtues as an adventure, gives us some new insights into the Bards' beliefs, in particular their theories on magery and sorcery and the eleven dimensions which they believed structured the universe. And, which is perhaps of more interest to readers of my original translation of the *Naraudh Lar-Chanë*, it is also an intimate portrait of the early years of Cadvan of Lirigon, who figures prominently in the larger events of the other Books of Pellinor.

I would like to sketch a few general notes for readers new to this remote but fascinating world. I have used the word "Bard" to translate *Dhillarearën*, which in the Speech means "Starpeople". They existed in every culture of Edil-Amarandh, but cultural conventions around Barding differed widely. Bards were people born with the Gift of magery and the ability to use the Speech. This gave them unique abilities, including a long lifespan and the capacity to speak to animals. The Speech was the language used in all spells and charms and, in Annar at least (although there is a voluminous list of writings from Annar and elsewhere which questions this rule), was considered the defining attribute of a Bard.

The Bards of Annar, as elsewhere in Edil-Amarandh, possessed both civil and spiritual authority, but it was considered a breach of the Balance (the central ethical guide of Barding) for Bards to be the sole authorities. Consequently, most regions had a double system of government – Bardic and secular, in order to check each other's excesses. In Lirigon, for example, the Thane, who figures only as a minor character in this story, was as important to governance as the First Bard, although in matters pertaining solely to the School, the Bards had final authority.

In Bards, the Speech was inborn: they never had to learn it. A Bard "came into" the Speech at some point during childhood, usually in pre-pubescence, although this appears to have varied widely. (Cadvan of Lirigon is said to have been five, while Maerad of Pellinor achieved the Speech at sixteen, which was considered unusually late.) Although it could be learned by non-Bards, and was sometimes used as a lingua franca, it only held its properties of magery when spoken by a Bard.

For those interested, the appendices in the later Books of Pellinor have more information on this fascinating civilization, the Speech, the history of Edil-Amarandh, and a list of further reading.

As ever, *The Bone Queen* is the result of the labour of many people besides myself. My husband, Daniel Keene, has once again been commendable in his provision of delicious meals at crisis points, and in his proofreading skills. I wish to thank my children, Joshua, Zoë and Ben, for their patience and support, and I'm again grateful to Richard, Jan, Nicholas and Veryan Croggon for their generous feedback. I owe a special debt to my editors, Chris Kloet and Emily Damesick, for picking up my grammatical infelicities.

None of this would have been possible without the work of colleagues who have gone before me, and who have helped me over many years. I owe particular gratitude to the profound Bardic scholarship of Kate Elliott and Courtney Schafer, who guided me through some obscure problems at a difficult point of this translation. Any oversights or errors that remain are all my own. Lastly, I would again like to acknowledge the staff of the Libridha Museum at the University of Querétaro, whose courtesy and unfailing helpfulness remain exemplary.

Alison Croggon
Melbourne, 2015

A NOTE ON PRONUNCIATION

MOST Annaren proper nouns derive from the Speech, and generally share its pronunciation. In words of three or more syllables, the stress is usually laid on the second syllable: in words of two syllables, (eg, *lembel*, invisible) stress is always on the first.

Spellings are mainly phonetic.

ae – a long sound, as in *ice*.

aë – two syllables pronounced separately, to sound *eye–ee*. *Maninaë* is pronounced Man–in–eye–ee.

au – ow. *Raur* rhymes with *sour*.

e – as in *get*. Always pronounced at the end of a word: for example, *remane*, to walk, has three syllables. Sometimes this is indicated with ë, which indicates also that the stress of the word lies on the vowel (for example, *ilë*, we, is sometimes pronounced almost to lose the *i* sound).

ea – the two vowel sounds are pronounced separately, to make the sound ay–uh. *Inasfrea*, to walk, thus sounds: in–ass–fray–uh.

eu – *oi* sound, as in *boy*.

i – as in *hit*.

ia – two vowels pronounced separately, as in the name *Ian*.

y – *uh* sound, as in *much*.

c – always a hard *c*, as in *crust*, not *ice*.

ch – soft, as in the German *ach* or *loch*, not *church*.

dh – a consonantal sound halfway between a hard *d* and a hard *th*, as in *the*, not *thought*. There is no equivalent in English; it is best approximated by hard *th*. *Medhyl* can be said Meth'l.

s – always soft, as in *soft*, not *noise*.

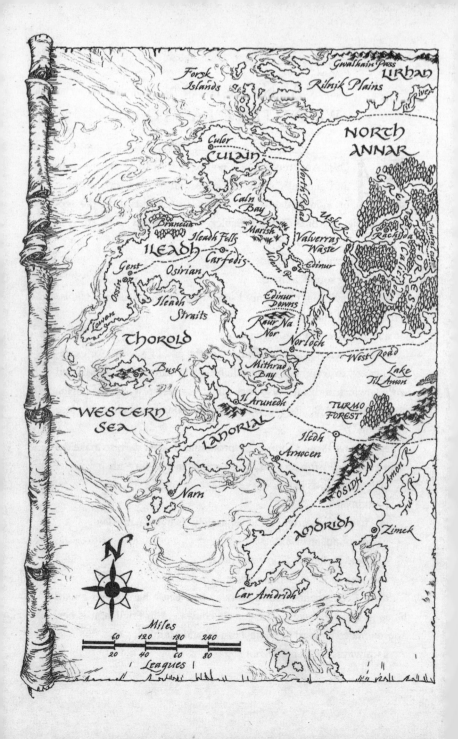

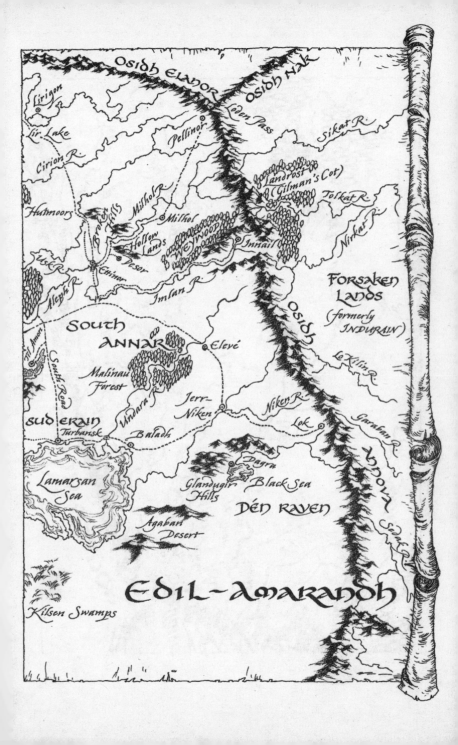

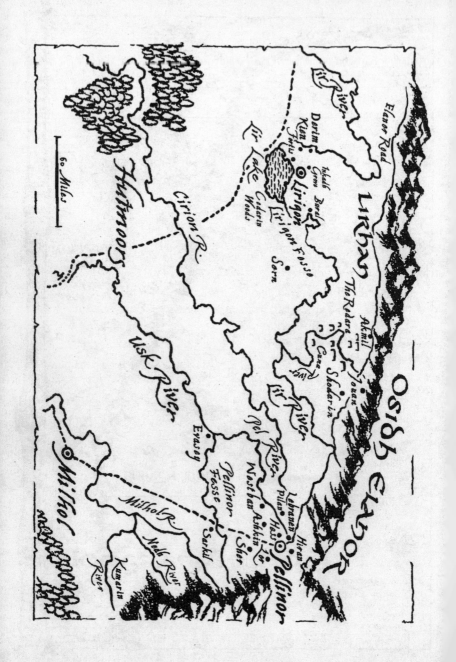

I

I

IT was towards sundown when they felt it: a shudder beneath them, as if the earth had twitched its skin. Afterwards some said that the light had flickered and briefly darkened, but what they saw was the shadow in their minds, a sudden knowledge that made their hearts stop beating for an endless moment before they started running.

One man, who was cobbling a boot on the porch outside his house in the spring sunshine, didn't run. He slowly stood up and watched the villagers racing past. He didn't stop anyone to ask what had happened: instead, he looked as if he were listening intently. He was a stranger in the village, so no one thought to pause and speak to him, but he bore them no resentment for that. Carefully, without hurry, he packed away his tools, and walked the half mile to the mine.

This man, who the villagers knew only as Cadvan, had arrived in Jouan, a small, unbeautiful mining settlement in the shadow of the northern mountains, almost three months before. He was tall and dark-haired like most of the Lirhan natives, and although he was young, perhaps in his early twenties, his manner made him seem much older. After enquiring politely whether there was need for a cobbler, and negotiating the right to live in an abandoned house on the edge of the village, he had quietly begun work. Most villagers looked at Cadvan askance as a foreigner, but they allowed that his boots were cheap and well made, and that it was useful to have a cobbler local-like, for quick repairs. His accent betrayed that he was from Lirigon, and they felt no need to question further. He in turn asked no impertinent questions of them.

Strangers were not unusual in Jouan but, unless they came seeking work in the mine, there was little reason for them to stay, and few attractions. The most common visitors were the traders who made their way to the north on carts pulled by oxen or heavy-limbed horses, to buy the coal that was piled in black heaps near the mine. As well as news from the outside world, they brought woollen cloth, leather, iron and luxuries for those who could afford them: spices from the south or a length of Thoroldian silk for a wedding dress. Coal was rarely used in Annar: it was useless for smelting ore, as its impurities spoiled the metal, but was highly prized by smiths. Jouan coal ended up in forges in Pellinor or Lirigon, or even as far afield as Baladh. For the traders, Jouan was the end of the road: the only thing north of the village was the Osidh Elanor, the high mountain range that bordered Annar. It was as far away from the world of Barding as anyone could get.

When Cadvan had first arrived, he had been appalled that people should live as the Jouains did, although he quickly found they bristled at any suggestion that they were to be pitied. The mine was a living – nobody starved, and, by their lights, the families of the best hewers were wealthy – but there was no argument that it came at a high price. Almost everyone in the hamlet worked at the mine, beginning as soon as they could climb a ladder and pull a basket. Cadvan saw very few villagers who were older than about forty years: if miners escaped the ill-chance of accidents, they were killed by lung disease and the toll of decades of back-breaking labour.

Cadvan had grown up in a place where Barding, the magery of the Light which sought knowledge in all things, was taken for granted, where illness or injury was always attended by a healer, and where human justice tempered the harsh necessities of survival. Until he left Lirigon, he had thought such customs general throughout Annar. Jouan, far from the great centres of learning, knew little of Barding, and cared less: its people had their own rites and traditions, which were nobody else's business. Ashamed of his ignorance, Cadvan was wise enough to keep his thoughts to himself. The village needed a cobbler: and so Cadvan had stayed.

As Cadvan walked up the long, bare slope to the minehead, he could see the mountains clearly before him, seeming closer than they were because of the clarity of the air. The lowering sun cast long shadows ahead. It had been a beautiful day, the first real sunshine of spring, and crocuses and daffodils were pushing up through the tussocks. A rabbit startled, and he watched its white tail bobbing up and down as it raced for its burrow. Rooks circled to their roosts and wrens called and squabbled in the hawthorn and blackberry bushes. It seemed too peaceful for catastrophe.

A few dozen onlookers were already gathered: women with babies on their hips, small children, miners who had been on the dawn shift, the tavern keeper and the smith, above-ground workers like the scramblers and pilers. They stared at the smoke that billowed out of the shaft and mounted high above them in a thick cloud, and at the broken windlass above the shaft, which creaked sadly as the terrified horse stamped and blew in its yoke, until someone unharnessed it and led it away. Some people were gathered in knots, talking urgently of what they might do now, but most stood staring at the mineshaft, waiting.

Those who had escaped the pit gathered a little distance away. They were mainly women and children, haulers who had been near the bottom of the shaft at the time of the explosion and had been able to climb out. Their eyes, the only part of them unblackened by coal dust, were shocked, blank holes in their faces. Some were injured, and the blood ran brightly, red rivers in the black grime on their skin. One man was being restrained by two others from climbing back down the shaft: he was shouting that his friends were down there, that he had to go down and get them. The others were soothing him, not attempting to argue: it was clearly impossible to enter the mine until the dust and gases had cleared.

Every detail seemed terribly sharp, outlined in the clarity of disaster. When he recalled it later, Cadvan remembered no sound: he knew that people were talking and shouting and weeping, but in his memory there was only a dreadful silence.

He turned to the man who limped up next to him, a hewer called Taran who had injured his foot a couple of days beforehand, and so had not been down the pit. Cadvan had helped him clean and bandage the deep cut, techniques that needed no magery, and had advised him to stay at home until the wound closed, or else he would face almost certain infection and the possible loss of his foot. Taran had screwed up his face at the advice, but Cadvan was glad to see that he had taken it.

"How many were down there?" he asked.

"Maybe three dozens," said Taran. His face was tight and pale. "Inshi and Hal went down this morning. Hal forgot her lunch." His expression crumpled for a moment, and Cadvan grasped his hand in sudden sympathy. Inshi and Hal were Taran's younger brother and sister. They worked as haulers, dragging the coal from the face in baskets so it could be winched up to the surface by the windlass: dirty, dangerous, body-breaking work at the best of times. If they hadn't come up by now, Cadvan thought, there was little hope that they were still alive.

Even Cadvan knew about the dangers of explosions. Gases in mines were a constant peril, but it was the firedamp that coal miners feared most. Any naked flame – even the spark of a metal tool on stone – could make it explode. That in turn could ignite the coal dust that hung thick in the air, driving a blast of fire through the pit. Deadly as that was, more people died of the bad air, the afterdamp, that followed. Cadvan thought of the people suffocating underground in the dark without hope of rescue, and shuddered.

"Maybe I can help?" said Cadvan diffidently. "At least, with those who are out. I have a few healing skills…"

Taran glanced at him, and nodded. "There's no healers here," he said. "Even a little is better than nothing."

Taking that as permission, Cadvan went to those who had escaped the mine. They were gathered together near a shed, surrounded by other villagers. He paused, suddenly shy of intruding, and approached a man who lay at the edge of the group, coughing violently.

"Can I help?" he asked the woman who held him. "I might ease the cough…"

The woman looked up at Cadvan. "You're that cobbler," she said.

"Yes," he said. "I know a bit about healing…"

The woman gave him a long, calculating look, but it was free of hostility. Then she shrugged and moved aside.

"I doubt you'll stop the coughing," she said. "When he sets off like this, it goes on and on." Cadvan knelt down and put his hand against the man's chest; underneath the convulsing coughs, he felt the rumble of diseased lungs struggling for breath. There were so many in the village like this man, withering away from the illness caused by breathing in coal dust. It killed most miners in the end. Many kept on working until they were unable to. The lucky ones found jobs overground before it was too late.

"Is he your husband?" Cadvan asked.

"Aye," she said, pushing back her hair. "Ten years we been together, Ald and me. The smoke set him off, I reckon."

Cadvan could find no injury, so he closed his eyes, sending out his Gift, trying to find the health in the blackened lungs beneath his hands. The disease was beyond his helping, beyond anyone's help; but he could ease the immediate crisis. Gradually Ald stopped coughing, and he sat up, looking at Cadvan narrowly.

"You're that cobbler," he said, echoing his wife.

"I am," said Cadvan. "But I know some other things too."

"He was sort of shining," said the woman, her voice high. "Shining, he was. It's witchcraft, that's what that is."

Cadvan turned to her, forcing himself to smile. "It's not witchcraft, but a Gift I have," he said. "He should breathe easy now."

"Shut your face, woman," said Ald. "He's a proper healer, he is. You should be thanking this gentleman here. I ain't felt this easy since I can remember."

A few people had gathered around to watch, and a buzz rose among those near by, drawing further attention. Cadvan studied the crowd, wondering if they would turn against him.

"Is there anyone else who needs healing?" he asked.

There was a visible hesitation; then a woman came forward.

"My Breta is cut bad," she said. "And she's burned by the fire."

Cadvan breathed out, realizing that in the moments before the woman stepped towards him, his whole body had clenched with anxiety. There was no reason why these people should accept him. Revealing his power here was risking suspicion and mistrust, perhaps even violence; but it ran against the grain not to help when there was such need. He nodded, and followed the woman, and began work.

Cadvan of Lirigon, Bard of Annar. Cadvan the cobbler, taking what business the miners could afford in an ugly mining settlement which had barely heard of the Light. I cannot marry these two things, thought Cadvan. And I cannot kill the Bard in me either. Unless, of course, I kill myself. And I have neither the courage nor the vanity to do such a thing. I have the despair, of course. I have plenty of that... Unconsciously, his lip curled with contempt.

He lay on his pallet in the small, patched house he now called his home and stared at the ceiling. It was very late the night after the explosion, so late that the first intimations of dawn glimmered on the horizon. He had driven himself to an exhaustion past sleep; all evening and into the night he had worked with the injured, and had comforted their families as best he could. The count was twenty-one missing and two dead. Fifteen of the missing and both the dead were hewers, all of them the main breadwinners in their families, because hewers were skilled craftsmen and bargained for the highest rates. The other six were haulers, five of them children under ten.

Sixteen had escaped the mine, and of those, eleven were injured. Healing broken limbs and superficial burns was straightforward; the sickness caused by gas and smoke was less simple but still treatable. But there were two among the survivors who had suffered a great deal worse, who had somehow used a last animal strength to climb the long ladder out of the shaft and spill onto the ground, despite serious burns that blackened their skin. Without salves or medicines, or even a modicum of hygiene, Cadvan had felt helpless: he knew that their injuries were beyond the help of healing, and that the most he could do, all he could do, was to alleviate their agony. And even that was not enough: magery could only do so much. When he first assessed the severity of their wounds, he had expected these two men to die quickly. But they had lingered on for hours, dying in the small hours of the night, before Cadvan had stumbled back to his hut, barely able to stand from weariness.

They were tough people, the Jouains: tough, proud and unruly. He had already learned to respect their stoicism; today had taught him how deep that went. The explosion was a numbing catastrophe: it meant not only deaths in almost every house in the village, but the possible destruction of their livelihoods.

The smoke had cleared from the shaft after nightfall, and the chief colliers had sent down caged finches on a rope to check the air. The birds had fallen off their perches at only one fathom. The colliers checked every hour after that, with the same result. Older miners shook their heads. Jouan had always been a safe mine, with no history of firedamp, but perhaps that had changed now. Perhaps the adits that ventilated the mine had collapsed in the blast. Perhaps the hewers had struck a large pocket of gas – firedamp or even blackdamp – that had made the entire pit noxious. Perhaps, they said, the mine would have to be abandoned altogether. Only time would tell.

Beyond listing the missing, nobody talked about the miners who were still below. There was nothing to say. They all knew that it was possible, just possible, that some had survived the blast and the poisonous airs that followed. Mining lore was full of these stories, of a desperate scramble to a lucky pocket of air, of heroic rescue against the odds, of the miracle that cheated their daily enemy, death. Every man, woman and child knew every morning that they might not return at nightfall. You could be knocked off a ladder, or just fall, as sometimes children did after a day of hauling, their hands too tired to clasp the rungs that led up to the daylight world; or a collapse of rock could stave in your head, as had happened only last month to one of the hewers; or any one of a hundred other mischances.

If anyone had survived underground today, they would be the unluckiest of all: until the damps cleared, there was no way in or out of the mine. They would die in the darkness, swiftly of the thickening air or slowly of thirst, beyond hope of rescue. Their last hours would be beyond imagining. After Nils had died, Cadvan had used his Bard sense to try to discover if there were any survivors. He set his ear to the ground and sent his Bard-born hearing as deep as it would go. He heard the groan and sweat of the earth, the slow grinding of the rock, the implacable trickle of water seeping into the mine now that the windlass was broken and could no longer pump the tunnels dry. He heard no human sound, no breath or heartbeat or cry.

He didn't tell the villagers. At first he thought he must, to save them the torture of illusory hope; but then he uneasily wondered whether he had any right to rob them of even that. The knowledge gave him some small comfort. He was as sure as he could be that no one had survived the accident, only to face the worst death of all, in the dark, alone.

If anyone deserved such a death, he thought, it was Cadvan of Lirigon. And yet he lived and breathed, facing nothing worse than his own nightmares. If any further argument was needed that the world was unjust, he would be the clinching evidence. Cadvan lived on, useless to anyone, while good people whose lives were needed, who were loved and missed, died without reason.

When sleep wouldn't come, Cadvan found himself obsessively retracing the choices that had led the rising star of the School of Lirigon, the man who had been hailed as the most gifted Bard of his generation, to his present disgrace and exile. In the bitter clarity of hindsight, there were no excuses: his own condemnation was absolute, more unforgiving even than his harshest judges in Lirigon. He had taken every step willingly and recklessly, heedless of those who had warned him... But here his mind flinched. He forced himself to finish the thought: he had been heedless even of she who loved him most, she who had paid the price for his folly as surely as if he had murdered her with his own hands. For such a crime, there was no redemption.

Sometimes, in his weaker moments, he wondered if this pit in which he found himself had been his destiny, a fate that he could not escape. It was a thought he always pushed away, as the cowardly plea of a man who would not face his own actions. All the same, the Dark had been there from the very beginning.

II

CADVAN had been raised with his four siblings by his father, Nartan, in a small Lirhan village, not far from Lirigon. He didn't attend the Lirigon School until much later than most children with the Gift. He was an attractive child, clever and quick with his hands; and he knew he was different from his brothers and sisters. He came into the Speech, the inborn tongue of magery that signalled he was a Bard, when he was about five, shortly before he lost his mother, Mertild. His father never quite recovered from the death of his wife, and was frightened of his son's precocity. He was often harsh with the boy, and when Cadvan's Gift became evident, he ordered him to tell no one. Even had he wished to, it was impossible for Cadvan to conceal it completely, and soon the whole village knew that he had the Speech.

When Cadvan was nine years old, the Lirigon Bards, as was the custom, came to Nartan's house to discuss his attendance at the School of Lirigon. Being a Bard was considered an honour in Lirhan; it was not a place where those with the Speech were shunned. Nartan was surly with the Bards, and would not hear of Cadvan attending the School. Perhaps he was reluctant to lose another member of the family, or perhaps he needed the hands of his eldest son to help with the younger children and his cobbling. The Bards told him that to leave a boy with the Gift untrained was asking for trouble, but Nartan turned a deaf ear. They said they would come the following spring and ask again, but Nartan turned his face away and would not speak another word, so they sighed and left.

Cadvan had not been allowed in the room during the visit, but he knew they were talking about him, and he eavesdropped easily enough using his listening. What he heard excited him, and he decided that he wanted to be a Bard more than anything else. His father cuffed him and told him to get on with his work.

After that, Cadvan conceived a great resentment against his father. He began to run wild, leading other children on his escapades. It was nothing very harmful: raiding orchards, throwing stones and other such mischief as occurs to small boys. Because he had the Gift, he could go hidden and speak to animals, which gave him the edge in their pranks. He was stretching his powers, but his use of them was wilful. His behaviour worried his aunt, his mother's sister Alina, who had a little of the Gift herself and was a perceptive woman; and she spoke again to Nartan, telling him he ought to send the boy to the School.

Nartan was a stubborn man, and he said he would not agree to his first-born going away. Alina told him he was a fool and was breeding problems for himself, but he wouldn't listen. The truth was that Nartan burned with a greedy love for his son, a love that he could not admit even to himself, and he could not face letting him go. It was often said that Cadvan was very like his mother.

One day, when Cadvan was about ten, a stranger came to the village on a black horse. He was tall and severe-looking, and he was dressed in rich clothes. He went straight to the cobbler's house, demanding that a strap on his horse's bridle be fixed at once. Nartan was not at home, so Cadvan took the job. Cadvan saw that the stranger's horse was ill-treated; its mouth was bleeding. This angered him, and he spoke to the man without respect.

"If you were more gentle with your hands," he said, "the strap would not be broken."

The stranger told the boy to hold his tongue, and then examined him more closely. What he saw interested him, and he asked his name. Concentrating on mending the bridle, Cadvan answered sullenly, not liking to be questioned. Finally, the stranger asked him if he had the Speech. Cadvan looked up swiftly, and took a long time to answer. At last he nodded.

"Why are you not at the School?" asked the stranger.

"My father will not let me."

The stranger heard the resentment in the boy's voice, and smiled to himself. He picked up a pebble from the ground and tossed it in his hand.

"How might I make this pebble fly, boy?" he said.

Cadvan shrugged. "Throw it," he said.

"Aye. Or give it wings." As Cadvan watched, the pebble turned into a butterfly and flew away.

Cadvan knew that illusions were the least of charms. "It's a trick," he said scornfully. "I haven't time for silly games."

The stranger laughed. "My name is Likod," he said. "I will be back." Then he mounted his horse and rode away. Cadvan stood in the road and watched him until he was out of sight.

The meeting disturbed him. He didn't like the stranger, and he liked even less the way he treated his horse; yet there was a fascination about him too that made him deeply attractive. For the next few weeks he waited for Likod to return, but he did not; and after a while Cadvan decided that he hadn't meant what he said. The conversation had made him curious, and he began to experiment more widely with the simpler enchantments – glimmerspells and other mageries of illusion.

Time passed, and Cadvan grew into a handsome boy. Every spring the Bards of Lirigon would ride to speak with his father, and every year his father spurned their offer. And every year the boy grew wilder.

It was around this time that the Bards of Lirigon began to be concerned about some disturbing, if small, incidents; and one of these happened to Cadvan. There were stories that shapeshifting wers had been seen in the wild lands near the Osidh Elanor, and rumours even of Hulls, the Black Bards who had traded their Names for eternal life, who had not been seen in Annar since the Great Silence. Also at this time, the raids of the Jussack clans pushed the Pilanel people out of their traditional summer grazing lands in the Arkiadera, and the chief of the Pilanel came south over the Osidh Elanor and asked the Lirhan Bards and Thane for permission to graze their herds in the northern Rilnik Plains.

Cadvan knew little of these things, although of course he heard gossip. Sometimes he would sit with his father at the inn and listen restlessly while the greybeards spoke darkly of bad portents. At such times, he would yearn to be at the School of Lirigon, because then, as he thought, he would learn great mageries, and would fight these evil things and be the hero he was meant to be. But he knew better than to mention his wish to his father. Sometimes he thought of running away to Lirigon, but despite his fierce desire, he could not abandon his father. And so he learned the trade of cobbling, and frittered away his spare hours thinking up new pranks to amuse himself and his companions. And all the time, a deep bitterness was nursing itself inside him.

One day, five years later, the stranger did return. Cadvan was working outside the house and he saw him riding through the village, looking neither right nor left. He stood up and watched the rider. The man glanced sideways at Cadvan as he passed the house, and pulled up his horse.

"Still here then, boy?" he said, with a touch of scorn.

Cadvan flushed and looked away.

The stranger dismounted and stared at Cadvan. "You'll be a man soon," he said. "And yet you still let your father tie you to his house? The world is big, my boy. You don't belong here."

He said no more than what Cadvan already thought, but the boy's face darkened at the man's mockery of his father. "I am with my own people," he said angrily. "Who are you, to speak thus to me?"

"You know my name," said the man. "Unless you are more stupid than I thought."

Cadvan wanted to deny it, but he did know his name. "Likod," he said, unwillingly.

Likod looked pleased. "So you have some wit. Or some memory," he said. "You have the Gift: from here I can see it is in you in no small measure. Why haven't the Bards of Lirigon taken you to where you should be? They betray their duty. Your training is no business of your father's."

Cadvan had no answer, because he had sometimes wondered the same thing. But Bards will not teach children with the Gift if their parents do not permit it.

"Come with me," said Likod. "I have something to show you. Your father is away from home, he will not know."

Cadvan wondered how Likod knew his father was out. Then he said, "I have to finish mending this boot. You can come back later, if you want."

Likod made to move away, but Cadvan would not go anywhere until he had finished his task. He bent his head down and concentrated on his work, ignoring the stranger. When he finished, Likod was still waiting for him.

Cadvan met his eyes and shrugged, as if he didn't care. He slowly put away his tools, and stood up to follow the stranger.

Likod led him out of the village and a short distance into a beech wood. It was high summer, and the light shone bravely on the leaves, but where Likod walked it seemed that a shadow followed him and the birdsong sank into silence. Cadvan felt fear settle inside him, and he began to feel sorry that he had come. But despite his doubts, he kept on following.

At last Likod stopped in a small clearing. He turned and smiled at Cadvan.

"Now," he said. "I will show you something you have never seen before."

He gestured and spoke some words that Cadvan didn't understand, and between them there began to gather a darkness, as if Likod were making a hole in the air. Cadvan now was very afraid and wanted to cry out, but his tongue stuck to the roof of his mouth and he could make no sound, and his feet were rooted to the ground. He was no longer aware of the woods or the sunshine around him: he could only watch the shadow gathering before his eyes.

The blackness thickened and roiled, and he heard a noise like rushing wind or water. And then, to his astonishment, Cadvan saw a picture form before his eyes: and the picture moved and was alive. It was of a glittering city, with graceful walls and towers, which stood by a great mere so still that stars were reflected on its surface. The city was built of white stone that shone as if it were carved of moonlight. It seemed to Cadvan that he entered the city and walked around inside it like a ghost, and that he peered through casements and saw men and women in fine robes speaking together, or making beautiful things; but none of them saw him.

The vision passed, and Cadvan came to, as if out of a swoon. Likod let down his arms, and the darkness disappeared. Cadvan stared at him with amazement.

"What is that place?" he asked.

"It is a place that is no longer," said Likod. "By my art, you glimpsed the ancient citadel of Afinil, which has been gone for many lives of men. Is that not wonderful?"

"Aye," said Cadvan, caught in enchantment. He hungered to see more. "What else can you show me?"

As Cadvan had suspected, Likod's aims were not benevolent. He was pleased that he had enraptured the boy, because he did not want him to be fearful. He had seen that Cadvan had a rare and untrained talent, and he wished to bind him, so the boy would be his slave.

Now that Cadvan was no longer wary of him, Likod lifted his arms again and put forth his power. But this time the spell was different, and Cadvan didn't like it; he felt that chains of smoke were winding around his thoughts, and he felt the stranger's voice inside his head, as if Likod's thoughts were his own. He thought that he would die from the black pressure in his mind.

Now Cadvan showed his native power, because he looked Likod in the eye, and, untrained as he was, he resisted the spell that would have imprisoned him. When Likod felt his powers so directly challenged, he was shaken; and he tried then to capture him by force, and abduct him on his horse. Even at fifteen, Cadvan was stronger than Likod, and he punched him in the face and knocked him over, and found in his panic such magery to strike him senseless. Then he stole Likod's horse and bolted away as fast as he could.

He didn't go home. Instead he rode to the School of Lirigon, which was more than a league away, and he didn't stop until he clattered into the courtyard and almost fell off the sweating horse. Nelac of Lirigon himself came running out to see what the disturbance was, and took the sobbing boy into his house and calmed him down. Nelac then rode to Cadvan's village and spoke for a long time to Nartan: and after that, Cadvan entered the School, and no more was said about cobbling.

And so, thought Cadvan, began the brilliant career of Cadvan of Lirigon. He had heard this story told so many times that he no longer knew whether it was true. It was part of the myth he had constructed around himself: even as an untutored boy, he had outwitted the Dark! He now wondered at his own vanity, his transparent folly. What troubled him most of all was that he couldn't really remember, from the inside. He could see the boy that he had been, but he seemed a mere puppet; it was as if those things had happened to another person, in another age of the world. He no longer remembered what that boy had felt; he could remember the colour of sunlight but not its warmth on his skin. His memories were like pictures in a book, that someone else had written to pass the time.

III

IN the days after the accident, Cadvan spent his waking
hours attending to the injured. He drove himself pitilessly,
answering every request made of him; it was two days
before he had any sleep at all. He was discomforted to find
himself acting as a counsellor and comforter to the bereaved:
it was a role to which he felt deeply unsuited. Words wouldn't
rise to his tongue: easy comfort in such a time felt like a lie. His
taciturn sympathy suited the villagers, who, although he didn't
realize it, respected him for it as much as for his unstinting care
of the injured.

He bitterly felt his inadequacy in the face of what was
needed: he saw only the pain he couldn't remove, the infection he couldn't entirely cleanse, the burns that he couldn't
heal. Healing hadn't been among the first of his interests at
Lirigon, and he cursed the shallowness and limitations of his
knowledge. He thought the silence of those he cared for was
a courteous cover for the same harsh criticisms he made of
himself, but it was simply that the Jouains were not given to
effusive gratitude. Instead, when he finally took himself to bed
and slept for sixteen hours, he woke up to find on his doorstep four eggs, a meat pastry and six golden apples hoarded
from the previous year's harvest, the first of many anonymous
offerings. He couldn't have borne to be thanked for a task he
thought botched and poor, but he was grateful for the food and
the delicacy of the villagers' tact.

The damps began to clear two days later, defying the

bleakest predictions that the mine would be forced to close. After the windlass was repaired and a makeshift ventilator erected, a party cautiously went down to explore the mine, and to begin the melancholy task of bringing out the bodies. The remains were winched up on a canvas sling, to be returned to those who gathered, with a patient, silent dignity, by the mine-head. Cadvan joined the whole village there when the first party went down, in case he might be needed; but when it was clear that the miners rescued only the dead, he didn't return. His work was with the living.

Most of all, he couldn't bear to witness the stunned grief that hit when all hope of hope collapsed. Many Jouains, no matter how grim the chances, no matter how rationally they knew there was no possibility of survival, clung to a secret belief that those missing were still alive, until the moment they saw the body come out of the shaft. To make things worse, the waterlogged corpses were sometimes unrecognizable: a few still kept hoping until twenty-one bodies made twenty-one deaths unarguable.

The first to be brought up was Taran's brother, Inshi: laid out on a bier, his corpse seemed tiny, like a broken bird. Taran, his face expressionless, went up to claim the body. Cadvan watched him walking beside the bier as two miners carried it down the hill to the village, and wished passionately that there was some comfort he could offer; but seeing Taran's rigid shoulders, braced against pain, speech died in his throat.

He liked Taran, who lived next door with his siblings: he was a tall, heavily muscled man with a deep fund of kindness. When Cadvan had first arrived in Jouan, he had dealt with Taran to buy the house, which had belonged to Taran's child-less uncle, who had lately died from the lung disease. Although he hadn't been asked, Taran had helped Cadvan to patch its walls and roof so it was weatherproof, laughingly brushing aside offers of payment. Although he had only recently reached manhood, he was a skilled hewer, the leader of his gang and the main breadwinner for his family. Both his parents were dead, his father the year before from a rockfall in the mine, his mother from a wasting sickness shortly afterwards.

Later, after Inshi's burial, Cadvan haltingly gave his condolences. Taran grasped Cadvan's hand, his eyes lit with sorrow. "Poor lad," he said. "Nine summers was all he had. An imp, he was. I'll miss him." His voice caught.

Cadvan cleared his throat, thinking of the mischievous boy he had glimpsed running past his door. "At least Hal got out," he said at last. Hal, a quicksilver girl a few years older than Inshi, had barely suffered a scratch.

"Aye. Aye. The best of friends, those two were, Inshi and Hal. You'd have thought they sprang from the same egg." Taran's face darkened with memory, and then he looked up, his mouth set firmly against his grief. "Truth be told, we were much luckier than some. If I hadn't cut my foot, I'd have been down there too. And how I cursed my luck at the time! Indira Huna lost her whole family, father, mother, brothers…"

Indira was blind, and had never worked in the mine. Cadvan had seen her walking around the village, feeling her way with a stick, although he had never had the occasion to speak to her. She was startlingly fair, her unseeing eyes dark and blank in her thin face, and was delicately built compared to most Jouains. Without a family to support her, she would find it difficult to survive. Taran looked sideways at Cadvan, and said, as if confessing something shameful, that he had asked Indira to live with his family.

"She is good with her hands, and a famous cook," he said. "So it would benefit both of us."

Cadvan met his eyes. "It's a kindness, too."

"Nay, I could do with the help in the house," he said. "The baby is walking now, and getting into all sorts of trouble…"

Cadvan smiled, and clasped Taran's shoulder briefly before moving off. All the furniture in Taran's main room had been shifted out of the front door to make space for the funeral meal, but despite this, the house was so crowded that exiting was difficult. On his way out, Cadvan glimpsed Hal, curled up at the top of the stairway, her dark head propped on her knees, broodingly watching the throng. She looked up and by chance met his eye: the desolation he saw in her face made Cadvan's breath rush out of him. She flinched, and Cadvan was abashed that he had unwittingly caught her in such private feeling. To cover his embarrassment, he gave her a brief, formal nod, and after a pause, she nodded back, her expression veiled.

Cadvan paid his respects at every burial, although he didn't know most of the dead and stood among the mourners as the stranger that he was. It seemed as if the burials would never stop, although in truth they were all over in a few days. Once the wakes and blessings were done, the village began to return to its normal rhythm.

There was a meeting among the gang leaders, who constituted the informal council that ran the mine. The miners had found no trace of firedamp, and they concluded that they had hit an unlucky pocket of gas. After much discussion, they decided to close the tunnel where the explosion had happened, and to follow another seam. The main problem they now faced was a much-reduced workforce. The only reason the toll hadn't been higher was because mining occurred in two shifts, morning and afternoon, to allow the miners some daylight hours in which to cultivate the gardens which produced most of their food.

After some impassioned argument – the rights to a mine were jealously guarded – the council decided to send news to Akmil and Shodarin, nearby mining settlements where some of them had relatives or associates, that there was room for five new teams. Jouan produced the highest quality coal in the region, the hard, black anthracite that was most sought by smiths, and that would attract interest. There would soon be newcomers in Jouan.

It seemed to Cadvan that routine asserted itself with astonishing rapidity. Once the mine was working again, it was as if nothing had changed. Only the twenty-three raw graves in the cemetery remained to tell of the catastrophe; and by summer even they were gentled by new grass.

The accident marked a sharp change in the villagers' attitude towards Cadvan: although he would always be regarded as a stranger, it was as if the village had breathed out and accepted him. It was nothing very obvious, but it made him realize, not without an inner sneer at his weakness, how much he had missed being part of a community. People who had previously given him the barest nod in passing now greeted him by name; when he went to the local tavern, his entrance no longer caused a brief silence. Sometimes the miners would invite him to drink with them, and he accepted out of courtesy, although he preferred to drink alone.

The Jouains were too polite to question him directly, but after the revelation of his powers, Cadvan became the object of lively curiosity. He was for a time the major topic of discussion in the hamlet, an interest only made sharper by his deep reserve. They judged that he could be no more than twenty years of age (in truth he was nearer thirty, but their work burned youth from the Jouains early, and men of Cadvan's age already looked old). Despite his youth, he carried the gravity of a much older man. He seldom smiled, and almost never laughed. It was generally agreed that he would be off one day, but for the moment he showed no sign of moving on.

Cadvan's black moods made the villagers wary of him, but they also earned him a curious respect. They treated him as one of their own afflicted, like Mad Truwy, who had to be avoided in his fits but otherwise was a good man. These moods happened every few weeks. In their grip, Cadvan didn't leave his house for days on end. The first time he didn't appear, it was thought he might have died in his sleep, and Taran, as his known friend, was sent in to check. He emerged quickly, and afterwards wouldn't say what he had seen, aside from roughly telling the inquisitive to leave Cadvan alone. Several children, daring each other, climbed the apple tree next to his house and peeped through his bedroom window to see what he was doing. They all reported the same thing: he was lying in his bed like a dead man, staring at the ceiling.

Cadvan emerged from these seclusions pale and haggard, and headed straight for the tavern. There he stood for hours in the corner, drinking mug after mug of the harsh apple spirit without showing any sign of drunkenness. The tavern keeper, Jonalan, said that in those moments he feared to speak to him: he looked like a man haunted by death. The next day he would be normal again.

It would have been considered the height of bad manners to pry into Cadvan's affairs when he clearly wished them to remain private, so the villagers were forced to shrewd guesses. It was clear that Cadvan was, or had been, a Bard, now fallen on hard times. The mean-minded thought that he had a Dark Past, and suggested that a terrible crime had exiled him from his kind; but general sympathy endowed him with Tragedy. Others, making the sign against evil, ventured that he was cursed. None of these guesses was so far from the truth, but the rumours gave him an unlikely glamour. Some of the local girls noted how handsome he was, and would greet him prettily in the road as he passed.

Fortunately for his peace of mind, Cadvan was oblivious to this speculation: if he had known how keenly he was discussed, he would have been deeply embarrassed. But the village gossip moved on after a month or so. Five new gangs from Shodarin, six families in all, provided plenty of new material; and then the talk died away altogether in the flare of a scandal that dominated the village all summer. It was discovered that Jorvil, whom everybody knew beat his wife, had been cheating his team, selling his coal for a higher price than he told his gangers and keeping the difference. He was lucky not to be murdered for it: such behaviour betrayed the core of the miners' code of honour. The verbal bargains struck with a gang leader were considered sacred.

Using his authority as a disinterested outsider, Cadvan arbitrated the dispute without bloodshed, hammering out a settlement that everyone (except Jorvil, who smarted under a sense of ill-usage) agreed was just. Cadvan privately considered that the most important part of his judgement was the condition which stipulated that if Jorvil hit his wife again, he would be run out of the village. Such violence was uncommon in Jouan, and the villagers considered it shameful and unmanly; but for all that, men were seldom punished for it, as it was considered a private matter. Perhaps, thought Cadvan, that might change. He hoped so. The previous week he had treated Jorvil's wife for a broken nose and bruises, and the fear in her eyes had set a cold anger in his bones.

By now, Cadvan the Bard in Exile was old news. He was an unremarkable, if slightly odd, part of the village landscape. His days were undemanding, but surprisingly full: like everyone else, he grew much of the food he ate, and there was the cobbling, and villagers routinely came to him for healing. He flatly refused payment for the healing, and so was often paid, anonymously, in kind. One memorable morning he woke up to find a nanny goat tethered to his porch, ruminatively chewing on some valuable leather he had unaccountably left out the night before.

Cadvan, who felt no need for a goat, sighed heavily, untied her from the porch and told her sternly in the Speech that she was not to eat his leather. She stared at him through her slotted eyes, and pointed out that if there were proper eating in reach, she would have no need for leather. He and the goat, whom he named Stubborn, struck a bargain: and thereafter she remained both untethered and (to the rest of the villagers, who were well-used to the depredations of goats) a mysteriously virtuous model of ovine behaviour. Certainly, although Stubborn occasionally lapsed and forced her way through a fence into a neighbour's garden, Cadvan's unprotected leeks and turnips remained untouched.

To stave off an encroaching boredom, Cadvan began to teach the village midwife, Eka, some healing techniques that needed no magery, and which would help her arts. Then somehow, towards the end of summer, he was teaching Hal as well. She had an innate talent, and she told him she would far rather be a healer than work down the mine. As autumn slid into winter, and then winter lifted into another spring, he realized, not without a grim humour, that despite himself he had begun to put down roots.

One morning in the early spring, Cadvan woke and lay staring into the darkness. He could feel the time in his bones: it was the icy hour before dawn, too late to turn to sleep again. He thought of rising to light a candle, but the air was freezing and his body was stupid with the remnants of sleep. Instead he set a magelight hovering above his head. Its blue, edgeless light bloomed against the walls, still bare, after all these months, of any decoration. He was possessed by an almost unbearable ache of nostalgia: how long since he had practised this trivial act of magery?

The dream that had wakened him refused to fade; instead,

grief thickened in his throat. This dream had been different from his usual nightmares, more vivid and somehow more real, even though his nightmares were full of terrible memories of things that had actually happened to him. And the sorrow it left in its wake was of a different kind: keener and deeper and larger. His suffering was a small thing, after all: when he died, it would die with him. The spring would succeed winter, the earth would burgeon with increase, bringing its gifts of life and death. Yet in his dream he had walked through a world in which the seasons were broken and the oceans were dying; he had seen dead lakes of strange, toxic colours covered with dark clouds of flies, and deserts, wasted by war and poison, where nothing lived, stretching further than eyes could see. There could be no consolation in such a world: a human life was vain, and its death meaningless.

Now he stared sightlessly before him, trying to shake off the horror of his nightmare. What if there were no spring, what if winter were endless? What if the song died in the throat of every lark, if the cuckoo no longer returned from its sojourn in the south, if the thawing waterways no longer sprang with breeding salmon and thick tangles of frogspawn, if the leaves fell in the forests and no greening answered their fall?

He took a deep breath and exhaled, watching the vapour curling white before his face. What had he dreamed? A vision of a world beyond healing, of the death of the Balance. A dream, he told himself. Only a dream… A thought struck him, and he almost laughed: perhaps his mind had drawn a likeness of his own soul, grown to encompass the entire earth. Ah, the petty egotism of Bards. Perhaps he would never be rid of his vanity.

At last he got out of bed, wincing against the bitter air, and shrugged a thick woollen cloak over his underclothes. He thought of blinking out the magelight – since his arrival in Jouan, he had refused to use magery of any kind, aside from healing – but he hesitated, and left it to follow him down the stairs. He lit a fire in the kitchen, again using magery. Its warmth quickly filled the room, and he sat down, looking about the house that had been his home for the past five seasons as if he was seeing it for the first time.

It was a far cry from the Bard rooms he had once taken for granted as his own, but it had a humble beauty. The house consisted of two rooms, one upstairs and one down. He and Taran had patched the broken roof and replastered the walls with lime, and there he had left his decorating. He possessed the minimum of furniture: there was a large pine table that he had bought from the local carpenter, two low stools, a bench and a cupboard. On the table was a clay bowl, in which lay six brown eggs, a loaf of dark bread and a big bunch of spring greens he had gathered the day before. A bowl of early apricots that someone had left on his doorstep sat on the cupboard, next to his neatly arranged cobbling tools and some curious pieces of black coal imprinted with the outlines of leaves that he had collected to study. Dry bunches of herbs, grown for medicine and cooking, hung from the ceiling and filled the room with their fragrance. It was enough. It was more than enough.

What he missed most of all was books. He had brought none with him, and there was no means of buying any in Jouan. Writing was unknown: miners kept track of their labour by making notches in sticks, and bargains were struck with a word and a handclasp, and stories told over firesides or remembered in song. Cadvan had a book of paper and a pen, hoarded in his cupboard, that he had brought with him from Lirigon, but he hadn't thought about writing since he had been here. It was part of the life he had laid aside. He still had his lyre, which was as much a part of him as music, but he kept it upstairs, hidden in a chest: no one in the village even knew he could play. He knew another musician in the village would be welcomed –

the Jouains loved music – but to play would have pained him, reminding him too much of everything he had lost.

He sat unmoving in the kitchen for a long time, watching the light creeping across the floor. For once, his sorrow didn't fill him with anger and self-contempt. He realized he no longer saw Jouan as an ugly, dull settlement: it was a place of complex life, of deep lore, of profound loyalties and relationships, which were no less significant than anything a Bard might study in the grand libraries of the Schools. There seemed no reason why he might not remain in Jouan for years. He might, after all, make something of his life that wasn't a lie.

IV

NELAC of Lirigon, Bard of the First Circle, foremost scholar of the Speech, famed healer and mage, stifled a sigh and stared down at the table that ran the length of the meeting hall in the School of Lirigon. Cut from a single cedar trunk centuries before and constructed with impeccable craftsmanship, it was a thing of rare beauty shown to visitors as one of the city's treasures, but Nelac was long used to its marvels. He wondered how many hours of his life had been spent sitting around this very table, listening politely to self-important fools drone on about matters of which they knew little and cared less.

Too many hours, he thought. Even a Bard's life, long as it was compared to others, was finite. And surely no life was long enough to compensate for the compound of tedium, exasperation and sheer, grinding depression that swept through him now. Noram of Ettinor had been speaking for the past hour, in a voice that might have been precisely judged to induce the nicest balance of boredom and irritation in its hearers. He was a thin, small-mouthed Bard who had built his scholarly reputation on an astounding ability to collect mountains of obscure facts, which he then arranged, thought Nelac, without the smallest skerrick of insight.

"In short," said Noram at last (here Nelac involuntarily smiled), "there is no reason whatsoever to reconsider judgement in this matter of Cadvan of Lirigon. As I have demonstrated in detail, there is no precedent in the *Paur Libridha* of Maninaë nor in any subsequent constitution of any of the Schools of Annar that warrants appeal against the sentence of exile for dealings with the enemy. I leave it to my learned colleagues in the Light to consider the evidence I have here compiled. More, I would suggest to those who would treat these traditions with disdain and contempt, that it is just these seemingly inconsequential examples of disregard that lead to the corruption of the Light. From such small beginnings grow the larger breaches, as the tiny breach in a dam portendeth flood."

Noram allowed himself a small, smug smile at this final flourish, and sat down. A number of Bards nodded and a couple clapped, but at least one of them, Nelac noticed, was doing so to cover the fact that she had dozed off. Nelac glanced at Milana, First Bard of Pellinor, who like Noram had travelled long and far to be at this meeting; she was pale with anger, her face carefully blank. Noram had supposedly been answering her, and his speech had been a calculated insult in the way it either brushed off or totally ignored her arguments.

In the silence that followed, Nelac accidentally caught the eye of Calis of Eledh, who sat opposite him. Her face too was expressionless: all the same, Nelac knew that she shared his stunned indignation. For a moment, seeing an answering sparkle in her eye, he wanted to laugh. Then he stood up.

"I have only one thing to say," he said. "My 'learned colleague' has indeed illuminated us with a legal history of the Schools, back to their very foundations. But he has traced a very different history from that outlined by Milana. For example, I find it curious that in all his learning there has not been one mention of the Way of the Heart. If we are to honour our traditions, as Milana reminds us, it is this tradition above all that Maninaë adjured us to observe. Is it not said, on the opening page of the *Paur Libridha*, that the Way of the Heart is the keystone of all knowledge? And did not Maninaë also say that a

Bard without compassion is no Bard at all, since love is the key
to insight, and knowledge without insight is an empty husk
which nourisheth not the body nor the mind nor the soul?"

Noram flushed with anger, but before he could say anything, the other Bard bowed.

"I must now beg your indulgence," Nelac said. "I have even
now an appointment for which I am unforgivably late, as this
meeting has continued much longer than I realized it would.
I ask your pardon, but I must leave. I have nothing further to
add to what I've already said, and you all know my decision
on this question. I ask Calis to register my vote in my absence."

Calis nodded gravely, and the Bards watched Nelac in
silence as he left the room and the heavy doors swung shut
behind them. No one saw Nelac of Lirigon, Bard of the First
Circle, foremost scholar of the Speech, famed healer and
mage, viciously kick the wall outside in an uncharacteristic
eruption of fury. He stood there for some time, breathing
hard, staring blindly at the stone, until a student passing by
on some errand jogged him out of his abstraction. He turned
to leave and only realized then how badly he had hurt his
foot: he could hardly walk.

The student paused and asked if she could help. Nelac
smiled ruefully.

"I seem to have had a foolish accident," he said. "I may have
broken a toe. I'd be grateful for your shoulder, if you could
manage that. My rooms are not far away…"

It was, as Nelac had said, only a short walk to his rooms in
the Bardhouse, but by the time he arrived, leaning heavily on
his helper's shoulder, he was sweating with effort. Luckily
the young Bard was strong: she was as tall as Nelac, broad-
shouldered and well muscled, and her red, curly hair was
cropped short. In answer to his polite queries, she told Nelac her

name was Selmana, that she was seventeen years old and had been at the School for six years, and that she studied the Making with Calis.

As they entered, Selmana looked around with ill-concealed curiosity: in all her years in Lirigon, she had never been inside Nelac's sanctum. It was a dull midwinter day and, aside from the grey light that filtered through the latticed windows, a fire crackling in a small hearth was the only illumination. Rich colours leapt in the shadows. Three couches were arranged around a low table by the hearth; they were covered in vivid crimson silk, echoing a hanging on the opposite wall that was worked in rich reds and blues. The other walls were shelved to the ceiling, and glowed with the gilt bindings of books and a myriad of curious objects: brass astrolabes and quadrants; zithers and lyres and flutes; a collection of unusual stones, steel-blue celestite and silver pyrite and rose quartz crystal. A table in the centre of the room was piled with scrolls and books and drifts of paper.

Selmana assisted Nelac onto one of the couches, and he breathed out with relief. "I think we could do with some light," he said. "Would you mind…?"

She saw a lamp by the low table and lit it with a word. It made the day outside seem even gloomier: although it was only mid-afternoon, the sky was heavily overcast.

"I swear it's going to rain," she said, to fill the silence.

Nelac grunted, glumly easing off his sandal and inspecting his foot. His little toe was poking out at an odd angle and was already turning black. He studied it dispassionately, and then, grimacing, set the toe straight. Once it was at the correct angle he pressed his hand over the foot. For a few moments he glowed with Bardic light. He set his foot on the floor, testing, and winced.

"Ah, well," he said. "Too much to hope that the bruising

would vanish, but at least I can walk now. It's astonishing that breaking something as tiny as a toe can be so crippling."

Selmana had been watching him interestedly. "Did you mend the bone?" she asked. "I can't do that. I broke my toe once and I couldn't walk for weeks."

Nelac smiled. "Easy enough, when you've had as much practice as I have. I hope yours wasn't as absurd an accident as mine."

"Me, I kicked an anvil because my father wouldn't let me be a smith," she said. "And I was really, really angry."

"How old were you?" asked Nelac.

"I think I was about eight."

"I kicked the wall because I was really, really angry," said Nelac. "But I am twenty-two times older than you were, so I have no excuse at all."

The girl's eyebrows shot up, and she looked faintly shocked. Nelac was far too old and serious a Bard to have such a tantrum.

"Oh," she said blankly.

"But I forget my courtesy," said Nelac. "My thanks for helping me. So Calis is your mentor, eh? A fine Bard, Calis. And a great Maker."

"Oh, she is!" said Selmana, her face lighting with sudden passion. "I don't know if I'll ever make things as beautiful as Calis does, but maybe one day... And I have to learn all these other things, and I'm not very good at the Reading. All those books!" She rolled her eyes in comic dismay, and Nelac laughed.

"I suppose she's given you Poryphia's *Aximidiaë*?" Nelac named a huge tome, the standard authority on working ore and metals.

"She did. It's hard going, you know. So big! But I expect you've read it through and through..." Selmana suddenly recalled that she was speaking to one of the most important

Bards in all Annar, and blushed vividly. "I'm sorry, I shouldn't
– I'm taking up your time—"

"Should you be elsewhere?"

"Well, not really…"

"If not, perhaps you would like to share a wine with me. I
have nothing important to do either. I told the Council I had
an urgent meeting, but I lied. I had to escape, or I would have
strangled someone."

Selmana gave Nelac a long, frank look. "You're not at all
what I imagined," she said at last. "You always look so…" She
stumbled, and blushed again.

"So…?"

"Oh, you know, important, and solemn, and serious."

"I am certainly all of those things," said Nelac gravely. "And
I would thank you to keep any reports of my solemnity and
seriousness unsullied."

At this, Selmana laughed out loud. Nelac limped over to a
table on which stood a green bottle stoppered with a large cork.

"I think we deserve something special, no?" he said, turning
to smile at Selmana as he twisted the cork and drew it from the
neck. He poured out two glasses of straw-coloured wine, handing one to Selmana. She sipped it hesitantly, and wrinkled her
nose. Nelac regarded her with amusement.

"It's an excellent wine, you know," he said. "It's made from
the white grapes picked on the slopes of Til Amon, which are
justly renowned for their flavour."

"The bubbles went up my nose," she said. "But it is nice."
She paused, and then spoke in a rush. "Were you are that meeting … it was about Cadvan, wasn't it? Did they decide to – are
they going to let him come back?"

"I don't know," said Nelac. "I left before the vote. And even
if they did, I don't know whether he would return. Do you
think we should allow him to?"

Selmana looked surprised at being asked, and then frowned, seriously considering the question. "If it were up to me? Yes, I think so. He did wrong things, and terrible things happened. And on top of that, many people don't like him, because they say he is arrogant and vain. And he *is*, you know. That doesn't make him a – a bad person. There are lots of Bards much more vain than him."

"Do you know him?" asked Nelac.

"I wasn't a friend of his, but I did, a little. Ceredin was my cousin…" A deep sadness flickered over Selmana's face. Nelac, his attention arrested, glanced at her sharply, and then looked away. There was a long silence.

"I miss Ceredin, so much. Every day I miss her." Selmana swallowed hard. "She – we are the only Bards in the family, and she looked after me, when I first came here and it was so strange. When she was killed, I hated Cadvan. I thought no punishment would atone for what he had done."

"And yet you believe he should be allowed to return?"

Selmana met Nelac's eyes. "I didn't think so for a long time. He wanted to talk to me, after, but I wouldn't speak to him, not for a whole year. But one morning I woke up, and it seemed clear to me. Ceredin came to me in a dream. And I remembered that she really loved Cadvan, and he really loved her. And she wouldn't have loved him like that without reason. She wasn't – foolish…"

"Ceredin was one of the most gifted Bards I have taught," said Nelac gruffly.

"She was kind. She was one of the kindest people I ever knew. I know what she would say. She would say that sending Cadvan away won't bring her back. Nothing will ever bring her back. And everything that happened was just a horrible accident…"

"Ceredin's death was wholly caused by Cadvan's folly, and

worse, by his dealing with the Dark," said Nelac, his voice hard. "Were it not for that, she would be alive today."

"I know." Selmana frowned again. "That's exactly what he said to me, before he went away. He came to tell me – to say sorry. He said he understood there could be no forgiveness, that no punishment was enough. Maybe he's right. But exiling him for ever seems – it's such a waste! People say we need good Bards now, and I know he's a good Bard. Maybe if he wasn't before, he is now."

"You comfort me, Selmana," said Nelac. He lifted his wine and saluted her. "And even if you struggle with the Reading, you know more of the Way of the Heart than some very deeply learned Bards I know." He drained his glass, and set it down precisely on the table. "For what it's worth, I think exactly as you do. Well, I've done my best. We'll all know the decision soon."

V

WHEN Selmana left, Nelac sat unmoving for a long time, staring into the fire. He wondered at his earlier anger: he had long mastered his temper, and the arguments today had hardly been unexpected. Yet he felt a compelling urgency that had nothing to do with these arguments. Was it simply that he loved the boy? He frowned, dispassionately examining his feelings. There was no doubt that he did love him: but his desire that Cadvan be permitted back into the world of Barding was surely more than that?

He called into his mind the image of the young man he had known. Cadvan was sensitive towards any kind of snobbery, and reacted aggressively. It was a juvenile hangover which Nelac had sought, without success, to discourage: some young Bards, envious of the drama that surrounded Cadvan's arrival in the School and of his obvious talents, had teased him mercilessly in his first years there. From such petty things could disaster grow...

The facts were bald enough. When he was made full Bard, Cadvan had come in contact again with Likod, who had shown him some sorceries that dated from the days of the Great Silence. As Cadvan admitted later, tormented by shame and regret, his curiosity overrode the strict laws that forbade sorcery; more, he had thought himself a powerful enough Bard to control the forces these sorceries summoned. And so the shadow rooted itself, and grew insensibly inside all his actions.

Nelac entertained an uneasy suspicion that Likod was a Hull, one of the corrupt Bards who exchanged their Truenames for endless life. Very few Bards attracted by the arts of sorcery became Hulls: indeed, Hulls had been unknown in Annar for centuries, although it was said some still lived, if living it was, in the south. If Likod was a Hull, he had made his bargain quite recently, within the past hundred years or so. As they out-lived their natural lifetimes, the bodies of Hulls shrivelled and became skeletal. They could conceal this easily enough from most people, but it was hard to hide from Bards. It could be that there was a new cabal of Hulls. This possibility, as much as anything else that had happened, disturbed Nelac deeply. If it were true, it would mean that the Dark was returning: only the Nameless One knew how to take the Name of a Bard.

Certainly, what followed bore all the hallmarks of the Dark. The arrival of Dernhil, the famous poet from Gent, had catalysed Cadvan's actions into disaster. Dernhil was a year younger than Cadvan, and his equal in intellect and magery. Cadvan conceived an irrational dislike of him, which stemmed from an unbecoming jealousy at having a worthy rival for his place as undisputed star of Lirigon. His dislike was fanned by Dernhil's amused responses to his provocations: Dernhil refused to rise to any of Cadvan's baiting. Eventually, Cadvan, a noted poet himself, had challenged Dernhil to a duel of poems. Dernhil won easily, and Cadvan took the loss badly. In a tower-ing rage, he had told Dernhil that, although he might be better at the mere crafting of words, Cadvan was the greater mage. He challenged him to a duel of magery.

Dernhil, with a rare display of temper, had accepted the challenge. Cadvan had told him to meet him at the Inkadh Grove, a dingle surrounded by ancient pines less than a mile from the School, at midnight. Later that day, perhaps from a sudden doubt, he had confessed to Ceredin what he planned to do. She had known nothing of his secret study of sorcery and was horrified. She begged him to lay aside his rivalry, but Cadvan was a man possessed and refused to listen. In the end, attempting to protect Cadvan from his own folly, Ceredin had also gone to the Grove. Out of loyalty, she had told no one else. Nelac bitterly regretted that she had not come to him.

There, Cadvan had summoned a revenant from the Abyss. And not just any revenant: in his arrogance, he had called the Bone Queen, Kansabur herself. She had ruled over Lir, as Lirhan was then called, during the Great Silence, when the Nameless One had held sway over all Annar. Even after all these centuries, the Bone Queen was still remembered in Lirhan with a shudder of dread, as a name to frighten small children, an evil shadow that haunted the folklore. Bards had longer memories, and knew what Kansabur's terror really meant.

Cadvan had told Nelac this much, but neither Dernhil nor Cadvan willingly spoke of what had happened that night. Cadvan had unleashed a monstrous spirit: the revenant had proved much stronger than Cadvan had imagined, and Kansabur had broken his control. When the other two Bards added their power in an attempt to banish it, they were brutally cut down.

The Bards of Lirigon had felt the jolt in the Balance the moment that Cadvan uttered the summoning, and had raced to the Grove: but it was too late. Nelac closed his eyes, remembering what they had found there. The trees, blasted with magefire, were still smouldering, giving a ghastly light, and the air was thick and sour with the burnt smell of sorcery. The three young Bards lay in a welter of blood. Dernhil was barely alive: he had suffered a deep wound from his shoulder to his thigh. Ceredin had been slashed almost in two. Cadvan had suffered no physical hurt: he was found unconscious, splashed with the blood of his companions, his eyes wide in stark horror. The revenant had vanished. It had taken more than a year to track the spirit, and to banish it back to the Abyss had taken all the powers of the First Circle. It was done at last: but the harm it had caused, that night and afterwards, could not be undone.

Bleakly, as he relived those terrible times, Nelac wondered again if there could be pardon for such a crime. Even with all the love he bore Cadvan, he found it hard to forgive him. Yet could one wrong be answered by another? Banishing Cadvan's gifts was to double the loss to Barding. But there was something else, some other reason that plucked at his deeper Knowing. It was an instinct that had yet to grow a mouth, a shadow that remained stubbornly without form. Again he groped towards it in his mind, demanding that it show itself, and again it vanished before him, mocking his fears.

How often, he thought, are one's convictions decided by trivial preference, rather than by a true desire for justice? He felt unusually troubled. Finally, he reached a decision and made his way to the guest quarters, to find Milana of Pellinor. He had need of counsel.

"Well, that was dispiriting," Milana said, as she poured him another wine. "I had thought better of my fellow Bards. Well, maybe not Noram. Right now I would gladly mince that man and feed him to the pigs."

"How did the vote run?"

"Me, you, Calis. Everyone else voted for exile for life, and it is confirmed by Bashar. I think it's shameful."

Although he had expected the decision, Nelac felt a stab of sorrow. He was silent for a time, studying the slender Bard who sat opposite him, her long black hair swinging across her downcast face, her startling blue eyes averted from his.

"My heart tells me this is a bad decision," he said at last. "And yet I scarcely know why, aside from my love of Cadvan. Tell me, why did you speak for clemency?"

Milana gave him a candid look. "For the same reasons as

you did, I imagine. You heard my argument. I don't know Cadvan as you do, but in the hunt for Kansabur I perceived his soul, and I know the Light is true in him. Bards should not be so swift to condemn…"

"Noram was one of those who resented Cadvan," said Nelac. "He often mocked his pedantry. But other arguments, such as Bashar's … they're not so easily dismissed." Those, he thought, were sober judgements from Bards who had thought long and deeply on the question. After all, Cadvan was by no means generally disliked. If he was arrogant, he was also generous: his gift for mockery had always been directed towards Bards who puffed their self-importance, or who used their status to diminish those they considered beneath them.

"You are troubled, my friend," said Milana. "This is about more than the harsh punishment of an errant Bard, is it not?"

"Milana, there is a shadow. A shadow pressing my mind. And yet I can't name it, I don't know what it means. I wonder if it is merely my sadness…"

"Perhaps you perceive a dimming of the Light," said Milana. "Our colleagues have been less than wise, and have permitted the desire for revenge to overcome their desire for justice. That is what I will carry home tomorrow. But…"

"But?"

Milana didn't respond for a time. She stood up and walked to the window, staring out with her back turned to Nelac. "There is a deeper Knowing at work here, my friend," she said at last. "I too feel it. And I don't understand why our friends are so blind to this. I feel a peril among us, that bears upon this decision. Is it fear, you think, that makes them so unwilling to listen?"

"Fear, certainly. Nothing more, I hope. But I have not before sat in such a debate, where the arguments of the Light had so little purchase."

"I can tell you that Pellinor would not have made such a

judgement." Milana turned around, and Nelac saw how anger still flickered in her eyes, a blue flame. "It goes hard when the First Bard is against you, and I have never felt Bashar was more misled. Cadvan is Lirhanese, and not in my jurisdiction, so I do not have the weight. I could understand his exile from Lirigon ... but for life? From every School? I know it sounds petty, but I resent being bound by this ruling. Had I the authority, I'd admit him to Pellinor, but that choice is taken from me."

"What is this deeper Knowing you speak of?"

"I fear for Pellinor. I couldn't speak of this at the Council, for I couldn't shape the connection." She paused. "You may not know that Dorn has foredreams," she said abruptly. Nelac lifted his eyebrows in surprise; he knew Dorn, Milana's help-mate, a Pilanel Bard.

"No, I didn't know," he said.

"We don't speak of them to others, as a rule," she said. "But he dreamed before I left for Lirigon. It was a terrible dream, and he wouldn't tell me the whole: but among other visions, he said he saw Pellinor burned and sacked. And afterwards he said, do not permit Cadvan to be sent away, for our children will need him..." She looked down at her hands. "Dorn and I have no children," she said. "It was a strange thing to say. And yet I knew, with all the foresight given me, that it was true."

"Perhaps he meant all children," said Nelac.

Milana shook her head. "Maybe I should have spoken of this. I regret now that I didn't. But it likely would have made no difference. Foredreams are rightly distrusted: how do we know they are not merely phantoms of sleep? And if they are true, how often do they set feet on the very path they prophesy? But when the vote was cast, Nelac, a dismal weight fell across my heart, as if our future had narrowed. I felt it was the first foot-step towards doom."

VI

TWO weeks after the First Circle confirmed Cadvan of Lirigon's formal banishment as a Bard of Annar, Dernhil of Gent abruptly pulled up his horse on the road to Lirigon, causing a farmer who was driving a cartful of hay hard behind almost to run into him. The farmer cursed him roundly, and Dernhil started and apologised, moving to the side of the road. The farmer, slightly mollified, drove past, staring at the Bard. As he reported later to his wife, Dernhil seemed like a man stunned: he remained by the road, his horse prancing impatiently beneath him, until the farmer passed the next bend and could no longer see him. "White as a sheet, he was," he said. "Didn't know if he was coming or going. He might still be standing there, for all I know." He sniffed, before dismissing the mystery. "Bards!"

Dernhil was oblivious to the farmer's curiosity. He had pulled up his mare, Hyeradh, when he rode over a hill and saw, for the first time in more than a year, the red-tiled roofs of the School of Lirigon in the valley below. The sight swept a wave of nausea through his whole body, bathing him in a cold sweat. All the terror and grief of that night in the Inkadh Grove seemed to possess him: for an endless moment it was as if he were back there, standing in the shadows of the pines as Cadvan woke the dead, as Ceredin ran towards him, crying out in dismay and horror... Dernhil was shocked by how even the distant sight of the School brought those memories back; it was as sharp as if it had happened yesterday, instead of two years before. He wondered if he could bear to return.

At last, prompted by his mount's increasing skittishness, Dernhil urged her on towards Lirigon. Infected by his mood, Hyeradh began to shy at things she would normally never notice: tree stumps, stray chickens, children playing. When a dog barked suddenly from behind a wall, Dernhil was nearly thrown off, forcing him to gather his scattered wits. But that last mile of road to Lirigon was harder than he could have ever imagined: he felt as if he were forcing himself, step by step, back into a nightmare.

Dernhil hadn't sent ahead to inform the School of his arrival. Norowen, who was at the gate, recognized his tall, slender figure with a cry of surprise and ran towards him. "Dernhil! By the Light, how lovely to see you. What are you doing here?"

He dismounted and returned her embrace. Norowen was one of the healers who had cared for him in the dark months of his illness, and they had become good friends; but glad as he was to see her, she too brought back dark memories. Was every association in Lirigon to be tainted with horror? He forced himself to smile, and replied lightly that he had a fancy to visit Nelac.

Norowen stood back, holding his shoulders and examining his face. "You look pale," she said. "It's a long journey from Gent, Dernhil. Are you recovered enough?" Seeing a flicker of irritation in his eyes, she let him go. "Now, don't be annoyed with me. You know you were my first concern for a long time, and I don't care to see my handiwork treated lightly."

At this, Dernhil laughed, and some of the strain vanished from his eyes. "And surely I was one of your worst patients!" he said. He clasped her hands and kissed her cheek. "It's good to see you again, Norowen. But I must see Nelac, and I had no chance of making him come to Gent. Look, I have to stable Hyeradh now, but perhaps we can eat together tomorrow?

I'm not planning to ride out straight away."

Norowen nodded, and watched with a frown as he led his horse away. He still walked with a slight limp, and there was a shadow in his brown eyes, which had used to be brimful of merriment. She wondered if that shadow would ever vanish: it seemed to her that Dernhil's mobile, expressive face now was set hard against an inner pain. Perhaps it never would go away entirely: Dernhil would never be able to unsee what he had seen, and he would bear the scar from the Bone Queen's wound until the end of his days. She sighed, and returned to her interrupted errand.

Dernhil made his formal visit to the First Bard, Bashar, who was too courteous to ask him his business or to refer to his last visit. Perceiving her guest's weariness, she welcomed him warmly, but she didn't keep him long. Then Dernhil was shown to his guest chamber, and was able to unpack his bag and wash off the grime of his journey. He saw with relief that the pleasant room he was assigned was in a different part of the house from that he knew.

Clean and freshly clothed, he threw himself on his bed and closed his eyes, feeling exhaustion sweep over him. He had by no means travelled hard since he left Gent, making the journey in easy stages, but his endurance was not what it had been.

Nothing was what it had been. When he pictured himself before the events in the Inkadh Grove, he no longer recognized the Bard he was: that man was a stranger, carefree and heedless, no more reckoning of danger than a child. Now he saw death everywhere, a dark pulse in everything living. The world was a different place, and he moved through it as a different person.

He rested only for a short while, then swept his long legs off the bed and stood up slowly, wincing. He went to the casement and looked out joylessly at the darkening day. From here, on

the second floor, he could see over the inner courtyard of the
Bardhouse, where a herb garden was planted between paths
of grey stone that were now blackened with rain. The sun was
obscured by heavy clouds that hung low over the School, draining even the red roof tiles of colour. He felt cold and comfortless,
although a fire burned brightly in the hearth behind him. Then
he shook himself, as if he could shoulder off his black mood,
and went to find Nelac.

Nelac was, as Dernhil had hoped, in his rooms. He answered
the door with a faint frown of irritation, which cleared as soon
as he recognized Dernhil.

"I'm sorry for the interruption," said Dernhil, looking over
Nelac's shoulder into the room, where a young Bard was star-
ing at him from a table covered with books and paper. "Shall
I come back later? I just wanted to see if you were free."

"No, no, it's fine," said Nelac, drawing him inside. "Selmana
and I were just about to finish." He directed a glance of amusement over at Selmana, who had shut the biggest of the volumes
with a loud bang. "I'm giving her some help with the Reading.
I suspect that Selmana wishes that it were true that you could
absorb knowledge from books by sleeping on them; but, alas,
the only way to do so is by reading them."

"If I slept on the *Aximidiaë*, I'd have the biggest crick in my
neck and I would never walk straight for the rest of my life,"
said Selmana.

Dernhil laughed. "So you are a Maker," he said. "If only
Poryphia had thought to write in proper Annaren, instead of
the language of her own time!"

"And if only everything she said were not so important!"
Selmana was gathering up her notes. "Maybe when I grow up I'll
translate it, so that other poor Bards don't have to suffer as I do."

"That is a fine ambition," said Nelac. "Do you know Dernhil
of Gent? Dernhil, this is a stray student of mine, Selmana."

Selmana shook Dernhil's hand. "I knew that I recognized your face!" she said. "I couldn't quite place it, but of course I saw you when you were last here." She seemed about to say something else, but checked herself, blushing, and glanced at Nelac. "I'll leave now, I see you want to talk. I'll come again next week, yes? You don't know how glad I am of your help…"

"But of course," said Nelac. As he showed her out, Dernhil stood by the fire, looking around Nelac's sitting room. Oddly, this time its familiarity was reassuring. Like most Bard quarters, it blended an attention to beauty with comfortable disorder; but what he felt most of all was Nelac's calming presence. He sat down on the couch and stretched his legs out towards the fire.

"Can I offer you a wine?" said Nelac. "I was planning to eat here later, and you're welcome to join me, if you're not too tired…"

"Is it that obvious?" said Dernhil.

"Only to eyes that know you well."

Dernhil smiled ruefully. "You're too courteous," he said. "I'm sure I look as bad as I feel. But yes to both wine and dinner, although I fear I might fall asleep on your most comfortable couch. I was hoping we'd have time to talk properly today."

Nelac handed Dernhil a glass and sat down, examining him gravely.

"I can't but wonder what brought you here," he said. "I didn't think to see you in Lirigon again."

"I can't pretend that it wasn't – hard – to come back," said Dernhil. "When I came over Veanhar Hill and first saw the School, I almost turned around and went home. I swear, Nelac, just that glimpse brought it back; it was like it happened all over again. I didn't expect that." He took a long gulp of wine. "But I had to see you. I've been longing to talk to you this past month, you don't know how much. There was no one else I could think of speaking to." His voice cracked, and he stopped.

Nelac leaned forward and gently patted Dernhil's shoulder. "My friend, be easy. You are here now, and there is plenty of time. But perhaps I am not so astonished that you are here after all."

Dernhil, who had been staring into the fire, looked up swiftly. "Is it the dreams with you too?" he asked.

"Dreams? No, not dreams," said Nelac. "I have reasons to worry." He waved his hand impatiently. "I'm right in thinking, though, that this has to do with Cadvan?"

"Yes. Yes, it has, but I don't know why. But, yes, we have to find Cadvan, wherever he has gone. If he's dead, then ... well, I don't know what we will do."

"I would know if Cadvan had died," said Nelac. His eyes unfocused, and for a few moments he seemed to be seeing into a far distance. "No," he said at last. "He's not dead: but he is far away, in thought as well as in body." There was a short silence, and then Nelac noticed Dernhil's empty glass, and refilled it. "But we will talk of this later. For now, my friend, I want to hear how things are in Gent."

Nelac kept the conversation to trifles until after they had eaten dinner, when most of the strain had left Dernhil's face. He knew Dernhil as the most private of people: he wasn't given to showing his deeper feelings, even to his closest friends, preferring to hide behind a mask of levity. It was one of the things that had enraged Cadvan, who read Dernhil's lightness as a studied insult.

Had Cadvan been in his right mind and disposed to be fair, Nelac reflected, he might have considered that, for all his apparent confidence, Dernhil was very shy. He might also have read Dernhil's poems with more attention: they contained all the feeling and thought that Cadvan claimed was missing in Dernhil's character. But Cadvan had not been in his right mind.

Nelac studied the young Bard in front of him. Deep shadows

were carved under his eyes, and even now he gave off a sense of inner tension barely held in check. When he had first arrived at Nelac's door, he had seemed to be at a breaking point. At least now the brittleness that had so disturbed Nelac had subsided.

"So tell me, Dernhil," said Nelac, breaking a comfortable silence. "Why are you here?"

Dernhil paused, gathering his thoughts. "It's difficult to say," he said. "It so easily sounds foolish…"

"Be sure that I don't believe you are a fool."

Dernhil glanced up swiftly, smiling, and then studied his glass thoughtfully. "Well. Begin at the beginning, I suppose. It won't surprise you to know that since – since that night, I've suffered from regular nightmares. When I left Lirigon, I wanted to forget, I never wanted to think about what had happened here again. I know it's not the Bardic way, but even knowing that, I couldn't go near those memories without the most awful pain. I still can't. Physical pain, I mean; the scar hurts, and when the memories possess me, as they sometimes do, I feel the wound almost as if it were still raw. The body and the mind are not two things, as some Bards say, but one thing together, however they might seem divided: if nothing else, this experience has taught me that."

"I expect you've always known that," said Nelac. "You are a poet, after all."

"I suppose so. In any case, as poets are commonly supposed to do, I began to drink too much. It helped to blunt the memories, and if I was very drunk, I slept too heavily to have nightmares. I can tell you that it's not very good for poetry, though… But I am only saying this because it's not as if I haven't suffered from bad dreams. They are more common than not: I know what a nightmare is, and how the terror of that night has inscribed itself in my memories and my body, no matter how much I wish it hadn't, and how it spills out in dreams and unwanted memories, as it does with other people who have suffered such things."

He refilled his glass, and was silent for a time. "These dreams are different. They started happening this autumn. I become more anxious in autumn, even in Gent; the weather is a prompt, bringing it back... And the first dream happened on a night which was very like the evening when we went to the Grove. It was a clear, beautiful night, do you remember? Almost like summer. Full of stars, there was no moon. Most of all I remember the scent – the hunaf shrubs were all in flower, that sweet, heavy smell. There are many around Gent, too, although I wish there weren't... Anyway, I went to sleep eventually, having had a large quantity of wine. And Ceredin came to me.

"I've dreamed about Ceredin before, but those dreams – well, they were just terrible memories. This dream was different, not like a dream at all. Most of all, it seemed entirely real.

"I was at my table in Gent, writing, and Ceredin walked in. I was mildly surprised, and said, but aren't you supposed to be dead? And she said, yes, I am dead. She looked very sad – sadder than anyone I've ever seen – when she said this, and I stood up and took her in my arms to comfort her. She kissed my cheek, and then stood back, looking at me in that way she had, open and serious and with that – that capacity for understanding that was her special gift. She told me that she couldn't stay for very long. 'I linger on the Path of the Dead,' she said. 'One day I will come to the Gates and will not return. Dernhil, I know that you cannot forgive Cadvan for what he has done. I do not ask you to forgive him or to forget. But you must find him, or else everything is lost.'

"I felt a pang in my heart then, for I realized that I had not forgiven him. The last time I saw Cadvan, before I left for Gent, I told him that I had; but I was lying to myself. Nelac, it hurt my image of myself." Dernhil smiled ruefully. "I had thought myself larger than that. I was overwhelmed with anger, this sheer, blinding rage: if Cadvan had been there, I would have punched him until I was exhausted...

"Ceredin touched my arm, and I remembered she was there. 'Forgiveness is harder than any of us realize,' she said. 'And you have no reason to love Cadvan. I do have reason. Because he hasn't forgiven himself, he will not hear me. You do not have to forgive him. You must not forget. Do not seek to forget, Dernhil. But he must be found, or else everything is lost.' And then, as I stared at her, she vanished before my eyes. And I woke up."

Nelac thought of Selmana's telling him that Ceredin had also spoken to her in a dream. "Did she visit you again?" he asked.

"No. The dreams that came after were quite different. They weren't like nightmares, although they sound like them; they were much worse. All of them were real, in the same way that the first one was real. I don't know how to describe the sense of them. At first they were quite specific. In one I saw Pellinor in flames, the School destroyed, its walls broken. In another, I saw a great army marching on Turbansk, and all the land behind it burned and littered with corpses. In another, I saw Innail besieged, and a great shadow rising over the Osidh Annova. Then – then it was as if I were lifted above Annar, like an eagle, and saw more widely. I saw the Great Forest all aflame and the Seven Kingdoms in rubble. Even the sky was on fire. The whole sky. And then there is just desolation, from one horizon to the other." Dernhil's voice shook and he covered his eyes with his hand. "Night after night, Nelac. Night after night I see all green and living things destroyed, all beauty laid to waste, everything I love trampled to dust. I've wondered if I am going mad. Sometimes I think I am. And behind all that, I keep thinking of what Ceredin said: we have to find Cadvan, we have to bring him back."

Nelac looked shaken. "Is there more?" he said.

"Yes. Perhaps this will make you doubt me…" Dernhil took a deep breath. "These are too easily explained as the residue of anguish or fear, but I am certain they are not. I have dreams in which the Bone Queen still walks in Annar. I see her in Norloch, on a throne in the Crystal Hall of Machelinor. The Crystal Hall looks just as it did when I last saw it, but in my dreams it is now a place of loathing and horror. I have seen her in Lirigon and Pellinor, too. In all these visions, she sees me and mocks me. And I am sure, in my deepest being, that Kansabur was not banished back to the Abyss, as we thought she was, and I think she walks on this plane."

Dernhil looked at Nelac directly. "I told a couple of Bards in Gent of this, but they just think I am suffering a disease of the nerves, and, with the greatest kindness, suggested I should stop work for a while. Seront gave me a herbal decoction that meant I slept so deeply I didn't dream at all; but it turned me into a dull, witless idiot and I stopped taking it … and then the dreams came back. At last I decided to come here and consult you. As soon as I left Gent, they stopped plaguing me, so that was something…" He hesitated, and then asked: "What think you, Nelac? Is it that I am going mad?"

Nelac was silent for a time, and then answered slowly, picking his words with care. "I might be tempted to think, like the Bards of Gent, that you describe the images of a wounded mind," he said. "It would be the simplest and most obvious explanation." Dernhil bit his lip, and looked away. "But I cannot say that to you. No, I don't think you are going mad."

Dernhil held his eyes for a long moment. "You don't know what a comfort it is, to hear you say that," he said.

"It is cruel to say so but, my friend, I would prefer to think you were ill. A wounded mind might be healed, with time and care. The other possibility is too terrible." He drained his glass. "I think that Ceredin did visit you. Such things are known to happen and, more, young Selmana, a relation of Ceredin's, told me a startlingly similar story... And you are not the only Bard to suffer such dreams. But more, you give voice to something – some pressure, some dread – that has been growing in my own mind over the past months. It presses not only on me; Milana of Pellinor speaks of it as well. Perhaps I don't have the sensitivity you have, Dernhil, to allow me to hear it. Or perhaps your very woundedness has opened a breach in your being that means that you can see these things more clearly."

"I have wondered if they were foredreams," said Dernhil. "But it seemed – presumptuous to take on the mantel of prophecy."

Both the Bards lapsed into silence, following their own thoughts.

"We argued long for Cadvan to be reinstated," said Nelac at last. "But we lost."

"If it weren't for these dreams," said Dernhil, "I might have agreed with those who argued against you."

"You misrepresent yourself. You yourself told the First Circle that he should not be exiled."

"Perhaps I said so because I thought it was right to do so," said Dernhil. "I can't like him, but I have never been more certain of a man's remorse and desire to atone for what he has done. But maybe I didn't mean it. Maybe all I wanted was revenge after all."

"For all that, you acted as you did, and it is our actions that speak in this world." Nelac stood up and stretched. "Dernhil, I'm glad you came here. I want to think further on all of this. But I'm an old man, and I'm weary, and now I must seek my bed."

"One thing seems very clear," said Dernhil. "We have to find Cadvan. Do you know where he went?"

"I have no idea where he might be," Nelac said. "He

wouldn't even tell me what direction he intended to ride in. He could be anywhere between the northern wastes and the Suderain."

"Typical of Cadvan, that he should make everything even more difficult than it already is," said Dernhil, as he stood up to take his leave.

Nelac smiled. "He was always one of my more vexatious students. And, in truth, one of the most loved. Not that he ever knew that. But then, he ever knew himself but slenderly."

Dernhil shrugged. "In that at least, he and I are alike," he said. "It is a painful knowledge."

VII

THE horseman trotted into Jouan as the sun vanished into a long summer twilight. Although there was only a sliver of a moon, it wasn't dark: the stars blazed so brightly their light cast shadows on the ground. Children playing tag in the village street stopped to watch the horseman, wondering what his business was: this wasn't one of the coal traders, and he certainly wasn't a miner. His horse looked fleet and fine-boned, unlike the labouring animals that pulled the drays and windlass, and one boy swore he saw a flash of gold under the rider's dark cloak.

Outside the tavern, the horseman stopped and looked around, as if he were uncertain what to do next. He noticed the children and beckoned. The oldest boy came forward cautiously.

"I'm told a man called Cadvan of Lirigon lives in this village," said the stranger, in an accent the boy couldn't place. "Can you tell me which is his house?"

"Who wants to know?" said the boy, more boldly than he felt.

"A friend," said the horseman. "An old friend…"

The boy looked up into the rider's face, but it was shadowed and he could make out nothing. He shrugged. "I don't know no Cadvan of Lirigon," he said. "But our cobbler's called Cadvan. Maybe he's the man you want. He lives in the second to last house in the village, next to Taran. You'll know it by the apple tree outside, the trunk is split."

It didn't take long to find the apple tree and the house.

Cadvan was sitting alone on the porch, with a mug of cider at his elbow. Yellow light spilled through an open door, half illuminating his face so his eyes seemed to glitter in deep shadow. When he saw the stranger, his body tensed and he sat up, watching silently as the rider dismounted and knotted the reins at the horse's neck so it wouldn't trip, before walking slowly up to him. The light from the house fell on his face and Cadvan recognized him. If he was startled, he didn't show it.

"Dernhil," he said, as casually as if he had been expecting him.

"Cadvan," said Dernhil, nodding.

There was a short silence while the two Bards studied each other. Their faces betrayed no emotion. At last Cadvan stood up, reaching out his hand in greeting.

"Welcome, friend. Will you join me?" he said, with a stiff formality. "I can only offer cider, I'm afraid, but it's crisp and good on a night like this."

"I thank you, but I should settle my mare first," said Dernhil. "She has borne me far today."

"I fear I don't run to stables in this establishment," said Cadvan. "You should try the tavern."

"I will," said Dernhil. "I thought only to find your house, not you. May I come back later?"

"Tonight?"

Dernhil nodded.

"Why not?" Cadvan lifted his mug. "We could talk over ... old times."

Dernhil heard the bitter mockery in Cadvan's voice, but didn't respond. He remounted Hyeradh and disappeared into the deepening dusk. Cadvan poured himself another cider. Now that Dernhil had gone, he found his hands were shaking.

Of all the people in the world who might have turned up in

Jouan, he thought, the last he would have expected to see was Dernhil of Gent. Yet at another level, deep inside, he wasn't surprised at all: it was almost as if, once he saw Dernhil walking up the path to his house, he had realized that part of him had been waiting for him.

Cadvan stayed where he was on the porch until Dernhil returned an hour or so later. Then, to the disappointment of the children who were spying on them from the bushes, the two Bards went inside and closed the door, shutting out the night.

"So," said Cadvan, handing Dernhil a mug of cider. "I can't imagine that you just happened to be passing through Jouan. No one just passes through Jouan."

"No, I'm not," Dernhil said. He looked up and met Cadvan's eye squarely for the first time. "I was looking for you."

"I can't think why," said Cadvan. "Surely you would rather forget that I existed."

"I imagine you feel the same about me," said Dernhil. Cadvan flushed slightly, and there was an uncomfortable pause. "Nelac suggested I look for you. He would have come himself, but he has duties in Lirigon he was loath to leave."

"It can't have been easy to find me."

"It wasn't easy," said Dernhil. "I've been searching since winter, and the merest chance led me here."

"Surely the Bards in their wisdom haven't decided to reverse my banishment," said Cadvan, with an attempt at an ironic smile.

"No," said Dernhil. "The exile was confirmed last winter. Nelac argued against it, as did some others, but…" He trailed off.

Cadvan swallowed, and turned away to hide his face. While he had been waiting for Dernhil to return from the inn, he had allowed himself to hope that perhaps, after all, he might be able to return to Barding. He could think of no other reason for a Bard, especially this Bard, to track him down. He should have known better. Somehow, hearing the confirmation of his exile was worse than the first judgement: his sentence was now final.

"It's no more than I expected," he said harshly. "And no more than I deserve."

"It wasn't … unexpected," said Dernhil. "For my part, I don't believe it a wholly unjust decision."

The two men looked at each other with barely concealed hostility.

"So you've come to enjoy my punishment, then?" said Cadvan. "I had thought better of Dernhil of Gent. Although I allow it's excusable, given what I did to you."

Dernhil flinched, but said nothing.

"There must be pleasure indeed in seeing my humble circumstances," said Cadvan, looking around his kitchen. "A neat moral indeed, to take back to the Schools: the vanity of Cadvan of Lirigon, contained in a hovel, reduced to nailing up the boots of miners. I'm sure your students will benefit from such an illustration."

"That is unjust," Dernhil said tightly. "And foolish. I had expected better of Cadvan of Lirigon."

"I'm no longer Cadvan of Lirigon, if you recall. I'm surprised you had any expectations."

Cadvan stood up and walked to the door, opening it so the night air flowed into the room. He drew a deep breath, trying to calm the rage that flared inside him. He knew he had no right to be angry, but that made no difference. How dare Dernhil sit in his kitchen with that superior air, too polite to comment on Cadvan's poor furniture and shabby clothes? It was probably all he could do not to sneer. How dare he remind Cadvan of everything he had thrown away? Of the life that was now closed to him for ever?

Dernhil spoke from behind him, his voice unsteady. "I have reason to come here, reason to find you. I didn't expect it to be easy, and I like it as little as you do."

"Then why did you bother?" Cadvan turned, and Dernhil saw, his heart sinking, that he wasn't trying now to conceal his dislike.

"Ceredin told me to find you."

At the mention of Ceredin, Cadvan turned white. "You dare – you dare to say…"

"You owe me at least to listen to what I have to say. I don't have the desire or the will to argue with you, Cadvan."

There was a long, tense silence, and then at last Cadvan sat down at the table.

"I'm listening," he said.

Later that night, Cadvan sat for a long time alone, attempting to untangle his thoughts. Dernhil's visit had deeply shaken him. It wasn't just the unwelcome memories that he called up. Those memories were always with Cadvan, whether he liked it or not; Dernhil's presence only made them more immediate. It wasn't even the shame, although his initial discourtesy towards Dernhil mortified him. His anger was only at himself; he had no right to direct it towards the person who, aside from Ceredin, he had caused most harm.

He attempted to put aside his feelings and think dispassionately about what Dernhil had told him. He had listened with his jaw set to Dernhil's description of his dream of Ceredin. Like Nelac, Cadvan had no doubt it was a real visitation. She had forgiven him? It gave him no consolation; it only deepened his shame. He deserved no such love, had never deserved it. Worst of all was the thought that Ceredin had attempted to speak to him, and he had not been able to hear. Had he been deaf even to Ceredin? Even after everything that had happened, even after her death, had he betrayed her again?

Once he had mastered his anger, Cadvan had looked at Dernhil more carefully, and seen the signs of weariness and long-endured pain. Dernhil's face was drawn, and his hands trembled slightly as he reached to pick up his mug. And yet he had travelled for months to find Cadvan, a man he had every reason to hate. Cadvan grasped at once the fears that Dernhil stumblingly attempted to express – when Dernhil had described his dreams, he immediately thought of his own dream, and shuddered – but he still had no real understanding of what he was supposed to do, or what Dernhil meant by insisting that he leave Jouan. He thought that Dernhil was equally unsure. Cadvan was now exiled from Barding, banned from entering any School. What possible use could he be?

Most disturbing was Dernhil's fear that the Bards had failed to banish Kansabur. The thought that, at the least, that harm had been contained was the one consolation of the whole sorry mess. Could Kansabur really have fooled some of the wisest Bards in Annar? Even Nelac had been sure that she had been banished into the Abyss… The Bards of Lirigon had hunted the Bone Queen for months, tracking her spoor from one haunting to another. This was a long and exhausting task, as Kansabur had no certain physical form. When Cadvan had summoned her, she had first manifested as the Bone Queen of Lirhan, taller and grimmer than most men, but nevertheless seeming, for all her sorceries, human and corporeal. But then she had become as insubstantial as smoke and vanished into the Shadow Circle.

It was a long time since Cadvan had considered much beyond the simple demands of his life in Jouan – it was more than a year since he had even read a book. But a Bard-trained memory, as Cadvan knew from his many wakeful nights, was as accurate as any written text. He knew already that he wouldn't sleep this night. He gloomily poured himself another cider and set himself to thinking over what he knew.

According to the Law of Theyan, Bards had theorized that the universe must consist of eleven Circles, each intricately bound within the others. The Knowing of the Eleven Circles was an esoteric lore known to few, and the little Cadvan understood had only been gained through bitter necessity. Even the wisest Bards could only describe four Circles: the others were called the Seven Unknowns.

"The Circles are not places," Nelac had told him. "It is only in the World that we understand place as place and time as time. They are neither within nor beyond nor beside our physical plane: none of those words mean anything in relation to them. We can but imagine them poorly, Cadvan: even a Bard's perception of them is shaped by our limitations, by what it is possible for us to see or feel or know. If we enter those other planes, we shape what we perceive, and it is only a rag of the truth. Perhaps it is just as well: we cannot bear very much reality…"

The four Known Circles were the World, the Shadow, the Empyrean and the Abyss. The World was the physical plane. The Shadow was the reality Bards could most easily enter: it was a dimension of energies that could manifest directly in the World, and which could be perceived in dreams or trances. It was where the dead lingered on their journey to the Gates, in the twilight of their souls when they still had some connection to the living. Cadvan thought of his own ventures into that realm, and shuddered: those memories underlay some of his worst nightmares. Yet Ceredin had spoken from that plane, to both Dernhil and Selmana. He wondered now if it was the fear that he had learned in those terrible and strange journeys to find Kansabur that had made it impossible for Ceredin to speak to him; simple cowardice seemed not quite as shameful as refusing to hear her voice…

The Empyrean, the third Circle, was beyond the Gates, the

irrevocable destination of the dead. Only one Bard, Maninaë, had ever gone that far and returned: and he had paid a terrible price, and ever after remained silent about what he had found there. The Abyss was more mysterious still, and no Bard had ever entered it. It was described as a place of unform, beyond human understanding.

"Neither depth nor height, neither mass nor nothingness, neither light nor dark, neither sound nor silence, neither life nor death, exist in the Abyss," Nelac had told him. "It is a place of unbeing, comprised of terrible energies. Sorcery is above all the study of the Abyss: sorcerers seek to find and use the vast powers that sleep within it. Such energies transform into grievous power when they manifest in the World: they do not belong here, and they can do nothing but injure everything they touch. They are not inherently evil, you understand: in the Abyss, where they are what they are, these energies are part of what hold our cosmos together. It is only when a human will seeks to bind and use them that evil is made. And this is why, Cadvan, Bards renounce with such absoluteness the study of sorcery. It is, in its very being, an injury to the Balance: and the Balance is at the very heart of Barding, and of the Light..."

Even now, so long afterwards, Cadvan blushed at the rebuke. Before she embraced the immortality offered by the Nameless One, the Bone Queen had been a mortal woman. Perhaps, Cadvan thought, she had not been so different from Cadvan himself: talented, ambitious, arrogant... Perhaps in the beginning she had told herself that she was working to a higher good, or at least did no harm. Perhaps she believed it even at the end. Power was its own reason. Bards, even corrupt Bards, tended not to be especially interested in wealth or luxuries or other trivial vices: so much the easier to be seduced by the pure thrill of power. Cadvan remembered the dazzle through his entire being as he exercised that strength when he summoned

Kansabur. For a few moments of exhilaration and terror he had felt himself capable of anything, anything at all: he could merely crook his little finger and empires would crumble, whole cities collapse into dust.

He had felt nothing like that elation when he and the Lirigon Bards had, at last, tracked down Kansabur and forced her – or thought they had forced her – back into the Abyss. Then the exercise of power had been an anguish so exquisite Cadvan still felt the echo of it in his bones: an intense labour that began as pain and finished as torment. Could it be true that they had failed in their task? He remembered uneasily that there had been a single instant – a flicker in the fraught moments just before the Circles had aligned and opened – in which the concentration of the Bards had faltered and broken against the will of their enemy. Could that have been the hole in the net? Yet the Bards, fearing that Kansabur might have fooled them, had searched for months afterwards for any trace of her, and found no sign; and the killings in Lirhan that had betrayed her presence in the World had stopped completely.

Cadvan wished he could believe she had been banished. In the deeper parts of his mind, a slow tocsin was ringing out an alarm. There was something he had forgotten, something that nudged at the edges of his memory, which he was now too tired to grasp. In the pit of his soul, he felt that Dernhil was right: but it seemed impossible. Perhaps Dernhil was mistaken, and was merely speaking out of an unfounded fear. Yet Nelac had been concerned enough to send Dernhil out to find Cadvan. That, more than anything, gave Cadvan pause: the Knowing of Nelac was not to be dismissed lightly.

The problem with fearing the worst, Cadvan thought sourly, was that too often it was the safest thing to bet on.

VIII

AS the early sun broadened over Jouan, stray beams crept past the edges of the shutters and played on the floor. Cadvan sat immobile, deeply wrapped in thought; lack of sleep left a heavy weariness in his body, but his mind was clear. He must leave Jouan with Dernhil. He wished that he felt as certain about everything else.

A knock startled him out of his thoughts. He looked up to see Hal peering in through the half-open door. Stubborn the goat was right behind her, demanding breakfast. Cadvan stood up hastily, realizing that he was late with the morning chores, and that he had completely forgotten that it was the day for Hal's lesson.

"Stubborn needed milking," said Hal reproachfully. "She's a bit cross, but she let me do it. I know she's saying she wants to be fed, but I already gave her a mash."

Cadvan swore and stood up, stretching the stiffness out of his body. "I thank you, Hal. I'm sorry to put you to the trouble. I know you have a lot to do. And *you*," he said to Stubborn in the Speech, "can stop calling me names."

Stubborn looked at him scornfully, flicked her tail and trotted off behind the house. Hal gave him her quicksilver smile, and edged into the kitchen. "I don't mind," she said. "I did mind her trying to eat my breakfast. When she couldn't wake you up, she came to me."

"She's a goat of remarkable intelligence and greed," said Cadvan. "I hope you kept the milk."

"I did," said Hal, sitting down and propping her face in her hands. "I knew you'd say that. Indira said she would make some curds."

Cadvan looked at his cold hearth with disgust. "And the embers have quite gone out. A poor householder indeed!" He busied himself kindling the fire and putting a kettle on the hob to steep some tea, wondering how to tell Hal that he was planning to leave Jouan. He had been teaching her for months now, and she was an apt pupil, quick and gentle. She was already an accomplished healer, and it seemed wrong to stop her education now. A sharp pang of sadness made him realize that he was fonder of Hal than he knew; not only of Hal, but of Taran and his noisy, cheerful family, and of many others in the village. Leaving Jouan would be a wrench.

"You're going to leave us, aren't you?" said Hal, interrupting his thoughts. "Your friend, that was here last night. He came to find you, didn't he? Has he come to take you away?"

Cadvan met her eyes, and nodded. Hal swallowed hard, and looked away.

"I must," he said gently. "Yes, Dernhil is an old … friend. And he has brought some bad news that I must attend. But, Hal, I am sorrier than I can say. I've enjoyed teaching you."

Tears started in Hal's eyes at that, but she blinked them back. "I've enjoyed it too," she said. "I'd like to learn more, but … I suppose it isn't to be."

Cadvan studied Hal's thin, intense face. As was common, Hal had a little of the Gift: not enough to make a Bard, but enough to ensure a quick, empathic perception that made her a very promising healer. She would never use the Speech, the inborn language that woke the powers of a Bard, but her talents were considerable. Her stoic acceptance moved him.

"You've learned a lot already," he said. "The truth is that I am not a very good healer, Hal. I know a little, as all Bards do, and I have the Gift. You're actually much more talented at it than I am."

Hal blushed with pleasure. "Eka asked me to help with that bad birth last week," she said, with shy pride. "And she said that Ulana would have died without me being there."

"She would have," said Cadvan, thinking of Eka, who was generally a good midwife, but hadn't spotted how seriously Ulana was bleeding. "I hope she paid you?"

Hal wriggled in her chair. "She gave me some coin," she said. "A bit."

"You could earn more, if you set up as a healer," said Cadvan.

"I hope so," said Hal. "I need to earn, but I don't want to go down the mine again. Not after ... not after the explosion. I keep thinking of Inshi. But people think I'm too young."

"You are too young. But time will cure that." Hal was curled up in the chair, staring at him. She was only a child, scarcely thirteen years old, but the resignation in her face was that of an old woman. Childhood burned out fast in Jouan.

"Hal," he said. "When this is over ... if I can – and I don't know if I will be able to, mind – I will come back to Jouan and see how you're faring. Even if I can't live here, I can visit a while and teach you more. If I had time and some books, I could even teach you how to read and write. Jouan needs a healer, and why shouldn't it be you?"

Hal jumped up and hugged him, her face blazing with sudden joy. "Would you?" she said. "Would you really come back, just to teach me?"

Cadvan unlocked her thin arms from his neck and stood her back from him, holding her shoulders. "Hal, I can't promise it. I have other duties and ... well, it might be dangerous. But if I can come back, I swear I will."

Hal regarded him sternly from underneath her fringe of hair.

"Don't die," she said. "I want you to come back."

Cadvan laughed. "I'll do my best not to die, then. Just for you."

They were so intent, neither noticed that Dernhil was standing in Cadvan's doorway until he cleared his throat. Cadvan invited him inside, and Hal, glaring at him, retreated to a corner.

"I don't mean to interrupt," said Dernhil, glancing uncertainly at Hal. "I can go for a walk, maybe, and come back later."

"You're taking Cadvan away," said Hal fiercely. "Why? Why are you taking him away?"

Dernhil, taken aback, looked to Cadvan.

"Dernhil, this is Hal, my next-door neighbour," said Cadvan. "Hal, this is Dernhil, a friend. You mustn't blame him for what he can't help. He is only the messenger."

Hal scowled, and ran out of the house. Cadvan followed her with his eyes, and sighed.

"I see I am not making friends here," said Dernhil.

"I've been teaching her," said Cadvan. "It's a crime to leave anyone so hungry for knowledge without the means of finding it. She's a talented healer, you know…"

Dernhil smiled. "Whatever the Schools say, you are still a Bard, Cadvan."

Cadvan glanced at him sharply, suspecting mockery, but there was none in Dernhil's face. He relaxed, and waved to a chair. "I can offer some sour milk, or some tea," he said. "But that's about it for refreshments."

"Tea would be most welcome," said Dernhil, sitting down. "So I'm to take it that you've decided to come with me?"

"Yes," said Cadvan shortly. "How can I not? Though I have no idea what you expect me to do."

"The truth is, I don't either," said Dernhil. "Nelac told me that we should come straight to him. Aside from that…"

A silence fell between the two as Cadvan boiled more water for the tea. He poured it out into two clay mugs, and sat down facing Dernhil. In the daylight he could see more clearly the signs of exhaustion on Dernhil's face.

"I think you've been travelling too hard," he said abruptly. "Have you stopped to rest?"

Dernhil shrugged. "Does it matter?"

"You look as if you're about to collapse."

"If so, it's my business."

"Not if I am to travel with you," said Cadvan. "I hardly want to be responsible for dealing you more injury."

At this Dernhil frowned, and then he looked up and met Cadvan's eyes, and reluctantly smiled.

"I see your point. Yes, the wound pains me still when I am tired. But I will not collapse, I promise you."

Cadvan nodded. "I need to make arrangements before I leave Jouan," he said. "That will take some days, I think. You should rest while you can, and then I will be in your hands."

Dernhil looked scornfully at his hands, which trembled slightly as they held the mug. "They are poor things to put trust in, I fear," he said. "But I thank you."

"There's no call for thanks," Cadvan said harshly.

"But there is. You need not have answered as you have."

"Like you, I have no choice."

"There is always a choice," said Dernhil.

For a moment it seemed as if the two Bards were about to argue, but then Dernhil laughed. "By the Light, if I have to fight even to show you gratitude, it will be a hard journey, Cadvan. Be less full of spikes, I beg you."

Cadvan met Dernhil's eyes and laughed, despite himself. His smile transformed his face: suddenly he seemed much younger, carefree and reckless.

"No spikes, then," he said. "At the worst, the odd prickle."

"Is that a promise?" said Dernhil.

"As good a promise as you'll get, which isn't much," said Cadvan. "Sadly, I seem to be made of spikes."

It was more than a week before Cadvan was ready to travel, although in truth it could have taken him a couple of days to dispose of his few possessions. When it came to the point, he found himself dragging his feet. He gave his house and furniture back to Taran, refusing payment, and he asked Hal to take Stubborn. He kept his cobbling tools, which had belonged to him since he was a child, and bought a horse and some supplies for the journey. The rest of his belongings scarcely filled a pack. He made his farewells, completed his unfinished cobbling orders and cleaned his house for the last time.

"We all knew that you would leave one day," Taran said, on Cadvan's final night in Jouan. They had just had another long argument about payment for the house, which Taran had again lost, and were sealing the deal with a drink in the tavern. "You're not the kind of man who would stay in a place like this."

"I'm sorry to leave," said Cadvan. "Jouan has been good to me."

"It went both ways," said Taran. "We've needed a healer here. And I think there would have been murder done over that business about Jorvil, if you had not been here."

"I can't say he loves me for it," said Cadvan, grimacing. Jorvil, the leader who had cheated his gang, still bore Cadvan a heavy grudge for his part in the negotiations.

"That one, he was born sour," said Taran. "Most are not like him."

Cadvan thought of the miners he knew. They were hardened by their lives, and were often harsh in their dealings, but Taran was right: Jorvil's bitterness and capacity for spite was unusual. "I hope you can keep an eye on his wife…"

"I will," said Taran. "We all will. Some things have changed since you arrived, and for the better. It hasn't done us any harm having a Bard around."

"I'm not a Bard," said Cadvan quickly. "Not any more…"

"I don't know why you're not a Bard, and I won't ask, because it's none of my business," said Taran, giving Cadvan a shrewd glance. "But whatever important people say in their stone castles, we make our own judgements about the worth of a man. You're a Bard to us. Our Bard."

At this, something lurched in Cadvan's chest. He turned away to hide his unexpected emotion. To cover the moment, Taran called for more drinks.

"You're very different from your friend," Taran said thoughtfully, putting full mugs on the table. "He's more…"

"More Bard-like?" said Cadvan, smiling.

"Aye, more like a Bard. Not that you don't seem like a Bard, you understand, but you also seem like one of us, somehow. He's a bit more … above us. More distant, like. Friendly and all, he's been nothing but courtesy since he's been here, I don't mean that he holds himself up…"

"He was born into Barding," said Cadvan. "I'm the son of a cobbler, and there are no other Bards in my family. Maybe it's just that."

"Maybe," said Taran. "Maybe it's something else, that's nothing to do with being a Bard or not, and is just about who you are." He paused, and then gave Cadvan a measuring glance. "Hal said that you think she should set up as a healer on her own. Did you mean that?"

"I did," Cadvan said.

"She won't go down the pit any more," said Taran. "I can't say as I blame her. You can scarce move in the house these days, for all the herbs she's drying and messes she's making…"

"She's already a brave healer," said Cadvan. "She has more

of a talent for it than I have, and she knows the basics. She could set up in my house, so she won't crowd yours."

"We could use the extra coin, for sure. But it's a big responsibility, for one so young. If things go wrong, she'll be blamed for it." He hesitated. "I hear that some are already calling her a witch."

Cadvan studied Taran's troubled face. "I suppose you mean that Jorvil is," he said. "He's wrong, anyway. A witch is one with a little of the Speech, and Hal has none of it. I think you'll find that more are speaking well of her, for the help she's giving them."

Taran nodded, but he still looked worried. "Aye. Aye. I hope you're right. She'll miss you sorely, will Hal. You saved her, after Inshi died. She was that cast down, I had never seen her like that before…"

Cadvan cleared his throat. "If she is honest about what she can do, she should avoid most problems," he said. "Hal has much quickness, but she also has a deal of common sense, and that will see her straight. And as you said, you need a healer here."

"I'll let her do it, then. As if I could stop her, anyway."

"If all goes well, I'll come back and see how she fares. How you all fare."

"Aye, she told me that," said Taran. "She says that you're not allowed to die."

Cadvan smiled, and a long silence fell between them. At last Taran looked up, meeting Cadvan's gaze. "I don't mind telling you, my friend, my heart is heavy. Something is amiss, in the middle of things. I don't know what it is. I just feel it, as if there's a shadow in the sunlight, and it's growing. Since before the accident, since even before you came here, but more after…"

Cadvan looked up, surprised. "What makes you say that?" he asked.

Taran shrugged, slightly embarrassed. "Maybe it's just fool-ishness," he said.

"No," said Cadvan. "If I've learned one thing while I've been in Jouan, it's that you're not a foolish man."

Taran grinned, but his eyes remained troubled. "Anyway, I know you probably can't say, Bard's business and all, but I can't help wondering... Maybe it's just nightmares."

"You've been having odd dreams?" Cadvan asked abruptly.

There was a short silence. "I dreamed of the explosion before it happened," Taran said. "I didn't tell no one before, because it would have been bad luck, and I didn't after, because there was no point. And there have been others, bad dreams. Forests dying. The sky on fire."

Cadvan studied the man beside him. It didn't surprise him that Taran had such sharp intuitions – since they had become friends, he had grown to respect his insight – but he was aston-ished by his dreams.

"Why I'm leaving is to do with that ... shadow," he said at last.

"Rather you than me, then," said Taran. "I don't want to know any more, even if you would tell me, which I warrant you won't."

"It's more can't than won't," said Cadvan. "We scarce understand what it is we have to do. I don't know if I can be of any use, anyway. But I have to go, whether it makes any differ-ence or not."

Taran finished his drink. "Time for home," he said. The two men paid and left the tavern. They lingered outside for a while, looking up at the starry sky, as Cadvan searched for words. He wanted to say, without embarrassing him, how important Taran's friendship had been; how much Taran's tactful kind-ness had mattered when he had arrived, utterly without hope, in Jouan; how deeply he had grown to respect him. In the end, he said nothing. He grasped Taran's hand and they embraced.

"Farewell, my friend," he said.

"May the Light protect you," said Taran. It was an odd thing for a miner to say: this was the blessing of Bards. He studied Cadvan with a deep, wordless compassion. "I don't know what you have to face out there, but I'm with Hal. You're not allowed to die. Make sure you come back one day."

"I will," said Cadvan. "If I can, I will."

II

IX

SELMANA sat up abruptly in her bed, sniffing the night uneasily like a startled animal. Something had wrenched her out of sleep: her heart was jumping in her chest, and the hair stood up on the back of her neck. She listened intently in the dark, and at last breathed out, telling herself that she was imagining things. And then she heard it again: a noise on the edge of hearing, a groaning that made her skin tighten with some unidentifiable horror.

She gestured and made a magelight, staring about the bedchamber. Everything looked the same as it always did. She had come home to visit her mother in Kien, as she did every fortnight or so, and this house was as familiar as her own hands: she had grown up here with her two brothers. Now both of her brothers were married and gone to their own houses, Selmana was learning to be a Bard in Lirigon, and her mother, long widowed, lived alone.

She waited for her heart to stop beating so fast, but the crawling sense of horror only seemed to intensify. She sent out her Bard senses in an agony of listening, so her whole body seemed a straining ear. She told herself that the noise must have been the tail end of a bad dream, but she knew she hadn't imagined it. At last she couldn't bear sitting there any more; she had to find out what was wrong. Snapping out the magelight, she scrambled silently out of bed, wrapping a soft woollen cloak around her against the night chill, and crept to the kitchen. She could hear her mother breathing in her bedroom, and the rustle of mice in the walls, and the sigh of the summer wind through the trees, and the rafters creaking: nothing more than the normal night noises. Yet the feeling was getting worse by the moment. Something was out there.

She stood uncertainly in the darkened kitchen, letting her eyes adjust. I'm a Bard, she thought. A Bard of Lirigon. She saw the kitchen knife and picked it up. Then she drew a deep, trembling breath, attempting to steady herself, and made a shield. It was one of the simplest transformations in magery, something every Minor Bard learned early, but her powers felt shaky and weak. She tested the barrier, found it wanting and tried again. This time it worked, and she felt a little better: at least now she should have some protection. She silently unlatched the door and, holding her breath lest the hinges creak and betray her, pushed it open and stepped out into the night.

The feeling of wrongness hit her like a blow. High above, a pale sliver of moon sailed through wisps of cloud, its slender illumination falling on the fields before her. The shadows under the eaves of the house were very black, but she dared make no light. She thought of running back indoors and slamming down the bar, but she firmly put that thought aside. I'm a Bard, she told herself again. I shouldn't be afraid. She could hear something breathing in heavy, shuddering grunts. She focused her perceptions: whatever was wrong was coming from the orchard, among the darkest shadows thrown by the trees. The ground there was stippled, grey and black and silver. Step by step, wincing at the smallest rustle made by her bare feet, she crept towards it.

She was almost at the orchard when she heard the groan again. It was much louder out here in the open: she stopped mid-step, her stomach flipping over with terror. What was it? It sounded like an animal in an extremity of distress: or perhaps a human, driven past the limits of speech by terrible pain.

It was there, at the far end of the orchard. She could see where the shadows thickened on the ground into a figure. Slowly she put her foot down, feeling carefully so she wouldn't snap a twig, and drew closer. Among the trees she felt trapped, as if she were entering a closed room: a silence seemed to have fallen around her, as if every living thing were holding its breath, hiding from some great predator.

Selmana tested her shield again, and strengthened it. The kitchen knife felt cold in her hand, and sadly inadequate. It was good steel, sharp enough to cut bone. It was all she had. She paused, and changed her grip so she was holding it clamped in her fist, ready to drive into anything that attacked her. Her eyes had adjusted to the darkness now, and she could see the tangle of shadow branches on the grass and the faint glimmer of the trunks under the leaves, but the clot of shadow before her resolved into no certain shape.

She had never been so afraid. She thought again about turning back. Even though she was a Bard, she was only a Minor Bard, and there was so much she didn't know. But she didn't turn back. She had come this far, and she would despise herself if she ran away now. She ran through the words of power in her mind, readying herself, and crept on, keeping to the shelter of the trees.

She could see it more clearly now, but she still couldn't make out what it was, although she could smell it. A rank scent, an animal. Then it seemed to twist and fall over, letting out the horrible groan again, and a cloud lifted from the moon, and the form condensed into something recognizable. It was a wild pig, a boar. It was trembling violently, and its flanks heaved in and out as it drew breath after shuddering breath. Its jaws were slathered with foam, and she could see the whites of its eyes. The grass beneath it was violently churned up: it had been in the same place for some time. She had never seen an animal in such agony. It was unbearable even to witness.

Even as she realized this, the air seemed to thicken, as if the darkness solidified into something malign that sought to invade her mouth and nose and ears, seeking a way inside her. All around was an awful pressure, a heaviness that pushed her down to her knees, down further, until her mouth was pressed against the earth. Her pulse pounded in her ears, as if she were drowning. Selmana twisted in panic, crying out the word for Bardic fire: *Noroch!* The white flame sprang out of her, a fierce blaze that flared vividly against the night, so she was blinded. For a few dreadful moments, she could see nothing, hear nothing, feel nothing. She only knew that the dreadful pressure had lifted.

She lay on the grass, gulping in air, conscious only of relief that she could breathe again. Then fear caught her up and she scrambled to her feet, grabbing the knife that she had dropped. She looked around, sobbing. Above her the branches of the apple trees still smouldered from the white fire, throwing a flickering light. The night was clean again. The orchard was just an orchard. Whatever it was had gone.

The boar was dead, stilled in the midst of its writhing so it seemed distorted and monstrous. The wildfire had burned it, and the sharp reek of singed hair mixed with the stench of its panic. She checked her shield again, and made a magelight so she could see the carcass. The sight made her gag. She had once seen a horse with colic, that had foamed at the mouth and twisted in anguish like this boar, and that had been horrible; but this was much worse. She turned away and walked about the orchard, circling every tree, looking for any clue to what had happened. Still nothing. She searched mechanically and thoroughly, not asking herself why she was doing this, even though her body was still racked by the tremors of aftershock.

Then she walked back to the house. She barred the door behind her and lit a lamp and stoked up the embers of the fire.

She poured herself a cup of the strong blackberry liquor her mother made and crouched by the hearth, warming her freezing feet. It was still the small hours of the night, but she knew she had no chance of going back to sleep. She didn't veil her listening: her ears were open, aware of every sound for half a mile about the house. For the first time she wondered why, despite her terror, she had gone out into the night: was it some kind of madness? She had been like some stupid insect blundering towards a flame. And she had only just escaped. She shuddered, drawing her cloak around her. Escaped what? She thought of the boar. The animal's torment was branded on her mind: no creature should ever suffer so. Poor innocent beast, she thought. And then: *It could have been me.*

When Berdh, Selmana's mother, rose before dawn to do her morning tasks, she was dismayed to find Selmana crouched by the fire. Her daughter was pale and haggard, with deep circles under her eyes, and she seemed to be talking wild nonsense. She told Berdh that she had to go back to the School straight away, and that there was a dead wild boar in the orchard that needed dealing with.

"But why now?" said Berdh, bewildered. "Your uncle is coming over from Derim, especially to see you. He'll be very disappointed."

"I know," said Selmana. Huys was her favourite uncle, a village smith like her father had been, and she had been looking forward to seeing him. "But it's important, Mama."

"And what's this about a boar?"

"In the orchard," said Selmana. "It's dead. But don't eat it, it's been sick. No, on second thoughts, leave it there, don't touch it. Don't go near it, it might be... Not until I come back... And, Mama, can Huys stay with you? I think you shouldn't be alone in the house..."

"My dear, you know very well I can look after myself. The Light knows, I have all these years," she said. "And Huys has his own duties to attend to."

Selmana stared at her mother. "There's something ... bad happening. I don't know what, but it's bad. Mama, you mustn't be alone."

Berdh studied her daughter, catching her urgency. Even though she had the Gift, Selmana had always been the most practical of her children: she wasn't given to nerves or flights of fancy. She patted Selmana's shoulder. "Huys will be here later this morning," she said. "Maybe he'll stay the night, if I ask him. Now, don't you worry about me. I'm sure I don't know what you're talking about, but I never do with Bard business. If you have to go, so be it."

Selmana took Berdh's hand and held it to her cheek. She wanted to curl up in her mother's arms and cry, as she did when she was a little girl. She set her jaw: now was not the time. She dressed and washed her face and saddled her horse, and made it to the School of Lirigon in less than an hour.

She found Nelac in his rooms, eating breakfast. He raised his eyebrows at her breathless entrance, and asked if she had eaten.

"No," said Selmana. "But..."

"Sit down," he said. "I can see you are big with news, and it's better heard on a full stomach. Besides, these delicious meat pastries deserve proper attention."

Despite her anxiety, Selmana couldn't help smiling. She realized she was ravenous, and devoured three of the pastries. They were, as Nelac had said, delicious.

"Now," said Nelac. "Tell me why you've burst in here, looking as if you've ridden in on a whirlwind."

Selmana blushed, and wiped her hair out of her eyes. "I couldn't think what else to do," she said. "Last night..."

She looked doubtfully at Nelac, fearing that he would

dismiss what she said as wild fancy. Nelac simply waited for her to begin. Haltingly, searching for the right words, she told him about waking so suddenly, how she had crept out of the house and found the tormented boar. To her own ears, the suffocating terror that had possessed her sounded stupid: in the sober light of day, it could only be the fears of a silly girl frightened by noises in the night. Nelac listened without interrupting, frowning.

"I'm glad you came to me," he said, when she had finished. "You were quite right."

Selmana felt almost giddy with relief. "I thought you might not believe me," she said.

"Why would I think you were making things up, child?" Nelac smiled at her. "After these months of teaching you, I know that's the last thing you'd do."

"You mean that I have absolutely no imagination," said Selmana.

"Say rather that you are not given to fancy, like so many of my students," he said.

"What was it, Nelac? Do you know what it was?"

"Not for sure. What I do know is that you were very lucky. If you had not shielded yourself, if you had not had the white fire, I hate to think what might have happened."

Selmana shuddered, thinking of the thing that had tried to invade her. Even the memory made her feel sick in the pit of her stomach. "It's some kind of ... haunt, maybe?" She thought of the stories she had heard as a child, of spirits who refused death and sought to return to the World by possessing the bodies of the living. Until today, she had never really believed them.

"Yes, something like that. Fortunately for you, it was not strong. If it is a mere haunt, then it is easily dealt with..."

"You think it might be something else?"

"I worry that it might be something worse. But let's not be

driven by fear, hmmm?" He stood up, brushing his clothes.
"I simply can't eat these pastries with dignity. Crumbs everywhere…"

Selmana giggled, looking down at the crumbs on her own
lap. "I'm messier than you," she said. "But they were very nice.
I feel a lot better now."

"Good. Are you ready to ride again? I think we should visit
your village."

Nelac and Selmana arrived in Kien just before noon, throwing Berdh into a fluster. "You should have warned me!" she
hissed at Selmana, as they prepared a herb tea in the kitchen.
"I've only that mess of stew I made for Huys! Thank the Light
I baked some loaves and that apple pie. What will he think
of me?"

"Oh, Mama, Nelac won't mind," said Selmana. "Anyway,
he didn't come here to eat."

They paused only briefly, to rest and to drink a tea, before
they walked to the orchard to inspect the dead boar. Berdh, and
Huys, who had arrived shortly after Selmana and Nelac, came
with them, full of curiosity. The boar looked much smaller in
the light of day, but the evidence of its suffering seemed more
stark. For a few moments they all stared at its grotesquely distorted form in silence.

"I've never seen that before," said Huys. "Looks like the
poor beast had a colic. But – look at that eye…"

Berdh made a noise in her throat and stepped back hastily.
One of the boar's eyeballs had popped out of the socket and
flopped down its cheek.

Nelac squatted down and inspected the animal closely,
screwing up his face against its smell. "One of its hams is dis-
located," he said. "I think it might have done that itself, in its
agony." He laid his hand on its hide, and his form glowed

briefly; then he shuddered and stood up, looking at Selmana.

"There's no sign of disease, although its innards are rup-tured," he said. "Perhaps it was a colic, although I've never seen a beast this bad."

"What else could it have been?" said Selmana.

"I'm not sure," said Nelac. He looked at Huys. "I have seen something like this before. Not in an animal, though. It was in a man."

"In a man?" said Berdh, drawing in a sharp breath. "What happened to him?"

"He was ... very unfortunate. He was in the wrong place at the wrong time." He looked at Berdh. "I think you'll not want to eat this beast," he said. "The body would be best buried. You can take no harm from it: whatever possessed it has gone now."

There was a short silence. "Are you talking about a haunt?" said Berdh, her voice wavering. "I thought they were just – stories..."

"Yes, something like that," said Nelac grimly. "You might as well go back to the house with Huys. I'll just look around here, and I'll join you when I've finished." Selmana turned to leave with her mother. "Selmana, can you stay?"

Selmana watched Berdh and Huys walk back to the house. "Are they in danger?" she asked, in a small voice.

"I don't think so," said Nelac. "No more than any of us, at least." He looked at the boar again, his face troubled. "I wish I could be sure of that, but I am as certain as I can be. Now, Selmana, if you don't mind waiting, I am going to enter the Shadowplains. I'll be absent for a little while, though it's always hard to tell how time passes there. If I am longer than, say, an hour, I want you to ride back to the School and bring Bashar here. Do you understand?"

Shadowplains? Selmana swallowed and nodded, although

she didn't know what Nelac meant. He smiled reassuringly.

"I'm sure it will only be brief," he said. "I ask in case of mischance."

This made Selmana feel no better, but she tried to hide her dismay. As she watched, Nelac's eyes went blank, as if he were blind, and just as suddenly his skin seemed to lose its blood: he looked as if he were made of marble. With a clutch of vertigo, she understood, with her deeper senses, what Nelac had meant when he said he would be absent. She didn't dare to touch him, but she knew that if she did, he wouldn't respond. His body was there, but he was not.

A few minutes passed with agonizing slowness, and nothing happened. Selmana realized that tension was singing through her whole body. She sat down cross-legged on the grass and looked around at the apple trees. Bees were buzzing in the grass amid the sunshine, and she could hear cows lowing in the distance. Somewhere a dog barked. Everything looked and felt absolutely ordinary, aside from the Bard standing in front of her, motionless as stone, and the twisted corpse of the pig.

At last Nelac stirred. He stumbled forward, as if he had fallen in through a door that had suddenly given way, and Selmana jumped up and took his arm so that he wouldn't fall. He steadied himself, and slowly sat on the ground, shivering and rubbing his arms. "It's cold," he said. "The frost is all over me."

Selmana bit her lip, but said nothing. The afternoon sun was almost uncomfortably warm, but where she had touched his hand his skin was as chill as a corpse. What disconcerted her more was that Nelac seemed lost; he looked around like a man who didn't recognize his surroundings. It reminded her painfully of her grandmother, when she had lost her wits before she died.

"Are you – all right?" she asked hesitantly. "Can I do something to help?"

Nelac stared at her blankly, and then it seemed as if his eyes filled up with himself. "Selmana," he said, and briefly gripped her hand so hard she gasped. "How long was I gone?" he asked.

"Not very long," said Selmana. "A few minutes, maybe."

"It's very far away," he said. "A long way there and a long way back…"

"Did you find what – what you were looking for?"

"No," said Nelac. "I found nothing at all. There should be some kind of spoor, a trace, but there was nothing…"

"Spoor?" said Selmana. Again she was confused: Nelac spoke to her as if she knew what he meant, but this was magery she didn't understand at all. Nelac now seemed to be deep in thought, and she didn't like to interrupt him. She watched the colour slowly returning to his face.

"My child," he said at last, breaking the silence. "Can you tell me again what happened here?"

Selmana repeated her story, but this time Nelac questioned her closely, forcing her to recall the details: the exact textures of her loathing, the weight of the terrible pressure that had pushed her down to the ground. "And then – nothing?" he said, when she had finished.

"It disappeared," said Selmana. "It was there, and then – it just wasn't."

"If it was a haunt, you would feel its presence," said Nelac. "You would see where it had been, as a hound perceives a scent. Even if it was—" He paused and stared into space, abstracted.

"Even if it was what?"

Nelac shook himself, and turned to face her. "The first time I saw something like this, it was the Bone Queen. She took the body of a shepherd named Miln, near Lir Lake, and left him broken and twisted, even as this beast. It was not the last time I saw it… Haunts do not do this: they are parasites, sucking on the life of those they inhabit, but they destroy minds, not bodies. Kansabur is … more violent."

"Kansabur? But didn't you – the Bards destroyed her, didn't they?"

"We thought we did," he said. "I fear she deceived us. After this, I am all but certain that she did. But how? When we hunted Kansabur, she left tracks, for those eyes that could see them. Now it seems that she is there, and then she is not, and there is no sign that she has even been, let alone a trace which might tell where she has gone…"

"You think it was Kansabur last night?" The horror rose in Selmana again, as thick as nausea. *"Kansabur?"*

Nelac took her hands between his. "I think it most likely," he said gently. "There are other signs that make me think so. The one consolation, if it is true, is that she is greatly weakened. If she had been in her strength, no shield of yours would have held her back. Nor would she have taken a beast as her flesh, if she could take a human. If we did not destroy her, we have at least crippled her."

"She was still very strong," said Selmana, in a low voice. "I – almost was—"

"Almost. But not." Nelac stood up slowly, as if his whole body ached.

"What about my mother?" she said.

"I will put a ward on the house," said Nelac. "If Kansabur is as weakened as I suspect, she will not be able to shift in daylight, and a ward will be more than sufficient to keep her out. But in truth, I think she would be unlikely to return here."

In the Shadow Circle, Nelac said, there are many kinds of spirits. A few, like the Elidhu, the immortal Elementals, move easily between the planes, equally at home in both. Some few Bards can also enter at will, but never without paying a price: it is not a home to us, he said, and to be present there is to suffer.

Some, like the souls of the recently dead, are simply passing through the Shadowplains, on their journey to the Gates of the Empyrean. Of those, a few never reach the Gates: they find themselves chained to the World, through suffering or grief or regret, and are lost between one place and another, longing for home but unable to find it. We know them as ghosts, and sometimes they can be seen, forlorn shadows flickering in the places where they once lived. Some others, like haunts, have more evil intent. Like ghosts, they are trapped between life and death, but they greedily desire life, and will pay any price to regain what they have lost. They are the spirits that will possess the living, twisting their minds into madness. They resent the living, and will destroy them if they can, but they are still spirits we can think of as human, aspects of ourselves.

"And Kansabur?" asked Selmana. She was in Nelac's sitting room, curled on his couch, staring into the fire that had been set against an unusually cold night. Autumn was coming early this year.

"Kansabur is not quite any of those." Nelac frowned. "Another kind of spirit is that which is summoned from the Abyss, by sorcery. Terrible creatures, like the Shika, which can erupt into our World on wings of dread. Mostly they sleep in the Abyss, but the Nameless One drove them into the Shadowplains and used them in the wars before the Great Silence. None could withstand them. And then there are revenants, the spirits of Hulls, who escaped banishment to the Abyss but who cannot travel to the Gates because of the pact they have made with the Nameless One. They are far more powerful than haunts. They have human memories, and they seek to return to the World. At first we believed they were all banished to the Abyss by Maninaë when he returned the Light to Edil-Amarandh, but alas! Some still yet hide in the Shadowplains, waiting for their master to rise and summon them again. And the Bone Queen is different even from these. Some say that she is more than a Hull, that she took the power of the Shika into her own being."

"Did Cadvan know this when he summoned the Bone Queen?" said Selmana. "How could he wake such a thing?"

"Yes, he knew that, although I am not sure that he understood it." Nelac leaned forward and poked the fire so it flared up. "He thought he could contain such power. As we all know, he couldn't."

Selmana thought of all the evil that had followed Cadvan's act: the death of Ceredin, Dernhil's terrible injury. She hadn't known that others had died, and it seemed to her now that Ceredin's death had been merciful in comparison. She remembered the boar, tormented beyond imagining.

"The council was right to banish him," she said. "He should never be allowed back again."

"There are many who think so," said Nelac. He gave her a measuring look. "You told me you thought otherwise."

"That was before ... before I understood what he had done. Properly, I mean. It's unforgivable, no matter how sorry he is. Even Cadvan said so." Selmana's voice was hard. "How can you forget such a thing?"

"To forget is impossible," said Nelac. "And yet my heart argues for forgiveness. Forgiveness is not about forgetting, child. It is about remembering, always. And if forgiveness is not possible, then I have no hope for any of us."

Selmana was silent. She thought of Ceredin in her dream, leaning over her bed and kissing her forehead. She had said something very similar. Her body had shone as if she were filled with starlight, and the sadness in her dark eyes had smitten Selmana to the heart.

She shivered and drew closer to the fire. "I suppose you're right. But I'm afraid of what he's done."

"What Cadvan did is one thing," said Nelac. "And that is certainly bad enough. But it's what he has unleashed that frightens me."

X

IT was two weeks' ride through lonely country from Jouan to Lirigon, and Cadvan and Dernhil took it at a leisurely pace. Now that he had found Cadvan, Dernhil seemed to have lost any sense of urgency. Which was just as well, thought Cadvan, since the horse he had bought in Jouan, a sway-backed gelding unimaginatively named Brownie, had no chance of keeping up with Dernhil's fiery Hyeradh. It had been the only beast for sale in Jouan, where horses were scarce, and had been a reluctant purchase. Cadvan had cured Brownie of worms and an open sore on his leg, and the horse had actually gained condition on their journey, but nothing would make it a comfortable ride.

Their plan was to travel to Lirigon Fesse, the region around the School, where Cadvan could take up lodging in one of the hamlets, while Dernhil went to the School to inform Nelac of their return. The vagueness of the plan bothered Cadvan almost as much as the thought of returning to Lirigon: why seek him out at such cost, disrupt the life he had made in Jouan, and drag him to Lirigon, if not for some clear reason? He had agreed to Dernhil's request, feeling that he couldn't refuse, but he spent long hours on horseback wondering what goose chase he had committed to. The only thing that cheered him was the prospect of seeing Nelac, who he had missed grievously in the past year and a half of exile; but this was balanced by his discomfort in returning home, where his shame was widely known.

Dernhil had idly proposed that Cadvan should stay with his father, or perhaps his sisters, when they returned, but the look on Cadvan's face had made sure he didn't suggest it again. Cadvan flinched from thinking of his family: there his humiliation was most raw. He knew that his relations had suffered from vicious gossip, and their pride in him had been destroyed; if they could welcome him back, which he personally doubted, their forgiveness would sting more than their rejection. He planned to find board in some place where he would likely not be recognized, on the other side of the Fesse.

He said nothing of this to Dernhil, who guessed more of his thoughts than he suspected. Their relationship remained constrained: Cadvan feared that his temper might again take hold of him, and thought it best to say as little as possible, and Dernhil himself was in no mood for chatter.

There was no direct route to Lirigon. For the first week, they followed cart tracks along the Cuna River, which flowed south past Jouan. South-west of Jouan were impassable forests, which hugged the curious rock formations known as the Redara, a haven for birds. Trading carts and other travellers were forced to follow the watercourses. This meant that the Bards had to ride south and then turn west. The weather remained fair, the days warm and bright, and the nights balmy. A day's ride from the village they began to encounter the forests of North Annar, with their foliage turning towards autumn; the sound of hoof beats was deadened by a thickening carpet of bright leaves. As they neared the Cuna's confluence with the Lir River, the woods thinned out to scrubby, rock-strewn wilderness, and the horses began to complain of the heat. On the day that they reached the Lir River, which would lead them to Lirigon, the weather suddenly changed; cold winds swept down from the mountains, bringing grey clouds and showers. Hyeradh and Brownie now plodded mournfully through the rain, their ears flattened back to their skulls.

That night, nowhere near any hamlet or farm that could

provide them with shelter, they made a poor camp under a dripping oak tree. Cadvan spent a fruitless half hour trying to coax a flame from some damp twigs, until Dernhil, returning from unsaddling the horses and scrubbing them down, set the kindling afire with a word. Like all Bards, Dernhil never used magery casually, but Cadvan's prim refusals irritated him beyond measure. He thought them hypocritical: was Cadvan serious in thinking that by refusing to light a campfire now, he made up for his earlier crimes against the Balance?

Cadvan cast him a surly glance as he poured dried beans into a pot to begin their dinner. It wasn't presently raining, but beyond the circle of their fire the night was utterly black, and the wind was damp and sharp. "It will rain again before dawn," said Dernhil, squatting down and stretching his hands to the flames. "I'd give anything for dry clothes, but I doubt I'll get them tonight."

"Not for a few days, if my nose doesn't mislead me," said Cadvan. "The rain is set in, I think."

Dernhil nodded gloomily. Travelling was exhausting, even at the best of times, and he was not at his best. The cold crept into his muscles, and he could feel his stamina faltering. He made no complaint, but he feared that even at their unhurried pace he might collapse: he had fainted and fallen from his horse more than once on his journey to Jouan. He hated his infirmity with a passion, and it stoked the resentment he felt towards Cadvan for causing it.

The two men ate their dinner in silence, and prepared themselves to sleep. They didn't set a watch; in the northern wilderness of Lirhan there wasn't much to fear. The worst that could happen was a curious bear sniffing at their provisions, and that was a danger easily dealt with by Bards, who could simply tell it to go away. Cadvan fell asleep quickly but Dernhil lay awake for some time. His body throbbed with pain. It began to rain again, at first softly and then more insistently, and an icy deluge of water that had built up in the leaves above fell on his face, trickling down his neck. He swore and wrapped his blankets and cloak more tightly around him. At last he dropped off into uneasy dreams.

In the dark hours before sunrise, Cadvan cried out in his sleep and Dernhil jolted awake. He curled up, hugging the warmth to his body, and tried to settle again, but the more he tried to relax, the more wakeful he felt. At last he gave up, and decided to poke the fire, now slumbering in ruby embers, and make himself a warm drink. It was no longer raining, and the wind had died down so that the night was very still: the clouds had parted and a little vagrant moonlight lit the surface of the river that ran beside them.

He was blowing on his tea, staring idly into the darkness beyond the river, when a woman spoke his name. He jumped, instinctively shielding himself, and looked around. He could see and hear no trace of anyone. Perhaps he had imagined it? He had just decided that his mind was playing tricks when he heard the voice again, much closer this time. He still couldn't tell from which direction it was coming, and could see no one near by. In any case, who would be here, out in the wilderness of Lirhan? He wondered whether to wake Cadvan up, and was just moving to do so when a slender figure stepped into the firelight, seemingly out of nowhere.

This was surprising enough: but then she let down the hood of the cloak that covered her face, and he saw that it was Ceredin. She stood before him, her dark hair loose about her shoulders, in a white dress that he remembered she had worn on the night of his poetry duel with Cadvan. Their eyes met, and Dernhil drew in a sharp breath. It was Ceredin to the life: her delicately arched eyebrows, her full lips and dark eyes, the tiny, faint freckles scattered over her nose. A dim illumination, delicate as starlight, seemed to inhabit her skin, but otherwise she appeared as solid and real as Dernhil himself.

For a few moments he was frozen with wonder. He wasn't at all afraid, but it seemed to him that he must be dreaming.

"Nay Dernhil," said Ceredin, although he hadn't spoken aloud. "You do not dream."

At last he found his voice. "How are you here?"

Ceredin smiled, and sat down by the fire, next to Cadvan's sleeping form. "I am not here," she said. "The Circles are bleeding and the ways are broken. I can't find my way to the Gates. I can see you on the Shadowplains, almost as lost as I am."

Dernhil felt a stab of fear. "I walk already with the dead? Do you mean I'm dying?"

"All of us walk with death from the moment we are born. There is part of your being that wanders in your waking life, and it is that I see in the Shadowplains. It is a living thing, and shines, and I know your form."

Dernhil shook his head in bewilderment. "I don't understand," he said. "I don't understand at all. Why are you lost, Ceredin?"

"Sometimes I think I see the Gates in the distance, and I am hopeful and walk towards them, and then they fade and shimmer and I find myself alone, on a dark plain, with whispering all around me. I cannot see who whispers, but I know there are many of them, and I think they are the voices of those who are lost like me."

Ceredin spoke without any emotion in her voice, as if she were speaking of something distant from her, but at this Dernhil reached forward without thinking, to take her hand in his, and she drew back hastily.

"You mustn't touch me," she said. "I am not here. I only seem."

Dernhil sat back, staring at Ceredin. There was, to his eyes at least, nothing insubstantial about her presence: he was torn between astonishment and a disconcerting sense that this encounter was, despite everything, absolutely ordinary.

"Should I wake Cadvan?" he asked.

"Cadvan cannot hear me, sleeping or waking," she said. "His longing fills his ears and drowns my voice. He cannot hear me, no matter how many times I say his name."

"Yet he burns to see you," said Dernhil.

"Yes."

Dernhil was silent for a time, pondering. In most tales, when the dead visited the living, it was to tell them something urgent. "Is there something I should tell him, then?" he asked. "Or is there something I should do?"

"There is a rift," said Ceredin. "It opens beneath the feet of the dead and the living. It opens within the World. There is a rift in the hearts of those who dream on the edges of the World, where the future opens like a wound. There is a great malice, broken into three and three. Each malice seeks the others."

"I don't understand…"

"Cadvan is hidden from himself, there is a shadow within him," said Ceredin, fixing Dernhil with her gaze. "Through Cadvan the rift has opened. The malice burned through him, and through him finds its shapes."

"Ceredin, I really don't understand," said Dernhil.

Ceredin didn't answer. She shivered and drew her cloak about her, as if a cold wind had sprung up, although the night remained still. "The Circles are bleeding," she said. "I am nowhere, yet everywhere hunted. I long for rest, Dernhil." Her voice, until now cool and distant, filled with yearning, and despite himself Dernhil leaned forward, knowing he must not touch Ceredin, yet wanting to comfort her.

"How?" he asked. "How may I bring you rest?"

But Ceredin stood up hurriedly, looking over her shoulder,

and without speaking stepped outside the circle of firelight. As soon as the night enfolded her, Dernhil knew that she was gone.

He sat motionless for some time, caught in the strangeness of what had just happened. Then he realized that he was still clutching his tin mug of tea, and that it had gone cold. He tipped it out, and hunted through his pack for his fast dwindling supply of medhyl, the drink Bards used to stave off exhaustion. He knew that sleep was now impossible, and he wanted to think. Ceredin's words baffled him: the only part he really understood was that she was lost in the Shadowplains, a spirit caught between one world and another. He had read of such things, and they were always sad stories: the thought that Ceredin should be so forlorn tore his heart.

She had said she was hunted. He thought that part of the riddle was more easily understood than the others: it must be the Bone Queen who sought her. He cursed himself for not having the presence of mind to ask her directly. Surely she would have said? Yet perhaps she couldn't be clear. She had seemed different from the Ceredin who had visited his dream last autumn: then she had been the woman he had known in life, but now she was estranged; even speaking seemed hard for her, as if she were seeking the meaning of words as she said them.

Then he wondered how he was to tell Cadvan. He could not conceal this encounter from him, but he quailed at the thought. Cadvan was sure to be angry, or pained, or full of self-contempt; or most likely, all three at once.

At dawn the wind changed to the west and the sky cleared, but it brought a sun with little heat in it. Dernhil and Cadvan pushed their reluctant horses across the ford at the confluence of the Lir and Cuna Rivers and started westward towards Lirigon. At noon, they found a sheltered dingle where they stopped for a midday meal. Out of the wind the sun was gentle and warm, and Dernhil stretched out on the grass with a sigh, closed his eyes and fell fast asleep. Cadvan watched Dernhil for a few minutes and then unsaddled and brushed the horses. He had noted the exhaustion on Dernhil's face that morning, and now decided that they would go no further that day.

By the time Dernhil stirred, the sun was low. He blinked and sat up, swearing softly. "Why didn't you wake me?" he said, moving over to the fire, where Cadvan was stirring a stew of dried fish in a pot.

"You were sleeping so blissfully that I didn't have the heart."

Dernhil rubbed his hands near the flames; the air already held an evening chill. "That was unusually merciful of you."

Cadvan said nothing. Dernhil watched his face for a while, bent in concentration over the pot. "Something odd happened last night," he said, clearing his throat. "I had a visit from Ceredin."

Cadvan glanced up sharply, his face expressionless. "Yes?"

Dernhil told his story swiftly and plainly, with a Bard's accuracy. Cadvan listened intently, his face averted, and when Dernhil finished, there was a long silence. Then he announced abruptly that they needed more firewood, and walked off. Dernhil watched him out of sight, shrugged and stirred the stew. It wouldn't do to let it burn.

Cadvan returned after sunset, with a smallish bundle of wood that he had clearly picked up as an afterthought. It was scarcely needed anyway: there was a good pile already that he had collected while Dernhil slept. Dernhil wordlessly doled the stew into bowls and they ate, staring into the leaping flames as darkness settled around them. After they had cleaned up, Cadvan brewed a camomile tea, and the two sat side by side, blowing on the hot liquid.

"Why do you think she can't speak to me, Dernhil?" said Cadvan, in a low voice.

Startled by the question, Dernhil didn't answer at once. "I think … she knows that you long for her, and it is that very longing that makes it impossible for you to hear her."

"It's so … unfair." He turned to Dernhil. "You know that poem of yours… *Could I but call you now, and hear your voice…*"

Dernhil finished the couplet. "*And yet my very anguish seals my loss.*"

"Yes, that one. I read all your poems again, after … when I was still in Lirigon. I was unjust to you, Dernhil. There are many ways in which I have wronged you, but I'm not sure I ever apologised to you for so stupidly criticizing your poems."

Embarrassed, Dernhil gestured dismissively, but Cadvan continued.

"Anyway, I feel like that poem." He leaned forward and poked the fire with a stick. "It's perhaps what wounds me most when I hear of Ceredin speaking to you. No, that's not the worst. What wounds me most is that she sounds as if she is afraid…"

"*Abandoned in the infinite…*" said Dernhil softly, quoting another poet.

"The immortal Lorica," said Cadvan, smiling painfully at Dernhil. "I think your work approaches her poetry, you know, in how you express… But I am not saying anything very well tonight. Forgive me for telling you this. I know what I feel about it is of the least importance." He paused. "Maybe I am talking about poems because they are the only place where it's possible to speak such difficult and complicated things." He gestured helplessly. "And it's not what I meant to say at all, anyway. I've been turning what Ceredin said over in my head, trying to understand…"

"I have been too," said Dernhil. "With small success."

"Some things are clear. She is speaking of the Shadow Circle. *There is a rift in the hearts of those who dream on the edges of the World, where the future opens like a wound."*

"She said that you are hidden from yourself," said Dernhil. "That there is a darkness within you…"

"That's not so hard to riddle," said Cadvan. "Nor this: *The malice burned through him, and through him finds its shapes.* It is clear how I opened this rift, and how the malice burned through me. Clear to me, anyway. But how does it *find its shapes* through me? I am a – conduit, perhaps? An unwitting doorway for Kansabur? How can that be so, and I not know it? Is this why you've been sent to find me?"

Dernhil met his eyes. "I don't know," he said. "To be honest, all I know for sure is that my nightmares stopped once I started looking for you. And I'd rather ride about the wilderness, even with you, than suffer those again."

Cadvan laughed. "If you were plagued with dreams like the one I had, I don't blame you," he said. "But listen: *A great malice, broken into three and three.* What does that mean?"

"Kansabur is divided into many, perhaps?"

"How is that so? It makes no sense. How can a spirit be split into different parts and yet exist? It makes me fear that I called more evils than Kansabur from the outer Circles…"

"Perhaps. But think you, Cadvan. Ceredin said this to me: *There is part of your being that wanders in your waking life, and it is that I see in the Shadowplains.* How can that be so? Yet Ceredin says it is. Are we less whole than we think?"

Cadvan was silent a long time. At last he said, "I know I am not whole. I think I never will be."

Dernhil glanced at him with quick sympathy. "I burn to speak to Nelac," he said. "Of all the loremasters, he is the one who might be able to solve these riddles."

"Aye." Cadvan drew his cloak closer around him. "I've missed him sorely. He can set a lamp in the darkest places. I know that better than anyone."

* * *

After that conversation, much of the constraint between the two
Bards vanished. Dernhil, used to Cadvan's reserve, was surprised by his confiding in him, and liked him better for it. To
his own chagrin, he was also pleased by what Cadvan had said
about his poems; he didn't like to admit it, because it felt petty,
but Cadvan's scorn had hurt him. On his side, Cadvan found
that his anger had subsided. To speak of Ceredin with Dernhil
had been painful, but it was also a relief.

Aside from a couple of showery days, the weather remained
kind, although the summer was now over. They rode through
pretty, if desolate, country. The Lir wound its way through
the tumbled landscapes of the Redara, where twisted towers
and strange cliffs of weathered stone poked through the forest
canopies, sometimes bare white rock, sometimes fringed with
grass. The region was loud with birdsong: great flocks of swal-
lows and starlings that nested in the cliffs swept through the
sky, beginning their migration south for the winter, as falcons
and other hunting birds circled high above them. The Bards followed a track that hugged the river until at last they emerged
from the Redara to the grass plains that stretched westwards
across Lirhan, all the way to the sea.

They began to encounter people again. In the past week they
hadn't seen a single soul, but here there were small, isolated
villages, or the lonely huts of shepherds, and they could beg a
bed of hay in a barn rather than sleeping in the open. From here
it was an easier ride to the Fesse of Lirigon, and they made it in
a few days. They arrived in the village of Bural, an hour's ride
from the School, on an overcast afternoon, with a rising wind
behind them and the smell of rain on the air. Bural was on the
other side of the Lirigon Fesse to Cadvan's home village, and
he thought it unlikely that he would be recognized.

"I won't be sad to sleep in a proper bed tonight," said Cadvan, as they stabled their horses at the village inn, which a sign over the door proclaimed was called The Fat Hen. "It looks as if a storm is building. I think we've seen the last of summer." He studied the inn's front room with approval: it was comfortable and clean, with promising smells wafting in from the kitchen.

"For my part," said Dernhil, "I want a meal that isn't composed of dried meat and pulses. I never want to see a pulse again."

Cadvan laughed. "Do you know how long it is since I tasted a loaf of good Lirigon bread?" he said. "Or a trout pie? Or a round of soft cow's cheese?"

"I can guess," said Dernhil.

"Too long. Much longer than you. Don't ride off to the School tonight, Dernhil. What hurry is there? I insist that you stay here. Food is best eaten in company."

Dernhil smiled, and they both bespoke rooms with the landlord, a stout red-haired man named Stefan, and met in the cosy dining parlour downstairs a couple of hours later, washed and brushed. Cadvan ordered a jug of the crisp Lirigon wine and they had a long discussion with Stefan about their meal. They settled for rabbit in ginger sauce with a dish of peas and saffron, a borage-flower tart and the local cheese.

"I could wish for clean clothes," said Cadvan, leaning back in his chair. "But otherwise, I am content."

Dernhil had been covertly studying Cadvan with some surprise: he seemed light-hearted, even joyous, as if he had temporarily forgotten everything that weighed him down. Dernhil had never seen this side of him before, and felt for the first time the force of his charm. It had often puzzled him that people he respected liked Cadvan so much, but now he began to understand why.

Dernhil raised his glass. "I think it's a cause for some celebration that we made it to Lirigon without a single argument."

"Yes. We could have stabbed each other to death out in the lonely wilds. Our bones might have been found years later, scattered by wild animals, an enduring mystery to the passing traveller…"

The meal arrived, and they ate with relish, pursuing a non-sensical conversation that touched on none of their serious concerns. Afterwards, as the storm that had threatened in the afternoon buffeted the trees outside, they sat together by the hearth and argued passionately about poetry. It was well after midnight when they made their way to their beds.

Dernhil lay awake for a while, thinking. He had seldom enjoyed an evening more: Cadvan had given his mercurial mind full rein, showing a wit, knowledge and depth of insight that made him a rare companion. Dernhil had travelled with Cadvan for two weeks without seeing a glimpse of this aspect of him. Why not? he thought with a flicker of anger; it would have made their journey so much more enjoyable. He had braced himself for all sorts of thunderclouds from Cadvan when they arrived in Lirigon, the scene of his disgrace, only to find himself confronted with an amusing, charming companion. No wonder his friends so often spoke of him with loving frustration.

Just before he fell asleep, Dernhil wondered if he was begin-ning to think of Cadvan as a friend. After everything that had happened between them, he thought, that would be odd beyond imagining: no one had caused him more pain. It was Cadvan who had opened the underworld in his mind, awaken-ing shadows he had never suspected lived within him. Ought he to be grateful?

He would rise early tomorrow, he thought. He needed to see Nelac for his own reasons.

XI

THE storm blew out after midnight, bringing in its wake
an eerie stillness. In her small chamber at the School
of Lirigon, Selmana laid down her pen and slumped
back in her chair. She had spent the evening making notes on
metallurgy from some obscure scrolls she had found in the
Lirigon library. Since Nelac had given her private lessons, she
had discovered an unexpected fascination with these writings;
although she still struggled to read them, she had begun to
wonder if she would write something herself, as Nelac had
once suggested she might.

Tonight that seemed a very distant possibility. She stared
dully at her notes: "Wherefore smelting is necessary, for by
this means earths, solidified juices and stone are separated
from their metals so that they obtain their proper colour and
become pure…" The words had ceased to make any sense, she
was too tired. She stood up and opened the casement, throwing
back the shutters that she had closed earlier against the storm,
and leant on the windowsill. The cold air was a balm and she
breathed in deeply. It was a moonless night, very black, with
a few vagrant stars peeking through the ragged clouds. She
lingered for a while, huddling a shawl about her shoulders, and
stared blankly over the dark roofs of the School.

Her first thought was for her mother. She looked east, wondering, as she had every evening for the past fortnight, if her
mother was safe. Selmana had returned to Lirigon reluctantly
after the ugly incident with the boar, feeling that she ought to

stay at the farmhouse in case something else happened. Nelac had said that he thought Berdh was in no more danger than anyone else in the Fesse, which was, when Selmana thought about it, little comfort. He had put wards about the farmhouse, as he had promised, and assured Selmana that it was most unlikely that Kansabur, if it were she, would return to the same place. But Selmana found it was impossible not to worry. She was having trouble sleeping: sometimes she startled awake, her heart pounding, terrified that a malign spirit was outside her window, or reliving the foul sensation as the revenant had tried to possess her. Even the memory made her break out in a sweat.

Selmana's answer to these anxieties was to throw herself into work. Despite Calis's demanding schedules in the crafts of the Making and the other compulsory classes for Minor Bards, she still had some idle hours: she dealt with them by cornering one of the Bards in the library and requesting a list of every book or scroll to do with metalworking. The Bard had been slightly startled, but the next day gave her what he called a "preliminary list". Selmana crossed out those in languages she couldn't read, and resolved to work her way through the rest of the recommended writings. There were fifty-four titles in the list, and so far she had stubbornly worked her way through five of the shorter scrolls. At this rate, she thought, she would be chained to her work table for the next half-century.

Still, a person couldn't work all the time. She should go to bed: but for all her exhaustion, she felt strained and wakeful. Tonight she was sorely missing Ceredin. If her cousin were still alive, she could have visited her room, as she had done so often when she was troubled. She didn't have to say a word: Ceredin always knew, with her quick, immediate sympathy, that something was wrong. She would have poured her a wine or a tiny glass of laradhel, a delicious golden liqueur brewed by Bards in the valley of Innail, and settled down to talk. It wasn't so much that Ceredin gave her advice, although when she did it was always good; it was the comfort of her company. They talked about everything under the sun, from the latest family gossip to the mysteries of the Speech. Ceredin had always made her laugh.

Selmana leaned over the windowsill, feeling the heaviness in her shoulders. It was a tiredness of the soul, she thought, deeper than physical weariness. That was harder to deal with. Her eyes were sticky and hot, and she rubbed them, thinking that even if she couldn't sleep, she should lie down.

When she looked out over Lirigon again, it had vanished. She blinked, and looked again. Where the School had been a moment before, a shadowy plain stretched before her, rising up to a black, cloudless sky studded with stars. For a moment she was utterly still: she thought her heart had stopped beating. She glanced back into her room: it was just as before, with the lamp casting its soft light over her work table, its image shining crookedly in the diamond panes of the window. The sill beneath her folded arms was solid and cold, and below her the wall ran unbroken down to the ground. And yet from the foot of the building nothing was the same at all.

I must have fallen asleep without knowing it and am dreaming, she thought. She breathed in hard, trying to calm her mind, and realized she was trembling. It is a very vivid dream. But in a moment I will wake and all will be well. She rubbed her eyes again, hoping that might make Lirigon reappear, but the empty plains before her remained unchanged. She looked up at the sky and saw with a shock that she recognized none of the constellations. They shone with a different light from the stars she knew: they seemed further away, but their light was more intense, somehow colder, and their groupings were utterly strange. There wasn't a whisper of wind, and the air struck with a dull chill, as if it had never been breathed. It was absolutely silent.

Selmana didn't know how long she stood there, staring out of her window, clutching the hard stone of the sill as if it were a spar that would save her from drowning. It was long enough for her body to stiffen so that when she moved, she gave an involuntary groan that startled her. She stepped back from the window, thinking that she should close the casement, bar the shutters and go to bed, locking out this unnerving reality that had suddenly appeared at her window. But what if it doesn't go away, she thought. What if I wake up and everything is just like this? She glanced over at the door of her room, which was closed fast, and with a shudder it occurred to her that if she opened it, she might not find the ordinary corridor and stairs of the Bardhouse, but something else, some other place.

She dug her nails into her palm until it hurt and then bit her finger hard, hoping the pain might shock her awake. It's a dream or a vision, it's not real, she told herself. But some deeper sense told her it was not a dream at all. It was impossible, but it was real. Reluctantly, taking deep, slow breaths, she turned back to the window, trying to control her mounting fear. The plains were still outside, a light grey under the black sky. There was no moon. For some reason she was sure there was never a moon in this sky, never any sun. And suddenly she knew what she was seeing: it was the Shadowplains the Bards spoke of, the second Circle, where the dead walked on their way to the Gates.

The moment she found a name, she seemed to see more clearly, and she felt less afraid. Nelac, she reminded herself, had walked these plains and returned. She stared out curiously into the endless night. Slowly, she became aware that the landscape was not, as she had first thought, utterly desolate: she could see forms like shrubs or small bushes, and she thought something like grass grew on the ground. Were they living plants, she wondered, or just the shadows of things, without substance or life? Were there animals, too? Was that fleeting form in the corner of her eye the shape of a bird? The cold began to bite into her and she shivered, drawing her shawl closer around her, and then leaned forward over the sill. There was a soft illumination in the distance. Something, a form of light, was moving towards her.

At first she wasn't sure if her eyes were playing tricks, but as it grew closer, the light resolved into a human figure, a slender woman, lit with a pale radiance the same colour as the stars. Selmana was almost sure, from her gait, that it was Ceredin, but she couldn't see her face clearly. Before she could decide for certain, the figure started and looked fearfully behind her. She lifted her arms in a sudden gesture of defiance or alarm, and vanished.

The plains were empty again, but Selmana sensed that something had changed. She squinted into the darkness, straining to see through the shadows. She could feel a new presence, a weight that pressed on her awareness. Then, as if the darkness rearranged itself before her eyes, she saw it. She leaped back from the window with a cry, covering her face with her hands. When she looked again, the Shadowplains had gone: the nighttime roofs of Lirigon again stretched below her window.

Relief flooded her body with sudden warmth. Hastily, her hands trembling, she drew the shutters and closed the window. She stumbled to her bed and sat down, staring at the wall, trying to understand what she had seen. She didn't know how to describe it to herself: it was like an image in a dream that wouldn't translate into everyday life, and which therefore slipped out of memory, leaving only its feeling behind. The strongest sensation was of horror. The Shadowplains had frightened her because they were uncanny, but this thing she had seen had terrified her in a wholly different way.

It had no form that she could fix her eye on. It shifted its shape, like smoke. But it wasn't like smoke at all, because at the same time it seemed to be material, as if the darkness had become glutinous. It had appeared like a disease, like a toxin erupting out of the ground. It had seemed to be many things, many non-shapes, running in and out of each other like mercury, but she was sure it was a single consciousness. It had no face, no eyes, but she had felt it was searching for her, that soon it would discover her sitting at her window.

Selmana shook her head. How could she describe this to anybody else? She couldn't make sense of what she had seen even to herself. The only thing that was clear was the feeling: an almost tangible wave of malevolent intent. It was like (but not at all like) a suffocating stench, that made you dizzy. You breathed it in and it became part of you, whether you liked it or not. It was like…

Selmana's thoughts faltered. She wondered if she should write her impressions down while they were still vivid in her mind, but as her terror waned and her body stopped shaking, she realized that she was so tired she could barely stand. There was one thing that she was sure of, one thing that was clear: it was exactly the same feeling, as distinct and particular as an individual voice, as that she had experienced in her mother's orchard a fortnight before. Exactly the same.

When Selmana woke the following morning, she lay on her bed staring at the shuttered window. She had to force herself to open it and let the morning in. Even though she could hear a chatter of morning birdsong and a cockerel crowing in the distance, she feared that she would see only the grey landscape: but there it was, the red-tiled roofs of Lirigon glowing in the early sun, the sky paling to the clear blue of what would be a beautiful autumn day. She drew in a shuddering breath of relief.

She dressed hurriedly and ran to Nelac's Bardhouse, but when she knocked on his door there was no answer. Biting her lip with impatience, she stood a while in indecision, and then made her way to her lessons for that day. She spent the morning trying to concentrate on the theory of the Speech, which was taught by Inghalt, one of her least favourite teachers. He seldom invited discussion and Selmana had twice fallen asleep in his classes out of sheer boredom.

This morning she was particularly distracted. Her sleep had been full of uneasy dreams, none of which she now remembered, and ever since she awoke she had been fighting a sense that something was tracking her, growing ever closer. It was absurd: what could happen here in the heart of Lirigon? And yet the feeling grew on her during the morning: the hairs on her neck prickled at odd moments, and she would turn swiftly, as if she might catch a glimpse of something that sniffed at her footsteps. Her friends noticed she was behaving oddly, and teased her for her jumpiness. She thought it would not be surprising to imagine things after her strange experience the night before. But the sensation wouldn't go away. She listened to Inghalt with half an ear, in case he surprised her with a question, fighting back her anxiety.

What did it mean, Inghalt was asking, when Bards said that it was impossible to lie in the Speech? "It means," he said, "that unlike other forms of language, the Speech has an indissoluble relationship to reality. This is why, in the mouth of a Bard, it can change reality. This is the core of the mystery of magery…"

At this point, one of her fellow students interrupted. "If that's really so, Bard Inghalt, then how is it that Hulls also used the Speech? Because we all know they did."

"Please don't distract us with juvenile questions, Gest," said Inghalt. "Hulls didn't use the Speech as we use it. Neither do those who are not born with it in their tongue, but who learn it in the same way they learn other languages. In such usages, the Speech is not the Speech…"

"But that doesn't make sense," said Selmana, suddenly interested. "It's the same words, isn't it? How can the words have a – an indissoluble relationship to reality – when they can be used in other ways too?"

Inghalt looked harassed. "The Black Speech is a mere side-alley to our subject today," he said. "Sorcery has nothing to do with us. As I said…"

"But the Hulls use the Speech to make charms, just as we do," said Gest, glancing at Selmana. "The Black Speech changes reality, and so must be one with the Speech in that way."

"And we all know that Hulls can lie," said another student. There was a rustling through the room: suddenly all the Minor Bards were paying attention.

It was a common game among the younger Bards, to try to lie outright in the Speech: they all knew how the words wouldn't form on the tongue or in the mind if you tried to say something that you knew was untrue. Sometimes the more talented among the Minor Bards could say things like "the sky is made of stone", but only if they concentrated very hard. Yet you could recite poetry – or at least, most poetry – in the Speech, and poetry often described things that were not real. Bards said this was because poetry explored more complex truths than literal realities. The smarter Minor Bards worked out that they could say something that was untrue if they believed it was true. How different was that from a lie? How different was a poem from a lie? If a Hull could lie in the Speech, why not a Bard as well?

"Perhaps the real question is not why it's impossible to lie in the Speech, but why it *is* possible?" said Gest.

Inghalt always sidestepped these questions, and today was no exception.

"As I said," replied Inghalt, his voice high with annoyance, "these are not uses of the Speech proper. Our subject today is the Speech proper, as used by Bards who do not stray from the path of the Light…"

"But surely they must be connected, the powers of the Hulls and of Bards?" said Selmana.

"It is a blasphemy to say so, young Bard, and I would thank you not to bring such ideas into my chamber," said Inghalt. And that was the end of that.

Nelac wouldn't have told me not to ask that question, thought Selmana. He would have tried to answer it… As Inghalt droned on, her mind drifted. Kansabur had once been a Bard, like all Hulls. She had never really thought about what that meant. She had always been taught that sorcery had nothing to do with magery, but was that the case, really? The question disturbed her: it seemed to grow out of her vision from the previous night as much as it did from Gest's needling of Inghalt.

Was it Kansabur she had seen on the Shadowplains? She was absolutely sure that it was same … *thing* she had encountered when she had seen the boar. Her mind flinched from the memory; two weeks later, it still made her feel sick. With a Bard's suspicion of certainty, Nelac refused to give the thing a name, but he clearly strongly suspected that was it was the Bone Queen, however diminished. Did it matter what anyone called it? Was it hunting her? The thought was paralysing, stupefying, and she pushed it away.

When she returned to Nelac's rooms at noon, he was still absent. She asked around, and found out that a messenger had arrived before sunrise, heavily cloaked, and that Nelac had left with him, riding east. He had left no word on where he was going, or when he might be expected back. Selmana was daunted by this news: he could be gone for days. She wondered for a moment whether it would be worth waiting for him in his rooms, but decided against it. After some hesitation, she found a piece of paper on the work table and wrote Nelac a note, which she left propped against some books.

She was hungry, but her stomach was in such a knot that she thought that if she ate anything she might be sick. She made her way to the dining hall, but none of her friends was there. She remembered belatedly that they had planned to take a basket of breads and cheeses to a meadow a short distance outside the School, to enjoy the autumn sunshine. She thought of joining them, and then discarded the idea, and then changed her mind again. She wanted company more than food.

Slowly she wandered through the streets of Lirigon to the North Gate. The streets were busy with people lured out by the warmth, going about their business or just talking idly, but she felt curiously alone. *But you are not alone.* The thought rose in her mind as if it were said by a voice not her own and she halted so suddenly that a Bard walking behind collided into her. She didn't respond to his apology, she didn't even hear him. She was suddenly cold with terror.

She stood, completely still, staring about her. She was in the Street of Potters. There was Aldan's workshop, with a pile of carefully stacked roof tiles dried for the kiln, and over there, throwing a lump of clay on the wheel, was Inkar. A black and white cat was curled up in an ecstasy of voluptuousness on Inkar's step, exactly where any customer would step on their way in. Everything was absolutely ordinary. It was exactly as it always was.

Except, Selmana realized with creeping horror, that there was no sound. A child was playing in the road, talking to a toy rabbit, but she opened and closed her mouth and Selmana could hear nothing. The potter's wheel, which she could see straight in front of her, whirred silently, and when Inkar thumped the treadle with his foot, it was noiseless. When had the world lost its voice? Was it just at that moment, or did the sound ebb out bit by bit, and she hadn't noticed until now? She stared wildly about her, feeling a pulse throbbing violently in her throat, and a woman took her elbow, mouthing something that Selmana couldn't hear. Almost beside herself, Selmana snatched back her arm, staring at the woman.

"Are you ill, child?"

And suddenly she could hear the world again. Unable to speak, Selmana shook her head, and she ran to the side of the road and retched. She brought up nothing but bile. The woman followed her, and patted her shoulder.

"You look like you've had a nasty turn, little kitten," she said.

Selmana stood up straight, wiping her mouth with the back of her hand. Despite everything, she wanted to laugh. Little kitten? She was taller than this woman by at least two hand-spans. It was difficult to tell how old she was: her face was creased with many friendly wrinkles, and she was very stout. She had on a bright red dress and gold rings hung from her pierced ears.

"I'm sorry," Selmana said. "Yes, I suddenly felt very sick, I don't know why."

"I'm Larla," said the woman. "My house isn't far, perhaps you should have a drink of tea and a rest... You might need a healer."

"Maybe it would be good just to sit down," said Selmana, with a rush of gratitude. "I don't know what happened then... But I feel all right now, really..."

"Come along then," said Larla, taking her arm and guiding her down a laneway to a house that was at the back of one of the potteries. The wall was covered by a vine that even now was turning to the vivid colours of autumn, and the door was painted blue. Larla sat her down in a kitchen that was full of bright objects – red and blue clay pots, polished copper pans – and swung a kettle onto the hob.

"A tea of linden flower will calm you down, and help your stomach," she said. "But it will take a little while. Let me know if you feel sick again in good time so I can find a dish. I just scrubbed the floor, you know. It's such a lovely day, and so it dried easy."

As Larla's comfortable chatter washed over her, Selmana began to relax. She wondered if she had imagined the silence. Perhaps she should see a healer and ask for her ears to be examined? For now she was content just to nod in response, to sit and watch Larla as she took some dried flower heads from a tin box and threw them into a pot. She walked with difficulty – a problem with her hip, she told Selmana – but all the same, she moved with an odd grace. Selmana sipped the mild tea slowly. For the first time that day, she felt safe.

"You're a Bard?" said Larla. Selmana nodded. "Then you'll know who to see, if you still feel sick."

"I think it's gone away now," said Selmana. "It was very … odd. I couldn't hear anything at all, all the sound of everything went away…"

"Anything wrong with your ears can make you dizzy. I had a bad cold once and my ears went and I couldn't stand up without falling over."

"Yes, maybe it was that. Anyway, it passed quite quickly."

"You stay here as long as you like. You're a better colour now. I was watching you, you went white, like all the blood had drained out of your body."

Selmana felt an impulse to tell Larla everything that had happened, all about the boar and the strange vision the night before and the terrible feeling she had had all day that something was following her, like a cat tracking the scent of a mouse. But Larla might think she had lost her wits. Perhaps she was a bit unbalanced: perhaps the incident at her mother's farm had thrown her. She was very tired, after all, and that in itself could make you see strange things... She told herself to stop being stupid. She shouldn't be flinching at shadows. So, after she had finished her tea, she thanked Larla and said she should take her leave.

"Are you sure, kitten?" Larla said. "You're very welcome to stay here for a while."

"I'm late for some friends."

The older woman studied her with a disconcerting shrewdness. Something in her gaze made Selmana wonder if she weren't a Bard, after all. "I'm half inclined to keep you here a bit longer, for all that you look a little pinker."

"I'm sure I'm well now," said Selmana.

Larla patted her hand. "If you're sure," she said. "The Light knows, I'm not kidnapping you. Remember I'm here, if need be."

When the door shut behind her, Selmana almost turned around and went back inside. She looked up at the sky, where a few fluffy clouds floated over the blue. It was still warm, but she felt a sudden chill as a wind sprang up and died away. The weather would change this afternoon. Perhaps she should return to the School after all, she thought: Nelac might have come back. She squared her shoulders and walked down the laneway, breathing out in relief. Everything was normal now.

And then, so swiftly she had no sense of transition, everything was wrong. A crushing sense of impending peril seemed to drop from the sky. The street was the same as before. The light was no different. Yet in the space of a moment she was terrified of something that she couldn't see and couldn't hear, but which she knew with every nerve in her body was about to pounce and devour her. Her instincts took over before she could even think, and she bolted, sobbing with panic.

She skidded around the corner into the Street of Potters, and stepped into darkness. The stars were above, distant and

bright and still. The plains ran level before her to a dark horizon. There was no sound. She whipped around, expecting to
see the laneway behind her, but all she could see was a dim hill
rising endlessly, cutting off the stars.

Lirigon had vanished.

XII

NELAC rode into Bural with the sun. Although the moon had long set, the sky had been darkly luminous for hours, dousing the brilliance of the stars and giving enough light to ride by. Only the dawn star, Ilion, shone undimmed: it burned low over the western horizon, bright enough to throw faint shadows in its own right. Nelac and Dernhil moved through a landscape of muted colours; shreds of mist curled about the fetlocks of their horses as they trotted through the meadows of Lirigon Fesse, with the rich smell of autumn leaf mould rising to their nostrils. Just before they arrived in the village, the sun sent its first rays over the edge of the earth, and the grasses, bent with heavy dew, sparkled alive in prisms of fire. Far away in the north the snowy tips of the Osidh Elanor, the Mountains of the Dawn, flared red and pink like the edges of petals.

Nelac pulled up his mare, Cina, and flung back the hood of his cloak. For a time they stood unmoving in the golden light, man and horse, while the disc of the sun edged over the horizon. Dernhil stopped beside him, and looked enquiringly.

"Such beauty, Dernhil,' he said quietly, in the Speech. "And yet – I can't say why – it fills me with so much grief." He paused. "It wasn't always so. Once, I found consolation in this…"

Dernhil opened his mouth to speak and hesitated, unsure what to say. In the Speech, Nelac's words had a deeper resonance, which stirred the sorrow in his own soul.

Nelac glanced across at him and smiled. "No doubt this is

the sadness of an old man, who feels his death pressing on his heels. Death is a mystery and a bafflement to us all! But once I thought this beauty and plenty would outlast me and mine. And the thought that it might not, that all this shimmering life might waver and die and never return – that is a sorrow, Dernhil, that I know not how to encompass."

"Even the mountains must be worn down to dust one day," said Dernhil. "And even the sun burn out its furnace…"

Nelac was silent. "Yes, all things must pass," he said at last. "But the dreams that haunt you, the fear that rises inside me… Ends and beginnings were always the warp and weft of the world's fabric. But this fear is different, Dernhil. To poison the Light, to burn the living world, to break the very axis of the Balance: how is that possible? And yet I feel it is, in my deepest being."

"Need it be so?" said Dernhil.

"Nay," said Nelac. "It need not. But we are so small… Those like the Bone Queen do not care, and so they are stronger: life is merely something in their way, which can be trampled or brushed aside. We cannot do that, we must stop to take care, and so we are hampered by the very things that matter to us most… Yet even the Nameless One, when he drowned all Annar in the Great Silence, did not destroy the Balance because he wanted to be evil. It was just what followed…"

Hyeradh stamped impatiently. *We are almost back to the stable*, she complained. *And it's cold. And I did not complain when you put the saddle on so early, although I would have liked to stay in the warm.*

Dernhil leant forward, patting her neck. *I am very grateful*, he said silently in the Speech. *And I will make you a mash when we return.*

Nelac smiled, and gravely apologised to the mare, who snorted scornfully. But for the moment he did not urge on

Cina, who remained silent and unmoving, her ears pricked alertly. He glanced over at Dernhil, and spoke in Annaren. "I'm sorry, my friend, for burdening you with my doubt. Despair is a bitter counsel, and the surest defeat of all."

"We must know what we face," said Dernhil. "It may be that we cannot stem what I have seen. And even if it is so, even if there is no hope, it is no reason not to struggle."

"So the wise have always claimed," said Nelac, gathering up his reins. "Although they fail to record adequately how difficult it is. And I wonder, Dernhil. Perhaps we will banish this threat now, but the real peril lives inside each of us – the lust to possess what cannot be owned, the desire to defeat death by denying life to others, the indifference that consumes us in our own ambitions, reckoning nothing of those unknown others who might pay the price for it. Each of us knows this, each of us carries this seed inside us…"

Dernhil was taken aback by Nelac's mood: a deep bitterness ran beneath his words. "But surely you have never chosen against the Balance, surely you have always worked for the Light," he said awkwardly, trying to feel his way.

Nelac glanced across at Dernhil, his eyebrows drawn into a frown. "Don't mistake me for something inhuman, Dernhil. I feel these things, and must recognize them as mine. And sometimes I understand that what is best in me is also the worst."

"Virtue was ever double-edged."

"Aye. And how keen is that edge? How do we know one side from the other, when it comes to our own desires? Be sure: what threatens us is not merely a skirmish between Bards and Hulls, Dernhil. It concerns us all, all of us who walk under this sky, all of us who will be born hereafter. I doubt there will be heroes in this story. And I am afraid…"

Dernhil knew Nelac had the gift of foresight, and his heart faltered. Nelac was the steadfast one, the bulwark to whom others turned in their own doubt, and he seldom revealed his inner thoughts. Dernhil was suddenly aware, as the sun lifted over them, how the years lay heavy upon the older Bard: he saw with a new clarity how deeply the lines were scored in his face, the fragility of the bones beneath the aging skin of his hands. For the first time, he wondered how old Nelac was. It had never before occurred to him to ask.

Dernhil cleared his throat. "If each of us plays our part, I can't see how we cannot find victory," he said. As he spoke, he felt the hollowness of his words.

"I wonder if there is any such thing as victory in this world."

Dernhil met Nelac's eyes, and the younger Bard saw they were full of a bleak light, cold and somehow pitiless. He looked away, shaken, and Nelac urged Cina on. It was a little while before Dernhil followed him.

They found Cadvan in the front room, broodingly watching the landlord, Stefan, as he went about his tasks. He looked up swiftly when the door opened and strode across the room to embrace Nelac. Dernhil suddenly felt awkward, as if he were a stranger at a meeting that ought to be private; it seemed to him that much passed between the two Bards in that brief greeting.

When Cadvan stepped back from the embrace, Dernhil saw that his eyes were bright. To break the moment, Dernhil rubbed his stomach, like a minstrel playing at being hungry, and brightly suggested that they should eat. Nelac cast him an amused glance, well aware of Dernhil's discomfort, and asked Stefan for a room where they could be private and break their fast. The innkeeper bustled off to prepare the board.

"Did you sleep at all?" Cadvan asked Dernhil. "I woke with the sun, only to find you already gone."

"I slept badly. No doubt I am unused to the comfort of a bed."

Cadvan frowned. "I did too, although I was weary to the bone. Strange dreams, although I remember none of them."

Nelac studied Cadvan's face. "You seem in good health, my friend, strange dreams or no. Dernhil tells me he found you in a mining settlement."

"Jouan," said Cadvan shortly. "I went there to be a cobbler." It was clear that he didn't want to talk about his time there, and Nelac didn't enquire further. Stefan showed them to a small parlour, bringing ale and a platter of breads and cured meats. They made their breakfast, talking idly of nothing in particular. Cadvan was wondering what he was expected to do, now he had made the journey back to Lirigon, but he was hesitant to begin the discussion. He thought that Nelac looked older than when he had last seen him, more strained.

"I suppose we should speak of the matter at hand," said Nelac, when the table was cleared. "Though I don't know where to begin."

"Here and now, I suppose," said Dernhil. "I had an encounter on our way here that you should know about. I spoke with Ceredin…" He glanced sideways at Cadvan as he told his story, but Cadvan stared down at his hands, betraying no emotion. When Dernhil finished his account, Nelac nodded slowly.

"There has been a strange incident in the Fesse also," he said. "Perhaps it is a sighting of Kansabur. I think it more likely than not, although I am trying not to leap to conclusions, in case I leap the wrong way." He paused, gathering his thoughts, and told them of Selmana's encounter with the boar, and of what he had seen and guessed himself. The Bards listened without interrupting. By the time Nelac finished, Cadvan's face was white.

"That is all too familiar," he said. "Remember the shepherd? And those others? Nelac, I searched the library at that time, looking for similar descriptions of possession, and there was not one account of a haunt that matched what happened to those people. I cannot doubt it is Kansabur."

"Me neither," said Dernhil. "It chimes too clearly with my
own dreams. I am sure that Kansabur escaped the Bards."

"I've been turning over and over the moments when we
thought we had banished her," said Cadvan. "Do you remember, Nelac? And I can't stop thinking about that strange – flicker
– that happened, just before the Circles closed. But we were
so sure, we hunted through the Shadowplains and there was
no sign…"

"Yes, I've been thinking of that," said Nelac. "Time doesn't
run in the other Circles as it does in the World, and she could
have changed her *when* as well as her *where*, although I have
not heard that it is possible to do that, except perhaps for the
Elementals… The Shadowplains, as you know, are linked to the
World, as a reflection relates to an object – but not exactly, and
there are strange distortions… But we were looking for spoor,
which is how we tracked her before. And there was no trace of
any spoor around that poor beast, nor in the Shadowplains."

"Then she has found some way to move without leaving
traces," said Cadvan. "She has become something else, other
than what she was."

"That may be so," said Nelac. "But perhaps her transformation is not quite so radical. I don't doubt that some kind of
change has occurred: perhaps the very pressures we brought to
bear upon her permitted Kansabur to discover another aspect of
her power. Part of our problem is that we don't understand how
sorcery works. In fact, we understand so little about the Circles
that anything we suppose is not much more than a guess."

"She is certainly not in her full power," said Cadvan thoughtfully. "If she had been, Selmana could not have resisted her."

"The clue is from Ceredin," said Nelac. "*There is a great malice, broken into three and three. Each malice seeks the others.* She
divided herself, and so escaped our vigilance and survived.

We no longer seek one thing, but many, and those many things leave no trace that we can see."

"Perhaps she seeks to reunite herself," said Dernhil. "Perhaps she can only do that in the World, not in the Shadowplains. Perhaps she needs a living body to sustain her. Perhaps she is like a deadly parasite, which needs a host strong enough to contain those different parts of her..."

Nelac was silent for a time. "If that is so, there are very few who could withstand such a parasite without deadly hurt," he said. "Only the most powerful Bards, perhaps, and perhaps not even them. When we were hunting her, she used living bodies as a hiding place, and she could remain there for only a few days before ... well, Cadvan, you remember what happened to them. And now it seems she is reduced to hiding in beasts. If her self is divided, so, it seems, is her power."

Cadvan had been sitting, half listening, deep in thought. "She never dared before to invade the soul of a Bard," he said. "It would have been too dangerous, it would have betrayed her presence to us at once. You say that Selmana told you that she felt as if something had called her out that night?"

"Not quite. She did say that she didn't know why she had gone out of her mother's house when she was so frightened, and that afterwards it wholly baffled her."

"Why Selmana?"

"Perhaps because she's young, and therefore vulnerable. But she's strong, as she showed when she drove off Kansabur. She's a Maker by inclination. I've been giving her some help with her Reading, and I think she will make a formidable Bard one day."

"Do you think she is in peril?"

"No more, I think, than any other Bard, if Kansabur is indeed hunting Bards," said Nelac. "And we cannot be sure that is the case."

"Selmana is Ceredin's cousin," said Cadvan in a low voice.

Dernhil's eyebrows shot up in surprise. "I would feel – it would be sorely unjust if that family suffered more because of what I've done."

By now the light was broad, and the sunshine outside shone through the latticed windows, glancing off their empty glasses. Cadvan pushed himself back in his chair and ran his hand through his hair.

"So," he said. "Here I am. Why is my being here so important? Why did Dernhil near kill himself riding through Lirhan to look for me? What shall we do now?"

"That's precisely what we don't know," said Nelac. Cadvan gestured impatiently. "Nay, Cadvan, do not think it has been a waste of effort."

"I thought you'd know what to do." The corners of Dernhil's mouth twitched: Cadvan sounded almost petulant.

"Surely you should know me better than that." Nelac glanced ironically at Cadvan. "Or did you lay aside all your Knowing when you fled to Jouan? Do not all questions begin in doubt and ignorance?"

Cadvan smiled reluctantly. "Aye. But I have a heavy culpability here, Nelac. I must right the wrong I made."

Nelac's brows bristled in a frown, and for the first time his voice was harsh. "You can't right it, Cadvan. You can't bring back the dead, or heal the grief of those who miss them, or make the anguish suffered as if it never was."

Cadvan flushed. "I do know that," he said. "I know that what is done cannot be undone. I just meant…"

"I know what you meant. But do not overestimate your importance: you did not begin this wrong. It began long before you made your own disastrous choices. And do not think you can end it."

A swift anger kindled in Cadvan's eyes. "Then what would you have me do?"

"As with us all: we find the tasks that are in front of us, and we deal with them as best we can. For the moment, I don't know. That doesn't mean that I won't know tomorrow. It doesn't mean there is nothing to be done. But better to be patient now than to act in haste and act wrongly."

Nelac left Bural in the early afternoon. Although he had told them that he felt clearer for their discussion, and that he would return the following day when they had all had a chance to think, Dernhil and Cadvan were both struggling with a strong sense of anticlimax.

"Nelac's right, of course," said Cadvan. "As he always is. But this makes my banishment from the Schools a matter of real tedium. Must I kick my heels in this forsaken inn while we wait for the Light to blaze up like a beacon and show us what must be done?"

Dernhil grinned. Cadvan was slumped back in a chair, unshaven and grumpy, his long legs thrust out before him. "I don't think that's quite what Nelac meant," he said.

Cadvan shot him a withering glance. "Don't you start being right as well," he said. "It's too much to bear."

"For my part, I need a wash," said Dernhil. "I didn't have time this morning. I see that it's market day in Bural. Maybe we should get out in the sunshine and buy some of the Lirhanese cheese that you've been missing so much."

Cadvan laughed, and they agreed to meet again in half an hour to inspect the sights of Bural. These were few indeed: it was a small village of perhaps three dozen houses, all built with the grey granite and red clay roofs common in the area. There was a meeting hall in the centre of town, and before that was a stone-flagged square dotted with a motley selection of stalls. Mostly they were selling food: hams and pickles, mounds of autumn fruit, fish taken from the Lir River, fresh in its scales or salted or smoked for winter. There was a knife-grinder in one corner, and in another two minstrels plied their trade, for the coins the villagers would throw into their hats. Various pigs and cows tethered by their owners, waiting for buyers, added to the general hubbub.

Cadvan bought a round of cheese, bargaining ruthlessly and with evident pleasure with the seller. After buying a loaf of the white wheaten bread particular to Bural, the Bards retreated to a nearby green, which was deserted aside from a few cows and a group of children playing tag, to make a rough picnic in the warm sunshine.

Dernhil had watched Cadvan curiously at the market: it struck him that Cadvan was at home in a way he had never seen him in the School. It wasn't simply that Cadvan spoke with the accent of Lirigon, and that Dernhil was instantly recognizable as a stranger; Dernhil was always deferred to as a Bard, although his clothing was plain, but no one seemed to think that Cadvan was anything but another Lirhan farmer.

"You're a skilful bargainer," Dernhil said, tearing a chunk from the loaf and topping it liberally with the soft cheese.

"My father taught me. I did most of the buying for the house, and he sorely hated seeing money go to waste."

"But you like it, too."

"I think all Lirhanese love bargaining," said Cadvan. "It's a game. Usually you both know where you'll end up. It's the getting there that counts."

"That's what I thought," said Dernhil. "I confess, I've always been one to pay the asking price of anything."

"Those stallholders would love you," said Cadvan. "And they'd also despise you as a soft Bard from Gent, raised on silken sheets, who never had to count his coins at the end of the week."

"Aside from the silken sheets, they'd probably be right," said

Dernhil. He yawned and lay back, shielding his eyes from the sun with his hands. A comfortable silence fell between them.

"When do you think you'll return to Gent?"

Dernhil sat up. "I'm not sure I should," he said.

"But surely your task here is done. You brought me back, like a good dog."

Dernhil spluttered. "Like a good dog! And you, I suppose, are the rabbit I've run to ground!"

"I am an excellent rabbit," said Cadvan, making ears with his hands.

Dernhil studied him. "No, you look nothing like a rabbit. And I, contrary to your outrageous assertions, am not a dog, good or bad." He turned over on his stomach and starting pulling grass stems from the ground. "Seriously, Cadvan, the truth is that I feel I haven't finished my part. Although I scarcely know what my part is. And I don't want to go back to Gent."

"Why?"

"Mostly, I'm afraid that the nightmares will return. But it's more than that."

Cadvan's face had darkened at the mention of Dernhil's nightmares, and he didn't answer him for a while.

"I think you're right to stay," he said at last. "But maybe that's just because I would be grateful for your company. I'd feel quite lonely, else."

Dernhil met his eyes, and then looked away, disconcerted by Cadvan's frankness. Clearing his throat, he said: "Well, I'll certainly stay for the meantime."

"Good," said Cadvan. He sat up, brushing crumbs from his jerkin, and sniffed the air. "The wind is going to change," he said. "It'll rain later."

As Cadvan had predicted, the wind that afternoon shifted north, running down from the Osidh Elanor heavy with rain, dragging a hint of ice in its wake. Gusts sprang up abruptly, sweeping over the grass in starts like invisible animals and thrashing the trees. They made it back to the cosy parlour of The Fat Hen just before the rain began.

Dernhil stared gloomily out of the window as the first big, slow drops intensified into a violent downpour. "It's so dark, you'd think it were nightfall!" he said. "I doubt that Nelac will make it here tomorrow, if it keeps on like this."

"Who knows?" said Cadvan. He flung himself on a settle by a newly lit fire. "The weather changed quick enough, that's for sure. Who's to say it won't turn again?"

"Is it always this unsettled in Lirigon? I don't remember it being this volatile…"

Cadvan shrugged. "It's autumn," he said. "We often get storms before the snow."

Dernhil didn't answer. Cadvan watched him as he stood in the window embrasure, the grey, changing light playing over his expressive face. The rain was beginning to lighten; the silver-edged clouds in the west suggested that the sun might even come out again.

"I wish it weren't autumn," Cadvan said. "Something tells me that we'll be travelling before long. In the cold and the rain."

"Do you think so?" said Dernhil, looking up. "But where, my friend? And why? If we're running on the hunting grounds of the Shadowplains, we might as well enter them from here as anywhere…"

"Just a feeling. Different doors lead to different places."

"I'm a bit weary of *feelings*," said Dernhil, with sudden venom.

"They're all we have to go on, it seems," said Cadvan. "Or almost all, anyway."

Stefan, the innkeeper, entered the room, looking harassed, and told them that the rainstorm had come on so quickly he hadn't had time to get all his chickens under shelter. These were Redfarthings, a breed famous for the quality of its meat and eggs, and were Stefan's pride and joy (as well as notable additions to his menu). He feared that at least two of them were missing. "I wish the rain would lighten up, so I could find them," he said. "They'll be off their laying for days, after all this."

"They probably found shelter of their own," said Dernhil soothingly. "Even in such a sudden shower as this."

Stefan suddenly recalled the Bards were guests and asked if they would like some ale, or wine, or perhaps a laradhel, of which he kept an excellent vintage in his cellars. They plumped for laradhel, and Stefan returned swiftly with a bottle and two glasses on a tray. He peered doubtfully through the window.

"I think I can check the hens now," he said.

"Good luck," said Cadvan, smiling. "I'm sure they will be fine. Redfarthings are far from a feather-brained breed."

"Feather-brained! No, indeed not!" Stefan looked briefly outraged at the thought, and then nodded anxiously and departed. There was a short silence after he had left, and then both Dernhil and Cadvan began to laugh.

"I wouldn't mock Stefan for anything in the world," said Dernhil. "And he has a way with a pie that would make him sought after in the high halls of Gent. But he – he does some-times look very like one of his chickens…"

Cadvan poured two tiny glasses of laradhel, and handed one to Dernhil. "I'm sure we'll hear if there is any disaster."

"Aye." Dernhil raised his glass, smiling. "Here's to Stefan's Redfarthings!"

XIII

ALONE in his bedchamber that night, Cadvan sat for a long time in the window seat, looking out over Bural. Now the storm had passed the sky was clear, save for a few wisps of cloud hurrying past, and the night chorus of frogs and crickets floated up in the still air. It was deeply peaceful, and for a while he allowed himself to sink into that peace, ignoring the black depression that pushed at the edges of his mind, building up like a flood at a dam.

When Dernhil had first told him of his belief that the Bone Queen still walked in Lirigon, Cadvan had thought it likely a result of Dernhil's trauma, a fear rather than a reality. Even Dernhil's encounter with Ceredin had left a space for reservation: something was wrong, that was not in dispute, but whether that wrong was caused by Kansabur, or was due to some other evil, had seemed to Cadvan uncertain. But Nelac's tale of Selmana and the boar, and especially of the being that had attempted to invade her body, had removed all doubt from his mind. Nelac might counsel caution, fearing to leap to hasty judgement, but, like Dernhil, Cadvan now felt no doubt at all.

How comforting that doubt had been. Cadvan's lip curled with contempt: in some corner of his mind there had lurked a cowardly hope that, whatever this wrong was, it wasn't his fault. Now it was clear that the business he had thought was over, his penance set, was not finished at all. Were such acts as his ever complete, could he ever atone for them? He thought of the long nights in which he had gone over his actions again and again, wishing with a hopeless passion that it were possible to go back. Even Bards can't change the flow of time, he thought. One lesson of the Balance was that an act, whether it was for good or ill, was irrevocable: one could heal, perhaps, but one could not undo.

These thoughts were as familiar as his own smell, and Cadvan was so sick of them, so tired of how easily his mind settled into the relentless tread of self-blame. Coming home to Lirigon, to the scene of his crime, was a mixed blessing: at first, to be back in familiar surroundings, among people who spoke with his accent and whose ways he understood, had been an unexpected joy; but it also reminded him heavily of why he had left. He thought of his brothers and sisters and, painfully, of his father, but then his thoughts flinched away; he hoped he would not see them. If he remained in Bural, on the other side of the Lirigon Fesse, it was unlikely. No one here had even recognized him.

Nelac had been right to rebuke him: it was only one step from self-blame to self-pity, a cancerous vanity. He surely knew better than that. And yet his hopelessness stemmed in part from feeling useless. Whether or not what was happening now was his fault was really immaterial: that was his private pain, and not the business of anyone else. If he could be of help in fighting the evil that stirred in Lirigon, he might perhaps feel a little better. But what help could he possibly offer?

Even though he was no longer a Bard of the School of Lirigon, no edict could take away his native powers: they still lived within him, and whether they were welcome or no, he laid them in the service of the Light. What little good he could do, he would do with a will, with every breath in his body. Nelac and Dernhil seemed determined that he was needed, but to Cadvan this was a mystery. Privately he thought it a mistake. He remembered again Ceredin's words: *Cadvan is hidden*

from himself, there is a shadow within him. Through Cadvan the rift
has opened. The malice burned through him, and through him finds
its shapes. It didn't mean that he was in any way necessary: it
simply meant that he had caused this present crisis. Worse,
Ceredin's words implied that he was blind to himself. Culpable
and stupid…

More than anything, he was disturbed by the idea that he
was hidden from himself. It chimed with a vague sense that he
couldn't see properly, that his Knowing was somehow muffled
or numbed, but he couldn't identify it. That deeper, inarticulate
sense was silent. He hadn't really noticed it before, assuming
any lack of perception was part of his woundedness, a scar, but
now he began to wonder. He searched his inner Knowing for
some intuition, some clue about what they might do next, but
there wasn't a single flicker. He gestured impatiently; he could
be no help in this quest. It was more likely that he would be
a hindrance, a stumbling idiot.

The blackness rolled in, with all its demons. There was
nothing he could do, no act of will that could keep it at bay: it
was like trying to stop breathing. For a long time he stared out
of the window, absolutely motionless: he saw and heard nothing at all, conscious only of the anguish that corroded his soul.
It was intolerable, and he had no defence against it. The only
way out, an option he had coldly considered and just as coldly
rejected, was to kill himself. After these spells, he would tell
himself that they were the price he had to pay for being alive
when so many others were dead, that it was the punishment
he so richly deserved. But while he was in the grip of this black
flood, he knew it meant nothing at all, neither punishment nor
salvation. This was the wound he had dealt himself, ulcerous
and ugly: it was the truth of his soul, riven by his own hands.
It wasn't madness, as he sometimes thought; it was the worst
sort of sanity. Sometimes he wasn't sure if he could survive it.

But he always survived. Somehow that seemed the worst thing
of all.

It passed, as it always did. Cadvan raised his head and realized with a small shock that he was still sitting in the window
seat. The air coming in the window was chill, and his muscles
were stiff and sore: he shivered as he closed the casement, and
stood up slowly and dizzily. He had no idea how much time
had gone by. The worst of it, he thought bleakly, was that it felt
as if he were trapped there for ever, that this lightless sea of pain
was the whole of his reality. It was like a fever that slept in his
blood, flaring now and then into crisis, and it left him exhausted
and drained. His first thought was that he would dearly love a
drink, but the inn was wrapped in sleep: the only way to find
one would be to steal downstairs and raid Stefan's cellar. He
felt too weary to make the attempt, and instead lay down and
wrapped himself up tight in the blankets in an attempt to gen-
erate some bodily warmth. He lay staring into the darkness,
feeling the beat of his heart as it slowed in his chest, the rasp of
his breathing, the surge of blood in his ears.

Both Dernhil and Cadvan rose early the following day, expecting a visit from Nelac. They breakfasted in the front room,
neither inclined to talk, and then settled down to wait. Dernhil
moved awkwardly, as if his old wounds were paining him, and
Cadvan's face showed the marks of sleeplessness, but although
each noted the signs of a restless night in the other, neither
mentioned it. They debated briefly whether to take the air, and
decided against it: Nelac might arrive at any moment. In any
case, the morning was heavily overcast, with bursts of showers,
and neither felt like venturing outside.

"It's not bad enough to forbid a journey, and I'm sure Nelac
won't be long," said Dernhil, squinting at the clouds through
the inn's front window. "But I confess I'd rather stay inside.

I'm sure I saw a *gis* board in the other room yesterday. Perhaps I could challenge you to a game, while we wait?"

Gis was a complex game of strategy beloved of Bards, usually played on a hexagonal board with black and white counters. Cadvan shrugged. "I've never been especially good at it," he said. "But I'm sure you'd relish another chance to defeat me."

Dernhil bit his lip at this reference to their ill-fated poetry duel: but Cadvan had spoken without malice, and he decided to ignore it. He left the room in search of the game, and returned in triumph with a wooden board and a soft leather bag.

"It sorely needed a dust," he said. "I think Stefan's guests are not over-keen on *gis*. And it took him a little time to remember where the counters might be. He fears some may be lost, in which case we'll have to play the simpler game."

Cadvan cast him an ironic glance: he hadn't missed the gleam in Dernhil's eyes. Some Bards were fanatical about *gis*, and wrote long tomes about the theory of the game. It could be played in several variants: the most complicated version gave each player ninety-six counters, and could last for days.

"I was speaking truth when I said I have little talent for *gis*," he said. "I fear you'll be forced to play with two dozen counters, whether there is a full complement or no."

"I never heard of a Bard who couldn't play *gis*," said Dernhil.

"Oh, I didn't say I *couldn't* play it," said Cadvan. "But I fear its higher applications have always escaped me."

Dernhil grinned. "Twenty-four it is, then," he said. "Though I warn you that some authorities claim that this version is actually more difficult."

They drew their chairs to the hearth and put the board on a low table between them, chatting idly as they placed the counters. The first game was over swiftly, with Dernhil beating Cadvan easily; they began another, but this time Cadvan, his competitive spirit fired, played more seriously. Cadvan lost that game too, and they started another. Slowly the hours passed, with no sign of Nelac.

After Stefan interrupted their game, asking whether they would be interested in a noon meal, Cadvan sat back in his chair impatiently, running his hands through his hair.

"It's not like Nelac not to keep an appointment," he said.

Dernhil glanced up, and then placed a counter slowly on the board, taking away two of Cadvan's. "I win," he said.

Momentarily distracted, Cadvan leaned forward and studied the board. "You win? How?"

"You can't possibly beat me from your position," said Dernhil.

"Surely not!" Cadvan picked up a piece and hesitated, seeing the truth of Dernhil's statement. "I see. Well, I am beaten roundly. Three out of three. I expect you could wish for a hardier opponent."

Dernhil smiled, sweeping the counters back into their bag. "Not at all," he said courteously. "I confess, sometimes your – *random* approach throws up interesting novelties. I suppose we should eat now. But what will we do? I had expected Nelac hours since."

"If I weren't banned from the Schools, we could just ride into Lirigon, and we wouldn't be stuck here," said Cadvan.

"Perhaps Nelac is seeking a stay on your banishment," said Dernhil lightly.

"That's a lost cause, I fear." Cadvan hesitated, and then spoke in a rush. "You know, Dernhil, it's a mystery to me what use I could possibly be. It seems to me that I'm an impediment, if anything."

"Ceredin insisted you had to be found, remember," said Dernhil. "And I know it to be true."

"But not *why*?"

Dernhil heard the trouble in Cadvan's voice, and answered

him gently. "No," he said. "I don't know why. The need to find you is the only thing that has been clear to me in this whole mess."

Cadvan started to respond, and then stopped himself. There seemed no point in telling Dernhil of the doubts that assailed him. "I hope nothing is wrong in Lirigon," he said. "It chafes, being forced to wait like this."

"It does." Dernhil met Cadvan's eyes. "I do fear..." He trailed off into silence.

"Fear what?"

Dernhil shrugged, smiling sadly. "That's the problem. I don't know."

XIV

*S*HE *knew neither pain nor hunger nor sorrow nor fear. She knew neither love nor delight nor pleasure. She merely was, as if she had always been there, standing on the slope of a grey hill, her feet crushing the ashen grass. She thought she could hear whispers on the very edge of her hearing, as if the air were full of lips. Perhaps they were calling her name. What was her name? She sometimes remembered that she had a name. She must remain hidden, otherwise no one might find her. She was afraid of no one. No one had no face. No one had no name. No one had a name. She had a name. No face a name. No one. Every one. Many and one. She was very afraid now. She stood on the slope where the stars let fall their hard light and strained her eyes, looking for no one. Who was no one? She remembered nothing, no, she remembered no one, she remembered a mouth of nothing, she remembered a devouring breath, but still she remained, surely she was someone, she was not no one, she had a name, her own name, if only she remained hidden from no one…*

Cadvan sat bolt upright, sweat pouring down his face. Impatiently he wiped his forehead with the sheet, and then he set a magelight hovering above his bed.

He was in his bedroom in the Bural inn. He set the light bobbing about the chamber: there was his pack, there was the casement, slightly open to admit the night air, there was the chest at the end of the bed, there was the candleholder with the half-burned tallow. It was a pleasant room, beamed and whitewashed and comfortably furnished, but it was very small,

and there wasn't much to see. All the same, Cadvan's scru-
tiny took some time, he examined each object closely before he
moved on to the next, as if he suspected it of being other than it
appeared.

When he had finished his inspection, he pulled his knees up
to his chin like a little boy, and hid his face until his breathing
had returned to normal and the sweat had dried on his skin.

At the moment of waking, he had been terrified, although he
couldn't say why. It was as if he were someone else. That was
the clearest thing about the nightmare: everything else was jum-
bled into a confusion of inexplicable horror. He, or she, was lost.
Perhaps he, or she, was dead? Perhaps he dreamed of Ceredin,
walking the Shadowplains, searching endlessly for the Gates?
But surely he would know if Ceredin entered his dreams? He
had no sense of her. But he hadn't dreamed about her, whoever
she was; he had *been* her. Surely it wasn't Ceredin?

He judged it must be the chill hours before dawn, but sleep
had fled. Cadvan idly thought of waking Dernhil, as he wanted
to talk; but then he discarded the idea. The evening before, they
had retired late after fruitlessly waiting all day for Nelac, and
Cadvan had watched the strain in Dernhil's face deepening as
the hours passed. Perhaps nothing was wrong, perhaps there
was a good reason for Nelac's absence, but it was unlike him not
to send a message if he was expected. They had talked distract-
edly of other things, passing the time, and when it was finally
clear that Nelac would not arrive that day, they had gone to bed.

Restlessly, Cadvan went to the window and flung open the
casement as wide as it would go. He leant on the sill, resting
his cheek on the frame. It was deep night, well after moonset;
although the sky was clear, a haze dimmed even the brighter
stars. He breathed in the cool air; below his window a stand of
lavender released its fragrance into the night. The scent comforted him. The Shadowplains didn't smell of anything; you

could see and hear them, you could feel the rough stone and the inert coldness of the air, but you could smell nothing. Nothing at all.

He had often had nightmares about the Shadowplains, since the hunt for Kansabur. This was different. He didn't know why he had been so afraid. It was as if a roof that he hadn't even known was there had lifted off his mind, and suddenly all his perceptions were alert and awake. And yet all this new perceptiveness had revealed was a sense of not knowing, an overwhelming terror of something that he couldn't see and couldn't name. It was too strange...

He sat very still for some minutes, gazing out over the dim landscape. Then, as if he had reached a decision, he hastily covered himself with a cloak against the chill, and rapped softly on Dernhil's door. Dernhil's room was opposite his, across a narrow corridor. When no one answered, he turned the handle and walked in.

Dernhil's chamber was as tiny as Cadvan's; there was room for a bed, a chest and a small, narrow table by the window. Cadvan sat down heavily, hoping the weight would wake the other Bard, but Dernhil only turned over, muttering something in his sleep. Cadvan shook his shoulder and Dernhil sat up at last, rubbing his eyes.

"Light's sake, Cadvan," he said. "I was fast asleep. What do you want? What time is it?"

"I don't know," said Cadvan. "It's the small hours of the night. I need to talk to you."

"Have you been drinking?"

"Drinking? No! Look, I'm sorry to wake you up."

"You don't look sorry," said Dernhil irritably.

"I had a terrible dream. And I was this woman, and I didn't know who I was. And when I woke up, I wasn't certain if I was really here..."

Dernhil hid his face in his hands. "Cadvan, you *have* been drinking. You can't wake me up in the middle of the night to babble nonsense at me..."

Cadvan grabbed Dernhil's shoulder and breathed in his face. "Can you smell anything on my breath?"

"Garlic," said Dernhil, screwing up his nose. "All right, I'll allow you probably haven't been drinking. But what..."

"I was afraid. I was in the Shadowplains, Dernhil. And I was as frightened as I've ever been."

There was a short silence and then Dernhil nodded, his face pale and drawn in the small magelight that bobbed above the Bards. He sat up, shrugging a blanket around his shoulders.

"In the Shadowplains, you say?"

Now he had an attentive audience, Cadvan hesitated, wary of the irony in Dernhil's glance, and then spoke in a rush.

"I think we're thinking about Kansabur in the wrong way."

"So, what is the right way?"

Cadvan stared at the ceiling, where the soft bloom of the magelight made criss-cross shadows of the crooked beams.

"Kansabur is hunting. Yes? She is stalking through the Circles, in the Shadowplains and in the World, seeking to bring herself bodily back into the World. It seems to me that when we made the banishment, she split, like a ball of mercury when you drop it on the floor, and all these parts fled into different corners, hiding from the Light. If she hid herself in a boar, she could be anywhere. Yet why do I have absolutely no sense of her?"

Impatience flickered in Dernhil's eyes. "Does it matter?"

"It nags at me. It seems odd that I should have no intuitions about this. At first I thought it was because I am stupid, ungifted in this way. But it *is* odd, Dernhil. I am too wounded by Kansabur not to have at least some weight in my Knowing... It's as if I have a scarf drawn over my Bard senses..."

"Perhaps you put the scarf there yourself. Out of fear, or..."

"Yes, I wondered that too. But ... tonight, I was somebody else, in the Shadowplains. It wasn't a dream, I was there. And it was as if everything opened in my awareness. It was as if I could only enter my own Knowing through the soul of another." He glanced at Dernhil, and saw that the other Bard was suddenly intent. "I can't help wondering if I am already ... caught, whether something of Kansabur's being passed into mine during that long struggle two years ago, and lives yet in my mind."

"Like a parasite, you mean?"

"Yes, like that. Feeding on my thoughts, hiding from me, hiding me from myself."

Dernhil sat back, folding his arms, and studied Cadvan closely, as if he were examining him for some flaw.

"I see no sign of that," he said at last. "It seems to me that your darkness is all your own."

Cadvan flushed. "I don't mean that," he said, his voice rough. "By now, you should know me well enough... I do not seek to evade my own acts."

Dernhil said nothing. His expression was neutral, watchful.

"I thought," said Cadvan, "that you might scry me."

At this, Dernhil's eyebrows shot up. "No, Cadvan, surely..."

"I'd ask Nelac, but he's not here. And there's no one else I would trust..."

"You mean, now?"

"Once you're properly awake," said Cadvan.

"Scry you? *Now?*"

Cadvan knew that what he was asking of Dernhil was outrageous, and so he saw no point in apologising for it. Scrying was the most intimate of acts, and was difficult and traumatic for both the scryer and the scried. Cadvan was asking Dernhil to look into his mind, to enter his very soul; he would expose his most private memories, his most painful and humiliating experiences, his most vulnerable hopes and joys.

"I think that if I am right, and Kansabur has left something of her essence in my being, scrying will expose it," he said. "That, perhaps, the hunter can become the hunted. There might be a spoor, some kind of trace…" He looked up. "Of course, it might be nothing."

"I'd rather you wanted to make love," said Dernhil, smiling crookedly. "That was my first thought, when you barged in here. I could easily refuse that."

"It's a much lesser question," said Cadvan gravely. Then he gave Dernhil a sharp look. "Would you really refuse me?"

"Probably." Dernhil's eyes brimmed with sudden laughter. "Honestly, Cadvan, have you no grace? What a thing to ask!"

Cadvan's rare smile leapt in his face. "It occurs to me that I might love you well enough."

Dernhil looked briefly astonished. "And to think that all these years I thought you hated me!" he said lightly.

"You know I don't hate you," said Cadvan. "I think you know I never did. Nor you me. And you, maybe more than anyone else I know, understand that there are many kinds of love." He gestured impatiently. "That's not what I'm asking, anyway."

"I know." Dernhil met his gaze darkly. "Only you would demand such a thing, in the middle of the night, from *me*, of all people!"

"Yes," said Cadvan, a soft mockery in his voice. "From *you*, of all people!"

Dernhil looked down at his hands and was silent for a time, thinking. Cadvan waited patiently, watching him. When Dernhil looked up, his face was open, and a smile lurked at the back of his eyes.

"Perhaps I love you enough to scry you, Cadvan," he said. "And that is a great deal more than you deserve."

"Have you scried someone before?"

"Yes, once. It was horrible."

"I haven't. I just have the words of the charm. I don't know what it's like." Cadvan hesitated and then spoke in a rush. "It's a feeling, no more, a sense in my Knowing," he said. "Not an idle feeling, or I wouldn't ask; but it may all be for nothing."

"I understand that," said Dernhil.

"You ... will have to forgive me."

Dernhil met his gaze levelly. "I understand that, too," he said.

Dernhil refused to scry Cadvan while he was still half asleep, and Cadvan refused to wait until morning. In the end, Cadvan ventured downstairs to the empty kitchen to make Dernhil a tea that would help wakefulness. It took him some time to find the right ingredients, but a search of Stefan's pantry turned up some dried milk-vetch and red medlar berries, which he steeped together in a kettle, and drew off into a clay mug. As an after-thought, he sweetened it with a generous spoonful of honey.

By the time he returned Dernhil had dressed himself, and had lit the candle on the table underneath his window; but he had also fallen asleep again. Cadvan shook him brusquely and he sat up, blinking, and drank the tea, grimacing at its sweetness.

"I think you need not have added the honey," he said.

"I thought it might make it more palatable."

"One day, when all this is over, I'll redirect you to the herbals you have clearly forgotten." Dernhil handed the mug to Cadvan. "Well. I am as alert as can be expected, I suppose. Shall we do this thing here?"

"Do we need to stand? Do we need more room?"

"I don't think it matters. I mean, you're supposed to be able to breathe openly."

After some discussion, the two Bards sat cross-legged on the bed facing each other. Cadvan suddenly felt sick with apprehension, and swallowed convulsively.

"Are you certain?" said Dernhil.

Cadvan nodded tensely, and Dernhil placed his hands on Cadvan's shoulders, instructing Cadvan to do the same.

"Now," said Dernhil, looking into his eyes. "Empty your mind. Expect nothing. There is nothing to expect. Fear nothing. There is nothing to fear…" He breathed in deeply, and then repeated the same words in the Speech, speaking rapidly in a low voice, before he began the incantation.

As the syllables of the Speech fell into his mind, Cadvan sensed a pallid light increasing behind his eyes. At first he flinched, and it dimmed; but the syllables of the Speech stilled him, falling gently into his awareness, and his mind opened and the light entered him, blooming more richly until it was like the golden radiance of a late summer afternoon, a honeyed flood building in his mind with an insistent pressure, opening its forgotten places. He was an infant, staring at a moth lying, perfectly whole and perfectly dead, on a stone-flagged floor; he was a five-year-old child, persuading an angry dog not to bite him, in its own language; he was a young boy, watching his aunt wash her hair in the kitchen, swinging back her head so her hair and the water flying from it made a silver arc; he was running from an orchard he had plundered of apricots, laughing; he was watching his father at work, admiring the skill of his weathered hands as he shaped the sole of a boot; he was leaning forward to kiss Ceredin for the first time, and her hair brushed against his cheek…

The flood of memories increased, overwhelming him. It was as if his entire life were happening at once in a single, endless moment, a vortex of texture and colour and smell and sound and feeling in which he had no foothold, so he was tumbled in himself, as helpless as a single leaf in a tornado. Now he couldn't flinch away, even if he wanted to; and a darkness was growing in the vortex, an angry eye of pain. There was no protection here: his nerves were raw and unsheathed, and he felt everything again, more bitter than rue: the sour taste of disappointment and malice, the white-hot agony of rage, the desperate chill of grief and loneliness; and still the memories gathered force, whirling him powerlessly through them, the scars of love and hope, of delight and anguish, of humiliation and pride and terror, of everything that made him who he was.

It was unendurable, he was sure he would break, and still it wasn't the worst; the worst yet lay hidden within him, and he was afraid he couldn't bear it, the black flood that must now erupt and erase everything. But there was no black flood, no undifferentiated sweep of despair and emptiness. It was all bitterly clear, each single moment vivid in its detail. The sweet, heavy perfume of hunaf flowers, the trees of the Inkadh Grove, every twig outlined against the heavily starred sky, the metal taste of the Black Speech on his tongue, the grim dead queen wrenching aside his circle of power and reaching towards him with her arms of bone, the blue-edged scythe of sorcery, the black sword sweeping in a deadly arc, Ceredin falling voiceless to the ground, a red flood erupting from her throat, her belly. He screamed in his mind, but there was no sound. And still the memories crowded the moment, layer upon layer upon layer, in this place where there was no time; the haunted Shadowplains, the tormented shepherd, Hal crouched in the corner of his kitchen in Jouan, frowning as she pummelled dried herbs in a stone mortar, Nelac embracing him as he stood for the first time after his illness…

And there, in a corner in this place of no corners, something else. Something like a stench that yet had a strange solidity; something that, in all this whirl of Cadvan, was not-Cadvan. In the fountain of himself, a malignant intelligence, formless and winding like vapour, but present, ever more present, scrabbling to hide itself from the inexorable light that poured through Cadvan's being. Cadvan was aware of a wave of disgust, as if his soul were retching. He could feel this thing tightening within him, as if it were some shelled creature closing its claws on his most sensitive skin, hundreds of little claws, each one needle-sharp and toxic, piercing him. And still the light grew larger and brighter, so that nothing might hide; and as the creature became more visible, so it gained solidity, its claws tightening and lengthening, driving deeper into him, until a red mist of torment obscured everything. Suddenly, bright and brief and vivid, he saw Dernhil, haloed with magery, speaking words that Cadvan could no longer understand, and a terrible pres-sure wrenched him, as if he were being ripped in two, and he thought he was going to die. And then he remembered nothing.

Cadvan opened his eyes and groaned. His entire body ached, as if he were a single bruise. It was a few moments before he recollected himself: he was lying on his back on Dernhil's bed. The first grey light of morning was beginning to filter through the window, which was swinging open on its hinges, broken. He stirred, and realized that Dernhil was sitting next to him, his arms wrapped around his knees.

Cadvan struggled to sit upright, wincing, and Dernhil turned towards him. His face was haggard, carved with deep shadows; he looked deathly ill. He made a wan attempt at a smile.

"I swear, Cadvan, that you will be the end of me one day," he said.

Cadvan was silent. In truth, he didn't know what to say.

"That was almost the worst thing that has ever happened to me," said Dernhil. "Almost."

Cadvan cleared his throat. "It was all the worst things," he said.

Dernhil smiled again. "And all the best things," he said.

Cadvan blushed with a sudden hot embarrassment. He felt raw all over, utterly exposed, like a newborn baby. Everything hurt. Yet at the same time, he was conscious of a new buoyancy within him, a sense of relief. It was said that scrying could do that, by bringing hidden wounds to the surface of the mind and draining them of poison. But there had been something else, there had been a parasite in his soul, a darkness that did not belong to him, and he knew it was gone. A surge of gratitude washed through him, and impulsively he grasped Dernhil's hand.

"Let me say this, before my pride or something else stupid forbids it," he said. "I owe you more than I can say. I..."

"You need not say, Cadvan."

Cadvan studied Dernhil narrowly, sighed and turned away, staring at the wall opposite. "It was done at great cost," he said at last.

"You were right," said Dernhil after a while. He spoke thickly, as if he were having trouble forming his words. "I don't know what you remember, but there was something there, a – fragment, if you like. It was a bitter will, winding deep into you. It was cruel work to tear it out. I am sure it was something of Kansabur."

"I remember a little," said Cadvan.

"It wasn't mindless, but it wasn't a mind, either." Dernhil laid his face on his knees. "Ah, I feel stupid with tiredness. I was able to cast it out of you. I thought for a while I had killed you doing it. And then it attacked me. It almost..."

Suddenly afraid, Cadvan looked a question.

"No, it didn't ... it's gone. I'm quite sure. I saw it, I can't even describe what I saw. Before I could do anything it had burst out of the window and fled."

"How long ago was that?"

"I hardly know. Not long."

"I fear what it might do," said Cadvan. "But I think that

neither of us is up to a hunt." He turned Dernhil to face him, examining him with concern. "You're not well."

"Just ... exhaustion," whispered Dernhil. "I feel as if all the life in me has drained out, for ever."

Cadvan sat up straighter and placed his hand on Dernhil's brow. Dernhil was right; there was no injury, but he had been taxed dangerously beyond his strength. Cadvan considered his own weariness, and put it aside.

"I practised one useful thing in Jouan," he said, swinging his legs off the bed. "Well, two useful things, if you count cobbling. I am not so bad a healer now." He told Dernhil to lie down and close his eyes, and then he laid both his hands on Dernhil's breast, summoning what power remained within him. Miraculously something answered his need, from reserves he didn't know he possessed; his hands burned silver with magery, illuminating the room brightly before the light ebbed slowly away, a last, soft luminosity clinging to Dernhil's skin. Cadvan knew that he was already dreamlessly asleep.

Cadvan straightened slowly, like a very old man, and shuffled over to the broken window, pulling the frame closed. The first rays of the sun were edging over the horizon, and the first birds were beginning their morning calls. He was surprised, when he thought about it, that they hadn't roused the whole inn. Perhaps there had been no sound, no cry that could reach ordinary human ears. Aside from the window, there was little sign of struggle; the candlestick had been knocked off the table, but that was all. He picked it up and placed it back carefully, and then stumbled across the hallway and fell onto his bed, too tired even to take off his cloak.

X V

NELAC had ridden swiftly back to Lirigon, smelling the coming change in the weather. His black mood continued to dog him: the meeting with Cadvan and Dernhil had, if anything, intensified his gloom. Two Bards, who should have been leading lights of their generation, grievously injured by vanity and folly: Cadvan, exiled into shame and guilt; Dernhil, scarred and haunted. And Ceredin dead: Ceredin, who might have been the greatest of them all, wandering lost and afraid in the Shadowplains, denied even the peace of death. All that possibility, all that promise, broken...

After he had stabled Cina, he walked slowly to his Bardhouse. The hour's ride to Bural and back had left him unusually weary and sore, but he put that down to his state of mind. Though it was true that he was getting old: he could feel mortality silting through him, as if every year left a fine dust that slowly built up in his veins. Two and a half centuries walking on this earth: perhaps he had another fifty years; perhaps, if he were lucky, another century. A generous lifespan, part of the Gift of a Bard, but still it wasn't enough. Or perhaps it was too much. With knowledge cometh sorrow, as the Chronicles said...

The sunny day was darkening swiftly. He entered his rooms just before the storm broke overhead with a deafening clap of thunder. An unlit fire was laid in the hearth, and all was in gloom. He snapped on the lamps with a gesture, and then, after a little consideration, lit the fire, as the temperature had dropped sharply. He poured himself a glass of spirits from a decanter on the low table and sat down heavily.

Carefully, piece by piece, he sifted through what he knew: Dernhil's visions of Ceredin and his terrible foredreams, Cadvan's dream in Jouan, the encounter with the boar... As Cadvan said, they pointed irresistibly to a single conclusion: the Bone Queen, stalking Lirigon in a new, insidious form. Although he had told Cadvan that they couldn't be sure, that they should consider all possibilities before leaping to conclusions, his inner Knowing had no such caution. Perhaps it was time to put that necessary scepticism aside and to face what had to be faced.

Unconsciously he sighed, and poured himself another glass. Cadvan's question kept coming back to him: *What shall we do now?* It was a fair question, but Nelac had no answers. How to track a foe that left no trace of its presence, and that had split into pieces? Was Kansabur, as Dernhil speculated, seeking to possess Bards to reunite her broken selves? Surely that was too dangerous, even for her? And yet...

Nelac stood up and paced to the window, peering out through the cascades of rain. The storms of the past two days disturbed him: they smelt odd, somehow. Too quick and too violent for this time of year: usually the autumn rains in Lirigon came in gentle bursts, heavy but brief. The unsettled weather seemed of a piece with everything else, in a way he couldn't trace... He shook himself. He was in danger of becoming an anxious old man, weaving everything he saw into a pattern of his fears.

He turned around, looking about his sitting room, and it was then that he saw the note propped on the books on his work table. He recognized Selmana's handwriting, and picked it up with a sudden clutch of foreboding.

Nelac – I need to speak to you, if you are anywhere close by today – last night something very strange happened and now

I am afraid. I was reading late past midnight and I looked out
of my window and everything was changed, I am sure I was
looking out on the Shadowplains, I saw Ceredin, I am sure, and
something horrible, it was just like the thing with the boar. It
wasn't any shape. And today I am frightened. Please, when you
return, can you send a message straight away? I'll be back in
my room this afternoon. Selmana. PS I am sure I am not imag-
ining things but I don't know how to write down what I saw.

Nelac looked up unseeingly at the ceiling, and then read the
note again. He swiftly cloaked and booted himself and went out
into the rain. He arrived shortly afterwards at the Bardhouse
where the Minor Bards lived, and endured a scolding from
Seriven, the Bard in charge of them, as he entered the door,
dripping rivulets of water onto the floor.

"Nelac! By the Light, what are you doing, venturing out in
weather like this at your age?" he said. "Look at you. You're
soaked to the skin!"

"At my age I can do what I like," Nelac said tersely. "And I
assure you that this cloak repels water very efficiently. I'm looking for Selmana."

Seriven pursed his lips, but something in Nelac's voice
stopped him from further upbraiding. "I haven't seen her all
day, since she went out to her classes this morning," he said. "I
know some of them went for a picnic, and maybe she went with
them. With any luck, they didn't get caught in that storm."

"Perhaps they took shelter elsewhere," said Nelac. "She said
she'd be back here this afternoon."

"Well, you know what young people are."

"Yes." Nelac paused for a moment, thinking what to do. "If
you see her, tell her I am back in Lirigon, and am awaiting her
in my rooms. If I'm not there, I'll leave word where I am. Make
sure you tell her."

Seriven's eyebrows lifted at the urgency in Nelac's voice, but he didn't ask any questions, and simply promised to pass on the message. He watched Nelac's departure with a frown. He hadn't before seen Nelac in such a state of agitation, and it disturbed him.

Nelac returned to his rooms, and dried himself by the fire, which was blazing merrily. There was nothing he could do now but wait: there was no point in chasing Selmana around Lirigon. From the moment he had read her note, he had been afraid for her. Most Bards had a mental bond to the people they cared for. Nelac had an inner web of connection to his students, which alerted him if something was desperately wrong. It was a vague intuition, and not always reliable, as he reminded himself. It was this sense, more than the disturbance in the Balance, that had warned him the instant that Cadvan had lost control of the Bone Queen. Now it was as if a small star in his inner constellation had simply gone out. He had no sense of distress or death, just an absence where there should have been a shining thread.

After an hour, the rain eased and slowly stopped. The hem of the clouds over the western horizon lifted, and a yellow storm light flooded through Nelac's window, illuminating the page he was attempting to read. He realized that he hadn't absorbed a single word for the past hour and put the book aside. For some time he just sat, watching the shadows darken to evening.

A light knock on his door pulled him out of his reverie. It was Seriven, looking worried. Selmana hadn't returned to the Bardhouse. Her friends had returned soon after the storm cleared, and said that they hadn't seen Selmana since the morning lessons, although they had expected her to come to their picnic. Disturbed, Seriven had asked around, and it seemed nobody had seen her.

"She's not at the library, and Calis hasn't seen hide nor hair of her today," he said. "Maybe she went off to visit her mother? She does that sometimes. But she would always tell me. And anyway, her pack is still in her room, and her horse in the stables..."

Nelac knew that Selmana was worried about Berdh, and it was just possible that she had gone to Kien, even if her horse was still in the stables. Perhaps she could have taken a lift in a cart. But surely not without leaving word? And especially not if she were anxious to talk to him?

"We should be looking for her," Nelac said.

"There's something wrong. I can feel it. I've been feeling it ever since you came to the Bardhouse..."

Nelac met Seriven's gaze, and for a few moments both Bards were silent. "I feel it too," he said at last. "But I cannot sense any distress. I don't think she is hurt or dead, but it is a ... curious feeling." He picked up Selmana's note from the table and held it out. "She left this, at around noon, as far as I can tell."

Seriven read Selmana's note, frowning. "The Shadowplains? That can't be right..."

"She was frightened," said Nelac. "I wish I had been here. I wish I knew what she was afraid of."

Seriven handed the message back to Nelac, his lips folded tightly. "Tell me, Nelac, is there a peril in Lirigon? Should I be warning the Minor Bards?"

Nelac was silent. "Not as yet," he said. "Before anything else, we must find Selmana."

"That shouldn't take long," said Seriven. "Perhaps I should send a message to her mother, to be sure she hasn't gone there?"

"If she is not returned tonight, we should send tomorrow morning. I don't wish to cause Berdh any unnecessary anxiety."

Seriven folded his arms and studied Nelac's face. "Don't think I can't see how worried you are," he said. "Are you going to tell me why? Or am I not worthy of your confidence?"

Nelac frowned. "Of course you are worthy," he said shortly. "The truth is, I don't know what it is I fear."

Seriven paused, as if he wished to speak further, but thought better of it. "I'll take my leave, then," he said. "I'll put out word, and let you know if I hear anything."

After he had closed the door, Nelac stood staring at the blank wood. He was all but certain that Selmana was missing now; he couldn't imagine that she would have left such a note, and not return to his rooms or to her own. He realized that he had been nursing a tiny hope that she was out with friends, or otherwise engaged in some harmless way that meant she had merely forgotten that she wanted to see him.

The following day word of Selmana's disappearance spread among the Bards, and some came to Nelac to tell him of when they had seen her. She had last been sighted making her way to the North Gate: after that, it was as if she had simply vanished. In the afternoon, increasingly worried, Nelac rode to Kien himself, to speak to Berdh. As he had expected, Selmana wasn't there. The visit took longer than Nelac had expected, since his courtesy forbade his hurrying away from a woman consumed with anxiety about her daughter. After he had left Kien, assuring Berdh that he would send word as soon as he heard any news, he visited Bashar, the First Bard of Lirigon, to arrange a meeting of the Circle. Bashar met his urgency with scepticism.

"Selmana is young," she said. "Young people can forget to tell others what they are doing, and cause all sorts of unwarranted flurry. Perhaps she has a lover whom she has told no one about? Or she decided to stay with a friend? It does happen,

Nelac. People have their own lives. I don't see why we should summon the whole School..."

"You have read the note she left me," said Nelac. "She was afraid."

"It seems very fanciful to me. You know as well as I do that the Shadowplains do not appear in the World and that one doesn't simply ... stumble into them. Why, she's not even a student of the Eleven Circles. As I recall, she is a Maker? Why is she talking this nonsense? More importantly, why are you taking any notice of it?"

"Perhaps it isn't nonsense," said Nelac impatiently. "And she is not a young woman given to fancy."

"I'm sure she will return and be embarrassed by all the fuss," said Bashar. "She has only been gone a day, after all..."

"My lady, whether or not Selmana is given to wild imaginings, you should know that I am not. And I am very anxious. Surely the incident with the boar should at least give pause..."

Bashar folded her lips tightly. "Yes, we are aware of that. But still I counsel patience. I respect your Knowing, Nelac, but you have been misled before by your fondness for particular students. On this business of Cadvan, for example. Our law is unambiguous about those who meddle with sorcery, and yet you argue..."

Nelac's impatience curdled into anger. "I wish I could be as certain as you," he said, his voice cold. "Alas, I am not; and you might perhaps remember that the laws teach that those who refuse doubt are blind."

Not trusting himself to speak further, Nelac turned on his heel and left, returning to his chambers in a rage. He knew his fury was unjust; what Bashar said was, on its own terms, wholly reasonable. He also knew that, in countenancing Dernhil's search for Cadvan and advising his return to Lirigon, he was breaking Bashar's own ruling. This made it impossible for him to speak openly of the deeper worries that drove him.

He reached his rooms and sat down heavily. Perhaps he was responding too hastily, perhaps his anxieties were irrational. It troubled him that his sense of justice was at odds with the considered ruling of the Bards of the Light. Bards were always argumentative, and often differed passionately; but all his life, Nelac had held faith in the collective wisdom that constituted Bardic law. He trusted that these arguments meant that all sides were considered fairly.

The decision on exiling Cadvan had been the first time that he had seen the process falter: he remained convinced that the decision had been driven more by fear and desire for punishment than by rational justice. Bashar's hostility on that question had taken him by surprise. It wounded him that she thought he had been simply arguing out of partiality for Cadvan, and that she so easily dismissed his arguments. How many others thought as Bashar did? And now it seemed that he was stepping further and further outside the law of the Bards. Was his Knowing misled after all?

Nelac realized with a start that the room had darkened as he had been thinking. He lit a lamp and set a fire in the hearth, the simple task calming his thoughts. No, he could not be certain; but that didn't mean the conclusions he had drawn were without reason. He stared into the fire, watching the flames dance about the wood they were consuming. The Shadowplains. Could Selmana have accidentally stumbled into another plane? Bashar was right: it simply wasn't possible to enter those realms physically: the soul of a Bard might wander those grey slopes, but the flesh always remained in the World…

He picked up her note and read it again. *I looked out of my window and everything was changed.*

He breathed slowly, in and out. He turned his perception inwards, seeking the edge from which he could leap outside his body, into the dizzying, unboundaried reaches beyond the World. And from there, gathering his mind, he walked step by step into the Shadowplains, where everything was changed.

XVI

CADVAN knew by the quality of the light that the morning was still young. For a few moments he lay there, idly listening to the noises floating through his window; a cock crowing, Stefan greeting a passer-by outside, a clop of hooves as a rider passed the inn. Then he realized he was wrapped in his cloak, and the events of the night before flooded back. He sat up abruptly and stared sightlessly at the opposite wall, wondering if it had been a terrible and strange nightmare. Yet he was aware of a new ease, as if deeply rooted illness had been driven from his body. He hadn't slept long, but it had been deep and untroubled, and there was a new clarity in his mind. There had been some – parasite – that was now gone. Even the thought of it made his innards clutch in disgust.

Now, he said to himself, whatever darkness I find in my soul is mine alone...

He poured some water from a ewer into a bowl, washed his face, pulled on his boots and went downstairs. The inn was quiet; Stefan was out, perhaps attending to his chickens. There was no sign of Dernhil. Cadvan wandered into the kitchen, where Stefan's daughter, Celb, was chopping vegetables, and asked for some bread and cheeses and tea. He broke his fast soberly in the front parlour, looking out of the latticed window. Banks of grey clouds were gathering overhead, and the smell of rain was on the wind.

He heard Stefan in the porch, stamping his feet and taking

off his overboots. He thought of asking if there had been any word from Nelac, but let it slide; surely Stefan would tell him if there were news. For a moment he felt guilty: there was too much that was urgent, too much to worry about. If they heard nothing from Nelac today, it was a sign that something was grievously wrong. But just now, Cadvan thought, just now I want to sit and be still and wonder what it is to be me.

That blackness, the inexorable wave that overwhelmed his being. Was it really part of him, or was it the foul thing that had insinuated itself into his mind, poisoning his thoughts? Was he now free of it? The thought lifted his heart. But, no, he said to himself, setting his jaw: that darkness, as Dernhil had told him last night, was all his own. His wounds lay in his own choices, his own crimes. What had lifted was something else entirely; it was as if a toxic mist that had muffled his Bardic senses had cleared. He was less blind now, that was all. But surely that was something…

He had been sitting for an hour when Dernhil came downstairs and sat awkwardly at the table. Both Bards were stricken by shyness.

Cadvan pushed the bread towards him and Dernhil studied it dubiously. "I'm not especially hungry," he said.

"Nevertheless, you should eat," said Cadvan. "I'll ask Stefan for some more tea."

Dernhil shrugged and broke some bread. Cadvan studied his face, hiding his anxiety: Dernhil's skin was pale, almost transparent, as if you could see the bones beneath.

"I slept very well," said Dernhil, giving him an ironic glance. "Better than I have for an age. You needn't worry, Cadvan; you can certainly cast a healing sleep."

"I asked too much of you, I fear."

Amusement flickered over Dernhil's face. "Asked? You *demanded*, Cadvan."

"Well, yes. Though if you had straightly refused, I would not have argued…"

"Yes, I know. But it was a terrible thing."

Cadvan could think of no answer and an uncomfortable silence fell between them.

"As it turned out, you were right to ask," said Dernhil at last, relenting. "And I am tired, which is only to be expected, but not so tired that it is a damage. Be sure I'm well used to monitoring my health."

"Good," said Cadvan, more abruptly than he intended.

"It is a strange … intimacy, scrying," said Dernhil, after a pause. "But intense and vivid though it is, the impression fades quickly. You can only absorb so much knowledge…"

Cadvan, grateful for Dernhil's tact, cleared his throat. "Yes. But the important question is what has happened to that – thing – you cast out of me."

"It's anybody's guess. Before I came down, I looked for any tracks, anything we could trace. But I felt nothing. Aside from the broken window, of course."

"We must tell Stefan about that," said Cadvan.

"I did already. He all but clucked, but he has forgiven me. And I asked him if there had been word from Nelac. No word at all. I'm worried, Cadvan. I'm sure something is wrong."

"It's yet early," said Cadvan. "In any case, I think we should ride to the School, rather than wait for Nelac."

"Both of us? You are *exiled*, Cadvan."

"Even so. I can hide my face. And this is too important. Will it tire you too much, do you think?"

Dernhil sighed, and contemplated his empty plate. "No, I'm not too tired," he said. "And I think you are right; but I fear the Bards will punish you."

"How could they punish me more?" said Cadvan.

"One of the punishments for breaking exile is death."

"And it has never been used, in all the annals of all the Schools. Not once. They could throw me out. But they won't know me; I've a little skill at disguise. The last person they'd expect to see with you would be Cadvan, formerly of Lirigon."

Dernhil laughed. "Perhaps," he said. "But it would still have to be a good disguise. There isn't a single person in Lirigon who would not recognize you on sight."

"Not if I am someone else," said Cadvan. "And I will be."

Later, as they travelled to Lirigon, Dernhil kept glancing sideways at the stranger who rode beside him. Cadvan had transformed himself utterly before they left the inn, using a charm of which Dernhil knew nothing. Once Dernhil had recovered from his astonishment, they had decided that Cadvan's new name was Garth, and that he was a local farmer with urgent news for Nelac. Garth could have been Cadvan's kin, a cousin, perhaps; he had Cadvan's high cheekbones and firm mouth, and his build and colouring. But his skin was wrinkled by wind and sun, his nose misshapen by an accident or a brawl, his expression good-humoured and open and perhaps a little simple. The transformation was startling. It was not a glimmer-spell, the illusion magery that was a source of much play and delight to Bards, because a Bard's eye could see right through a glimmerspell if they wished. Dernhil was fascinated.

"I have never heard of such a charm, Cadvan," he said. "Where did you learn how to do this?"

"It's Garth, remember?" said Cadvan. "I met a Pilanel a few years ago, who taught it to me when I cured his prize horse of founder. And I have kept it close and secret ever since. It is sometimes useful."

"I don't know much about that people," said Dernhil. "I am told they are powerful *Dhillarearën*, for all their lack of Schools. But many Bards will not trust them."

"Those Bards are foolish," said Cadvan. "The Pilanel are a wise and ancient race. And they have, as you see for yourself, some useful mageries of which we know little. It is as well I ride a poor horse; it completes the disguise."

"It's complete indeed. I thought this would be a perilous enterprise, and I'm not even nervous! The chief difficulty will be convincing Nelac that you are who we say you are."

"Nelac will know," said Cadvan.

When they arrived at the School of Lirigon, the rain that had threatened since dawn began to arrive in little squalls and eddies. They passed through the gates without remark, and Cadvan rubbed down Brownie in the communal stables. Nelac's horse, Cina, was still in her stall, which reassured them that he was still in Lirigon, and Dernhil gave her a message just in case Nelac passed them by mischance.

As he walked through the grey-cobbled streets, lined with poplars now turning to the gold of autumn, Cadvan felt his chest constrict; this was where he belonged, and he could never be a part of it again. They passed a Bardhouse where a group of musicians sat in one of the ground-floor rooms, playing one of the Canticles of Light. Cadvan halted, involuntarily overwhelmed as the music flowed over him. His whole body ached to be part of the world of Barding, to know this difficult beauty living again in his hands. Dernhil turned to him, taking his elbow in sudden concern, and Cadvan started and smiled painfully.

"I'd almost forgotten," he said. "I feel like I'm haunting a house where I used to live."

"It's always hard, coming back," said Dernhil. "But we must hurry, or we'll get soaked. The weather's beginning to set in."

The cobbles were already dark with rain when they reached the Bardhouse where Nelac lived. No one was about: the household was already busy at classes or other business. Dernhil knocked on Nelac's door, but there was no answer. He swore softly.

"He's out," he said. "I hope we didn't pass him on our way here."

"I doubt he's far away," said Cadvan. "He won't mind if we wait."

He pushed the door open, and they entered Nelac's sitting room. Inside was dark and chilly, and a fire had fallen to ash in the grate. Dernhil woke one of the lamps, and it was only then that they saw Nelac slumped on the couch. Cadvan ran to kneel beside him, taking his hand. It was as cold as the earth. Colder.

"Has he died?" whispered Dernhil, at his shoulder.

"I don't know." Cadvan felt for a pulse, first in Nelac's wrist, then at his neck. "I can feel nothing. But…"

"I'll get help."

"No, wait." Cadvan put his hand on Nelac's forehead and began to glow with Bardic magery. As he did so, the Pilanel charm was broken, and his disguise fell away. "He's not dead," he said at last. "But he is absent. I don't know how long he has been away. Long enough for the fire in the grate to burn out…"

"Absent? What do you mean?"

"My guess is that he has entered the Shadowplains, and has yet to return."

"Do you think he has been here all this time we were waiting? Why did nobody find him?"

"Perhaps nobody thought he was here. People are reluctant to interrupt Nelac, after all. But my guess is that he has been here since last night."

"What shall we do?"

Cadvan stood up, considering. "I think you should light a fire and warm the room," he said. "I'll try to find him."

"In the Shadowplains?"

"That's my best guess."

Dernhil bit his lip. "You know that you're no longer disguised? If we're found here, and Nelac as one dead, I don't know what will happen... They might think you killed him..."

"Then we had better find Nelac, no? Bolt the door, so no one can interrupt us. If this doesn't work, you'll have to find Bashar and tell her what has happened."

Dernhil stood up, and started pacing the room in agitation. "I'm not sure. I think I ought to find Bashar now. I know nothing of the Shadowplains, Cadvan, only what I have seen in dreams, and that is bad enough. I wonder how you can find anyone in there..."

"I know more than I care to remember," said Cadvan. "One thing I do know is that time passes differently there, if indeed it passes at all. You can spend what seems like days in the Shadowplains and when you return here, only a little time has gone by. If Nelac has been here since last night, I am sure he is trapped."

"And if even Nelac may be trapped there, why not you?"

Cadvan hesitated. "It's a risk, certainly. But I think it's a gamble that I must take. My Knowing is open now, Dernhil, and I think ... it's difficult to explain, but perhaps I can trust it. Let me try."

Dernhil halted, and met Cadvan's eyes. "And if you end up like Nelac?"

"Then call Bashar, and we will deal with what we must deal with. But I think I will not."

After a long pause, Dernhil nodded.

"Light the fire," said Cadvan. "It's cold in the Shadowplains."

It was cold in the Shadowplains, but while you were there you didn't feel temperature. Here was no smell, no taste: only a sensation that afterwards you thought of as a memory of taste, a tang of acrid air. You knew hardness, softness, light and dark, length, breadth and height, you could hear whispers and cries and the sound of your feet treading down the shadows of grass. Distance was very different: far and near meant as little as they did in dreams. You moved around as if you had a body, but somehow you knew it was an illusion, a memory formed by the mind to cover the unfamiliar. As some of your senses shut down, others, of which you were scarcely aware in the World, sharpened and blossomed. It made it hard to describe being in the Shadowplains: the meanings words had in the World had little purchase. As Bards often said when they recorded their experiences, it was like attempting to describe colour to someone who had never in their lives been able to see.

Even fear was different: it had a muted quality, as if it were a feeling that was witnessed rather than experienced. Cadvan was frightened now. As the sky opened above him, still and dark with its scattering of white stars, he felt horribly visible, as if the ground itself were aware of him. It usually took a while for the Shadowplains to coalesce from indeterminate shadows into something that was seeable, but this time it was quick, snapping into instant, clear focus.

For a time, how long he couldn't tell, Cadvan didn't move. He stood in the middle of a long slope, which gradually shelved down into a wide valley. At the bottom there was a winding darkness, which looked like a river, although Cadvan already knew that there was no water there. Rather, it was a course filled with a dark vapour, its surface curling and wisping in strange formations, responding to air currents that were undetectable in this windless place. Bards in Lirigon called it the River of Forgotten Souls. Behind Cadvan the slope ran up and up, like a vast wave, and at its top he could see sharp outcroppings of stone.

Gradually the sense that he was being watched ebbed away,

as if whatever had noted his arrival had lost interest in him. Cadvan wrenched his mind into focus: it was too easy in the Shadowplains to lose yourself, to become like the shades that he could see drifting along a pale path that meandered down the slope, without memory or desire or hope. It was this leaching of yourself that Bards warned was the chief peril of entering the Shadowplains: it was as if your soul slowly evaporated, leaving only a husk. It was no place for the living.

Cadvan gathered his will and stepped onto the path, grasping for the intuition he had felt in Nelac's study. There, he had sensed Nelac, faint but unmistakable, in the inner constellation that mapped the presences of those he loved. That was all he needed to listen to, that echo of love: he fastened his mind onto the thought. He looked uncertainly up the slope, and then turned down towards the river. He walked slowly and deliberately, as if his heels were dogged with loathing.

The long slope seemed at once crowded with people and yet empty. Somehow everyone was at a distance: although he saw many shades wandering up and down the path and across the grey grasses, none ever came close to him, and he never passed anyone. He wondered if Ceredin were among the souls he saw, but pushed the thought aside. It could only distract him. He felt strangely heavy, as if his limbs were made of mud, but he forced himself on. He was nearing the river, and could see the coils of vapour on its uneasy surface. Nelac was near by, he was sure, but he couldn't see him.

Cadvan had always tried to avoid the River of Forgotten Souls when he had entered the Shadowplains. Once, he had been forced to cross it, treading the Bridge of Tears, a stone arch unmade by hands that linked the shores, and it had seemed to him that the vapour entered his soul like ice, numbing his thoughts. But that time he had not been alone. Perhaps Nelac had gone too close to the vapour. Cadvan halted, questing for the faint light that had guided him, and turned to walk along the shore. And at last he saw something: a still, dark figure, motionless on the bank of the river.

Cadvan no sooner perceived Nelac than he was beside him, saying his name. Nelac didn't respond, and Cadvan took his arm and shook him. The old Bard turned and looked at him incuriously, gently removing his arm from Cadvan's grasp, and turned back to face the river.

"Nelac," said Cadvan again. "It's me, Cadvan. You must come back."

Again Nelac turned, but no recognition flickered in his eyes. "I knew a man named Cadvan once," he said slowly. "You have something of his likeness…"

Cadvan took Nelac's arm again, and this time Nelac didn't resist. "Come," Cadvan said. "You must leave the river behind."

"Come where?" said Nelac.

"Come home." Even as he said these words, Cadvan felt uncertainty rising inside him: what did home mean? Surely it did not exist, surely it was a dream… With an effort, he recalled Lirigon, the sunlight falling through the latticed window of Nelac's chambers, the red-tiled roofs, the streets of grey stone, the apple orchards of the Fesse where he had run as a boy. But it was as if these memories slid away as soon as he recalled them, as if they peeled off and dissolved in the vapours of the river.

"Home," Cadvan said stubbornly, and pulled Nelac's arm. Nelac took a step, and then another, stumbling like a blind man. "I have come to take you home. But first we must leave the river…"

Cadvan turned his face to the slope above them and began the long trek upwards, dragging Nelac with him. Nelac didn't resist, but would not walk on his own; if Cadvan didn't push him along, he simply stood where he was. Cadvan's only thought was to leave the deathly river as far behind as possible.

He placed one foot in front of another, step by step by step, and every inch was a slow anguish.

At last he could go no further. He looked back: the river was further away than he had thought, lost now in shadow. Cadvan wondered how long Nelac had been in the Shadowplains: in this timeless place, it could have been years, it could have been centuries. How could he bring Nelac back to the World, if he had lost his memory?

"Nelac," he said, feeling his voice die on the unmoving air. "Nelac. I am Cadvan. You gave me my Truename. The ceremony was held in the courtyard of your Bardhouse and afterwards we sat in your chambers and drank laradhel and we sang the Song of Making. Do you remember? You named me."

Nelac remained silent and unresponsive beside him. Cadvan would have wept, except that this was a place too dry for tears. Desperately he turned to face him, taking the old Bard's face between his hands and staring into his empty eyes.

"Do you not remember me?" he said. "You are the father of my magery. You opened the door so I could be myself at last. If I have closed that door for ever, it is no reflection on the gift you made me. Nelac, you Named me. You said I was black and silver, like the storm cloud that surges out of a still sky. You looked into my darkness and there found my light. I owe you my life. I remember how the star music surged through me, and I became a Bard at last, when you revealed to me who I was. I am Inareskai, Nelac. Do you not remember?"

As he said his own Truename out loud, Cadvan felt an echo of the cold and beautiful star music he had heard in his Instatement, and the light in the Shadowplains shifted. It was if he had shouted in a place of terrible silence: everything around him was aware again, and a shadow was present where there had been nothing before. But at last Nelac stirred. He took Cadvan's hands and held them between his own.

"Inareskai," he said.

"Home," said Cadvan. He could feel the shadow gathering around him, like a predator bunching its muscles to pounce, but he kept his gaze locked on Nelac's. "We have to go home." He summoned an image of Nelac's sitting room in his mind: the only thing he could remember was the red couch, laved with the light of a flickering fire. Everything else was vanishing into vague mist. As the red silk flared in his mind, he felt Nelac's thought groping towards it in recognition, and knew that their minds had melded.

A terrible pressure was building around them, but Cadvan ignored it: all his remaining will was concentrated on Nelac. And even as he felt the shadow leap, like a giant whip at last releasing its energy, they stepped out of the Shadowplains and opened their eyes on Nelac's chamber, and good plain daylight roared into Cadvan's sight.

Dernhil stepped forward and caught Cadvan as he slid to the floor, and helped him back onto the couch. Nelac gasped and stirred, like a man pulled from deep water, and Dernhil began to chafe his hands, looking over his shoulder to Cadvan.

"What happened?"

"I scarcely know. Was I absent for long?"

"No, though it felt like an age." Dernhil nodded towards the fire, which was just now beginning to catch the wood. "A few minutes, if that."

Cadvan rose clumsily and knelt beside Dernhil, studying Nelac's face anxiously; it was ashen, although he was now breathing evenly. Nelac opened his eyes, and focused painfully on Cadvan. At last he spoke, so quietly that Cadvan had to lean close to hear him.

"That was a near thing," he said.

"It was, my friend. Too near."

A long silence fell, and gradually Nelac's colour began to

return. He sat up, pushing the two younger Bards away.

"Laradhel, Dernhil," he said. "There's some on the table over there. And make mine a large one, eh?"

Dernhil and Cadvan's eyes met, and they almost grinned. Dernhil busied himself pouring the golden liqueur into three silver goblets, and Cadvan stood up, stretching, and stamped his feet. His whole body felt full of pins and needles. He was shaking so badly he could barely hold the goblet that Dernhil gave him, but he grabbed it between two hands and drank it in a single draught. It went down like smooth fire.

Nelac couldn't hold the goblet at all, and Dernhil had to help him. "Another, I think," he said when he had finished, and this time he smiled. "I feel as if this cold will never leave my body."

"You were here all night, I think," said Dernhil.

Nelac's eyebrows shot up in surprise, but he said nothing until Dernhil had refilled his cup. He drank the next goblet swiftly and leant back on the couch.

"I think I have my wits back, or at least most of them," he said. "But perhaps not. I could swear that you are not supposed to be here, Cadvan."

"No, I shouldn't. But it's perhaps as well that I am."

"And no doubt you're both wondering how I, the most wary of travellers in the land of shadows, could have fallen into a trap that even a Minor Bard should know to avoid?"

"Something like that," said Dernhil. "Even though I don't know what you're talking about."

Nelac drew a deep breath. "I'll try to tell you, but it's hard…" he said. "It's like remembering a dream, which vanishes as you awaken. Well. I was looking for Selmana. I saw her, in the distance. She was shining, but it was with a light that was not of that place, and I remember being astonished: she was there in her flesh. It shouldn't be possible, but there she was."

"Selmana?" said Cadvan. He sat up, fixing his eyes on Nelac.

"Aye." Nelac paused for a long moment. "Aye. Selmana disappeared yesterday, and the moment I heard I went cold – this is no ordinary absence... I spoke to Bashar, who was inclined to think nothing of it. That did little to dispel my anxiety. I thought that Selmana might be in the Shadowplains, and so I went there. And there she is." He shook his head. "Everything we know about the Circles says this is an impossibility. But the Shadowplains are changed in their nature..."

"It is changed," said Cadvan. "I felt it at once. I have always loathed the Shadowplains, they are not a place where mortals might walk with ease, and never have been. But this time..." He shuddered.

"I could hide myself, that wasn't so hard," said Nelac. "What bothers me more is that sense that something has slipped... The usual protections didn't seem to work, and I couldn't move through the plains as I have before. I couldn't reach Selmana. I remember walking and then running, but she never came any closer. And the more I tried to reach her, the harder it became. I felt that I was bleeding to death from some invisible wound, as if my life were leaking out of me." He faltered, frowning. "And then, I remember nothing. Rags, rubble, ash. Nothing."

XVII

WHEN Lirigon vanished before her eyes, Selmana was so afraid that she couldn't move a muscle. She had no idea how long she stood on that dark slope. After an unmeasurable time, she realized that she was hidden from whatever it was that had been tracking her. Bit by bit the paralysing fear began to ebb away. She looked about her. She could almost hear voices, whispers at the very limits of hearing, but she could see no one: the plains seemed to be deserted. It seemed that she had always been there, and always would be there, but this didn't disturb her. Time meant nothing: she could have been standing there for the merest flicker of a moment, or a year, or a century.

After a time she sensed a presence. It was as if someone had spoken, although she had heard no voice. Cadvan? She looked around uncertainly. Surely it wasn't Cadvan? And then, as if answering her thought, she saw his form, not quite corporeal, seemingly sculpted out of light. He was looking right through her, but she knew that he was aware of her. She reached out impulsively, her lips forming his name but making no sound, and as she did her sight became deeper, as if their beings merged into a single mind, although it still seemed to Selmana that he stood before her. His form became transparent, an intricate weaving of skin and organs and bone, and through those she saw the play of Cadvan's thoughts, a shimmer of living colour. And something clambered and clung inside him, a vile, shapeless parasite. Even as she flinched in horror, Cadvan vanished, and she was alone again on the grey slopes, beneath the black sky where the stars never moved.

But now time flooded back, the past and the future filling her endless present, and she remembered who she was. She was Selmana of Lirigon, student of Calis of Eledh, a Maker, an apprentice to the humours of earth and metal and stone. She looked down at her hands in wonder: with these she had already taken iron and silver and had shaped them, and she had written down words in new orders that had different meanings, and she had left the prints of her fingers on skin and clay and rock. She thought of the many small ways her hands had changed the world: they had seemed so insignificant at the time, but each gesture, each touch, each moment of Making, had brought forth a shift. Not always good, she saw now: but not always damage, either. The complexity fascinated her, but it was daunting: she understood that she wasn't a discrete body, a mind with a boundary of skin, but a shimmering web of actions and relationships that reached further than she had ever imagined. She remembered the First Law of the Balance, which every Minor Bard learned as soon as they entered the School, and now it seemed no longer an abstract rule but a way of being, pregnant with complex meaning.

First, do no harm.

First, do no harm. And yet, nevertheless, and even in the best circumstances, harm was done. How was it possible to know what was harmful and what was not? How did anyone know the far-reaching effects of any action? How was it possible to choose?

Rapt in these contemplations, Selmana forgot where she was. The Shadowplains no longer seemed hostile: the stars were not lifeless, as she had thought, but merely flickered in another state of being. She wasn't hungry or cold and her body didn't pain her in any way. She simply was. She could have stayed there for ever in this strange ecstasy, caught out of time, following the glowing threads of her thought.

The grasses bent and the shadow trees wavered. She thought a wind sprang up, but there was no wind in this place. Something was shifting again. Arrested, but still unafraid, she searched for the source of this change. Now the plains were full of figures, of the forms of people. She knew that they hadn't suddenly appeared: rather, they had been there all the time, but somehow sideways to her sight. Unlike her vision of Cadvan, these were shadows, delicately outlined by starlight. There were so many, she realized with wonder; had they really been around her all the time? And now their voices were clearer, although she couldn't understand any words.

The dead. Even as the words fell into her mind, a shade stood before her: dark-eyed, dark-haired, slender, her head bowed. Selmana stared at her in wonder.

"Ceredin," she said. "Are you still here?"

Ceredin nodded and looked up. Their eyes met, and with her wider perception Selmana saw in Ceredin's face the echoes of everything she would never now become; the wise woman, the great Bard, the mother, the Maker. A terrible grief and anger surged through Selmana; she was suddenly aware of her heart beating in her chest, of cold air inflating her lungs. Ceredin blinked, and looked away.

"I have no sorrow," said Ceredin. "Pain is for the living, Selmana. The dead are not in pain."

She laid her hand on Selmana's. It was a searing agony, as if Ceredin's hand were fire, and Selmana ripped her arm away with a cry.

"You are strange here," said Ceredin. "You are what should not be in this place. The Shadow cannot see you, because you are impossible here. And yet if you return to where you are possible, you will be seen and hunted."

Selmana had forgotten that she had been afraid. She bit her lip. "Why can you see me, then?"

"I can see you, but I am dreaming," said Ceredin. "I often dream of those I love." She fell silent. "I find it harder and harder to use the words of the living," she said at last. "Where I am, I can see past and present and future all at once, like the sea, and in that sea there are many visions. I know less and less which is when and what may happen and what may not. But I am fading. I am becoming a Knowing without a self to Know."

Selmana listened in stricken silence, her eyes burning with tears. Ceredin met her gaze again, and for a fleeting moment Selmana saw her cousin as she had been in life, vital and ardent and unafraid.

"I think no tears have ever been shed in this dry land," she said. "Do not weep for me, Selmana. Weep for the living. Weep for what may come if this Shadow is not fought back."

"But I weep for you, Ceredin. Because I love you."

Ceredin paused, studying Selmana's face. "Love is maybe all that remains of me," she said uncertainly. "You love what I have been. You cannot love what I am."

"You are all the things you awoke in me, all the memories I have of you, all the things I want to become because of you," said Selmana, with sudden passion. "Of course I love who you are…"

Ceredin's form wavered, and for a moment Selmana feared that she would vanish. "Nay, Selmana," she said. "That is both true and untrue, and that Knowing is part of the sorrow and gladness of the World. But I am not in the World. I have seen and I must say what I have seen, and I say it out of love. But I am no longer anything you can know.

"Listen well, because I cannot stay. We are hunted, we of the wild blood. She hunts us to fix her in the World, for we may have bodies where others do not. The Circles have ruptured and now the laws are changed. The Abyss opens on the Shadowplains, the Shadowplains open on the World, the Empyrean is shut. Be wary! And yet you must trust your selves, you must trust your Knowing. You must be wakeful, always."

"Ceredin, I don't understand…"

"She is divided and small in her power, but all her divisions are linked by her will. She wishes to find her way back whole into the World, and she is both more and less powerful than you realize. She answers the will of her master, who will return hereafter. She will scorch a path for his return. But we are not alone in our fear, others move through the Circles, though they remain hidden. They help us, for they have the greatest stake in this. You must remember what I am saying…"

Selmana nodded, numb with dread.

"Do you truly remember?" said Ceredin fiercely.

"I remember," said Selmana. "I promise I remember."

Ceredin reached forward and grasped Selmana's hand again, and this time she did not let go. Selmana screamed, held in a vice of pain, and the flame spread through her whole body until it was beyond bearing, until she lost consciousness of everything except her physical agony. And then, quite suddenly, the pain was gone as if it had never been, and she was kneeling in the Street of Potters in the dim light of afternoon, and it was raining.

Selmana scrambled to her feet, bewildered. All the houses were shuttered against the rain, which beat down heavily in great cold sheets, drenching her instantly. She hunched her cloak around her and wiped the streaming water out of her eyes, trying to order her thoughts. She no longer felt as if she were being stalked by some unseen presence, but she had no doubt that it would be searching for her. Her one thought was to speak to Nelac. She ran blindly through the streets of Lirigon, her head bowed against the downpour. The streets were deserted: the rain was heavier every moment, and the sky was darkening, and lamps flared in the houses she passed as if it were nightfall.

A passing student glanced at her as she stood in the hallway of the Bardhouse, catching her breath and dripping water on the floor, and she hunched her shoulder, turning away. At first there was no answer when she knocked on Nelac's door and she bit her lip in frustration. Who else could help her, if Nelac was not here? Where could she go? She beat her fists on the door again, wondering what she should do. Should she speak to Bashar? But Bashar scarcely knew who she was. And then, to her intense relief, she heard someone inside answer, a voice that was familiar but that she couldn't at once place.

"Who is there?"

"It's me, Selmana," she said. "I have to talk to Nelac. Is he there?"

"Selmana?" She heard the man's astonishment. There was a brief pause, and then a bolt was drawn and the door opened to reveal Dernhil. He took one look at her and pulled her into the room.

"It's not fit for man nor beast out there," he said, as he bolted the door behind her. "Come in and warm yourself."

"I—" Selmana saw Cadvan, standing at Nelac's shoulder staring at her, and stopped in astonishment. What was Cadvan doing in Lirigon?

"Selmana," said Nelac, coming forward to embrace her. "By the Light, this is beyond hope! I cannot tell you how glad I am to see you. But first, let's get you dry. You are soaked to the skin!"

Shortly afterwards, Selmana was ensconced on a couch, warmly wrapped in a spare robe of Nelac's. She wanted to cry with relief: this room was real and ordinary, full of solid, every-day objects, a haven against the storm outside and the chaos of her thoughts.

"Oh, Nelac," she said, "I've had such a strange day. I don't know how to tell you what happened. I scarce understand it myself. Did you get the note I left this morning?"

"I did, Selmana," said Nelac. "And I have been searching for you ever since. But, my dear, you left it two days ago."

"Two days?" Selmana faltered. "Is it really two days?"

Nelac nodded. "I think you have been in the Shadowplains, am I right? At least, I saw you there, or thought I did. Time is not the same there as it is here."

"You were there too? But I didn't see you…" She paused, and turned to Cadvan. "I did see Cadvan, though. I could see right into you, as if you were made out of glass…" She looked away, troubled.

"What did you see?" asked Cadvan, after a silence.

"I don't know how to say it," she said slowly. She thought of Ceredin, and anger surged through her. "You shouldn't be here. Why are you here? This all happened because of you, and you are black inside, Cadvan, you are rotten, an evil eats at your soul, and you should be banished."

Cadvan flinched and looked away, but made no answer.

"I think I know what you saw, Selmana," said Dernhil gently. "I saw it too. A parasite of a kind, maybe? I struggled with it last night, and it is cast out. It was a hard battle, and I am still weary from it. But I swear to you, by the Light, that I know everything there is to know about Cadvan, the good and the ill. And for all his many faults, that horror is now gone."

Selmana met Dernhil's steady gaze, her rage ebbing. "Maybe," she said. "I know what I saw."

"As do I," said Dernhil. "I have no reason to lie. But it seems to me that you did see Cadvan, and somehow what you saw made him know what was within him, and that is why he came to me and asked me to cast it out."

"I dreamed of you," said Cadvan. "It must have been you."

Selmana studied him doubtfully, but said nothing.

Nelac had been listening, his brows drawn in thought. "Be not too quick to judge, Selmana," he said. "We have been talking, Dernhil and Cadvan and I, this past hour, attempting to make sense of what is happening in this world. I can vouch for Cadvan; I do not believe that darkness lives in him now. But I begin to wonder where else it might dwell. I am full of fear, as are we all: but let us not speak out of fear. There is too much we don't understand. In any case, I wish very much to know what happened to you. Can you tell us?"

Selmana nodded. "I'll try," she said. "But it's hard to describe…" Haltingly, she told the Bards of how she had seen the Shadowplains from her window as she was reading late at night, and of her feeling the next day that something was hunting her, and then of how she had stepped from the Street of Potters into the Shadowplains. She began to explain what had happened there, stopping in frustration as words failed her. Nelac prompted her with simple questions, and bit by bit she found the words. When she had finished speaking, she felt exhausted, as if she had undergone a long and wearying examination.

"It is too strange," said Dernhil abruptly. He stood up restlessly and walked towards the window. The rain was falling so heavily that he couldn't see more than a few paces through the gloom. "Even the weather is strange," he said, turning around. "I don't remember this kind of rainfall in Lirigon. It is like the rains in the Suderain, when the seasons turn."

"Weather is weather," said Cadvan. "We don't fully understand its laws."

"I remember reading that the Elementals can change the weather at will," Dernhil said. "They can summon rains and snow and frost, even in the midst of summer, if they are angered."

"It is claimed so," said Nelac. "I confess, I haven't studied the

Elidhu. It is a long age since Bards had anything to do with them."

"Did Ceredin mean the Elementals, when she said that others would help us?" asked Selmana hesitantly.

"Surely not," said Nelac. "She must have meant the dead, who, like Ceredin, are trapped in the Shadowplains. They would have the greatest stake in this affair. The Elidhu allied with the Nameless One, and it is a bitter memory among Bards, who do not trust them. It is hard to see why they should help the Light."

"Some say they were enslaved," said Dernhil. "They were also part of the Light in Afinil, remember?"

"We know almost nothing about the Elidhu," said Cadvan. "Let's concentrate on what we do know, which is difficult enough! Also, I'm hungry. I have not eaten one morsel since dawn, and this has been a long day…"

Nelac laughed. "That's easily dealt with," he said. "And I will take care of it soon. But we must debate now what to do. I have several thoughts. Firstly, it seems clear that Kansabur has divided herself, as Ceredin says, most likely in the conflict when we believed that we had defeated her."

"There was that moment when the Circles were all open to each other," said Cadvan. "An instant when everything faltered and frayed, when I thought that we had lost: and then it passed, and it seemed that the battle was finally won… I've been going over and over it, trying to remember, and I keep thinking that something has been erased from my memory, a kind of scar, maybe. But I am beginning to think that Kansabur transformed in that instant, that at the moment of extremity she found some other way of being, in order to escape us."

Nelac nodded. "Aye, I am thinking something similar. And if that is so, she is much diminished. But she is gaining strength now, which bodes ill. I think this is part of some much larger strategy. I can't but remember how the Black Bard Likod came to you, Cadvan, when you were just a boy. What seeds were laid then? Was the plan even then to return the Bone Queen to the throne of Lirhan? I have begun to suspect that Likod is a Hull, not merely a Bard who has turned from the Light: and if he is, he has been a Hull for less than a century, maybe. There is only one being that I know of who can transform a Bard into a Hull, and that is the Nameless One. And if that is true, he must have returned, against all the will of the Light."

Dernhil rose and walked to the window, and stood there looking out, his back turned on the others. "You name my inmost fear, Nelac," he said. "All I can say is such a thought is the very substance of my dreams, and if they are indeed fore-dreams, then no other could create such desolation..."

A silence descended on the Bards. Selmana, who had been listening intently, stirred restlessly. "But why use Cadvan?" she said. "If the Dark wanted to summon the Bone Queen into the World, couldn't they have done it themselves?"

"Perhaps they cannot," said Nelac. "Hulls give up a great deal of themselves when they permit their Truenames to be devoured. It could be that the Dark needs magery to bring the Bone Queen back into the World. But I'm only guessing. Maybe in gaining the powers of sorcery, and so gaining the dominion they desire over people and things, they lose the capacity to create life. The Dark doesn't only fear the Light: it envies it, with a deep and bitter jealousy."

"I could only summon Kansabur's spirit," said Cadvan. "And that was deadly enough."

"If she were more than spirit bound with sorcery, she would be deadly indeed," said Nelac. "Then she could remain in the World and wreak her vengeance on Lirigon. For I have no doubt she desires vengeance." He sighed. "But I think also that they used Cadvan because the Dark seeks to divide Barding from within. It has certainly been effective. Which leads me to my other thought: if Cadvan could carry a part of Kansabur's being concealed in his, without the least suspicion that he did so, then it is entirely possible the same thing has happened to me. I have entered the Shadowplains twice in the past fortnight, and both were a trial in ways they should not have been. Indeed, the second time was almost fatal. And my Knowing lately has been – muffled, as if I cannot quite hear myself, which is too like what Cadvan has told us. So, Cadvan, I think that first you should scry me, since that seems the only way to be sure."

Cadvan looked up, surprised. "Nelac, I thank you for your trust. But I have never scried anyone before. And after the night and morning I've had, I'm not sure I could do such a thing today."

"I think nevertheless you are the one to do it, and that you should do it soon," said Nelac. "I think that every Bard who was present for the banishing of Kansabur must be scried. If indeed she escaped us, and it now seems undeniable that she did, then that is when it must have happened."

"Who was there?" asked Dernhil.

"There were six of us," said Cadvan. He counted the names off on his fingers. "It was me, Nelac, Bashar, Calis, from Lirigon. Also Milana of Pellinor and Enkir of Il Arunedh."

"Perhaps they will not agree."

"Calis will, I am sure, but I am uncertain of the rest," said Nelac. "They will need to understand its urgency. We must tell Bashar what we know and what we fear, but I hesitate. She would not listen to me yesterday, all but saying that my Knowing is misled, and she may equally dismiss what we say now."

"You can't tell her that Cadvan is in Lirigon," said Dernhil. "Or at least, not at first. It is her edict that you break, and she will be the less likely to accept what you say."

"It goes against the grain to conceal anything, but I fear you're right." Nelac sighed. "The other puzzle is Selmana."

He looked across at the young Bard. "The Impossible Selmana! It seems to me that you are key, somehow. I wish I knew why you could just step, by accident, through the Circles. What is different about you?"

"I don't know," she said. "I'm just the same as anybody else."

"But the fact is that you're not the same. Of course, we are all different, each from the other, and each of us has their own Gift. But there is something in you that is clearly very different."

Selmana blushed under the intensity of Nelac's gaze, and he laughed and released her. "I am sorry, Selmana, but it is very curious. This is outside my knowledge. We should let Seriven know you are safe and send word to your mother, they have been most anxious, but I think for the moment you should remain here. I am loath to leave you on your own." He stood up and stretched. "Ah, I'm tired in my very bones. Perhaps food will help."

It rained all afternoon and into the night, a punishing downpour driven by high winds. Inside Nelac's rooms, the four Bards scarcely noticed: the relentless rain gave them ample excuse to be private. They had decided that they would stay overnight in Nelac's chambers, and a feeling of holiday, as if they were children camping out in midsummer, began to take hold of them. Selmana had one of the merriest meals of her life that afternoon.

Cadvan scried Nelac at twilight, after they had eaten and rested. Scrying was usually a private business, conducted only between the two Bards concerned, but Dernhil insisted that he and Selmana be present in case something went wrong. Selmana watched with fascination, her legs curled beneath her on the couch, as Cadvan looked into Nelac's eyes and cast the charm. The Bards seemed to fall into a trance, their figures shining with magery. For a time nothing happened, and Selmana shifted restlessly, feeling pins and needles in her feet. Then everything seemed to happen so quickly that she could barely follow it.

Cadvan cried out, and at the same time Nelac collapsed. Selmana saw something on the floor, a thick, moving shadow on which she couldn't quite fix her eyes. She gagged and instinctively scrambled to the far end of the room in panic. Cadvan and Dernhil stood shining before her, their arms raised, speaking words of power that scorched the air. A bolt of light pinned the shadow to the floor, and it writhed horribly around it, like a pinioned animal. She could feel the thing's rage and hatred, as if they were sweated into the air, and she was very afraid of what would happen if it escaped. But then tendrils of light seemed to cage the shadow, spearing it with small lightnings and enclosing it in a net of blazing silver that slowly, with a terrible slowness, began to shrink. Little by little the net tightened, until it was the size of a melon, and then a fist, and then a walnut, and it grew brighter and brighter as it became smaller. And finally, when it was an intense pinpoint of brilliance, it seemed to explode in a great soundless rush of energy, and there was nothing there.

Dernhil and Cadvan let down their arms, and the light inside them died. Cadvan rushed to Nelac, who lay gasping on the ground. As Cadvan caught him up, he opened his eyes.

"Twice rescued in one day!" he whispered. "My dear friend, I hope I never have cause to ask this of you again."

Cadvan's face was grey with exhaustion, but at that he smiled. "However many times a day you need me, my friend, I hope that I shall always be there," said Cadvan. "But I can't pretend that it's easy."

Nelac stood up slowly. "At least you don't have age weighing you down," he said. "I'm not as young as I was. More's the pity. That hurt almost as badly as anything I have suffered." He looked across at Dernhil and Selmana. "All well?"

"Up to a point," said Dernhil, grinning tiredly. "We destroyed the fragment."

"It is good to know that it can be destroyed," said Nelac. He leaned against the wall, breathing hard. "A beginning, at least."

III

XVIII

THE rain poured all night, ceasing just before dawn. The rising sun cast a grey light over a drenched landscape. Lir Lake was already swollen after the recent rains, and the downpour burst its banks, swamping some shoreline villages. Elsewhere the wind had torn down trees and blown tiles from roofs. Lirigon, set on a high ridge by the lake, had largely escaped flooding, although sodden drifts of autumn leaves and rubbish were piled in the streets.

Alone in her chambers, Bashar rubbed her temples and leant back in her chair. Requests for help had been coming in from all over the Fesse since the evening before, and she had had little sleep. She had just finished a long discussion with Berhard, the Thane of Lir, trying to determine where there was most need. Obviously the shore villages had suffered the worst damage, she would send the Makers there, but thought had to be given to other emergencies as well. Two people had been injured by falling trees, a man had been killed when a roof tile had struck his head, and many people were flooded out of their homes. She studied the list before her. The only certain thing was that there would be more to do as the day broadened.

At least the rains had stopped. Coglint, the Lirigon Bard most learned in weatherlore, had told her that there may be more rains later in the day, although he thought that they would not be so heavy. But for those who no longer had roofs, or were working in the open, more rain would add to the misery. The downpour over the past day had been unremitting.

It didn't come in buffeting waves of showers, as was usual in the plains of the north; it had been a constant, suffocating assault. She wondered how the sky could hold so much water.

A shadow fell across the door, and Bashar looked up, irritated: she had said that she was not to be disturbed while she worked out the duty lists. When she saw it was a stranger, she frowned.

"My lady Bashar," said the stranger. He bowed and entered the room. He was a tall man, grey-haired and pale-skinned, with deep-set, unsettling eyes, and was dressed all in black.

"Forgive me, but you mistake your entrance," she said, with icy courtesy.

"Indeed I do not." The man walked insolently across the room and sat in front of her. "Allow me to introduce myself. My name is Likod."

Bashar frowned: she knew the name, although she couldn't quite place it. His cool assurance angered her. "I am presently engaged," she said. "If you have need, see the Thane of Lir. Please leave." She returned her gaze to her lists, dismissing him, and picked up her pen.

"But I don't wish to leave," said the man. "My business is not with the Thane of Lir, my lady. It is with you."

"How did you even enter here?" said Bashar.

"I have my means," said Likod. "You Bards do not, after all, know everything, as you so fondly imagine."

Likod moved his hands so swiftly her eyes couldn't follow the gesture. An instinct made Bashar recoil as if she were avoiding a striking snake, and then she froze. In that moment, she realized she was bound fast.

Likod studied her, a cold amusement flickering in his eyes. "I can enter the stronghold of your power at my pleasure, and I can hold you here for as long as I desire," he said. "You have no way to prevent me."

Bashar struggled fiercely in Likod's bonds, too angry to be afraid. At last she spoke, but thickly, as if her tongue were made of wood.

"You scum," she said. "I know who you are."

Likod shrugged. "So, you can speak." He snapped his fingers and Bashar's tongue was locked. "Alas, if only you knew: you are held by the lightest of chains. If I wished, I could tighten them so you could not even breathe, so the very organs of your body would be strangled. I realize you have been taken by surprise, I'll allow you that, but even had you been wary, you could not resist the power that I have. For I am far beyond the pathetic limits of the Light, my lady. You cowardly Bards, babbling of the Balance, will never understand this. So you must be made to understand..."

He stood up and approached Bashar, taking her face between his hands. She twisted impotently in disgust, and he laughed, and kissed her lightly on the lips. "Never let it be said that I am immune to the beauty of Bards!" he said. "It might be the only reason that they can be tolerated. But even then..." His smile snapped off, and she saw the abyss behind his eyes, the arid emptiness of his ambition. "Even then, that beauty is only the barest of justifications for their delusions..."

Bashar realized then that Likod intended to scry her, and such was her fear and panic that she almost wrenched herself free. There was a flicker of surprise in his eyes. He spoke and a hidden claw within her clutched at her throat and silenced her, a parasite that paralysed her will even as she perceived it with a horror that made her choke. Nothing could now stop him: he would scour her most intimate being, and he would use that power to possess and dominate her mind. The world closed around her until the only thing she saw was Likod's eyes, which were now lit with a cold flame, a cruel and pitiless power. She heard herself screaming, but she knew she made no sound, and her scream echoed in the caverns of her mind until at last it faded, obliterated by pain.

A short while later, Calis knocked cursorily on Bashar's door and entered without waiting for a reply.

"Sorry to interrupt, Bashar, but Berhard is asking after the healers," she said. "I'm just heading to the lakeside with the Makers."

Bashar turned and contemplated her calmly. "All Bards are to repair to the School," she said. "It's only a little rain. The villages can be dealt with later, at our leisure. It is not as urgent as they claim, they are always exaggerating. The Fesse makes too many demands and gives too little in return."

Calis was taken aback. "No, Bashar, the need in the villages is real. It could have been much worse, but some are flooded out and need our help. And there may be more rain later, we need to build levees. We're leaving now."

"They have their own crafters," said Bashar. "Let them be responsible for what is theirs. As I said, all Bards will be working in the School."

"But the School was barely touched!" said Calis. "You can't be serious."

"Indeed, I am serious. This morning I've given some thought to our obligations, and I cannot see why we are so continually drained by the demands of the Fesse. It isn't supportable."

"You're talking nonsense," said Calis. "Of course it is."

"If the people of the Fesse want the magery of Bards, they will have to pay. This is my decision."

"But they do pay," said Calis, beginning to lose her temper. "What madness is this? In any case, you have no authority over Bards that isn't freely granted, and if you're talking rubbish, you have none at all."

Bashar looked briefly nonplussed by Calis's bluntness.

Her eyes blurred and unfocused, as if she were listening to some unheard voice, and then she shook her head and smiled. "Forgive me, Calis. I am perhaps misled by anxiety at our short resources. For now, do as you see fit."

Calis studied her warily. "You're exhausted, Bashar," she said. "Get some sleep. You're no good to us if you are not well. And remember, we need healers."

"I am not in the least tired. All the same, this question of responsibility must be discussed."

"I'll speak to Norowen myself about the healers, if you are too busy with your own responsibilities," Calis said crossly, and left, slamming the door behind her.

Bashar blinked, and paced slowly across the room, back to the window.

"We must be more careful," she said. She cocked her head, and was silent for a time, as if she were listening to that silent voice. "Until it is time for an open assault. Soon, soon, but now is not the time." She turned and studied the sky, where more clouds were gathering. A few vagrant drops were beginning to fall.

XIX

THE silence when the rain stopped woke Cadvan just before dawn. Dernhil and Selmana were still asleep, and Dernhil was snoring softly. Early the previous evening, shortly after the scrying, the three younger Bards had rolled themselves up in quilts on pallets in Nelac's sitting room, insisting that Nelac rest in his own bed. Cadvan had fallen asleep as soon as his eyes closed, dropping into the blankness of utter exhaustion.

He sat up, rubbing his eyes and yawning. Like all Bards, Cadvan had powers of swift recovery, but the past few days had left a silt of weariness in his body. On the other hand, the new ease in his being since Dernhil had scried him made up for much of the fatigue. But he felt grubby, as if every crevice of his skin were slick with old sweat and dirt. A bath! He couldn't remember when he had last had one.

Making a dim magelight, he raided Nelac's commodious storage room for clean raiment and a drying cloth. He was about to leave the chambers when he remembered that he must not be recognized. He cast a light version of the Pilanel charm, enough to conceal his identity, and then let himself out, bolting the door behind him. This early, the Bardhouse's occupants were still abed, though he heard movement in the streets outside. He guessed that there must be flooding somewhere. No doubt Nelac would be called upon to help if there were any emergencies, which might cause complications. Well, they could think about that later.

In the Bardhouse bathing room he turned on the copper taps and shaved as he waited for the stone bath to fill. Then he eased off his clothes and sank with a sigh into the hot water. For a while he simply lay there, letting the heat dissolve the aches and pains in his muscles as the lavender-scented steam rose and cleared his head. It felt like a stolen luxury. It *was* a stolen luxury: he was breaking his banishment, after all.

This was an aspect of Barding that he had missed sorely. Bards had developed bathing to an art; not for them a hasty sponging down in a cold river, or breaking the ice in a basin on a winter morning. In Lirigon, water was gathered in a cistern on the hill above the School and cunningly pumped using gravity into every house, where it was heated in copper pipes. The bathing rooms were comfortably furnished, decorated in colours that were meant to induce tranquillity and meditation. Cadvan studied the cranes painted in flight on the opposite wall, and for a few precious minutes he was utterly content.

He remembered with a start that he shouldn't linger, scrubbed himself thoroughly and dressed, and returned to Nelac's chambers not half an hour later. The sun was yet to rise, and the other Bards were still asleep. For a moment he thought mischievously that he should wake them, but relented: there would be time enough later. He drew a screen around Nelac's table, so the light wouldn't disturb the sleepers, and idly opened a book. Another luxury he had missed; he had taken none with him to Jouan, just as he had never played music there, as if his banishment meant he had no right to any of the things he had loved as a Bard. The truth was that they had reminded him too painfully of what he had thrown away. More cowardice; it would have been useful to have books in Jouan. He could have used them to teach Hal her letters.

The sun rose and broadened and the other Bards woke and took themselves to the bathing room and discussed breakfast. Cadvan remained absorbed in his book behind the screen, waiting until they were ready to convene about how best to approach the Circle about what they knew. Lirigon's dawn chorus was especially loud; the School's birdlife was celebrating the end of the rainstorm. For once, Cadvan felt at peace; the thought of his exile didn't chafe him today. Even if he could never enter Lirigon again, he could read and play music and enjoy the pleasure of clean clothes on freshly bathed skin. Barding wasn't everything. It wasn't even mostly everything.

Then, quite suddenly, his head jerked up from his book. He sent out his Bard senses, questing. He couldn't say what had alerted him: an instinct of peril, of violent intrusion. He put the book down and stood up, peering over the screen.

"Do you feel that?" he said.

Dernhil, who was folding away his bedclothes, glanced at him oddly, and then smiled. "Oh, it's you," he said. "You should warn me before you change your face, Cadvan…"

"Something's wrong. Really wrong."

"I don't sense anything," Dernhil said, after a pause. "What is it?"

Cadvan shook his head. "Something's happened, something … violent. And now…"

"Kansabur?"

"I don't know." Cadvan lifted the screen and put it back where it belonged, frowning. "I'm so tired, Dernhil, of chasing shadows, this constant, formless … not knowing. I begin to long for a monster that just turns up, like in the tales, all horns and fangs and breathing fire, and all we have to do is to chop it to bits."

Dernhil smiled. "Be careful what you wish for."

"At least we'd know what we're up against. All this stuff inside our heads. How do we tell what is us and what is not?"

Dernhil didn't answer for a time, as he carefully stowed

the bedclothes in a carved chest. Then he turned to Cadvan. "Maybe that's the real question," he said soberly. "We *can't* tell, for certain. There is no real division. Even if we cast out what is driven into us, we are left with ourselves. If we can do good, we can do evil. If we are Bards, we can be Hulls, too: that possibility stirs inside us, as a condition of our being Bards at all. Perhaps the Light and the Dark, they are not so different..."

"That is bleak indeed," said Cadvan. "And best not said to most Bards."

"Aye," said Dernhil. "But I confess, it's a thought that haunts me. After all, as we know from our first lessons, the Dark was made by human beings: and so was the Light. And so both reflect our failings..."

The door opened, and Selmana entered, her hair wet from bathing. She stared at Cadvan. "Who are you?" she said.

"Selmana, meet Cadvan," said Dernhil. "He can change his face, which you must admit is useful."

"A glimmerspell?" said Selmana. "But..."

"No, something else. I'll explain later," said Cadvan. "Is Nelac about, Selmana?"

"He went to arrange breakfast," she said doubtfully, looking from one Bard to the other. "What's wrong?"

"Something has happened in the School."

Selmana paused, as Dernhil had earlier, sending out her Bard senses. "I don't feel anything ... wrong," she said.

"I don't know why you can't feel it," said Cadvan. "Pain. It's like pain. I'm not imagining it."

"Maybe," she said slowly. "But there is always someone in pain, maybe you are just picking up on something ordinary. Something that isn't a threat, I mean."

Cadvan thought, and shook his head. "No, whatever has happened is linked to the Dark," he said. "We have to speak to Bashar."

"But you heard what Nelac said last night. She might think we're imagining things."

"Given what you and Nelac have to say? Surely that would make anyone sit up and take notice." Cadvan began to walk about the room, agitatedly running his hands through his hair, until footsteps sounded in the corridor outside, and he turned in relief.

Nelac entered bearing a tray of freshly baked pastries and laid them on the table, glancing sideways at Cadvan. "That disguise is disconcerting, my friend. You are hungry? This was the best I could do, I'm afraid; Ithan is beside himself feeding messengers from the Fesse asking for help with the flooding."

"Maybe that's the problem?" said Selmana, turning to Cadvan. "Maybe there are people hurt, and…"

"I keep telling you, it's not like that."

"Let's break our fast," said Nelac equably. "And then you can explain to me what is troubling you."

Cadvan glanced impatiently at the other Bards, and then shrugged and joined them at the table. The sweet smell of the pastries reminded him that he had woken early and was, after all, very hungry. For a while they ate in silence.

"It stinks of sorcery," said Cadvan abruptly. "But it's not the Bone Queen. And it's here, now."

Nelac contemplated his half-eaten roll. "I see," he said. "I am not doubting you, Cadvan. Yet I am certain that I would know if the Dark had invaded the School. More than walls protect Lirigon; there are wards woven into the very stone."

"Kansabur was tracking Selmana in the streets of Lirigon," said Cadvan. "Selmana saw the Shadowplains through the windows of her Bardhouse. Perhaps there are ways through the wards that we don't know about."

"And you still sense this peril?"

"Yes. For a while it was just getting worse and worse, and

it almost made me sick. Now it's like an aching tooth that's just lying quiet." He lifted his hands in frustration. "I wish you could feel it. I can't ignore it."

Nelac finished eating, and brushed the crumbs from his hands, calmly studying Cadvan. "One of the things that seems to be happening at present is that none of us knows anything in common," he said. "Each of us dreams and fears in solitude and understanding between us is riven. We are each alone with what we know. This isn't how Barding works; we know best when we know together, when our understanding is held in common."

"Perhaps we could try melding our minds," said Dernhil.

"But you can only do that when you cast a charm," said Selmana. She looked around the table, suddenly uncertain. "Or maybe that's not true. But that's what Calis says."

"It's certainly the easiest way, Selmana. Not the only way. Then let us cast a small charm," said Nelac. "It needn't be significant. The saying for clear contemplation suggests itself? Do you have that one, Selmana?"

She nodded; it was a spell often used by students on the brink of a test. The Bards linked hands and said the necessary words, bending their thought to the weaving of the charm. As soon as Cadvan began to glow with magery, his disguise fell away, and she felt relieved; his altered appearance made her uneasy, and gave her a little shock every time she looked at him. Bards shouldn't be able to hide themselves, she thought. Somehow it wasn't right.

Bards had many ways of linking their thought. Scrying was the deepest and most profound, the complete entering of another's mind; at the other end of the spectrum was a lightly sensed web of relationship, as Nelac had of his students. Melding was more formal, the mutual permission to share their powers to strengthen magery. The last time Cadvan had done this was almost two years before, in the terrible hunt for Kansabur.

He turned his thoughts from the memory; this time, the making was graceful and full of light, a gentle coming together Quite suddenly, almost as if a lock clicked over, he was one of four minds, and the music of the charm became subtler and stronger, as many fingers of light doubled and tripled its simple patterns.

And then, with relief, as their powers entwined and strengthened and a pool of clarity opened between them, Cadvan knew that the others felt the dark pressure that was troubling him. Selmana gasped out loud. As the other Bards recognized it, Cadvan's sense of its presence amplified and became clearer, coalescing from a vague shadow into a specific memory. A man who sawed at the mouth of his horse so that it champed on a foam of blood. A man who had attempted to trap him in a foul web of sorcery. A man who had shown him the forbidden books, sneering at his Bardic hesitation as weakness.

I know who it is, he said, into the minds of the others, and he showed them the image of his memory and told them a name.

"Likod!" said Dernhil out loud, breaking the charm in his astonishment. He turned to Cadvan. "That is Likod? You are sure it's that same man?"

"That same Hull, I think," said Nelac. "And you're right: here in the School, and hidden. And it has broken something."

"Or someone," said Selmana. "It has broken someone."

Nelac shot her a sharp look from beneath his bristling eyebrows. "Yes. Or someone."

A peremptory knock on the door, followed by someone rattling the handle, made him rise from his seat. It was Calis. "Why is your door bolted?" she said impatiently, when he opened it.

"Sometimes a Bard desires a little privacy," said Nelac dryly. Calis was the only Bard he knew who would barge into someone else's rooms without the courtesy of waiting for permission.

"Well, are you going to invite me in?"

"I'd rather not," said Nelac, forbidding questions with a glance. "How can I help you?"

Calis looked as if she were about to argue and then thought better of it. "I need healers to help in the villages."

"But do you need me?" said Nelac. "I have other urgencies this morning…"

"I'm taking some Makers with me to the lakeside villages, and thought you could come with me. There's no huge emergency, but we are told there are injuries. One unlucky death, I believe, and the family needs the rites. Norowen is going north to Lepolan, but I could do with a healer."

"What about Gerant?" said Nelac, naming Norowen's assistant at the healing house. "He would deal as well as I could. Better, even."

Calis gave Nelac a measuring look. "This isn't like you, Nelac," she said. "I was sure you would come."

"Floods aren't the only thing we must deal with today," said Nelac.

Catching something in his tone, Calis hesitated. "I wish you would tell me what is of greater importance today," she said. "Coglint says there will be more rain, and we must restore what we can before it arrives, and ensure that there is no illness later. I like this weather not at all. Bashar is in a fey mood and is no help at all this morning. And now you…"

Nelac took her hands.

"Calis, my friend, go and do what you must do. If you love me, let it be known that this morning I am busy with other duties."

Calis met his eyes and was silent. "I will, my friend," she said at last. "You disquiet me. I wish that you would take me into your confidence. But now there is no time."

"Trust me, Calis," said Nelac.

"I do," she said, with sudden seriousness. "I always have.

I'll return later, when our tasks are done. I think we must talk."

She took her leave, and Nelac bolted the door behind her.

"We can't just stay holed up in here, like rabbits hiding from a fox," said Selmana. "What's the point of that?"

"Indeed we can't," said Nelac. He was frowning. "I think we should visit Bashar."

XX

AFTER a day locked indoors, Selmana was tired of confinement. At the same time, Nelac's chambers had been a haven from the strangeness of the past days. She felt the difference as soon as she stepped into the street: her senses were now rawly open, and a feeling of deep unease washed over her, as if the ground were no longer solid, the sky a mere illusion that might at any moment dissolve. Perhaps Nelac had woven extra wards about his rooms, she thought. To protect him from invasion? Or to keep things in, maybe? Perhaps to protect the rest of the School from his own work?

She glanced across at Nelac, who paced beside her, his face closed in thought, thinking that she knew very little about him. He was a powerful mage, everyone knew that, but Selmana was suddenly aware of what that meant. Once physically strong, he was now at the cusp of old age, his hair almost white, his hands beginning to knot and darken. He seemed perilous to her, a font of energies that pulsed with capacities that she could barely guess, potent and hard-willed and beyond her predictions. She perceived, with a shiver of clarity, that Nelac possessed powers that could lay waste to everything she knew. If he should choose, she thought. But he does not choose...

Nelac smiled, as if he read her thoughts. "It's a strange sky up there," he said. "I would almost prefer to stay indoors, even though it was beginning to feel as if we were caged."

Selmana glanced at the clouds. Nelac was right; she had never seen clouds like that before. They loured in strange

formations that covered the entire north sky, a raft of lumps
that hung dark and ominous, like huge grapes, or the egg cace
of some gigantic insect.

"Perhaps they'll hatch some monster," she said.

Lirigon was busy; people were sweeping up rubbish or
checking their homes for damage, talking in small groups or
hurrying on errands. Bashar's chambers and the meeting hall
were a short distance away, on the other side of the Inner Circle,
which was the hub of the School. In the middle of the space,
with a notebook propped on his knee, they met Coglint, who
greeted Nelac with a brusque nod.

"What do you make of this sky, Coglint?" asked Nelac.

"It is remarkable," he answered. "I've read of such clouds,
but I've never seen them with my own eyes; they are very rare.
They've formed very swiftly, over the past half-hour."

"What weather do they tell?" asked Selmana.

Coglint glanced at her indifferently, dismissing her as a
Minor Bard. "The records are not clear," he said. "Sometimes,
as I understand, they simply disappear."

"I think these will not vanish," said Nelac.

"It's hard to say," said Coglint. "But they are certainly still
increasing."

"The wind increases too, and swiftly. I prophesy a storm,"
said Nelac.

"Surely not." Coglint looked irritated. "There's no sign of
that in my readings. More rain, I think, but hardly on the scale
we've seen in the past day."

"A storm beyond imagining," said Nelac. "I hope you've
warned the School to batten down."

"Bashar has issued the appropriate notices," said Coglint. He
started fiddling with his instruments. "If you'll forgive me…"

Nelac nodded, and the Bards passed on.

"Why did you say there would be a storm beyond

imagining?" said Selmana. She was afraid now.

He looked back at her and laughed. "Partly because Coglint annoys me," he said. "He is good at weatherlore, but apt to think he is the only Bard who knows anything about it. But also because I fear it might be true. I smell something in the wind. A will directs it."

"This wrong, it is thickening here," said Selmana. "Could it be that Likod has entered the First Bardhouse? Surely that isn't possible, Nelac?" The thought appalled her; she began to feel as if a hollow were opening in her stomach.

"There are wards here that would destroy any emissary of the Dark the moment they set their hands to the door," said Nelac. "But I don't know what is possible any more."

They passed into the Bardhouse with no further speech. As she watched Nelac stating his errand to Bashar's housemistress, Selmana began to wish fiercely that she had not come. She had no business here with the high Bards. But the others had insisted she go with Nelac, to tell Bashar her tale in her own words.

They knocked on Bashar's door, and her musical voice told them to enter. The First Bard was seated by the broad arched window at the far end of the chamber. The room was unlit, so it was thrown into a strange gloom, and she appeared to them as a silhouette against the light. At her elbow were the remains of breakfast and an unfinished glass of tea.

"Good morning, Nelac," she said.

"This is Selmana, Minor Bard of Lirigon," said Nelac, bringing her forward. "She has something of importance to tell you."

"You know very well that we are busy today," said Bashar. "I wonder that you waste my time."

"If it weren't important, I would not be here," said Nelac. Selmana heard the edge in his voice and quailed inwardly. If Bashar wouldn't listen to Nelac, what chance was there that she would listen to a mere Minor Bard?

Nelac paused, to permit Bashar to invite them to sit down, but she simply waited for Nelac to speak. Selmana was feeling more and more awkward; after her first glance, Bashar hadn't looked at her once since they entered the chamber. Nelac began to tell of Selmana's vanishing into the Shadowplains, and of his own almost disastrous search for her, when Bashar interrupted him.

"You demand my time, Nelac. I have no time, and especially not for wild tales such as this." Contempt flickered across Bashar's face, and Selmana felt Nelac tense beside her. "I've been courteous with your fears and imaginings. But who do you bring with you? This is Selmana, you say? A Minor Bard?"

Selmana felt her cheeks redden as Bashar gestured towards her, and wished more than ever that she had not come. The First Bard's scorn was palpable.

"You came to me two days ago in a panic, claiming that this student had disappeared in mysterious circumstances. I told you not to be concerned. And here she is, safe and well! What story has she told you? Perhaps she covers some shameful escapade. I would not be so trusting of children's tales, Nelac."

Selmana glanced anxiously at Nelac, who stood very still for a few moments, as if he were striving with himself.

"I would argue that in my time I have earned the right to be heard, even by the First Bard, in the midst of her most important affairs," he said quietly. He was looking intently at Bashar, and he thought he saw in her face a fleeting uncertainty, a sudden pained hesitation; but it passed so swiftly he couldn't be sure.

"Indeed you have, dearest of friends and colleagues," said Bashar. "But this? Childish fancies and fears, Nelac. There is work to do, and you waste your time in nonsense about the Dark?"

"Nelac said nothing about the Dark," said Selmana abruptly. She was shocked by Bashar's dismissiveness, and felt anger stirring inside her.

Bashar turned and looked thoughtfully at her. "You must be the latest of Nelac's little ducklings," she said. "He has shown poor judgement of late in choosing his favourites." She returned her gaze to Nelac. "My friend, I swear by the Light, if you do not collect your thoughts and put your powers where they are needed, action must be taken, however reluctantly. Your championing of that scion of the Dark, Cadvan, has not gone unnoticed. There are many who speak of their disturbance and doubt. We begin to wonder where your true loyalties lie. Do not forget what happens to those who betray the Light."

The threat was naked in Bashar's voice. Nelac looked warningly at Selmana, who had opened her mouth to speak, and bowed.

"Such discourtesy unbecomes you, my lady," he said. "I would remind you that there has never been need nor reason to question my commitment to the Light. My apologies for our intrusion. We won't disturb you further."

"Report to Norowen," said Bashar, nodding in dismissal. "You are slated for duties. Perhaps your student might actually be of some use there." She returned to her contemplation of the sky, and the two Bards left in silence.

Outside the Bardhouse, Nelac took a deep breath. His expression was unreadable, but he seemed suddenly older. They walked across the Inner Circle in silence, wrapping their cloaks against the wind. Selmana looked around uneasily: it was already a gale, and the sky seemed more sinister every moment.

"I didn't know the First Bard was so..." Selmana trailed off and looked at Nelac. She smarted with humiliation, but felt more the lack of respect that had been shown to Nelac.

"That was not the First Bard," said Nelac shortly.

"What do you mean?" Selmana went cold, as if all the blood in her body had ceased to move. She thought she could begin to guess what Nelac meant.

"I think that Likod has scried her by force," said Nelac, after a pause. "The Dark can do such things. And if scrying is done against a Bard's will, the mind can be broken, and the body can become a puppet to be used at will. It happened often during the Wars of the Silence, according to the records. But no Bard would do that, surely. Only a Hull would do such a thing…"

Selmana felt sick at the thought of such violation. "So you think that Likod is definitely a Hull?"

"There has always been rumour of Hulls who survived the defeat of their master," said Nelac. "If Likod is a Hull, he must be newly made. Even though the Nameless One can offer them immortality, he cannot prevent their bodies from aging. Likod is not even old. And only the Nameless One can create Hulls."

Selmana shuddered and thought about what she had been taught about Hulls. She had read of them in old tales out of the Great Silence when the Nameless One had ruled all Annar, forcing the Light out to the Seven Kingdoms, where it remained defiant through the long years of tyranny. That Hulls should be in Lirigon seemed impossible; they were part of a distant past that was long over, that belonged only in dusty, half-forgotten books and children's tales.

"But how could a Hull enter the School?"

"I wish I knew." Nelac sighed heavily. "It seems likely to me that Bashar, like Cadvan and I, had something of Kansabur hidden in her soul. And perhaps that opened a gateway, a chink in her protection, which meant she couldn't resist Likod, for all her native power. But that doesn't explain how he could have passed the wards, unless Bashar herself took them down. Perhaps he can step through the Circles, from Shadow to the World, in ways we don't understand, and so bypass them."

"Will Bashar be all right?" said Selmana, in a small voice.

Nelac halted, turning to face her, and Selmana was startled by the grief she saw standing in his eyes. "No," he said, his voice harsh. "If I am right in my guess, and I think I am, there is no returning from what has been done to her. The Hull might be expelled from her mind, but even if she survives that, she will be forever after broken and diminished. Sometimes Hulls do this to Bards for no reason except their own amusement, to laugh at their torment." His voice broke and he was silent for a time. "Bashar was a great Bard, wise and just. A true friend, through all our differences. To think of what has happened to her is beyond bearing."

"That was unsubtle," said Cadvan back in Nelac's chambers, after Nelac had reported their visit. "One would think that the Dark would have more guile."

"The Dark has its own blindnesses," said Nelac. "They cannot imagine that others should have desires different from their own, and they only desire power. Likod believes a First Bard would wear her authority as tyranny, because that is what he would do."

"Had Likod been cleverer, he would not have cut you off with such impatience," said Dernhil.

"The Dark was ever arrogant in its cruelty," said Cadvan. "I should know."

"For my part, I'm surprised by how little concerned he was to conceal his hostility," said Nelac. "But do not underestimate his cunning. Perhaps he thinks to provoke us into making an unwary accusation against Bashar, which he can then use to discredit me."

"We should not stay in your rooms," said Cadvan.

"I think that Likod believes we are presently thwarted. We can do little in the School without Bashar's help. All the same, I agree it would be wise to go elsewhere."

"Will Bashar survive this?" said Dernhil.

"Perhaps," said Nelac. "Some Bards did. But the records say that they were never the same afterwards. We must do what we can to help her, but I fear it is already too late."

There was a bleak silence.

"Now," said Nelac. "We should prepare ourselves." He took a key ring from his belt and led them to the general storeroom in his Bardhouse. Selmana's eyes opened wide in wonder: here was kept anything Bards might conceivably need to do their work. Neatly stacked on shelves that went to the ceiling were spare instruments, reeds and strings for flutes and lyres, stacks of fine paper and bundles of pens, a small armoury of weapons, including short swords and the slender bows Bards preferred, shields and light armour, and astrolabes and other delicate instruments. Nelac looked at the other Bards and chose swiftly, throwing them practical travelling clothes: breeches, jerkins and stout boots, the thickly woven cloaks of sheep's wool that were a particular craft in Lirhan, and some packs and saddlebags. "Take these," he said. "There are other sizes, if these don't fit."

They retired to his living room and changed. Selmana, who was shy, used the screen for privacy. Then Nelac took their Bard clothes and folded them away for laundering, and they packed their bags: kits for horse care, travelling victuals such as pulses, nuts and dried fruits, goose grease for their boots, a flask of medhyl each, flints for lighting fires, soap and salt, and other things they would need for a long journey.

"Are we going away?" asked Selmana uneasily.

"Not yet," said Nelac. "And perhaps not at all. But we may have to flee Lirigon."

Selmana swallowed hard and looked at the heavy pack at her feet. She felt very uncertain and inexperienced next to these sober-faced Bards. She had never been outside the Fesse of Lirigon in her life. "So what do we do now?"

"Now?" said Cadvan. He was back in disguise, but he smiled, and she saw fleetingly through the dour face of the Lirhanese farmer a glimpse of Cadvan, mercurial and joyously reckless. "Now we hunt down the Hull. And we destroy it."

"It?"

"Bards don't permit Hulls the dignity of sex," said Dernhil gravely.

There was a brief silence, and then Selmana burst into snorting laughter. "Oh, I'm sorry," she said, gasping as she tried to control herself, conscious of a hysterical edge in her voice. "But that sounded so funny."

But Cadvan was laughing too. "It's true," he said. "They have no sex. When they reject death, Hulls reject the life of their flesh. It no longer matters to them. And so the bodies of others don't matter to them either: they become only objects for them to use at their will. They are not man nor woman nor any other of the five sexes. And they do not love."

"So why do we always speak of the Nameless One as if he is a man?" she asked. "And why do we say Kansabur is she? Aren't they Hulls? Or are they special Hulls?"

"The Nameless One is not a Hull," said Nelac, who had been listening, smiling faintly, as he checked over his pack to ensure he hadn't forgotten anything. "No one knows what spell he used to bind his spirit within the World, but he has kept it for himself alone. And the Bone Queen? Well, she was a Hull, but the rumour is that she was also something more: it is said she reached into the Abyss and took the Shika, the Terror of the Abyss, into her being, and that is the source of her dread. I don't know if that is true. But when she ruled over the Realm of Lir, she took a queenly form, dire and beautiful to those without the eyes of Bards. Bards, of course, saw her otherwise. So in Lirhan, we call her *she*. You should know already that Bards are not always consistent." He stood up and looked at the others. "Well, are we ready?"

"I am," said Dernhil. "But I confess that I have no idea what you plan to do."

"We should shield ourselves, so Likod can't track our magery. And for now we need a place to conceal ourselves within Lirigon, where we won't be easily found. I am thinking of your friend Larla, Selmana."

"Larla?" Selmana turned in astonishment, remembering the kind, fat woman who had helped her in the Street of Potters.

"She is not a Bard, and so Likod will not even think of her," said Nelac. "She has powers beyond magery. And she is also an old friend of mine." He hefted his pack, grimacing. "Let's leave. The skies will open soon."

The rain began in earnest just before they reached the Street of Potters, following one of the major streets that ran, like spokes from the hub of a wheel, out of the Inner Circle. The strange clouds covered the entire sky, hanging very low above them, almost as if they might brush the red roofs of Lirigon. There was no thunder or lightning, just a heavy downpour driven almost sideways by the wind, which was still rising. The Lirhan cloaks, woven of wool cunningly waterproofed, kept out the rain, but within minutes they were splashing through deep puddles. Even the boots, made with the best Lirhanese cobbling, as Cadvan had pointed out, were not enough to keep Selmana's feet dry: she stepped unwarily into a small river rushing down the street and the water overtopped them.

Nelac led them unerringly to Larla's blue door. They crowded into her little porch, trying to escape the rain, and water streamed from their hoods onto the scrubbed threshold. Larla answered the door swiftly, almost, Selmana thought, as if she had been waiting for them, and spoke over Nelac's greeting.

"Come in, come in," she said. "It's wild out there." She fussed around as they entered, taking their cloaks and hanging them in her entrance hall, where they dripped lugubriously onto the floor, pointing to a storeroom where they could stow their packs and urging them to take off their boots and dry them by her fire. "Now, come into the kitchen. Lucky I'm on high ground here, and my house is nice and low, it's the high houses next door that'll catch the wind, you mark my words. There'll be no flooding in *my* street. But look at your boots, Nelac! Wet feet run up to wet noses, and the last thing you want is a cold!"

Dernhil caught Cadvan's eye and they both grinned; they had never seen their mentor treated so cavalierly. Selmana sniffed: something was baking, warm and homely and sweet.

Larla asked them for no explanation; she didn't seem in the least surprised to have four Bards turn up at her door. She seated them at a big table in her kitchen, chatting brightly as she poured tea from a pot that might have been made for their arrival.

"I'm glad to see you, young kitten," she said to Selmana, as she handed the cups around. "I was that worried about you, when I heard you'd gone missing."

"So were we all," said Nelac. He leaned back in his chair and regarded Larla with open amusement. "Am I right to assume that we were not unexpected?"

Larla returned his gaze innocently, with her eyebrows raised. "Why would you say that?"

"Perhaps you are awaiting other guests," he said, indicating the kettle. "I trust we're not inconveniencing you?"

"No, no, not at all. Yes, of course I was expecting you. I saw you in my basin, as sure as sure, as I was washing my small clothes. Though I wasn't very certain of the time, and it is just good chance that you turned up when I was taking the weight off my feet and making a brew."

"Good chance is what we've been short of lately," said Cadvan. "It's very welcome."

Larla cast him a narrow look. "I think I know you, young man," she said. "Though I cannot call your face to mind."

"Perhaps you do," said Nelac, smiling. "This is Cadvan, once of Lirigon, in other guise." Larla's eyebrows shot up, but she made no comment. "For now, Larla, I'm curious. What do you make of what is happening here, in Lirigon? Because it seems to me that you might understand something that we do not."

Larla looked suddenly serious. "It's not likely that I do," she said. "You've read all the books, and I try and try, but I just can't get my head around all those letters, they slip and slide and make no sense at all. I'm that troubled, Nelac. I sniff and look into corners, and all I can tell is that something's awry, the weaving's knotted in the making of things, in the shadows where you don't look. I couldn't even knit this morning, the stitches kept dropping, and I couldn't read the yarn."

"But you could see us?"

"Aye." Larla blew on her tea and gave him a sly look. "But I confess, I did call to you, my friend. I was a bit worried this morning, when the knitting went wrong, and it was like there was a black knot in my head, and I thought to myself, Nelac, he's the one to talk to. And like I said, I saw you in the basin, you and your young friends here, and I felt a little better after that, knowing you'd be here later."

Dernhil was listening with a puzzled expression, looking as if he wished to laugh but didn't quite dare. Larla glanced at him. "I know who you are, young Dernhil of Gent," she said. "I don't mind if you laugh at me. I did like coming to hear your poems. I like a handsome man, I do. And your poems do get inside a person, like you already know something."

Dernhil blushed vividly, and stammered an apology. "No, I wouldn't dream of…" he began, but Larla cut him off.

"I know," she said kindly. "I was just teasing. But we're wasting time. What are you Bards going to do about all this, eh? There's something bad here, something bad right in the middle, and you can't tell me there isn't. Selmana knows, she can see, though I didn't realize until after she had left my house. But nobody seems to notice, they're too busy with their little floods, as if that's the only thing going on."

As she spoke, the shutters on her little house rattled violently, as if the wind were clawing to get in. Selmana shivered.

"This storm isn't little," said Selmana. "It's part of everything. It's there to distract us."

Dernhil looked up. "Perhaps the Elidhu set their power with the Dark, as is said in the tales," he said.

"Not always, if the old accounts are true," said Cadvan.

Selmana stirred impatiently. It would be just like Bards, she thought, to plunge into a learned discussion about the history of the Elementals, while the world was torn to rubble around them. "Yes, but what must we do *now*?" she said. "How do we destroy Likod? I mean, we can't just walk up to the Bardhouse and chop off his head."

"No," said Nelac slowly. "We can't do that. And we are not well placed: the Dark has struck at the centre of Lirigon, and from there Likod will direct affairs as suits the Dark's wishes. I believe a strategy long-prepared is now unfolding. Perhaps it was the plan from the beginning, when Likod first spoke to you as a child, Cadvan. We don't know what the Dark will do next, but I fear it will be swift and strong. And we have no time."

"Then are we going to hide here, as we were hiding in your chambers, scurrying from place to place like frightened mice?" said Cadvan. "Is there nothing we can do?"

"I did not say that," said Nelac. "It is well to understand what confronts us. The Dark is moving fast, and so must we: but equally a careless move made in haste would spell disaster." He paused. "I only know one way of undoing the possession of a Bard. Another Bard must take the Hull into himself. I will do this."

There was a shocked silence, and then Cadvan jumped out of his chair. "No," he said. "You can't."

"I can, and I will, Cadvan," said Nelac mildly. "Do not argue with me."

"But won't you end up like Bashar?" said Selmana.

"No," said Nelac. "Not if all goes well. That is, of course, a risk."

"But we know nothing about Likod's powers," said Cadvan. "We know nothing about this thing that is Kansabur. You don't know what you will be facing. This is reckless beyond measure. If anyone is to take that risk, it ought to be me. We can't afford to lose you, Nelac. And in any case, it all started with me, and the price is mine to pay."

"What did I say about your vanity, Cadvan?" said Nelac. "Of course it didn't begin with you. If we are correct, it began in the days of Afinil, when Sharma of Dagra rejected his Truename and wove the binding spell that bent the laws of the Circles and made him into the Nameless One. But this task is mine. I am the only one among you with the Knowing to do this. And only I have the strength."

Cadvan opened his mouth to argue further, but Nelac glared at him. For a moment Nelac's anger seemed to outline him in a restless silver light. Cadvan slowly sat back down in his chair without speaking.

"If that is what must be done, then how shall we do it?" said Dernhil. "I think you should not go alone."

"Selmana shall stay here," Nelac said. At this she cried out in protest, and he glanced at her kindly. "No, Selmana. I have other plans for you. It's not because I doubt you. Dernhil and Cadvan are to come with me."

Larla smiled at Selmana. "Don't worry, kitten," she said. "You're still a babe, and there's nothing to be ashamed of in that."

"If we don't return by tomorrow morning, Selmana, I want you to leave Lirigon and travel to Pellinor as swiftly as you can. You must speak to the First Bard there, Milana, and tell her what has happened in Lirigon. She is a dear friend and wise and she will listen. Go to my mare, Cina. Tell her my Truename, Validur, as a token. She knows the way and she will bear you. Trust her: she is the best of beasts."

All three Bards stared at Nelac with their mouths open. Only Larla, who was listening intently, her restless hands busy with some sewing, seemed unsurprised. Nelac had said his Truename openly before all of them. No Bard ever revealed their Truename lightly, and if they did, it was only to those they trusted with their lives. Selmana was abashed and shocked by his confidence; it underlined their peril as nothing else had. She swallowed hard. Leave Lirigon on her own?

Nelac took a gold ring from his finger. "This is the Ring of Silur, a treasure of Lirigon. It has the virtue of fitting any hand that wears it. When you reach Pellinor, show it to Milana. She will know you bear my word."

Selmana took the ring and studied it curiously: it felt cool and heavy in her hand, and was inscribed with strange runes that she didn't recognize. She slid it onto her middle finger. Her hands were larger and rougher than Nelac's, and at first it seemed that it would be too small; but as she put it on, the metal seemed to shrug and it slid easily onto her middle finger.

"I'm sure you'll come back, though," she said. To her annoyance, her voice wavered. She didn't want to seem afraid. "And then I can give you back the ring. It's too precious for me."

Dernhil smiled reassuringly. "We'll come back," he said. "Of course we will. Nelac always plans for the worst."

"The truth is that we may not," said Nelac. "But if I thought we had no chance of success, I wouldn't suggest this course. Now. We are decided, yes?"

"*You* have decided," said Cadvan, with a flicker of humour. "We but follow in your wake."

"You're going out in this storm?" said Larla. "You will

scarcely stand up against the wind!"

"It will work to our advantage, I think," said Nelac. "Likod will not expect us in this chaos. We'll use shields against the tempest." He stood up, suddenly brusque. "Cadvan, you can't use magery without breaking the Pilanel charm, yes? That's a little inconvenient. Dernhil will have to shield both of you: I don't want anyone to recognize you, even though there's little chance of anyone seeing anything in this weather."

The room was now charged with purpose and grim urgency. Perversely, given her earlier impatience, Selmana was alarmed by how quickly things were moving. The three other Bards pulled on their boots and cloaks, still damp from their earlier walk, and made the shields that would protect them from the storm. A quick embrace in Larla's tiny hallway, and they were gone. The brutal wind tore through the door and blew the wall hangings so they fluttered wildly, and it took the strength of both Larla and Selmana to wrestle it shut. The hallway seemed strangely quiet. Selmana stared at the blue door, suddenly feeling lost. The tea that Larla had poured for them when they arrived wasn't even cold, and now she might never see Nelac, Dernhil and Cadvan again.

"We'll have to wait now, kitten," said Larla. "Waiting is the worst thing, much worse than having to do something." She gave Selmana a shrewd look. "Now then, Nelac wouldn't send you to Pellinor if he didn't think you could do it."

"I don't think I could," said Selmana forlornly. "I've never been anywhere."

"Of course you could," said Larla. "Lucky I was making some honey cakes, because I sniffed the weather and I knew we'd be holed up inside. They'll be ready just about now."

XXI

IT was scarcely two hours since Nelac had spoken to Bashar, and in that time the wind and rain had steadily increased. Cadvan linked arms with Dernhil to ensure that Dernhil's shield covered both of them, but also because it was difficult simply to move forward. The wind snatched the words from their mouths, and if they had need they spoke, as Bards will sometimes, into each other's minds. The shields didn't keep out the cold, which bit through their cloaks and numbed their hands. It was probably almost noon, Cadvan thought – it was hard this day to tell the time – but Lirigon was plunged into murky twilight. He could only just see Nelac's form, a mere pace away. The streets were shin-deep rivers that coursed so fast that, without magery, they might have been swept away. They passed blurred blooms of light, where people had lit lamps in their homes. Anyone on lower ground would already be flooded.

Cadvan felt his will tiring: every step was hard won. When they reached the Inner Circle, the wind hit them with renewed force, eddying with unpredictable violence in the open space. They worked their way around the edge of the Circle towards Bashar's Bardhouse, broken branches and leaves whipping around their faces. Huge hailstones hit the stone flags and smashed like small boulders before melting into grey sludge. If it hadn't been for the shields, Cadvan thought, they would for certain have been cut or knocked out by flying debris.

They finally reached the portico of the First Bardhouse. The great double-leaved door was locked, but Nelac drew out a bunch of keys and let them in. The three Bards tumbled breath-lessly into the entrance hall and then turned to fight the door shut. Nelac locked the door again and leaned against the wall, breathing hard. The Bardhouse, usually bustling with comings and goings, was eerily deserted. It was normally well-lit, but now the high hall was thrown into gloom; the long windows were all shuttered, and only a single lamp glowed at the far end, where stairs wound up to the next floor.

"Where is everybody?" whispered Cadvan.

"I imagine the Bards are out at the villages, trying to help with storm damage," said Nelac. "The Light knows what's hap-pening in the Fesse… But we cannot think of that now. It was more than wind and rain we were fighting there, my friends. There is a will in this storm."

"There is," said Dernhil. The dim light threw shadows of strain over his face. "I think it is not a human will."

Cadvan studied Nelac anxiously; he looked frail and already weary. But even as he watched, Nelac gathered himself, straight-ening his shoulders, and his age seemed to fall away. "The storm is the least of our worries now," he said. "Dernhil, Cadvan, whatever we face in here will demand everything we have, and more. I fear that we may not prevail, but I fear more not making the attempt."

At this Cadvan's heart sank. Dernhil stood unmoving, his mouth drawn into a grim, determined line. Nelac drew them close, speaking directly into their minds, using the Speech so his instructions would be clear and unambiguous, burned into their memories.

Now, listen well. Listen with all your listening: I have never been more serious. When we enter Bashar's rooms, I want you both to fol-low my lead. Say nothing unless you must, and do nothing until there is need. It may be that an impetuous act, an act made out of fear or anger, could ruin us all. Whatever happens, be mindful.

He paused, to let his words sink in. *There will be a struggle, and it will be difficult to perceive. Watch carefully. You will know me if I say my Name. If I do not, if I cannot say my Name, then you must kill me. The battle will be yours then, to fight as you must.*

Kill you? said Dernhil.

Nelac's face softened. *There are things that are worse than death, my dearest friends. I know I could demand nothing more terrible of you, but I ask this out of the love I know you bear me.*

An appalled silence stretched out between them, and then both Cadvan and Dernhil nodded. Cadvan was white to his lips, and his eyes shone.

"I would do this thing, because you ask it," he said out loud. "But if it comes to that, it will be the worst thing the Dark has done to me."

Nelac grasped his hand. "I believe it will not come to that," he said. "Nothing is certain. But know you must do this thing, if I am defeated."

"What shall we look for?" said Dernhil.

"Watch with all your senses," said Nelac. "You will know."

Cadvan took a deep breath to still the shaking in his body. It was one thing to be afraid for himself; it was quite another to be afraid for Nelac, who, he realized with a pang, he loved as if he were his father. More than his real father, he thought; and then he felt ashamed. A vivid memory rose unbidden in his mind, from when his father began to teach him how to cut and shape leather. It was before his mother died, and he had been perhaps five years old. He saw his father's face, patient and gentle, his skilled, strong hands. Nartan loved him, and deserved his love in return. It wasn't his father's fault he had a Bard for a son, instead of the cobbler he wanted. He hadn't deserved the pain that Cadvan had brought him. How was his family surviving this storm? Why hadn't he thought of them since he had returned to Lirigon?

He deliberately pushed the thought of his father out of his head. Now wasn't the time. But perhaps there would be no time after... To distract himself, he stared at Nelac's cloak as he walked up the stairs in front of him. It was made of green and red wool cunningly crossed into a pattern of repeating leaves, the work of a master weaver. The thought of the skill and patience that had gone into making that cloak made him want to weep.

It was hard to stay focused. The sense of wrongness in the Bardhouse was palpable, like a constant dissonant noise that keened below the cacophony of the wind, or a heavy toxin in the air that blurred and weighted his thoughts. Cadvan was almost certain that he was walking to his death. He realized very clearly that he didn't want to die.

Dernhil touched his arm, and Cadvan started out of his distraction. *I am afraid too*, he said into Cadvan's mind. *The only time I was more afraid was in the Inkadh Grove.*

Cadvan took his hand and clutched it hard before letting go. Nelac had spoken of love: it was love that the Dark didn't understand, it was through love that Cadvan might find the clear space where he could stand and fight. He felt no less afraid, but a small chink of hope opened in his mind.

Bashar's quarters occupied the whole of the top floor of the Bardhouse. They didn't need to discuss where she was: with their heightened senses they could feel Likod's presence as if it were a source of feverish heat. The Bards were still shielded, and their footsteps were muffled by rich carpets as well as the wind, but it seemed strange that they had encountered no one. Cadvan thought that the house must be utterly empty; even through the shield, he should have sensed the under-flicker of magery. Where were the other Bards?

At last they stood in front of the carved double doors that led to Bashar's private meeting room. Nelac pushed them open and a gelid light poured out, dazzling after the gloom of the hallway. Cadvan blinked, swaying with the force of its power. He glanced involuntarily over to Dernhil, who stood beside him, his mouth set, his eyes blazing with something like hatred or contempt.

This is the empty heart, said Dernhil. *This is the void.*

The light came from Bashar herself, but it wasn't the illumination of magery: it was a fierce cold, so fierce it burned, a pure, deadly energy that radiated from her skin. Cadvan flinched at the obscenity of what he saw: Bashar was reduced to an instrument of Likod's will, her powers used to his ends. She was motionless, but other senses told Cadvan that she was deep in a complex sorcery that occupied all her attention. Bashar hadn't even noticed that they had entered the room: she stood by the window, her arms outstretched. The arched casements were wide open, but some force kept the storm outside. The air inside the room was utterly still. Then Cadvan realized the window no longer opened on Lirigon: outside was no worldly storm, but a sight-defeating darkness, a vortex of impossible energies riven with fires that were beyond the spectrum of human sight.

Nelac strode forward, throwing back his hood from his face. He burned with the silver-gold radiance of magery, but it was dim next to the light that beat out of Bashar. Cadvan and Dernhil followed for a few paces and then stopped, tense and uncertain, all their perceptions painfully alert.

Cadvan wondered what malevolence Bashar was calling with such concentration: for it seemed to him that something was being summoned. He could feel the edges of a presence, a dread that cut beneath the fear he was feeling now. He opened his deepest listening and suddenly, as if a lid were lifted, he perceived the sorcery that Likod was weaving through Bashar's power. He recoiled; with a thrill of terror, he realized that he knew the spell. Likod had shown it to him during the last of their meetings.

"Even the Nameless One himself is loath to use this summoning," Likod had said, as he unclasped a book sealed with lockcharms so strong they made Cadvan dizzy. "Beware! To read it is perilous. Only the greatest may do so, and even then it may burn out your eyes. Do you dare?" Cadvan had hesitated and Likod had laughed. "Of course you do not dare!" he said.

Cadvan had dared. Knowing the absolute bans against sorcery, knowing the peril, knowing the punishment visited on mages who flirted with the knowledge of the Dark, he had dared. He had read all the sorceries that Likod had shown him, but this was the last: after that, ill and shaken for days, he had decided that he needed no more knowledge of the Dark. He had congratulated himself for knowing his own limits; he had never been tempted to invoke the spells until he challenged Dernhil. Later, after the disaster in the Inkadh Grove, he had often wondered at himself. But Bards were inquisitive: seeking knowledge of all kinds was at the heart of Barding. Cadvan was driven by an overwhelming curiosity.

Likod had cunningly pricked his vanity, flattering him with a respect that underlaid his open scorn – Cadvan was, after all, the Bard who had, wholly untrained, broken Likod's attempt at chaining him. Likod's mockery was sly. Cadvan wholly believed that the Light was more powerful than the Dark, that the purity of his allegiance and his will would protect him from its malignity, and Likod did nothing to disabuse him of that idea. Surely, Cadvan had thought, it is better to know than not to know. Surely the Light would ultimately benefit from his insight into the Dark. And so he had looked. He had survived the looking, but reading the spell had frightened him more than anything he had yet encountered in his life.

It was the sorcery that summoned the Shika from the Abyss.

The Shika. The winged terror. In all the annals of Barding, there was no description of them: those few who survived their presence said they defeated all knowledge, that they were beyond human perception. They were the purity of fear that tore through the deepest levels of being. They were unbodied force that could make the very stone shake with terror, that could bend time itself and enclose it in a prison of torment, a nightmare that reached beyond the ease of death. They could never remain long in the World when they were summoned, and even the Nameless One only called them in the last resort. And now Likod was summoning them, not as a last resort but as a first play, to destroy the very heart of Lirigon.

All this flashed through Cadvan's mind in less than a moment, as he watched Nelac raise his hands with careful deliberation, preparing his own magery. Bashar still seemed unaware of their presence. How was that possible?

Likod is summoning the Shika, Cadvan said into Dernhil's mind. *I fear that window opens on the Abyss…*

Then he must be stopped.

The sheer wasteful recklessness of Likod's gesture made Cadvan cold with rage. So Likod planned to wholly destroy the Light in Lirigon, using the worst weapon he knew. Cadvan hoped bitterly that Likod would die of the spell. But it was Bashar who would die, not Likod. He wondered where Likod was: this kind of possession required him to be close by, but there was no sign of the Hull. How much of Likod's being was enmeshed in Bashar's mind? Where was his body?

The force of the sorcery was increasing with each moment, a terrible pressure that beat on them unbearably, as if it would scrape the flesh from their bones. And then there was another voice in the room. Cadvan almost stumbled with the relief of it. The light in Bashar dimmed and almost went out, and she turned to face them, swaying. Her eyes made Cadvan flinch:

her irises had vanished, so they turned sightless and white.

Nelac lowered his arms, and a dazzling light leapt into the room, pitiless and fierce. The spell shattered, and its force hit the chamber in a brutal wave. Bashar stepped back and almost fell, her mouth opening in protest. A thread of smoke trickled from her lips and dissipated in the air. Nelac spoke again, and the thread thickened into a plume of blackness that hung suspended between Nelac and Bashar. And then, as if she had suddenly snapped to attention out of a trance, Bashar stood tall and straight, and the smoke curled back into her nostrils, like an animal fleeing into a burrow.

Dernhil and Cadvan felt the breaking of Likod's spell as a stunning blow: Dernhil's shield shook and faltered, and he staggered back. At once Cadvan lifted another, stronger shield over both of them, and his disguise fell away. In the chaos of the breaking spell, Cadvan heard a rattling beat of insectile wings, a voice that came from no earthly throat. A gout of terror beyond reason pulsed through his body. In that moment he thought that even if they all died in what followed, it was better than the coming of the Shika.

Even though it was broken, the spell was still in motion; its splintered energies were now released into the room, spilling in glittering shards of sorcery, gleams of razor-sharp power that hung spinning half-seen in the air, defeating the eye as they winked in and out of visibility. The window seemed to blink, and Cadvan knew that outside was no longer the Abyss, but the storm that was hammering Lirigon. A gust of hail-laden wind blasted into the chamber. A glass ewer crashed to the floor, and loose paper whirled in eddies about the room. Dernhil stumbled to his knees, and Cadvan took his wrist and hauled him up, meeting his eyes in urgent query.

I'm all right, said Dernhil. All the blood had fled his face. *What should we do?*

Nelac said to do nothing.

Yes, said Dernhil. Cadvan could feel his frustration, which was close to panic. *Up until the point where we had to fight for our lives…*

I don't believe Bashar has seen us, said Cadvan. *Her eyes see elsewhere.*

Cadvan's head began to buzz, as if his eardrums might burst. He was shaking with the effort of keeping the shield strong, but when Dernhil recovered from the breaking of his own shield, they melded their powers, and after that it was a little easier. Sheltered from the worst of the chaos that was ripping the room apart, the two Bards stared in wonder and fear at the strange struggle before them.

Nelac and Bashar were absolutely still, as if they were both statues carved of different spectrums of light. The narrow space between them was filled with a writhing shadow, which moved now this way, now that, under the influence of two opposing forces. For a long time the issue seemed to sway in the balance; then, it seemed all at once, the shadow coiled into Nelac's mouth, like a fat, black snake, and vanished. Bashar instantly collapsed to the floor and lay as one dead.

Nelac turned and stared at Cadvan and Dernhil, as if he only now realized that they were present. Cadvan saw with a clutch of fear that his eyes were white, as Bashar's had been. Then, as in a nightmare, he saw Likod step in through the open window, as if he had been standing outside in mid-air. There was a perceptible click, as if something snapped into focus, and the fragments of sorcery that were spinning about the wrecked chamber began to collect together, linking bit by bit into threads that wound about each other, re-weaving the spell. The illumination that streamed out of Nelac was now the wrong colour, the same fierce cold that had possessed Bashar.

It's over, thought Cadvan, with a wondering despair. We

are lost. He glanced at Dernhil and saw the same desolation in his face.

Nelac closed his eyes and lifted his hands, and Cadvan waited numbly for the word that would set the spell in motion again. He knew that he and Dernhil should stop it, but in his horror he was unable to move. It was all he could do to stay upright, to keep himself alive in the midst of the murderous currents of power that swirled around them.

The word was never said. Nelac's eyes snapped open, and the blind whiteness was gone. His eyes were his own again, and they burned with a blue fury. He sent a blast of force against Likod that made him stumble, but Likod recovered almost at once and set a thick curtain of smoke about him, against which the white fire faltered and went awry.

Now the Bard and Hull were locked in combat, Cadvan felt the pressure lift slightly, and he realized he could move and think. The spell was still weaving itself together, as if it had a life beyond the will that had set it. The metallic taste of sorcery thickened in his mouth. Perhaps, he thought, nothing could stop it now, even if Nelac prevailed…

He knew this spell; once read, it imprinted itself for ever, like a brand or a scar. Later, ashamed and sickened, he had tried everything to remove it from his memory, but he only had to think of it and the scorched letters crawled across his vision as pitilessly as when he had first looked inside the book. Perhaps, knowing this spell as he did, he could find how to undo its inexorable process, its strange unlife. Gingerly at first, fearing that he might distract Nelac, he sent out his will and began to examine the spell. It burned, and he flinched, and then set his jaw and tried again.

At once he was puzzled; it was the same spell he had read, he was certain, but other energies moved within it that he couldn't read. Perhaps it was two spells, woven together. It resisted him with a force that made him gasp. He shook with strain, blinking sweat out of his eyes, but didn't dare even to wipe his face. With part of his awareness, he saw Nelac sway and almost fall.

Cadvan decided to ignore the parts of the spell he didn't understand. There was a beginning in this weaving, a first thread that, once found, could undo all the others. The sorcery ran backwards and forwards across three Circles, forcing each open to the others, and its construction was intricate and hard to follow, sharp and toxic. But he thought he knew where to look: and at last, when he had begun to despair, he saw a glint of sorcery shaped to trigger and amplify the spell in endless repetitions, a form of constant remaking that would patiently repair any breakage. With all the force of his despair, Cadvan said a word to reverse it, praying he was not mistaken, that he had found the right word. It writhed and flickered and disappeared, and he felt, with an immeasurable relief, the spell beginning to unravel, collapsing inward on itself. As it unravelled, the sorcery wound about it was exposed. His gorge rose: it was loathsome, like something thick and rotting, a heaving of undead flesh writhing towards a parody of life.

Likod, immediately aware of what Cadvan had done, whipped around to face him. In that moment his attention was distracted, and Nelac brought his arms down like an axe and said the word for ending. It flew from his lips like an arrow of white fire launched at Likod's throat. Cadvan saw Likod's eyes widen in shock in the instant before it hit him: a dark shield filled the room like smoke, and then he wasn't there.

A foul weight lifted from Cadvan's mind. He realized, with a sob of relief, that the sorcery that had puzzled him had vanished with Likod. He wondered if this other spell permitted Likod to step bodily through the wards of Lirigon, into the high chamber of the First Bard. Yet this sorcery wasn't broken, as the summoning had been, and with a chill he understood that it was merely removed; he could feel its forces at work, close at hand, even though he could feel no trace of Likod's presence.

But there was no time to think. Cadvan and Dernhil started forward, but Nelac forbade them with a look. He spread his arms wide, and the unbound shards of sorceries spinning about the room gathered before him in a field, as iron filings crowd around a lodestone. Slowly and painstakingly, he touched each sliver with the tip of his finger. As he touched each part, it curled up like burning paper and disappeared. The erasing of the spell seemed to take for ever, but at last it was done. The buzzing in Cadvan's ears stopped, and there was only the noise of the wind and the rain.

"Close the windows, Cadvan," said Nelac. His voice was hoarse, as if he had burned his throat.

Dernhil grabbed Cadvan's arm, forbidding him to move, and Cadvan turned, startled.

"Your Name," Dernhil said to Nelac. "Say your Name."

Nelac frowned, as if he could not remember. "My Name?" he said. "You know my Name, Dernhil."

"Say it." The tension cracked in Dernhil's voice.

Nelac laughed. "Validur," he said. "My Name is Validur." And he crumpled to the floor, next to Bashar.

Cadvan latched the windows and shuttered them, his hands shaking. It was suddenly pitch-dark, so he set a magelight and hunted down the lamps, turning on any that were not broken. Clear Bardlight leapt into the room.

Dernhil was kneeling beside Bashar, his hand on her forehead. "She yet lives," he said. "Nelac too. His pulse is strong and there is no injury; I think he will revive soon. But Bashar…"

Cadvan put his hands on Bashar's chest, wincing as the sense of damage flowed up through his fingers. Physically she was unharmed, but her mind was torn and splintered, a pulp of anguish. He concentrated, melding with Dernhil: together they could stem some of the pain, but they could do little to close the wound. Likod had riven her mind as brutally as if he had attacked her body with a cleaver, and the only thing that had kept her alive was his will and intent. She hovered now on the very brink of death. Drawing on their deepest reserves, Cadvan and Dernhil did what little was possible, patching the smaller injuries, numbing pain where they could, setting sleep where they couldn't. When they had finished, they sat back on their heels.

"She'll live now, I think," said Dernhil. His voice was empty with exhaustion. "I didn't know that could happen to a Bard. I wonder whether we should have let her go..."

Cadvan met his eyes, and looked away with a feeling like shame. The impulse was always to heal, always to save; and yet they were also taught that healing on the precipice between life and death sometimes meant a choice. He was not a good enough healer, he thought, to have yet faced that choice. He remembered what Nelac had said in the hallway earlier. Perhaps some things were worse than death.

In the intensity of their attempt to save Bashar, they had all but forgotten Nelac. He stirred and sat up, groaning, and looked around the wrecked chamber.

"She lives?" he asked.

"Aye," said Dernhil. "But she needs a healer beyond our capacities."

"I have nothing left," said Nelac. "Nothing." He hid his face in his hands.

Even speaking hurt, thought Cadvan. He wondered dully who they could call to help, if no one was present in the Bardhouse. He listened: was he imagining it, or was the wind dying down?

"The storm is passing," said Dernhil. "And those voices are

gone. It is only the wind that keens now."

For a time all three sat unspeaking, too exhausted to move. Cadvan's ears caught the sound of motion in the Bardhouse, voices and footsteps, and he thought they should call for help; but even that felt beyond his means. At last, Nelac stood up, grimacing. "Come, my friends," he said. "Our task isn't finished." He stumbled over to a nearby shelf and picked up a bottle, which he unstoppered and sniffed. "Medhyl. I thought so. I don't know why I hadn't the foresight to bring some here myself…"

Nelac took several sips before passing the medhyl to Dernhil and Cadvan. Its herbed, clean taste woke Cadvan's palate, and he felt its virtue at once, lifting the hollowing exhaustion that followed the making of powerful mageries. He leant over Bashar, wondering if there was anything else he could do to help her, when footsteps sounded in the hall outside.

"Nelac! By the Light, what has happened here?"

All three Bards turned in surprise and relief. Coglint and Noram of Ettinor stood at the threshold, ashen with shock. When Noram recognized Cadvan, his face darkened.

"Bashar is near death," said Nelac. "We have done what we can, but she should go to Norowen."

"What have you done?" said Coglint. "What evil have you brought here?"

"There will be time for explanation after," said Nelac. "Now there is sore need." But Noram was already calling for help, and they heard voices and feet running. Coglint shielded himself, and ran to Bashar and lifted her, gravely studying her face. Noram didn't take his eyes off Cadvan.

Two Minor Bards ran in and Coglint issued hurried instructions. Before long, bearers carefully lifted Bashar onto a stretcher and took her away. Hard on their heels, four soldiers bearing the livery of the Thane of Lir entered the room.

"No," said Nelac in alarm. "Coglint, Noram, you misunderstand what has happened here."

"I see a Bard who has had traffic with the Dark, and I see the work of the Dark," said Noram. His voice was hard. "Would you have me doubt the evidence of my eyes? I do not know what caused you to betray the Light, Nelac. And you, Dernhil, of all people! I am deeply grieved. But it seems that Bashar was correct in her fears."

The soldiers drew their swords and warily approached the three Bards. Nelac drew back his shoulders, his form flickering with rage.

"Lemmoch!" Such was Nelac's authority that everyone in the room halted, suddenly still. "Stop this madness! Think for a moment. Since when have you had cause to doubt my service to the Light? Dernhil has more reason to hate the Dark than anyone here but Bashar. More is at work than you know. Before you judge what has happened here, *listen*."

Coglint hesitated, and began to tell the guards to wait, but Noram cut him off. "Why have you brought this exile into Lirigon?" he said, hatred palpable in his voice. "Tell me that, Nelac. By your own acts you stand condemned. You are caught in the very act of treason, and you'd parley in the midst of the ruin you have made?"

He nodded to the armed men. "Take them," he said. "They will languish at the pleasure of the First Circle until judgement is called against them."

"You fool," said Dernhil. "Nelac just saved the School from the worst attack it has yet suffered. And you'd imprison him?"

"It's no use arguing with these idiots," said Cadvan impatiently. He was cursing that he hadn't thought to hide himself.

"No," said Nelac. "This is not the time to argue." A lightning blazed out of him, and the soldiers and other Bards froze, their faces tight with fear. With a supreme effort, Nelac had broken their mageshields and set a charm of fastening, a making so simple that even a child could do it without thinking, and their feet were bound to the floor.

"Coglint, Noram," said Nelac in the Speech. "I am sorry to do this to you, but you must understand that all of us are imperilled, and hasty judgement now endangers the whole School – perhaps all of Annar. Understand that none of us wishes you harm."

Coglint was pale with anger and fright. "You dare to attack me!" he said. "Me, a Bard of the First Circle! And you have the hide … in the very act of murder…"

"I did not seek Bashar's death," said Nelac. "I attempted to save her from a fate that you can barely imagine. And yet you will not hear what I have to say. You command I be imprisoned, on no authority but your mistaken appraisal of what has happened here. I wonder that you did not help Bashar earlier. Where were you? Black deeds were done this day and you stood by."

Doubt clouded Coglint's face. "I don't know what you mean," he said.

"Did you not notice that all was not well with Bashar this morning?" said Dernhil. "Where were you both when the Dark entered this house? Were you bewitched?"

"The Dark stands before me," said Noram. He stared at Cadvan with contempt.

"And you brought it here, Nelac," said Coglint sadly. "Why? What has possessed you?" Anguish was raw in his voice, and Dernhil blinked and looked away.

Let them take me, said Cadvan into their minds. *I am the crime here.*

We would gain nothing if you were imprisoned, and we would lose too much, said Nelac impatiently. *I don't know what has happened in this house, but it seems to me that everyone is ensorcelled. Even if Likod has been cast out of the School, he has set his poison here…*

"Let's go," said Dernhil. "I can hear others coming. Cadvan, conceal yourself." When Cadvan hesitated, he pushed him. "*Now*, Cadvan."

I'll not make that Pilanel charm here, while others are watching, Cadvan said. Noram was still staring at Cadvan, his eyes hard with hatred, as he vainly attempted to undo Nelac's fastening charm. *If we are to leave, we should leave now.*

Nelac hesitated. *If we flee this place, it will confirm their suspicions,* he said. *Perhaps we should wait…*

Think you that others will believe us, or them? said Dernhil.

Nelac glanced at Noram, and reached a decision. *We must leave, though my heart misgives me,* he said. *We dare not risk what might happen.* He looked Coglint in the eye then, and said in the Speech: "You do not know what harm you do this day, when so much harm has been done. I know you doubt me, but I have never spent myself in the service of the Light more than this morning. I pray you will understand this, before it's too late."

Coglint disdained to answer him, but he looked as if he wanted to spit.

They left Bashar's chambers swiftly, casting their hoods over their faces. The house was alive with movement, and they passed unnoticed amid the bustle, wondering at its earlier desertion. Nelac must be right, thought Cadvan: Likod must have ensorcelled the entire Bardhouse.

They emerged blinking into the daylight. The storm had lifted altogether: a greenish light poured through ragged clouds, touching the buildings with an unearthly hue. Broken branches and torn rubbish littered their path, and everywhere was the sound of trickling water. Lirigon seemed uncannily still, in the numb aftermath of violence.

They crossed the Inner Circle, expecting any moment to hear alarms and the beginning of pursuit, and at last reached the relative shelter of the streets. Nelac stumbled then and almost fell, as the exhaustion of the past hour struck home. Dernhil and Cadvan supported him between them, hurrying as fast as they could back to Larla's house. The heaviness in their limbs made this journey seem interminable, almost as hard as when they had pushed through the storm; but at last they reached Larla's blue front door. As if she had been keeping watch, Larla flung it open almost as soon as they knocked and drew them in, checking up and down the street to ensure that no one saw.

"Oh my," she said. "We're in such trouble now, my dears."

XXII

ARLA'S oaten honey cakes were delicious, even by the standards of Lirigon, where they were a local speciality. While the other Bards fought their way through the storm, Selmana ate five, one after the other, staring broodingly into space. Larla made little attempt at conversation; indeed, the clamour was now so loud it was difficult to talk. Instead, she busied herself with stoking the oven, and began to chop onions and carrots and herbs, throwing them into a glazed pot. Selmana was obscurely comforted by Larla's unfussed domesticity, but wondered at her blithe confidence that her house would be unharmed. How would Nelac and the others make their way through such a tempest, even with mageshields? A crash near by, audible even over the hammering rain and roaring wind, made her jump: she remembered the old pine up the road, a tree of huge girth, weathered and gnarled by many winters. If it fell on the roof, Larla's house would be broken open like an egg. Larla looked up and studied the ceiling, frowning briefly. "Missed!" she said brightly, and went back to her chopping.

Larla was right: waiting was hard. Selmana could feel panic fluttering in her stomach, a dread that ran through her blood like a low-grade fever, but she tried to ignore it. She had no reason to be afraid, she told herself. She was sheltering like a mouse in its cosy burrow, her nose twitching with alarm. The image almost made her smile; she couldn't think of anyone less mouse-like than herself. She had overtopped her mother when she was seven years old, and by the time she was thirteen she was as tall as her father, and almost as strong. She reached for another honey cake and munched it slowly, thinking of her childhood.

She hadn't known she was a Bard until quite late, at around ten years old, and it had come as a relief, illuminating the difference within her that until then had slept merely as strangeness. She couldn't remember a time when she hadn't wanted to smith metal. She had haunted her father's forge as soon as she could walk. At first her father had tolerated her, calling her his little assistant and permitting her to pump the huge bellows she could barely reach, blowing the forge coals to white heat. He had even taught her some simple techniques, and she had learned the deep pleasure of shaping metal. She had loved the musical ring of the swinging hammer, how flakes of hot iron flew in bright sparks around her, the power of her hands.

But when she grew older he had forbidden her to come to the forge, saying that it was no job for a girl. When she had pointed out that Rabla in the next village was a smith, and a good one, he had mumbled into his beard. It was fine for Rabla, but not for his own daughter, and that was that. His ban cast her into profound misery. Her mother argued that smithing was an honourable job, for both man or woman, but her father was implacable. Perhaps, her mother had said as she comforted her, if she'd had sisters, he might have let her have her head … but Selmana was the only girl in the family. In her impotent rages, Selmana thought it was only just that neither of her brothers shared her passion for smithing: both of them followed their mother, and became farmers.

But when the Speech opened inside her, her life opened too. Now she could learn everything she desired, now no one could tell her that her passion was wrong because she was a girl. Even her father was proud to have a Bard in the family, and they had reconciled their differences before he died. She missed him sorely, but that at least was a comfort. Until Ceredin had been killed, Selmana had been wholly happy: her life had work and meaning and purpose. She had heard talk of the Dark, but it had no connection with her life: it was a force that belonged in history books or in distant places she would never visit.

And now... She drew in a deep breath. Now the ground had opened beneath her feet, revealing depths that she hadn't imagined. Now the familiar world was turned inside out and she saw through different eyes. The change had happened so fast she could scarcely keep up with herself. She knew now that the Dark wasn't the opposite of the Light, nor even its absence, but something much more disturbing: a seed that lived in the very heart of the Light. No wonder Inghalt refused even to discuss the idea: it shifted the sure ground of Barding to a landscape of doubt and peril. She was certain that Nelac, accounted as one of the wisest scholars of the Way of the Heart in all Annar, had known this all along.

Maybe that's why he argued that Cadvan should not be exiled, she thought. Perhaps Cadvan understood the Dark better than anyone else. She stared at her hands, calloused and scarred by her work. With these hands, she could choose to dominate the lives of others, to treat them as things; or she could create the possibility of delight and love, she could nourish the promise that lay within every mind. She shuddered with the weight of the responsibility: it was curled into every moment of her life, every tiny gesture, every trivial choice. How could anyone live with that?

There was another crash, closer this time, and she started out of her abstraction. Larla, who was by the stove stirring her pot of stew, met her eyes and shrugged.

"Aren't you worried?" Selmana had to shout to make herself heard.

Larla gave the stew a final stir and put a lid on it, settling close to Selmana so she could hear. "Time enough to worry when the roof blows off," she said. "I believe it won't, but there will be many houseless people at the end of this. And worse, maybe, if Nelac can't do what he must."

Again Selmana wondered who Larla was. She wasn't a Bard, but she had something of a Bard's aura. Larla caught the question in her eyes, and laughed. "I have the Sight," she said. "It is a Gift, if not the Gift of Bards. I don't know what you are taught there in the halls of learning, and I know there are Bards who have contempt for such as I am. But Nelac never did."

"He said you're old friends," said Selmana, her curiosity piqued.

"Aye, kitten. Old lovers, as it happens, and then deep friends. That was long, long ago, although I suppose it wasn't so long ago for Nelac, Bards being what they are. I often wonder what time means to them."

Selmana politely hid her surprise, but it didn't escape Larla's shrewd gaze. "I was never pretty, but I had a charm all my own," she said. "As do you, my love. You'll never be beautiful in the way of your cousin, but there are many kinds of beauty."

Selmana blushed, discomforted by Larla's direct gaze, and changed the subject. "So if you have the Sight, maybe you know if Nelac will return?"

"There are things I can't see," Larla said, and for a moment Selmana saw how anxious she really was. "There are knots that must untie themselves as they will."

A new blast of wind drowned out her words as she spoke. Dernhil was right, Selmana thought; there was more to this tempest than the accidental weather of the world. The creeping dread, briefly forgotten, returned worse than before. There was an afternoon to get through, and then the night: and if the others weren't back by morning, she was ordered to ride, by herself, all the way to Pellinor. She pushed the thought away, twisting the ring on her finger. They would come back. They must.

Larla was clearly someone who always liked to be busy. She pulled a pile of yarn from a basket underneath the table and began to roll a thread into a ball, inviting Selmana to help. The rhythm of the work was comforting. Selmana had no idea if it was still morning, or how long it was since the other Bards had left the house. Time seemed to have stopped altogether; she had the odd feeling that she'd always been in this warm, colourful haven, winding yarn in calm yellow lamplight, while the unreal storm howled over their heads.

Then, for no reason that Selmana could see, Larla's head jerked up, snapping to attention. For the first time that day she looked frightened. "Is something wrong?" asked Selmana.

Larla couldn't hear what she said, but she caught Selmana's meaning and nodded, her face tight. She leaned forward and spoke into Selmana's ear, so close that her whiskers tickled. "Listen," she said. "Listen so I can see."

Selmana had kept her listening closed because of the cacophony; to open it was to be bruised and battered. Cautiously she sent out her senses, questing for clues, her blood pulsing loudly in her ears. Everywhere was the deafening noise of wrongness, but she couldn't discover why Larla was suddenly so agitated; everything seemed the same as before. She shook her head.

"Something is opening, kitten. Something I don't understand. A door is opening, and behind it is something terrible, something that waits to devour us…"

Selmana stared at her stupidly. "I don't know what…"

"Not in the storm," said Larla impatiently. "It's not in the storm. Don't listen to that. Beyond it. Beyond the World. Outside everything."

With intense relief, Selmana shut her listening against the tumult outside. She wants me to listen in another way, she

thought. But how? And then, as if something clicked, she understood. Of course there was another way. She had always known,
without quite being aware of it. It was a way of looking *between*...
She closed her eyes and concentrated, attempting to unfocus her
mind; and there, on the edge of things, she sensed a cold and
terrifying presence, a broken flutter like wings of delirium. She
snapped open her eyes, staring at Larla.

"That's it, my kitten. What is it?"

"I don't know," she whispered.

"Try and see. It is closer, it is closer all the time... Something
is calling it in..."

The last thing Selmana wanted to do was to look closely
at whatever it was she had glimpsed, but she obediently tried
again. This time it was clearer, but the sense of horror that filled
her was almost intolerable. It wasn't so much a presence as an
absence, a consciousness that was so beyond her knowledge
that she couldn't comprehend it. She screamed without knowing that she screamed. Even at this distance, it was an affliction
like madness. There were huge wings, or something like wings,
which beat in a rhythm that had nothing to do with the pulse of
warm blood. She tried to snap her mind closed but somehow
she couldn't, and she met Larla's eyes, pleading to be released.
But Larla wasn't looking at her: she was staring, fear naked in
her face, at something beyond Selmana. Selmana turned to look
and saw nothing: and then terror obliterated everything else.
The next thing she knew, she was curled in a ball underneath
the table, her head wrapped in her arms, and Larla was pulling
her arm, trying to drag her out.

"I can't," she sobbed. "I can't stop it."

"I'm sorry, kitten, I wanted to see and I couldn't by myself,"
said Larla. "Come out, there is nothing here. Oh, that was a bad
mistake. I'm so sorry. Come out now, come out."

Gently, as if she were a frightened animal, Larla coaxed

Selmana out from underneath the table, and at last she stood in the kitchen, staring wildly around her, shaking from head to foot. Selmana was surprised that she could see the kitchen at all: her inner eye told her that everything was pitch-black, and in that blackness was a shadow darker even than that, which now seemed to beat with the rhythm of her own heart. She no longer knew who she was, the boundaries of her skin dissolved and she bled into the darkness, and the darkness was her. The only mooring was Larla's warm, living hand: it was the one solid point in a universe that spun around her. Selmana held on as if she were drowning.

"She's here," Selmana said. "I can feel her here. I can't keep her away, oh, Larla, what will I do, what will I do?"

"Don't let go, my dear. The wings have gone away, I think the door is closed."

"It's not the wings." Selmana could scarcely speak through her chattering teeth. "It's not the wings. It's her. She's here. She's me. She wants me…"

Larla put her arms tightly around her. "No, my lovely, you are you. She has no part in you. She has no right to you. She wants to trick you, yes, she does, but it's only trickery… She's gone now, she's not here. Come, my kitten. You are here, not there. I'm sorry I asked, I was so afraid, but it's all right now. Come, my love…"

"I opened to see and I saw her and I can't stop seeing her and she wants to eat me alive," said Selmana, through choking sobs. "I can't stop her. She's here now, she's here and everywhere…"

Larla kept talking, a soft, gentle monologue as she stroked Selmana's hair. And gradually, so slowly that at first it was scarcely perceptible, the horror that had opened within Selmana began to dispel. She became aware of her body again, warm and real in the soft yellow lamplight of Larla's kitchen. She felt the tears on her cheeks and her hair tangled over her face and the bruises on her knees from when she had thrown herself underneath the table. And then, quite suddenly, a shutter within her blinked and closed, and the terrible sense of unbeing was gone, and she was just herself.

She unclenched her hands, becoming conscious that she was holding Larla hard enough to hurt, and stood up straight, wiping her hair out of her eyes. She realized, with embarrassment, that she had wet herself in her terror.

"I'll get some cloths and dry clothes," said Larla. "We'll have to clean you up now. I'm so, so sorry, that was something I shouldn't have asked. I didn't know. Sometimes I am just a silly old woman…"

"It's gone," said Selmana, wonder in her voice. "I thought it would never go, that I was going to be like that for ever…"

Larla stroked her cheek and kissed her. "I told you it was trickery," she said. "We'll talk about it later. It's too close now." Then she smiled and cocked her head. "Listen."

At first Selmana didn't understand, and then she realized that it was quiet. Larla unlatched the shutters and threw them back and daylight flooded into the room. Selmana blinked.

"Blessed peace," said Larla. "I thought I'd go deaf with all that hammering. We'll see the other Bards soon, I expect. They've done what they had to do. So let's get you respectable."

XXIII

GLAD of something concrete to do, Selmana washed herself and changed into the woollen breeches and thick silk underclothes she had stowed in her pack. She rinsed out her soiled clothes, fending off Larla, who insisted that she should do it. After some argument, Larla gave her a wooden tub and heated some water, and had to be content with instructing Selmana on how best to scrub woollens. Selmana listened with half an ear, squeezing the fabric until the water ran clean, and hung her clothes in Larla's tiny paved courtyard. Larla tutted over her plants, sadly shredded and bruised by the storm, and began to sweep up the litter, a sludge of grey, unmelted hail and torn branches and leaves. Selmana looked up at the clearing sky, feeling the clean wind like a blessing.

Alone in the kitchen while Larla busied herself about her garden, Selmana found that she was very content to wait. A deep tiredness, as if she had laboured all day in a forge, had settled in her very bones. She listened for the return of the other Bards, hoping that Larla's confidence wasn't misplaced. She realized she trusted that the old woman was right, that the crisis had passed with the storm and that Nelac, Cadvan and Dernhil were unscathed, and she wondered why. Was it that Larla made her judgements with emphatic confidence? And yet on reflection they were, perhaps, little more than an expression of hope… She remembered then with a shudder how lost she had been, and how Larla had held her and brought her back, and thought that there was something more at work.

The more she knew of Larla, the stranger she seemed. Selmana knew that it wasn't uncommon for people to be born with aspects of the Gift, but without the Speech that defined a Bard; she had long suspected that her father, who was a famous smith, had something of the Gift in his hands, and had passed it on to her. She had at first assumed that Larla was a wise woman, like the midwife in her village. But now she wondered if Larla's eccentricity concealed another kind of power. Of all the places Nelac might have taken refuge in Lirigon, where almost every building was thick with charms and wards, he had chosen Larla's house. And she had been notably unworried that the storm's violence, even at its height, might damage her home. Who was she?

Selmana studied the bunches of dried herbs hanging from the ceiling, the basket spilling over with undyed yarn, the pine table scrubbed to whiteness, the shelves that lined every wall, packed with brightly glazed pots and curios and glowing jars of preserves. Everything spoke of unwearying and meticulous domesticity; Selmana couldn't pick up one sniff of magery. If Larla had powers – and now Selmana was certain that she was, in her own mysterious way, very powerful indeed – it had very little to do with the magery of Bards. Whatever it was, it was deeper than Speech, and followed its own rules, living closer to the heartbeat of things. Remembering Inghalt and his priggish definitions of Bardic lore, she thought with a sudden irritation that the Light could do with more of Larla's kind of wisdom. Selmana loved the Light, but sometimes Bards could be blind…

Her meditations were interrupted when Larla came bustling through the kitchen and hurried to the front of the house. Selmana looked up in surprise – she had heard no sounds of arrival – and followed Larla into her tiny hallway as she pulled open the door. All three Bards stood outside, Nelac supported between the other two, and Larla all but hauled them inside, agitated with her news; but when he saw Nelac she bit her lip and was silent. Selmana was shocked at their faces; all of them were pale, but Nelac seemed to have aged a decade since she had last seen him. She took his arm to support him, asking what had happened, but Larla stopped her with a fierce glare.

"Enough now. There'll be time enough to talk," Larla said. "You all look like ghosts of yourselves. And I mean you too, kitten." Before they spoke about anything, Larla insisted that the Bards eat the stew she had made, and she brewed a tea of peppermint and camomile, explaining that it would steady their nerves. When everyone had eaten to her satisfaction she sat forward in her chair, her chin on her hands, and studied her guests.

"You all came back, and for all your raggedness, none of you is hurt, and that's a blessing," she said. "But, my dears, something very strange happened while you were gone, and I can't read it."

Selmana shuddered. "First there were those wings, which made me so afraid," she said. "I don't know what they were…"

"We do," said Cadvan grimly. "They were the Shika."

"I'm sure I don't know who the Shika are, and I'm sure I don't want to know," said Larla. "But listen: just as I heard them, there on the edge howling like they were going to tear everything to pieces, I saw the Bone Queen in her black armour. She came with the wings."

The Bards looked stunned. "Kansabur?" said Cadvan at last. "Are you sure? I mean, how do you know?"

Larla hesitated, and her gaze turned inward. "I just knew, like she'd said her name out loud," she said at last. "When I felt the… I asked Selmana to listen, because I couldn't see with my own eyes, so I thought to look through her senses. And I saw the wings, and nothing has frightened me more in this life. I knew they were drawing closer and closer. But then they were gone as if they were never there. And then I saw the Bone Queen."

"I saw her too. It was her, I know it was her," said Selmana, her voice trembling.

"Where?" asked Cadvan urgently.

"I don't know where I was," said Selmana. "But I saw her, first like a shadow, like I saw her in the Shadowplains and with the boar, and then it was like ... all the shadows ran together with the wings and she became ... solid... And I knew she was hunting me, that she might see me, and that the wings were hunting with her, and there was no escape..." She gestured impatiently. "I was so afraid. I don't know how to say it."

"I think I know what happened," said Cadvan grimly. "It was that other sorcery..."

"What other sorcery?" Dernhil looked surprised. "Surely there was just the summoning?"

"There was another spell wound through the summoning. It seems to me that Likod was intending more than the destruction of Lirigon," Cadvan said. "Maybe the Shika were called to bring their potencies to Kansabur, to knit the Bone Queen's shadow-flesh so that she might step into the World. It was often said that during the Great Silence she made the Shika part of her being."

"What is she?" whispered Selmana. "Is she part of me, now? I felt that I had lost myself in her. Should you scry me?"

"No, my dear, there is no shade of her in you," said Larla. "Not one single bit."

"How do you know?" Dernhil said sharply. "Cadvan didn't know. Even Nelac didn't."

"But I did know, you see," said Larla, folding her hands so primly in her lap that Selmana wanted to laugh. "I knew that Nelac was sick with something dark inside him. I told you so, didn't I? Though I might have saved my breath, for the notice you took."

Nelac smiled at this. "You did tell me," he said. "Though it's not true I didn't listen."

"And I saw when it was gone, when you arrived here today. You might be Bards, and learned and all, but that doesn't mean you see everything. My problem is that I see many things but I don't understand a lot of it, because I don't have the learning. Or the Speech, come to that. I can't do charms."

"Is Calis ... is she touched by the shadow?" asked Selmana abruptly. "Can you tell?" The thought of her adored mentor infected by Kansabur, without the knowledge to protect herself, was more than she could bear.

"I don't know Calis, as to speak to," said Larla. "I only really know Nelac, among the Bards."

"Calis?" said Nelac. "I'd say not, at a guess. She was undeceived, unlike Coglint... I wonder about Coglint and Noram."

"They could just be stupid," said Cadvan.

"I don't know. The only way you can sense that presence within you, as far as I know, is that your Knowing is shrouded, hidden from you." Nelac spoke slowly, as if it hurt even to talk. "Is the Circle wholly infected? I am too weary to guess, my friends. I can scarce think. But I do believe Kansabur intended this day to take Lirhan as her kingdom. We were attacked on all fronts. And we were to be utterly defeated."

"That, at least, didn't happen," said Cadvan. "But I fear we failed elsewhere."

"We won through by a whisker." Nelac grimaced. "And not without hurt. I can't remember when I have felt more diminished... And yet the urgency remains. If Coglint and Noram prevail in their suspicions, we will be made outlaws, and will be powerless to alert Lirigon to the peril we know assails us." He paused, and added heavily: "Bashar's injury is the worst grief."

"Is Bashar dead?" asked Selmana. The other Bards were silent. "What happened?"

After a short pause, while he waited for Nelac to speak, Dernhil told her what he had seen. "Bashar yet lives, to my knowledge," he said. "But it hurts even to think of what I saw when we tried to heal her. I've never seen damage of that kind…" His voice broke. "Even if she lives, what sort of life will she have? Will she ever be free of that pain?"

No one answered him, and a heavy silence fell around the table. Selmana wished that she hadn't asked; she wondered if the same thing might happen to her, if the Bone Queen found her.

"I don't understand what you did," said Dernhil, turning to Cadvan. "But I am sure you broke the sorcery."

Cadvan nodded, and said painfully, "You see, I knew the spell. Likod showed it to me once."

Dernhil looked as if he wanted to ask further, but he perceived Cadvan's shame and changed the subject. "Who is to say we are innocent, if Bashar cannot? And if we are perceived as agents of the Dark, who will listen to us? But if we are forced to flee, who will warn the School of the Bone Queen, if she has indeed regained her power? And where should we go, and what use would it be?"

Again no one answered. Larla broke the silence. "If the Bone Queen is returned to her power, she is not whole, yet. She wants something…"

"She wants *me*," said Selmana, in a whisper.

Cadvan was frowning. "The Shika cannot remain in the World for long, because they are not of it," he said. "If most of Kansabur's power is drawn from the Shika, then maybe she can't, either. She is not human enough. And yet all her ambition is in the World…"

Nelac, who had been silent, looked up at this. "I begin to

see what you mean," he said slowly. "She needs mortal flesh, to exist in the mortal plane. But why Selmana?"

They all turned to look at her. Selmana stared back, her jaw jutting. "I'm just a Minor Bard," she said. "I'm not important."

"That's where you're wrong, kitten," said Larla. "It seems to me that you're very important indeed. You have the Sight. You can step into the Shadowplains as easy as if you're just going for a walk to the market. None of us can do that."

Selmana felt herself trembling. "But I don't want that," she said. "It's nothing to do with anything I decide, it just happens. I don't know why it happens."

"The only beings who can step between the Circles with ease are the Elidhu," said Dernhil thoughtfully. "Perhaps it's something to do with them after all?" He examined Selmana keenly, and she turned away, a flush riding up the skin of her neck.

"I don't know anything about the Elementals," she mumbled. "They're nothing to do with me."

"There is too much that is outside our knowledge," said Cadvan. "And yet we have never needed knowledge so badly. I feel as if everything I have ever been taught is a waste of time."

"Nay, do not say so, Cadvan," said Dernhil. "Say rather than learning never ends."

Larla was looking at Nelac, her brow creased in concern. "That's enough of talk," she said. "You should all get some rest. As for you, Nelac, you look near death."

"But what will we do?" Dernhil looked at Cadvan. "It won't be long before they're looking for us."

"The storm will have left much damage and hurt," said Nelac. "There will be enough to do after this, without setting out a hunt for us."

"I think we cannot count on that," said Dernhil.

"We should speak to Calis," said Nelac. "And I think, if we are to leave Lirigon, we should head for Pellinor. Milana will help us, and I think Enkir is there."

"Enkir hates me," Cadvan said. "I doubt he'll listen to us."

Nelac frowned. "He condemned your act, as is only just, but he is fair as well as stern. And if he dislikes you, what of that? It would be a good chance if he were there. If Kansabur hid in me and Cadvan and, most likely, Bashar, when we attempted her banishing, it's possible she has done the same to Milana and Enkir. And most importantly…" He trailed into silence.

"What?" prompted Cadvan.

"Pellinor has a stake in this. Lirigon first, as we now know, and secondly Pellinor. I fear for Pellinor."

"Enough," said Larla, standing up and briskly brushing her hands. "You should rest, the lot of you. And all of your clothes are wringing wet, I'll need to dry them. I have pallets aplenty, and blankets." No one answered, but Nelac nodded. "If you like, I can look for Calis, and ask her to come here later. One thing at a time, yes?"

"Oh, I almost forgot," said Selmana, looking at her hand. "Your ring." She drew the Ring of Silur off her finger and gave it back to Nelac. It was a relief, taking off that token: if her fate were to travel to Pellinor, at least she wouldn't be travelling alone.

XXIV

THE Bards slept through the afternoon, while Larla prepared a pie for supper. Once she had finished baking, she ventured out into Lirigon to see how it had weathered the storm. Nelac rose before the others, just as she returned home, and they shared a cup of tea while they waited for the younger Bards to wake.

Lirigon had fared surprisingly well. "Suspiciously well, Nelac," said Larla. "I thought that this was a storm to throw down houses and tear off roofs, but it's mostly a few wet floors and missing tiles. People holed up and nobody seems to be hurt, though most everyone was scared. The only real harm is to the trees: a lot of poplars snapped clean in half, and the big pine down in the Street of Potters, and a mess of branches everywhere that will give everyone firewood for months."

Nelac smiled. "Perhaps that's not so strange," he said. "All the houses here are granite, after all, and many have wards of protection."

"Aye," said Larla. "But there's more. There was no storm outside Lirigon. The Fesse was untouched. That tempest fitted itself exactly inside the walls of the School, like a foot into a shoe. You can't tell me that's not odd."

"Are you serious?"

"I am indeed," she said. "Well, it's good, isn't it? If those winds had hit the Fesse, there'd be such a mess to clean, and injured livestock and who knows what else, on top of the problems with the floods. But, no. I talked to Irant, you know, the herbalist who lives down at Fortis? And he told me he had never seen anything so strange in all his born days. Those clouds were all over the Fesse, and everyone thought they were in for something bad, and then, he said, all at once it was like a hand rolled the clouds into a ball and pushed them down on top of the School. They could hear the noise miles off, but he was busy cutting cowbane in the sweetest weather they'd had for days."

"I know of no weatherlore that can do that," said Nelac. "Perhaps Dernhil is right, and Elementals were at work. I didn't doubt, from the beginning, that there was sorcery in the weather…"

"The word is out for you three," said Larla. "The crier has been in the streets, and you are all named outlaw against the Light, and are to be arrested on sight. There's a mort of gossip running around about that, but nobody seems to know why. I never heard a word about Bashar."

"I suppose that is only to be expected," Nelac said. "However much I wish it otherwise."

"I asked around and found Calis at the Hall of Makers too."

"Ah, good. Did she agree to come here?"

"Yes. I didn't have to persuade her. She's very upset. She missed the storm, she was out in the Fesse helping with the floods, and she can't believe that the Circle wants to imprison you as an enemy. I told her that you wished to speak to her, and she said she'd come, and she promised to keep it a secret. She's a sharp woman, I didn't have to explain anything. I like her."

"She's always been one of the best here," said Nelac. "She's Selmana's mentor, did you know?"

"Well, the girl needn't worry about her," said Larla. "There's no dark parasite in Calis."

Nelac fell silent, watching as Larla drew the proving dough from beside the stove and began to knead it. The good, sweet smell of warm yeast filled the kitchen.

"It's such a grace to be able to watch you at work, my dear," he said. "I never saw more capable hands in my life."

Larla threw him a mischievous look and blew him a kiss. "You should know."

Nelac smiled with deep fondness, his eyes twinkling, but said nothing. Larla shaped three knotted loaves, which she put into the oven, brushed the flour from her hands and sat opposite Nelac, her face suddenly serious.

"You'll have to leave tonight."

"I know."

"And you should take Selmana with you."

"I wonder," said Nelac. "I am thinking that perhaps it would be better if she stayed here… Calis is a strong Bard, and would care for her."

"She's in danger here. The further she can get away from Lirigon right now, the better. There's something in her that the Bone Queen wants, and you can't let her get it."

"I wish I knew what it was," said Nelac.

"I can't guess either, but I know it's something that she is. She has a mixed Gift, Nelac. It's not so far from mine, but I can see that she's all Bard, too. It's a kind of double seeing she has. I thought that you couldn't have both: it seemed to me that words make the Sight go awry, and if you have the Sight, then words don't work for you. And then suddenly there's Selmana being everything at once. There's a power in her that's got nothing to do with the Speech, nothing to do with words. She knows it and she doesn't know it. And she's frightened, as well she might be."

Nelac's face darkened in thought. "You're right, Larla. I know you're right. I wish I had some of that double seeing myself."

"So where will you go?"

He looked at her straightly, his doubt open. "I fear my ignorance. These young Bards … they need my knowledge, but they think it's greater than it is. They think I am wise, and in some ways I am. But here I'm feeling my way, blindfolded, my ears stoppered, and I know that a chasm is yawning before our feet…"

Larla took his hand and kissed it. "Nelac, you are a kind, good man," she said. "That counts for more than being a good Bard. I trust you."

"I am not only kind and good. Much of me isn't kind or good at all. How can I trust myself?" he said.

"You must." Larla studied him, suddenly serious. "Perhaps the chasm will gobble us all up, but it won't be because you're not mindful or brave or don't do what you must. And that's all anyone can ask of you, or anyone else."

Cadvan dreamed. He was walking through a meadow in high summer, the lush grass and tangled wild flowers brushing against his knees. Grasshoppers leapt away like green springs as he disturbed them and bees zigzagged lazily, nuzzling the red anemones and the small yellow orchids that nodded amid the grass stems. Hidden crickets zithered around his feet. The sky arched above him, a deep, translucent blue. Somewhere in its cerulean vapours, so high up he couldn't see it, he could hear the trilling of a lark.

It wasn't a place he had seen in his waking life, but with the clairvoyance of dream he knew that it was near Pellinor, one of the meadows that nestled on the lower slopes of the Osidh Elanor. He was walking towards a rocky ridge that jutted into the sky. He was in no hurry, but all at once he reached his destination, where a dark-haired woman was waiting for him. She stood with her back to him, looking up the sheer face of the mountain that towered above them. She wore a circlet of cornflowers and daisies that she had plucked from the meadow and woven together, and her long robe was as blue as the sky. She was playing a small lyre. Each note came to him with unusual clarity, as if that note had never been made before and would never be made again. Cadvan thought he had known the melody all his life, but he had never heard it before.

Part of him assumed that the woman was Ceredin, returned past death, restored from the broken past to the future that had been promised them; but as he grew closer, he realized she was shorter, and that her hair was so black that the sunlight struck it with a blue shimmer. It wasn't Ceredin.

When she heard his step, she stopped playing and turned around, smiling, to embrace him. He knew then that he loved this woman, that he had loved her for a long time. There was a wildness in her vivid face which made him catch his breath, and for a time he forgot everything in the gladness that flooded through him. He reached for her name, which seemed to be on the tip of his tongue, just at the edge of memory, but he couldn't find it. And then she vanished, and he was all alone on the side of the mountain, trembling with mingled delight and loss.

After that Cadvan's dreams became troubled: he saw in swift succession the same visions that had tormented him in Jouan; the burning sky, the lifeless lakes, the desolations where green would never grow again. Somehow these visions were linked to this woman, as if they were two futures, both equally possible, but each cancelling out the other. He cried out and Dernhil, slumbering in the same room, was briefly roused and muttered in irritation. And then, mercifully, a blank curtain drew across Cadvan's mind, and his nightmares dissolved into the healing forgetfulness of sleep.

When he woke it was late evening, and the naked stars were brightening over Lirigon. He remembered nothing of his dream, although a residue of its gladness remained, an unexplained lightness. For the first time since he could remember, he felt hopeful.

IV

XXV

A S she had promised, Calis came to Larla's house at sunset on the day they left Lirigon. She was heavily cloaked, and looked haggard and strained, barely acknowledging the Bards' greetings. When she saw Cadvan she pressed her mouth into a grim line. Selmana noted that she was shielded, and bit her lip. That sign of mistrust brought home how serious their situation was; if even Calis thought they might attack her…

"Well, Nelac," Calis said brusquely. "I don't have a lot of time. I can make no promises on what I will think about what you have to say, except that I will give you a hearing. But I will say to you that my first allegiance is to Lirigon and to the Light."

"As is ours," said Cadvan.

Calis's eyes blazed with a sudden anger which she as quickly concealed. "As things stand, I am not inclined to believe that," she said. "I will listen, for the love I bear Nelac. But you have brought the Dark into Lirigon. I want to know why I should not bring you to the First Circle for judgement."

"You have seen Bashar?" said Nelac.

Calis nodded, and her face crumpled.

"Does she yet live?"

"Aye, but barely. And I am told that you three did this, that you were discovered in the very act of sorcery that has all but destroyed her. Nelac, how could you? What possible reason… What were you thinking?"

"It isn't like that," said Selmana hotly. "It's not that at all!"

She spoke much more loudly than she meant.

Calis studied her coldly. "Then what is it like?"

"Today the Dark sought to destroy Lirigon," said Nelac. "That these walls are not now in ruins and our people lying cold in the streets is because I and Cadvan and Dernhil fought back the sorcery that would have destroyed everything we hold dear."

Calis met his gaze, her eyes hard. "I'm listening," she said. "As I promised."

Nelac took a deep breath, and related everything that had happened since Cadvan had left for Jouan. He chose his words carefully, leaving out no details, and it took some time. Calis sat without speaking, her face downcast. Selmana watched her, trying to guess what she was thinking, but it was impossible. Hearing Nelac pull the threads together, making sense of the strange and terrible events that were shaping their lives, was an odd relief.

When Nelac finished, Calis sat for a time in silence, staring at her hands, which were twisted in her lap. It seemed to Selmana that she was struggling with herself, but again she couldn't tell what she was thinking. What if Calis didn't believe them? What then? She glanced at the others, who sat waiting for her response, their eyes averted. Only Larla watched Calis, frowning slightly, her body tense.

Finally Calis looked up at Nelac, meeting his eyes for the first time, and Selmana saw that the anger had drained from her face. In its place was an immeasurable sadness.

"I don't know which is worse," she said. "To think that you, my dear friend, had been seduced by the Dark, or to know the peril which you tell me stalks us. No, I do know. It is worse to think that you betrayed us. But I cannot be glad of the other." She wiped her cheeks with the back of her hand impatiently. "I saw Bashar an hour since... By the Light, I thought my heart was torn in two. The healers say that it is likely she will never speak again, even if she lives…"

Her voice broke, and Nelac reached forward and took her hand.

"I remember, when we first met … so long ago, now," said Calis. "I loved her on sight. I thought she was the most beautiful human being I had ever seen. And now…"

Selmana looked away from the naked pain in Calis's face. In the silence that followed she felt a pang of jealousy: would anyone ever love her that much? She pushed it away as a petty thought.

"Of course I'll help you," said Calis, when she had mastered herself. "I judge that you speak truly. Indeed, you give shape to many doubts and fears that have long troubled me. I too spoke with Milana, after that meeting…"

"Nelac says we should go to Pellinor," said Selmana. Despite everything, she felt a flare of excitement: Pellinor! It was famed as a centre of the Making, one of the Three Arts – Reading, Tending and Making – which comprised Bardic Knowing. Bards were taught all three, but most found themselves drawn to a particular area once they were instated as a full Bard. Some of Selmana's friends still weren't sure which they preferred, and some people never did decide; but for Selmana, ever since she could remember, before she even knew she was a Bard, it had always been Making.

As a small child she had loved shaping things with her hands; she was fascinated by all the techniques of crafting and the intricacies of material things, wood and fibre and stone. She knew very early that she was a smith, that her deep love was the lore and craft of metal. When she became a Bard, she counted herself lucky to study with Calis, whose skill and learning in metallurgy was respected through all Annar. The only person who rivalled her knowledge was Milana of Pellinor. Pellinor had always been in her future: Calis had said she would write to Milana when Selmana was instated, recommending her as a talented Maker worthy of special instruction. But she could never have imagined that she would flee there seeking refuge, an exile from her home.

Calis smiled at Selmana with understanding, as if she read her thoughts. "Perhaps you will be in danger anywhere, but it seems that Lirigon most imperils you. As for you three: the decree is that anyone who conceals your presence is also a traitor and will be punished just as you will be. Noram and Coglint say that they saw you performing sorcery. Cadvan's breaking of the ban of exile counts against you sorely. It is believed that Cadvan has bewitched you both to do his will... And the mood in Lirigon is ugly, Nelac. You are already condemned. Even if you told the Circle everything you have told me, it could easily be read as the wiles of the Dark."

Cadvan stirred uncomfortably. "The more I regret being seen," he said.

"It is unfortunate, yes. But I think it is not the whole reason for the misjudgements in Lirigon."

"All the more reason for us to be here." Cadvan gestured impatiently. "Likod even now wins this throw. Lirigon needs us. How can they outlaw Nelac? Even if I am condemned, Nelac surely deserves a hearing before such a decision is taken. Coglint wouldn't even listen..."

Calis paused. "I'll demand that the Circle hunt Kansabur," she said. "That at least may be argued for. Otherwise, I think you must leave tonight: it will be more difficult the longer you delay. But all the gates are watched."

"That useful disguising spell," said Dernhil. "Can you cast the charm on others, Cadvan? Or perhaps teach it to us?"

"I don't know," he said. "I would have to turn it inside out. I can try."

* * *

It took a few attempts, but in the end the disguising charm did work. At first Cadvan tried to teach them, but the enchantment was tricky and only Selmana had some success with it. Pilanel magery was little known among Bards, and widely distrusted or dismissed as primitive magic; some thought of it as akin to sorcery. Certainly, the thoughtstreams of Dernhil and Nelac couldn't catch it. Finally Cadvan was able to refigure the charm, and transformed Dernhil and Nelac with some rough changes of hair and eye colour, and gave them stouter outlines. The effect wasn't as startling as it was when Cadvan cast it on himself, but they looked sufficiently changed to pass any suspicious eye. They hoped.

Then, with heavy hearts, they farewelled Calis and Larla and made their way to the Bard stables, which were in the outer ring of the School. An icy wind had sprung up, and the streets were empty, aside from a few stragglers hurrying to shelter. Selmana saw that most of the rubbish from the storm had already been cleaned away; if it weren't for the broken trees, there would be little sign left of the tumult that had battered Lirigon that day. For some reason, she found this disquieting.

The stables, as they had hoped, were deserted. The horses had all been fed and bedded down for the night, and aside from Cina, Nelac's mount, they complained sulkily about being taken out. Selmana stroked her mare, Jacindh, breathing in her familiar smell; at least this was something she knew, in this newly strange and frightening world. Cadvan studied Brownie, and said he couldn't face another journey on his bony back. He bade him farewell, and chose one of the horses kept for general use, a tough and fiery chestnut mare called Brera.

Cloaked and hooded, they trotted through the darkening streets, heading for the East Gate. It was watched by a single Bard, a man Selmana vaguely recognized, which was unusual; mostly the Thane's men did gate-watch. He was just lowering the bar when they arrived. He asked their business, which was also unusual, and demanded that they show their faces. Selmana heard the tension in his voice and her pulse pounded in her throat: what if the disguising charm was not enough? Jacindh danced beneath her, feeling her anxiety. They drew back their hoods, showing their faces, and Nelac, playing the family patriarch, said he was returning to his farm in Bural with his sons and daughter-in-law.

"We're late because it took so long to see a healer," he said, his voice loud with complaint. "It was chaos here. My daughter was hit by a branch in the storm. She's with child and we wanted to be sure all was well. We have to get home tonight, there are tasks neglected."

Alarmed by Nelac's invention, Selmana tried to look pregnant and unwell. The Bard peered into their faces and demanded their names.

"I'm Stefan of Bural," said Nelac, without hesitation. "This is my daughter, Celb, and these are my sons, Halep and Idris. Can we go through?"

The Bard wrote the names down, and then he nodded and opened the gate.

"You just made it," he said. "The word is that after the last bell no one will be let in or out of Lirigon."

"It's been a bad sort of day," said Nelac.

"Aye, that it has. I'll be glad to get home."

"So will we," said Dernhil.

Outside the School, they pushed their mounts along the north road. Its white stone glimmered before them, winding through the dark fields of Lirigon.

"I didn't like that he wrote down our names," said Cadvan, when they were out of earshot.

"Me neither," said Dernhil. "I hope that Stefan of Bural doesn't get visited by suspicious Bards. His cooking deserves better."

Cadvan laughed. "Indeed it does," he said. "When all this is over, I'm planning to revisit his pigeon pie."

When all this is over, thought Selmana. She wondered if it ever would be over, or if they were now all condemned, like Cadvan, to homelessness, fleeing both the Light and the Dark. She passed the first leg of their journey in unrelieved gloom. Although the wind was cold, the night was clear and a huge moon, almost at the full, rose over them. Selmana rode unspeaking, stunned with tiredness. The hoof beats echoing on the stone road filled her with melancholy; with each step everything she had ever known fell further and further behind her. Nothing would ever be the same again.

No Bard roads, the broad stone thoroughfares that linked the Schools of Annar and the Suderain, linked Pellinor and Lirigon; but even if there had been, the travellers would have chosen another route. Their first aim was to steer clear of other Bards. They rode due north from Lirigon, avoiding the impassable rock formations of the Redara, planning to take the little-used byways that ran along the foothills of the Osidh Elanor, the Mountains of the Dawn.

Selmana had often ridden out to distant villages in the Fesse, but she had never in her life been out of Lirhan. She had loved those light-hearted summer excursions, when she and her friends would make camp and sing long into the night. Well, the others would sing: although she knew the words of all the lays, Selmana herself was, unusually for a Bard, completely tone-deaf. Sometimes, for a joke, she would be asked to sing; it was her party trick, because it always reduced her companions to helpless laughter. That life seemed so far away, as if it had happened to someone else. This was a different kind of journey, and not only because winter was hard on their heels. There was little pleasure in their camps, and no singing.

The other three Bards were experienced at this kind of travel, and she was surprised by their toughness: she found it hard to keep up even with Nelac, who was clearly ill. She was shocked by how freely they used magery: all of them used charms, to light fires, or to bind branches into shelters against the rain, or to heal the strains of their exhausted horses. She had been taught never to use magery lightly. Only Cadvan observed the conventional restraints, calling on his powers only to ease his horse or to help Dernhil; he never cast a charm to ease his own aches. Dernhil teased him about it.

"Time is against us," said Nelac, catching her disapproving glance one evening. "And we must use the powers we have to move as swiftly as we may. That's what they're for."

"I suppose so..." she said doubtfully. "It's just that I've always been told never to do that."

Dernhil grinned. "One of the best things about being a full Bard is that you learn that you can break the rules," he said. "And what are a few words of fire when the Balance itself is in peril?"

Put like that, it was hard to argue, and Selmana found that she was soon using magery as much as the others. It did make a great deal of difference. Without magery, their journey would have been an intolerable trial of endurance; with it, it was simply damp, cold and exhausting.

XXVI

C ADVAN wasn't sure if he was more relieved or sad to
leave Lirigon. Returning had only reinforced his exile:
it had reminded him of everything he had pushed out
of his mind since arriving in Jouan. He embraced the physical hardship of their journey: this gruelling ride through wild
country was the truth about his life, the reality he must now
accept, without the deception of hope.

On this second departure he found his thoughts dwelling,
for the first time in months, on his family. His main concern
when he was in Lirigon was not to be recognized by anyone
who knew him, but he could have visited his home, if he had
wanted, if there had been time. His banishment meant that he
was forbidden from the Schools only: a harsh punishment for
a Bard, but merciful in that otherwise he was free to go where
he willed. But he couldn't face seeing his kin. When he had
left the first time, he had thought it was for ever, but somehow
this second leaving felt more final. Now there might never be
another chance. Now he could no longer show his face even in
the Fesse.

Despite everything, somewhere in the back of his mind had
glowed an unacknowledged hope that he would speak again
to his brothers and sisters, that he would at last find a way to
reconcile his differences with his father. Perhaps, after a few
years, there might have been a way. He realized that now that
hope was all but gone. Unless he could clear his name of the
attempt to murder Bashar, he would never be able to return to

Lirigon. His father and siblings would die, forgetting him, perhaps hating him, and he would live on, hating himself for what he had done to them.

Some of his most painful memories played over and over again in his mind. One of the worst had happened not long after the terrible events in the Inkadh Grove, when he had lain feverish and near death in the healing house. Cadvan had only fragmented memories of that time, when dreams and waking had merged in a confusion of pain and terror, but he thought his family had cared for him. He wasn't certain, as he had never asked them; he still wondered if some of those faces he had seen – his father, Nartan, holding a cup to his lips; his sister Juna clutching his hand as he cried out in anguish – were phantoms of his illness.

One memory, however, was clear and unambiguous. He had woken, quite suddenly, in his right mind. He lay on his back staring at the white ceiling of the healing house. His body was light and empty, as if all his muscles had dissolved into air, and he felt too weak to speak or move. After a while he became aware of voices, familiar voices, and slowly realized his two brothers, Ardur and Ilios, were seated by the window on the far side of his chamber. They were talking together, unaware that he was conscious. At first he wanted to call out to them, but then he heard what they were saying.

"It goes hard with his pride," Ardur said. "I think the old man has fought with everyone in the village."

"Pride was always his problem." Ilios, his youngest brother, was the most like Cadvan, restless and mercurial. "I never felt it from him, it must be said. It's hard for me to love him. But he had such pride in the Bard…"

"Aye. Aye." Ardur glanced over to the bed. "If Cadvan knew how he boasted about him. Or how he was used as a club to beat about our heads. *You'll never be the half of Cadvan…*"

Ilios grunted. "Sometimes I hated him for that," he said. Cadvan, listening, wondered if he meant him, or their father. Perhaps Ilios meant both.

"Still, it's low to scrawl filth on the front door," said Ardur. "I'd give a mort of coin to know who did that."

"It could be anyone. A black mark has fallen on all of us now."

"I think the old man will die of humiliation," said Ardur.

"Perhaps it would be better if our brother died. More just, anyhow." Cadvan flinched at the bitterness in Ilios's voice.

"Nay," said Ardur softly. "We can't think that. For all that he's done wrong, he's still our kin." He stood up and walked over to the bed, and Cadvan felt Ardur's gaze upon his face. He laid still, his eyes shut, pretending he was asleep.

"Well, brother, I guess I might as well speak as not, though I doubt you'll hear me," said Ardur. "I wish you good health and a good life, though it looks like you'll have neither now. We've come to say goodbye. We're going south to find our fortunes, and I don't think we'll be back." He stood for a while unspeaking, and then Cadvan heard steps as Ilios joined him.

"He's dead to me now."

"Nay," said Ardur, his voice rough. "You don't mean that, not in your heart. Remember him as he was, brother."

"Do we even know what he was?"

Ardur didn't answer, and there was a long silence. Cadvan felt the touch of fingers on his face, brushing back his hair, and then the sound of footsteps leaving the room.

Cadvan couldn't remember what had happened after his brothers had left; that was the first time the blackness had rolled in. Afterwards he had been delirious for days. Later, from his sister Juna, he discovered that his brothers had decided to leave Lirhan after Ilios's betrothal to a local girl was forbidden by her family, who were shocked by the scandal. Ardur was already planning to move to Desor, where he had once journeyed with their father to trade at the famous market there, but Ilios had never wanted to leave Lirhan. The departure of his brothers was the moment when Cadvan began to realize what he had done to his family.

Juna, a capable, gentle woman, never spoke of how Cadvan's crime had affected her. Tera, like Ilios, had hero-worshipped her oldest brother. As far as he knew, she never came to his sickbed. Tera and Ilios were the youngest siblings, and Cadvan had helped to raise them from babyhood. Perhaps he had injured those two most. Once his recovery was certain, only Juna visited him in the healing house.

The last time he had seen Nartan was just before he left for Jouan, when he had ridden over to say farewell. It was the beginning of winter, and a bright sun with no warmth cast a merciless light that carved sharp shadows of the leafless trees. Cadvan had stood outside the house where he was born for a long time, gathering the courage to knock on the door.

Juna answered and led him to the kitchen, where Tera and Nartan waited. His sisters stood together awkwardly by the table, their hands clasped, their faces pale. Cadvan saw, with a constriction in his throat, that sweetmeats were set out, as if for a celebration. That would be Juna…

Nartan sat apart by the big hearth, and his eyes were fixed on his son's face. He seemed much older. He had always been a big man, strong-shouldered and well-muscled, but now Cadvan could see how age crept into his body, hollowing out his face, greying his hair, withering his arms. For the first time, he seemed frail.

For a few moments everyone was frozen, not knowing what to do or to say. Then Juna stepped forward and embraced Cadvan. He held her fiercely, feeling her heart beating against his.

"I'm sorry," he whispered.

"So am I," she said. She stood back and tried to smile, wiping her cheeks. "Oh, Cadvan…"

Tera hadn't moved, and her face was stony. Cadvan tried to meet her eyes, but she turned away and mumbled something he couldn't hear.

"Let's have a wine," said Juna. "And drink the cup of farewell."

She had set out the best glasses, and poured the wine in silence, handing one to each of them.

"Sit down, Tera," she said. Tera sat at the far end of the table from Cadvan, her mouth set. Nartan took the glass automatically, as if he didn't know what it was.

Cadvan sipped the wine, and cleared his throat. "Nartan, I thank you for having me in your house," he said. His words fell heavily into the silence, clumsy and awry. He glanced at his father, and looked away, clearing his throat again. "I know that you cannot forgive what I've done. I know I've hurt you deeply."

He paused, but no one said anything. Now his father had turned to look into the fire, his wine untasted in his hand.

"I'm leaving Lirigon," Cadvan said. "I can no longer stay here."

"You and your brothers," said Tera viciously. "None of you have any *guts*. You should stay like us and face the shame."

"Tera, I … I'm not permitted… I'll probably be exiled."

"I knew no good would come of this Barding," said Nartan. "I knew right at the beginning, when you first had the words. It's not for the likes of us."

"I can't help what I am," said Cadvan.

"It's from your mother's side, for sure."

This was an old argument, and Cadvan felt the old anger stir inside him. "If you'd sent me to the School when I was first asked, none of this might have happened," he said, before he could stop himself.

"So it's my fault now, is it?" Nartan cast him a look of contempt.

"Let's not argue," said Juna quickly. "There's no point."

"No, it's too late for arguing," said Nartan. "And no point in having him here, like I told you."

Cadvan felt himself trembling. "I shouldn't have come," he said. "I promise you won't see me again. I just wanted to say ... before I left, I wanted to say how sorry I am. I know it's not enough, but I wanted to say it. I'm sorry for the shame I've brought upon you."

"It's not the shame," said Tera. "It's not that..." And suddenly her face crumpled and she put her head in her arms and began to cry. Cadvan looked on helplessly, longing to comfort her but not daring to, as Juna leaned forward and stroked her hair.

"I don't want us to be sorry for what is not said, or what is said too late," said Juna, when Tera's sobs had subsided. "That's why we're here. I love you, Cadvan, and I always will, no matter what bad things you did. You must remember that."

"I don't deserve that," said Cadvan.

"Love isn't about deserving. It just is."

Another unbearable silence stretched out between them. Cadvan glanced quickly at his father, drained his wine glass and stood up.

"Juna, you are wiser than many Bards," he said. "I wish I were as wise as you. Tera, Nartan, I don't want you to regret anything you said or didn't say to me. I must atone for what I've done, but you need feel no shame. You have done nothing wrong. Nothing. The shame is all mine."

He paused, and then spoke in a rush. "I came for one other reason. Maybe the only good one. Nelac has promised me that he will see to all of you when I am gone. If you are troubled, or if things get too bad, go straight to him."

Nartan shrugged. "What could a Bard do?" he said.

"You must promise," said Cadvan fiercely. "Promise that you will ask him in need, whatever that need is. I can't do anything to help you, but Nelac can. If he had known in time, he would have stopped the pettiness that led to Ardur and Ilios leaving Lirhan. You know his voice is heard. Juna, will you?"

Juna nodded.

"I'll leave then," said Cadvan. "Remember what I said."

He took Juna in his arms and kissed her hair, smelling that familiar Juna smell that was so much part of his childhood and would now be lost to him for ever. Then he reached out his hand to Nartan. His father looked at him briefly, hard and cold, and turned away without taking his hand.

Cadvan turned on his heel and walked blindly out of the kitchen. His only thought now was to leave this torment. It was so much worse than he had imagined. Even his father's rage would have been better than his bitter, uncomprehending pain.

Cadvan was at the front door when Tera rushed down the narrow hallway and flung her arms around him, sobbing passionately.

"Don't go," she said. "Cadvan, don't go. I do love you, I do. I didn't mean it. I don't want you to go."

"Tera." For the first time, Cadvan felt tears burning his eyes. "Little sister. I have to go. I don't have any choice."

He hugged her close, and then held her at arm's length, holding her gaze. "Tera, I love you too. Never forget that. Look after our father. And Juna. I know it's been hard on you all, but don't forget that Juna needs to be cared for too…"

She looked up at him, her face red with weeping, and nodded, swallowing. Cadvan kissed her forehead, and let her go. He opened the door and let himself out of the house. His whole being felt completely numb. He wondered if he would feel anything again.

* * *

As he relived them, these memories were vivid and raw to Cadvan, as if they had happened the week before. Only the death of Ceredin hurt more. How many people had he wounded? Was it worse to harm those who loved you? What about the strangers who had suffered, who had died, because of what he had done? They had been loved too, and their pain was no less.

He thought of Juna's words. *Love isn't about deserving. It just is.* He felt them as a brand on his soul. No one who loved him had escaped. No matter what he did with his life from now on, some things could never be atoned.

Perhaps because Dernhil knew the worst of him, Cadvan found his companionship comforting. Dernhil guessed much of what troubled him; after the scrying, he knew Cadvan almost as well as he knew himself. Maybe, Dernhil thought, he knew him better, because he could stand outside his guilt and see him whole. Sometimes, in a small but generous gesture or in his unexpected smile, Dernhil saw a grace within Cadvan that touched and surprised him. And he was grateful for Cadvan's healing; without that nightly succour, he knew he wouldn't have withstood their journey. Cadvan was correct when he rebuked Dernhil for not taking sufficient care of himself; he resented his bodily weakness and preferred to ignore trivial pains. Each night now he slept dreamlessly, and he felt his muscles knitting together, finding new strength. In truth, for all his tiredness, he felt better than he had for months.

He wondered at the fate that had blighted Cadvan's life. Sometimes Nelac had spoken of it as a plan of the Dark, that had seen in Cadvan a gateway to its own ends; if so, then Cadvan had been merely a pawn, however willing. And there were more disturbing thoughts. Yes, sorcery was forbidden to Bards, and for good reason; yet if Cadvan had not known the spell that Likod had woven to destroy Lirigon, not one of them would now be alive. How to riddle that? Dernhil reflected that the machinery of the Light had as little mercy as the Dark; it seemed to him that Cadvan was pincered between the two. The White Flame, the centre of Barding, was very cold.

None of the Bards spoke much at first; the events in Lirigon had left them weary to the depths of their souls, and the long days gave them no respite. Of all of them, Nelac felt it most: the victory over Likod had come at a high cost. Over the first three days, Selmana noticed that both Dernhil and Cadvan were covertly watching him, subtly slowing their pace if he slumped in the saddle. He was never permitted to keep watch at night. She understood their concern; new lines were carved deep in Nelac's face from his nose to his mouth, and his eyes seemed sunken in his head. At night, when they stopped to rest, he barely spoke at all. She was astonished by the iron will that drove him on.

Gradually the deathly greyness began to ebb from Nelac's face, and she felt like weeping with relief. Over the past months, she had come to love him, and his frailty hurt her. She understood why he was so beloved of his students; he wore his learning lightly, unlike many Bards who were far less dis-tinguished, and was endlessly patient. And he was funny; no teacher had ever made her laugh so much, or made learning a thing of such pleasure. He was like the father she would have loved to have. Even as the thought rose, she felt ashamed; her father was her father, and he was owed her respect. But he had never understood her as Nelac did, and she hungered for that understanding.

Once they left the Fesse, there were no more roads. They followed a series of winding tracks, always northwards. Sometimes there was not even a path, and their progress was agonizingly slow as the horses picked their way through moors tumbled with boulders or through woodlands tangled with brown bracken that brushed the horses' bellies. Cadvan, who by tacit consent was guiding them, never seemed to doubt his direction. On the fourth day they reached the track that ran along the foothills of the Osidh Elanor, a byway mostly used by the Pilanel people, and after that their journey was easier. They saw birds and foxes and hares and once, in the distance, a pack of hunting wolves, but they encountered no people at all.

As the days passed, Selmana found herself fascinated by Cadvan and Dernhil's friendship. They were very different, but she perceived a likeness in them all the same, a quickness of spirit that flowed above private depths. She knew their history, as did everyone in Lirigon, and was at first surprised to see the easy companionship that had grown between them. Cadvan checked Dernhil's wellbeing each evening, joking that he would never forgive him if he collapsed; they would sit a little apart from the other two, talking softly as Cadvan wove his healcharms. If she overheard scraps of their conversation, it was never about anything important: trivial things that had happened that day, or some abstruse joke. But she felt the current of feeling that ran between them, and wondered.

"I thought they were enemies," she said one night to Nelac.

"On the contrary," said Nelac. "Those two were fated to be friends. The shame is that it took so long."

Selmana drew a deep breath. "It would take me a long time to forgive something like that," she said. "If I ever could."

"I'm not certain that Dernhil has forgiven him," said Nelac. "I think he has discovered that he likes and trusts Cadvan. If there is one good thing that has happened in the past days, it is that."

Selmana frowned. "You know, Nelac, I don't understand how you can be friends with a person who has done you such wrong, if you have not forgiven them."

"That wrong still stands," said Nelac. "Myself, I think it will take Dernhil a long time to forgive Cadvan. It is not an easy thing. One can love and even trust, and not forgive."

"I guess I don't understand people very well sometimes. I don't understand anything very much." Selmana hunched her cloak closer around her.

Nelac cast her an amused look. "In your own way, my daughter, you are much wiser than I am," he said. "Think of what Larla said."

Selmana gave him a fleeting smile. "That's hard to believe," she said. "I know so little, really."

"No, it's true," said Nelac. "All you are is young, but age is no sure measure of Knowing. I know Bards far older than you, who have read many books and studied arcane lore, who have not your perception. And in some ways you are far beyond me. In this dark time, you are my lantern. You throw light where I see only shadows."

Selmana stared broodingly into the campfire. All day she had been feeling homesick; it was a sharp ache through her whole body. She missed her mother, and she missed Lirigon. She worried uselessly about what was happening at home all the time, knowing that there was nothing she could do if anything was wrong. She wondered if Nelac suffered from homesickness; like all Bards, he travelled widely, but never with the fear, surely, that he might never be able to return... She glanced at him sideways. It still surprised her to see him squatting beside her, an old man stirring a pottage over a fire. Before she had met Nelac she had regarded him with awe, a great Bard far beyond her ken. If anything, her respect for him had increased; and yet in knowing him, the awe had vanished. He might be a great mage, but he was also a man, like any other man.

"What do I show you?" she asked. "It's not like I see anything..."

"For one thing, you are showing me that the Bone Queen is nowhere near by," he said. "And that is a comfort."

None of them had mentioned Kansabur since they left Lirigon, and Selmana looked at Nelac in surprise. It was as if he had broken a silent agreement.

"How do I show you that?"

"You aren't afraid."

She drew in her breath, surprised and a little discomforted that, even as she had been studying the others, she too had been observed. But Nelac was right: she wasn't afraid.

She had spent many of the numbing, cold hours of travel thinking over what had happened in Lirigon. From this distance, it seemed unreal. The hauntings that had stalked her in Lirigon, the vertiginous sense of a world that was no longer solid beneath her feet, had retreated. Maybe it was just that she was so tired; she wasn't used to this kind of endurance riding and, even with the charms that Bards used when they travelled swiftly, every part of her hurt with unfamiliar strains.

The feeling of horrible visibility that had plagued her since she saw the dying boar had retreated. She only realized how oppressive it had been when it lifted: for weeks, some deep part of her had felt that a malignant eye was always searching for her. In the moment when she had glimpsed Kansabur in Larla's kitchen, it had been intolerable. When they left Lirigon the edge of that horror blurred, and now was barely perceptible. But still she sensed that she was being hunted, that far away, in the distant shadows of the night, something was haunting her tracks… Selmana shuddered and unconsciously drew closer to Nelac.

"It's a bit grandiose, to say that I'm wise," she said. "Is a mouse wise for smelling a cat?"

Nelac smiled. "Yes, it is," he said. "For one thing, the wise mouse doesn't get eaten."

XXVII

IN only eight days, they reached the rutted track that branched off north to Jouan. Cadvan hesitated, and asked his mare, Brera, to halt. A wave of nostalgia swept over him, taking him by surprise. It was less than a month since he had left, and yet the friends he had made there, Taran and Hal and others, even his goat, Stubborn, had woven themselves into his life more deeply than he had realized, and he felt a tug of longing. Already his time there seemed so long ago... The others looked at him curiously, and pulled up their mounts beside him.

Only Dernhil knew why he had stopped. "Shall we ride on to Jouan?" he asked.

"It's barely noon," said Cadvan. "We'd find welcome and shelter there, I don't doubt, but we'd lose a day."

Selmana looked up hopefully at the mention of shelter. She was tired of travel rations and of sleeping on hard ground. She was tired of the rain and of cheering up her dispirited horse and of her numb hands and sore thighs and damp clothes. Even one night indoors would be a blessing.

Cadvan was having a silent debate with himself. For all his desire to see his Jouain friends, he felt a strange reluctance at the thought. Hal would at first think that he had returned as he had promised, his task done, ready to teach her. He could see how her face would fall, how she would pretend it didn't matter. He couldn't bear the prospect: Hal was too used to disappointment. He should return properly, or not at all.

"No, now is not the time," he said at last, and spoke again to Brera, urging her on. Selmana slumped back in her saddle.

"Why not?" said Nelac unexpectedly. "There's an inn, I assume?"

"Aye, for traders," said Cadvan.

"The notion of a hearth and a table and a bed attracts me wonderfully. And we would travel the faster for the rest."

"But we can't afford to lose even a day."

"We're almost halfway to Pellinor, by my calculations; we've made good progress. We can afford a few hours."

Cadvan glanced at him expressionlessly for a few moments and then shrugged, and turned Brera up the track. Selmana brightened up instantly. A bed! A roof! It seemed the summit of luxury. Nelac winked at her and urged his mount along the track behind Cadvan.

The sun still stood high in the sky when they reached Jouan. The mountains seemed very close today, lowering over the tiny hamlet, their peaks vanishing into mist. A knot of small children watched them as they rode to the tavern: they saw at a glance that these were not their usual visitors. At first they didn't recognize Cadvan, but then a small boy, a cousin of Hal's, set up a cry. "It's Cadvan!" he said. "Hey, Cadvan!"

Cadvan waved and the boy ran off. He wasn't surprised when Hal came running up, her face alight with joy, as they dismounted outside the tavern. She halted when she saw the other Bards.

"Hello, Hal," said Cadvan.

"Hello, Cadvan," she said. "You're back, then?"

"Only for the night," he said.

Just as he had imagined, Hal's face fell. She swallowed hard. "In that case it – it was good of you to think of coming all the way here." She glanced again at the other Bards. "I'll go, I see you're busy. But Taran will be so pleased to see you."

She made to leave, but Cadvan stepped forward and embraced her. She flung her arms around his neck and hugged him tightly, and then stood back, uncertain and shy.

"It's good to see you, Hal," Cadvan said. "Why don't you come to the tavern when we've taken care of the horses, and I'll introduce you to my friends?"

"They look very grand," she said. "I don't think…"

"They're no grander than me," said Cadvan. "They're only Bards. And besides, I want to know how you all are."

A shadow passed over Hal's face. "Taran will be that glad to see you," she said again. "But he's down the mine now. I'll tell him you're here when he gets home."

"Is something wrong?"

But Hal just shook her head and left. Cadvan watched her run off. She was still half a child, the grown woman she would become nascent in her gangly legs and awkwardness. But she was old beyond her years, her life already tempered by hard losses. She deserved so much more…

The tavern keeper interrupted his reflections, coming out to welcome his visitors, and Cadvan turned to the business of hiring rooms and stables. When Jonalan recognized Cadvan his face lit up in welcome. "I must have known we'd have a visit," he said. "I killed the pig for winter just two days since. I'll roast a ham tonight and there'll be a feast. Only one night! I could have wished it longer. You've been sorely missed."

"You are well loved here," said Dernhil later. They had washed and changed their clothes, and now he and Cadvan sat by the tavern's big hearth, each with an ale at his elbow. For the moment, they were alone; Jonalan was off arranging for their filthy travelling gear to be cleaned and Selmana and Nelac were still both upstairs.

Cadvan glanced at Dernhil and shrugged. "As you know, I worked as a healer as well as a cobbler," he said. "Bad at it though I was, I was still better than no healer at all..." He felt a strange reluctance, almost a shyness, in speaking about his time in Jouan, even to Dernhil.

Dernhil smiled. "I think it is more than that," he said. "You can't help the Bard in you. That girl you were teaching, I saw her face. What's her name? Hal, isn't it?"

"I was no Bard here," said Cadvan harshly. "I made boots."

Dernhil was silent for a time, studying him. "I think you are too ready to diminish your own good, Cadvan," he said. "That's as foolish as not acknowledging your faults. Worse, maybe."

Anger flickered across Cadvan's face, and then he caught Dernhil's sceptical eye and laughed. "I'll admit it, then," he said. "I'm not wholly evil."

"Merely arrogant, stubborn and irritating, but these are forgivable faults. Maybe."

"You go too far, Bard."

"Or not far enough." Dernhil sipped his ale, still steadily regarding Cadvan. "One day I will present you with a careful and thorough dissection of your character, and you will be forced to see yourself in proper proportion. Neither really bad nor really good..."

"Indeed, I am the very model of blandness," said Cadvan.

"You are many things," said Dernhil. "But bland isn't one of them."

"And you think that this portrayal will be a stern lesson to me?"

"I have no doubt of it. It's time you learned what you are."

"And you think that then I will learn to forgive myself?"

Dernhil paused, suddenly serious. "I don't know," he said at last. "Should you?"

"I don't know." Cadvan looked away. "Even if I could, I'm not sure I have the right. Others must do so first."

"That may take some time."

"Time." Cadvan drained his ale. "I'm not sure we have much of that."

Upstairs, Selmana sat on the rough bed in her tiny room, her gaze fixed on the latticed shadows the thin sunlight threw over the floorboards. The unexpected respite made her aware of her body's fatigue, as if every string that animated her limbs had been cut: even the thought of standing up and walking down the narrow stairs seemed too much. The room was warm, and she had washed and put on clothes that weren't stiff with sweat and grime, and the ease in her skin was delicious. After the enforced intimacy of the past few days, it was pleasant to be alone.

She let her thoughts drift. She had gathered, although she hadn't asked and no one had told her, that this was where Cadvan had hidden himself when he had left Lirigon. That awkward, skinny girl... What was the story there? Her face had transfigured when she saw him, a blaze of surprise and hope. She had looked as if she were welcoming a loved brother, long lost... With a stab of sorrow, Selmana had a vivid vision of Ceredin at her table in her chamber, a slight crease between her brows as she studied a scroll, puzzling out its meaning, before she turned with a smile to greet her.

"Selmana." Her name fell into her hearing as if it were spoken into her ear, but there was no one in the room. It was Ceredin's voice. Selmana jumped, startled out of her abstraction. Please, she thought, not now, please let everything be ordinary, please let me have imagined that...

She blinked. The room still looked the same, but something had happened to the light: everything seemed drained of colour, every object seemed unreal, a ghost of itself. And then, with no sense of transition, Ceredin was standing before her, a slender form of shadow. Selmana could see the opposite wall through her body. She clutched the edge of the bed. The fur coverlet slid beneath her fingers, soft and warm and real.

"She is tracking you," said Ceredin. Selmana didn't need to ask who "she" was. "She can smell your spirit, your blood. She craves you, as she craved me."

All Selmana's sense of safety fell away. "She is tracking me?" Then the implications of what Ceredin had said struck her, and she stared at her in horror. "What do you mean, she craved you?"

The shade sighed, as if an unseen wind blew through her. "She sought me, even as the Dark sought Cadvan. She desired to take me for her own use. But she couldn't devour me. Cadvan saved me that, at least…"

Selmana stared stupidly, trying to order her mind. Ceredin wished to warn her of some peril, and she must ask the right questions. But what were the right questions?

"What should I do?"

"Be wary, cousin. This World is not as that other place, and she sniffs around in the other place, now here, now there, trying to find the mark. The tissue between the Circles is broken, here a rip, there a wound. Here the borders are rent, here the doors will fly open. See, I can speak to you, even here… Be wary. She hungers for us, for we who have the Sight: we are the blood she needs to knit her sorcery into flesh, so she may tear open the wounded Circles and pour each into the other, and summon the armies of the dead…"

Bewildered, Selmana swallowed. A dark chord of alarm was vibrating in the deepest levels of her being. "The armies of the dead?"

"Already she is a torment the dead cannot resist. We can only flee and hide, and she hunts us down, one by one, and bends us to become agents of her will."

A sob gathered in Selmana's throat. "Not you, Ceredin, surely not you?"

"Not me. Not yet. But she is so close now. So close… And

the dead are so many. Should she break the Gates…"

Ceredin's form was fading even as Selmana watched. "No, stay!"

"I cannot. Ever I become less. Even in death I am a shadow. And yet I cannot depart…"

And then she was gone. Selmana stared wildly about the room, her heart hammering, a sick dread rising through her body. She had thought herself safe and hidden, but it was an illusion. Who could protect her? How could she protect herself?

Her fingers trembling, she unlatched the door and tumbled downstairs. Cadvan and Dernhil were deep in conversation at a table by the hearth, but they turned as she entered, the smiles fading from their faces.

"What's wrong?" asked Dernhil.

"Ceredin…"

Dernhil drew her down to sit beside them. "A deep breath, Selmana. Yes. That's right. Now, what's happened?"

Selmana glanced at Cadvan, who was watching her, his face tight. "Ceredin just spoke to me," she said. "It was a warning. She says Kansabur is close, that she is tracking me, she says Kansabur will rouse the … the armies of the dead, and that she can break the Gates."

"She can break the Gates?" repeated Dernhil, paling. "Surely that's not possible?"

Selmana hesitated, attempting to recall Ceredin's exact words. "She said: *She hungers for us, for we who have the Sight.* She meant me and Ceredin, so Ceredin must have had the Sight as well. *We are the blood she needs to knit her sorcery into flesh, so she may tear open the wounded Circles and pour each into the other, and summon the armies of the dead…*"

Cadvan stared at her. "Ceredin had the Sight, like you?"

"That's what she said." Selmana brushed her hair back from her face; her tears had made it stick over her mouth. She hadn't realized that she had been crying. "She said Kansabur wanted to devour her, but she couldn't." She breathed in again, trying to fight down her panic. "Nelac said he knew she had lost our scent, because I wasn't frightened. But she hasn't. That's what Ceredin said. She's been trying to track us, in the other place. She must mean the Shadowplains…"

There was a long silence. Then Cadvan spoke, his voice bitter. "I thought I knew the worst," he said. "I had thought Ceredin's death was the most terrible thing I could have done to her. But it seems I was wrong."

Selmana impulsively took Cadvan's hand. "No, she said you saved her," she said. "She said: *Cadvan saved me that, at least*."

"At least." Cadvan's expression frightened Selmana. "Well, that's something, that she's only partly devoured by the dead thing that I summoned into life…"

"Stop it, Cadvan," said Dernhil sharply. "I too was there, and I remember how you leapt before Ceredin. You can hate yourself as much as you like later, but now is not the time."

Cadvan met his gaze, and then looked away. "I failed. And now she is dead."

"What matters is that we understand what Ceredin was trying to tell us."

"Nothing good."

For a moment, Selmana feared Dernhil would punch Cadvan. His lips tightened as he bit back a retort. "No," he said slowly. "Nothing good. But now that we are warned, we might protect ourselves. Better to look at what we must face now, than to gnaw the past with useless regret."

Cadvan stared into the fire, as the colour slowly returned to his face. "Aye," he said at last. "You are right, of course. And now it seems we must save the dead as well as the living."

XXVIII

KANSABUR the Mighty, Tyrant of Lir. Avatar of Despite and Terror, Supreme Grace, Adamant of the Law, Regnant Jewel of the Northern Realm and Tributaries, Defender of the Truth, Absolute Ruler of the Dominions of the North. She had many titles in her centuries-long reign over the ancient realm of Lir, but the people she ruled called her the Bone Queen. They saw the fields where bodies lay unburied, rotting into acres of bones tumbled together under tangles of weeds. They remembered the pyramids of skulls that were piled as grim warnings to rebels outside her prisons and torture halls. Those Bards who survived an audience with the Queen of Desolation reported a Hull clad in sumptuous robes, eyes of red fire burning in a white skull, skeletal hands adorned obscenely with the dark flames of rubies. To those without the eyes of Bards, her sorcery clothed her with a beauty beyond the reach of mortals, a shimmering illusion of desire and dismay.

Yet even at the height of her power, Kansabur was but a slave. The Nameless One was said to call her his cat, and if he beckoned, she leapt to do his bidding. She feared nothing in her dominion: all her terror was reserved for the Black Hand of the South, the Lightless Silence of the Real, the Eternal Despite, the Nameless One himself. If she was cruel, he was crueller; her malice and cunning were shadows of his atrocity and guile. No matter how numerous her spies, how ruthless her armies, how rich her treasuries, how fearsome her prisons and barracks, they were toys compared to the deep-delved dungeons and factories of torment in Dagra. He alone had the power to humiliate her pride and daunt her malevolence. The Nameless One perceived her secret hatred and cultivated it, for it made her more cruel. She was one of his most useful tools. But as with all his minions, who worshipped and feared and hated him as the shadow and dread of their own ambitions, he knew that she would attempt to supplant him if she dared. He was careful to ensure that she would never, quite, dare.

Nelac lay on his bed in Jonalan's tavern, staring at the ceiling. As he did every day now, he was running through the Lore of the Silence, thinking through everything he knew about the Bone Queen. Til Niron, a Bard who had escaped to the Isle of Thorold in the Great Silence, wrote one of the most famous accounts, which Nelac recalled as if he were reading it; she was one of the few who survived being brought before the Bone Queen at the height of her power. Was Kansabur returned as slave or absolute tyrant? Nelac found himself swinging one way and then the other: sometimes he was certain that she was but the forerunner, blazing the way for her master.

In Lirigon the records of the Bone Queen's reign were extensive. Nelac had read most of them, grim though they were. The library held scrolls that dated back to the Silence, kept by Kansabur's servants and officials: here, meticulously notated in brusquely written ledgers, were countless crimes: massacres of whole villages accused of rebellion; torture and imprisonment of anyone considered to be a threat to the reign of the Dark. A careless word, or even the testimony of a malicious neighbour, was enough to ensure torment or death. Nelac sighed, remembering some of the sadder entries: *Nokin, ten years, son of Traitor Kern of Skiln, confessed: death.* Behind those indifferent words were unimaginable worlds of suffering.

Northern Annar had been the realm of the Dhyllin, the people whom the Nameless One had most hated. The Dhyllic realm stretched from the Osidh Elanor to the Aleph River, and was famed for the beauty of its arts and the depth of its learning. Even the Elementals, the immortal Elidhu whom Bards distrusted as allies of the Dark, were said to gather with the Dhyllin, sharing their knowledge and delighting in the arts of mortals.

Most famed was the High City of the *Dhillarearën*, Afinil, which rose by a lake whose water was so clear that to drink from it was said to be like drinking light. Sometimes Nelac dreamed of Afinil, walking in wonder through its vaulted stone halls and hanging gardens, the star music of the *Dhillarearën* sounding through his mind as an ache of loveliness. Afinil had been erased so completely that no one knew exactly where it had been. Even the mere had been destroyed, its site lost in a maze of swampland. The fruitful country around Afinil, vineyards and forests, gardens and orchards, was now a haunted waste called the Hutmoors. Travellers went out of their way to avoid the Hutmoors: the land was poisoned still with the wounds of that war and the wind itself was said to weep with voices raised in endless lament.

The Nameless One had levelled all the Dhyllin's fabled cities. The Light had been driven out of Annar, the Song of the *Dhillarearën* had withered and died. So much knowledge had been lost in those dark centuries. The Light could never be what it had been; the innocence of the age of the *Dhillarearën*, when day and night had been two sides of one whole, was gone for ever. The Dark was born out of Sharma's greed and ruthlessness, his desire to possess and rule, and he had made himself the Nameless One. Now Bards were trained in warfare and combat, and their cities were walled, keeping a garrisoned vigilance against the Dark even after centuries of peace.

And even so, the Dark had found a chink in the armour. Nelac thought it was possible, even likely, that the Bone Queen

sought to rule in her own right. But even if her remaking pres-
aged nothing else, even if it didn't foreshadow the Nameless
One rising again in the south, it filled him with fear: if she
regained her full powers, she had the strength and will enough
to drown all Annar again. The White Flame, the Knowing of
the Light, was kept alive in the Seven Kingdoms grouped
around the borders, which held out, over all those centuries,
against the onslaught of the Dark. If the Nameless One returned
now, thought Nelac, his first thought would be to destroy the
Seven Kingdoms. He would hate them as much as he hated
the Dhyllin. But the Seven Kingdoms were hard to attack and
harder to govern, jealously preserving their independence. The
Dark would need to be strong indeed to think of crushing them.
Annar, the largest realm of all, was always the weakest. The
Seven Kingdoms had survived the fall of Annar once; could
they do it again?

As she had during the Great Silence, Kansabur would find
allies. In her time, the Bone Queen had had many willing servants. Thinking of Bards like Noram and Coglint, Nelac's belly
lurched with contempt: he could see so clearly how they would
fall, listening to their fear. Milana's alarm after the discussions
about Cadvan's exile was well founded: a just mercy in the face
of wrongdoing was the easiest to argue against, the hardest to
defend in times of crisis. And once that was swept aside, it was
easier to ignore other principles, little by little, act by act, until
they embraced the most unthinkable atrocities of the Dark,
while telling themselves they were merely obeying necessity
and reason. Already there was rot at the centre, where they
most needed to be strong. Cadvan's crime was clear, and could
be reckoned with: Nelac feared much more an insidious corruption, that spread slowly and invisibly, unnoticed until it
was too late…

He wished he were not so tired. The battle with Likod had

emptied him as nothing in his life; he thought he would never be free of that dragging weariness. Even Bards couldn't escape age. He knew that Cadvan and Dernhil were vigilant, and tactfully checked their pace to suit his. He hid his fatigue as much as he could, but his weakness humiliated him. Once he would have pushed on past Jouan, instead of arguing for a bed… But, he thought, aching bones will not be argued with, and it was true that he would travel the faster for even a short respite.

He put his hands behind his head and contemplated the beamed ceiling of his room, turning his mind from gloomy thoughts. He had been surprised by the accommodation, but it seemed that Jonalan's traders expected more than the communal dormitory he had anticipated when he had walked into the taproom. A private room was a luxury… He heard Cadvan and Dernhil talking as they clattered down the narrow stairs outside his room, and then, without intending to, he fell fast asleep.

Taran walked into the tavern an hour later. He was scrubbed so clean his skin was pink and his hair was still damp; noticing this, Cadvan thought, with private amusement, that Hal must have supervised his bathing after he had finished his shift at the mine. She could be very stern. Taran nodded to the dozen other Jouains who were already packed into Jonalan's tiny snug to welcome Cadvan back. News travelled swiftly in Jouan.

"Taran," said Cadvan, his face lighting up. He stood to greet his friend, grasping his hand.

"Hal tells me you're just passing," said Taran.

"We are. You remember Dernhil?" Taran nodded and Dernhil held out his hand. "And this is Selmana, also from Lirigon."

Selmana greeted him courteously, suppressing her panic. All these good people, so eager to greet Cadvan and to tell him the latest news of the village, were wonderful; but the Bards needed to attend to Ceredin's warning. And yet Cadvan betrayed no sign of impatience, chatting with the miners as if they had all the time in the world. She had never seen him more at ease with people, even in Lirigon when Ceredin was alive. Then, even at his most expansive, she had always sensed a reserve. All Bards were private people, she reflected, but Cadvan had always been more withheld than most.

"I'm right glad you're here," Taran said quietly to Cadvan, after everyone had exchanged courtesies. "I'd appreciate a talk."

"Something troubles you?"

Taran nodded. "These are troubled times here," he said.

"Later, then," said Cadvan. "Perhaps I should come to your house?"

"Come over before the evening meal," said Taran. "I don't doubt Jonalan wants to feast you, or I'd invite you myself. We'd all be grateful."

The conversation became general after that, and Taran left soon after. Dernhil, who had overheard his request, followed him with his gaze and looked enquiringly at Cadvan.

"What do you think is wrong?"

"It might just be a deal gone wrong," said Cadvan. "I sometimes helped them out with things like that."

"I think it's more than that."

Cadvan hesitated, and then met Dernhil's eyes. "I think so too," he said. "He's no fool, Taran. He's had those dreams, like you and I." At this, Dernhil's eyes widened in surprise. "And putting that together with what Ceredin said..." He looked down into his mug of ale. "I think we shouldn't have come here, Dernhil. I don't want to bring trouble on these people."

Another miner interrupted them, wanting to greet Cadvan, and Dernhil glanced across the table at Selmana, who was squeezed into the corner chewing her lips, her hands twisting in her lap. She caught his eye and he nodded. He whispered something to Cadvan and drew Selmana away from the crowd.

"They just want to speak to Cadvan," he said. "I'm not sure we're needed."

"No, they don't want to see us," said Selmana. "Why doesn't Cadvan send them away? Should we set wards, Dernhil?"

Dernhil took both her hands in his. "First, we should not let fear rule us. Wards may do something, but I'm not sure that they will stay Kansabur, if she is hunting in the Shadowplains. Likod bypassed them wholly in Lirigon."

"Yes, but…"

"Tell me, Selmana; have you any awareness of the Bone Queen?"

Selmana shook her head slowly.

"Then our peril is not immediate, even if it's close. I feel nothing wrong, but I'm uneasy. Nothing feels right, either."

"I've forgotten what 'feeling right' feels like," said Selmana. "Everything's wrong."

"We'll see what Nelac has to say, eh?"

She followed Dernhil upstairs, where he knocked on the door of Nelac's room. When there was no answer, he pushed the door open, suddenly anxious. Nelac was lying on top of the bed, snoring gently.

"I'm loath to disturb him," he said, turning to Selmana. "He is more weary than he will let us see."

"He'd say we should wake him."

"Aye." Dernhil touched Nelac's shoulder and said his name. When there was no response, he shook him, at first gently and then more roughly. Selmana's stomach tightened: a Bard should wake instantly. What was wrong? At last, after what seemed an age, Nelac stirred, and then he cried out and scrambled upright, his face rigid, staring sightlessly in front of him.

"Nelac," said Dernhil softly.

Nelac clutched his arm, and his eyes slowly focused on Dernhil's face. "Dernhil. Selmana. Thank the Light." He rubbed his hand through his tousled hair. "I'm not sure ... where I was..." Nelac swung his legs off the bed and picked up his pack, searching impatiently through it until he found the flask of medhyl. He took a sip and wiped his mouth, and then directed a sharp look at Selmana.

"Tell me, is Kansabur close?"

"I can't feel her presence," said Selmana. "But that doesn't mean she isn't close. I saw Ceredin, she said the Bone Queen is tracking us."

Nelac drew his breath in sharply. "Ceredin?" he said. "Our messenger from the dead..." His face darkened with sadness. "How I miss her. There was a Bard with a great capacity for love. It is that love that ties her to us, even now..."

He was silent for a long time, and Dernhil and Selmana exchanged glances. Nelac caught the look. "Nay, my wits aren't wandering," he said. "I'm just ... tired to the very depths of my soul. Everywhere a fog of dread." He was silent for a time, gathering his thoughts, and the others waited without speaking. "I saw Kansabur," he said at last. "Not formless this time, but as the Iron Tyrant of Lir. Perhaps as you glimpsed her in Lirigon, Selmana."

"Did she see you?" Selmana's voice cracked, remembering that moment of terror.

"No. I feared very much that she would, that I would be imprisoned in that eye... But she didn't see me." Nelac shook his head, trying to rid himself of the aftermath of his dream. "It could have just been an ordinary nightmare. It wouldn't be wholly surprising; I was thinking through the records of Lirigon when I fell asleep. But, no, it hadn't that quality. I've not been afflicted with such visions as you and Cadvan have suffered, Dernhil, but you say that they are not as other dreams..."

"No," said Dernhil shortly. "They are not."

"That I did fall asleep, against my intention, is strange in itself." He paused. "I thought at first I must have entered the Shadowplains. But then it seemed to me that I was elsewhere."

"It's said we sometimes wander through the Shadowplains in our slumbers," said Dernhil.

"It is also said the dreaming soul is protected there, unlike the waking Bard, shielded by its innocence. But there was no protection. I was lucky, I think." Nelac shuddered and drew his hand across his eyes. "This was a place with no dimension, no height or breadth or anything I could recognize," he said at last. "And Kansabur was there. She was the only thing I could properly perceive. But I knew with other senses that the dead were there, and I knew they were afraid." He paused again. "Tell me about Ceredin, Selmana. I can't speak my dream, it is too confused."

Selmana told him of her vision of Ceredin. He interrupted her at times, demanding Ceredin's exact phrasing. He was now fully alert, with none of the confusion that had disturbed Selmana before. Then he fell silent again.

"What think you, Nelac?" asked Dernhil at last.

"The armies of the dead," said Nelac. "That has a fell sound." He sighed heavily. "And, alas, it makes my dream the more clear. I was with the dead, but I think it was not the souls of the Shadowplains. I was in a place beyond, different in every way. I can't describe it; it was stranger and darker, dull and heavy with terror. But it seemed to me in my dream that this terror was a new thing, that it hadn't always been there."

"Do you mean the Third Circle? The Empyrean?"

"I think so. If Kansabur is there before us, the Gates are broken already. Yet I can't believe that: such a shattering would shake all the Circles, none of us would not know it. I could have been witnessing what is to come."

"What did you witness?" asked Selmana, in a small voice.

Nelac looked up, his face drawn, and tried a few fumbling

phrases, and then shook his head. "I wish I could say," he said. "There are no words that will shape it for you."

"Should we leave Jouan, do you think?" she asked. "Ceredin said we are not safe."

"I'm not sure," said Nelac. "I am thinking that perhaps it isn't coincidence that Cadvan was drawn here. The Knowing can call us, perhaps most strongly when we are least aware of it."

"Cadvan said that he doesn't wish to bring trouble on these people," said Dernhil. "Perhaps for their sake…"

"I'm thinking that I'm tired of fleeing from shadows," said Nelac. "If there is a breach in Jouan, as Ceredin said, trouble is here already. Can we leave these people to face it alone?"

Downstairs, Cadvan contemplated the row of drinks that stood in front of him, bought by the folk of Jouan to welcome him back. Many people, he noted ironically, had remembered his fondness for the local apple spirit. If he consumed them all, the result would be unseemly. In order not to insult them, he took tiny sips from each, before placing the mugs aside to be tactfully removed by Jonalan. He needed a clear head.

The Jouains' enthusiasm embarrassed him: he knew them as an undemonstrative people, but they were welcoming him back like a lost son. Yet he couldn't deny that it pleased him too: when he left Jouan, he had had no idea that he would be missed, except by those who were dear to him, like Taran and Hal. The whole village seemed to have turned out, and there was already an air of festival.

All the same, he became increasingly aware of an underlying anxiety in the villagers. Faces fell when he said he was only staying overnight. "It's hard that you can't be here longer," said a toothless grandmother called Kipa. "Since you left, it's like our luck has gone." Others hushed her, as it was discourteous to pressure a guest, and she grinned to cover the moment and punched his arm.

Cadvan reflected that he could hardly be said to have brought Jouan luck; the explosion had happened not long after he had arrived. He thought of Taran's hints, and listened more closely, but nothing quite explained the anxiety he was sensing: there were accounts of accidents, of Old Tirn's death from the lung fever, which had been well-advanced when Cadvan left a month before, the birth of a son to Odil and Bren, who lived near Taran. A few spoke of Hal, who, it seemed, had taken over Cadvan's healing duties with honour. He wondered where the other Bards were, but felt no need to find them; if they needed him, they knew where he was. An hour before the evening meal, he made his farewells, and took the familiar path to Taran's house.

Taran was waiting for him in his crowded kitchen. Cadvan smiled involuntarily when he entered; it was all cheerful activity, chaotic and orderly at once. Hal, pounding herbs in a mortar and pestle, gave him her quick smile. Her two younger brothers, who still worked as haulers in the mine, were squabbling amicably in a corner, playing Knuckles. Indira stirred a pot by the hearth, a toddler on her lap. She turned her pale face when Cadvan entered, smiling shyly. He went to her and touched her shoulder, and her fingers fluttered about his face, feeling its shape. "Cadvan," she said. "I can't mistake your tread."

"It is good to see you, Indira," he said. He sniffed appreciatively. "That's a brave stew you're making. It smells like a feast for kings."

Indira laughed with pleasure. "You speak too high of me," she said. "It's just a mess of herbs."

"But made by a master of the art," said Cadvan, smiling.

"I swear we're all growing fat, since Indira came," said Taran. "You should taste her bannocks." He hesitated, and then suggested, over the protests of his brothers, that he and Cadvan take a walk. "I can't hear myself think in here," said Taran, frowning them down. "And there's no rain, for a wonder. We won't be long, and then you can tell Cadvan whatever you want."

He shut the door behind him and the two men began to walk up to the minehead. Dusk was already drawing in, with the early nights of approaching winter, and the first few stars were beginning to open in the darkening sky.

"Your family seems well," said Cadvan.

Taran glanced at him. "We're doing fine," he said. "Aside from what troubles us all."

"What is it?"

Taran was silent for a time. "It sounds foolish," he said. "It seems to me to be Bard business, there's stuff I don't understand."

"I'm sure it's not foolish," said Cadvan.

"Remember I told you about that dream? I've had more, since. I wake in a cold sweat, shaking all over, they're that bad. The thing is, I'm not the only one. Hal too. And some of the hewers were turning up for work looking like they hadn't slept at all, and we started talking, and it's almost everyone in Jouan. There's some now that are afraid of sleeping. Mad Truwy is mad most of the time these days, he's been afflicted more than the rest of us. Quite a few are talking about a curse, and say we're haunted. And there's many that has noticed it only happened when you went away, and are thinking that you kept bad spirits at bay."

"I could have as easily brought a curse upon you," said Cadvan.

"None of us thinks that," said Taran. "Well, Jorvil says something like that. Remember Jorvil? But no one listens to him. He was born twisted."

But I did bring the curse, Cadvan thought. He didn't say it aloud; it would only have distressed his friend.

"I'm thinking that this has something to do with why you left," said Taran. "And I don't know if you can drive away the nightmares, but I thought it worth asking. Me and the others, we'd be grateful even to understand what they are. Maybe as a Bard, you know about these things. I mean, we all have bad dreams now and again, but these…"

"Yes, they're different," said Cadvan. He wondered where else, across the length and breadth of Annar, the same thing was happening. He hesitated, and then asked what kinds of dreams they were.

"I don't like to think of them," said Taran. "None of us do. But often it's about the dead. Our dead, I mean. They're not good dreams, and they grieve us. Often we can't even talk about them, so odd and horrible as they are."

"Is there – anything else?"

"What I told you before. Everything destroyed, but this time it's worse: the dead marching across smoking ruins, armies of them. And the Queen of the Dead before them, holding a great black sword, and her eyes burning like coals." He paused. "I wouldn't say, normally, but it's all of us been dreaming the same things."

"There's been a lot of death here, recently," said Cadvan slowly. "It could be that's why the – the borders between death and life are thin in Jouan. In dreams sometimes these worlds open up to each other…"

"But this is more than that, surely," said Taran. "I mean, we've all had visits from our dead. Mostly we don't speak of it, it's private. But this … this is a different thing. It's bad."

"Yes," said Cadvan. "It's bad."

XXIX

AS Cadvan returned to Jonalan's tavern, a chill night fell swiftly. The waning moon was yet to rise, and the shadows were very black. Mists rose from the ground, curling about his feet, so he had to pick his steps carefully along the path that wound between the houses. If he hadn't known the village so well, he might easily have become lost: each building looked much the same as its fellows, shapeless lumps of darkness, their windows shuttered against the cold. His footsteps sounded loud to his ears; the wind had died down and the night seemed to stretch emptily around him, huge and ominous.

He found Nelac, Selmana and Dernhil in the snug, where they were deep in conversation with Jonalan. "You took your time," said Dernhil. "We were about to send out a search party."

"For which, my apologies," said Cadvan, throwing his cloak over a settle. "I got to talking with Taran's family, and they all like to talk. Did all your customers go home, Jonalan? I am sorry for that."

"It's no great matter," said the tavern keeper. "It was a fine afternoon for those of us here. Dark comes early now and we don't stay out after sunset these days. The whole village is as skittish as rats."

"Taran told me why," said Cadvan.

"Yes, some of us thought it would be easiest coming from him, as you know him best and all, and everyone knows he's not a mooncalf," said Jonalan. "But Nelac here asked whether we'd had any odd things happen lately, and one thing led to another." He stood up and drained his ale. "But I'm thinking you'll be wishing for your dinner. I'll go and see how that ham is doing. Dana is great with pastries, but it's me who knows how to roast a pig so it melts in your mouth."

Cadvan slid into the settle beside Dernhil. "It seems you already know what I heard at Taran's," he said. "I'll say straight out, I fear for these people. And I am wondering too if this is happening elsewhere. I can't believe Jouan is alone."

"You think this is part of some larger plan, perhaps?" said Dernhil, his dark eyes alert and thoughtful. "It may be simply a side effect of the Dark's assault. After all, the Circles are knocked awry, out of their harmony, and we don't know how this violence ripples out. Perhaps part of Likod's aim in Lirigon was to break the Circles further, to open broader paths between the Abyss and the Shadowplains and the World... And the Empyrean, which might be worst of all. Perhaps this is what Kansabur does with her new strength." He paused. "I wish we knew what is happening in Lirigon."

"All the more I resent the stupidity of our having to flee," said Nelac. "There you see clearly how the Dark uses fear to prosecute its own ends, even in the heart of the Light."

"Jonalan was saying the dead walk at night," said Dernhil. "That's why nobody goes out."

Cadvan looked surprised. "Taran didn't mention that," he said. "He told me the dead were returning in dreams. Hal said so too." He fell silent, thinking of Hal, who had seen Inshi, her dead brother. She had spoken of it reluctantly, in a private moment while she was showing him how she had turned Cadvan's old home into a healing house. "He's so frightened, Cadvan. I don't like to think of him like that," she had said painfully. "I thought that at least he would be free of fear and sorrow. That's what is said, but maybe it's a lie. Maybe death is worse than being alive. Do you think so?"

Cadvan hadn't known how to comfort her. "None of us understands what happens in death," he had said at last. "But there is a darkness there now that is not part of it. It isn't death, it's something else…"

"Can you make it go away, Cadvan? You and your friends?"

Cadvan brought his mind back to the present and looked challengingly at the other Bards. "I'm thinking we can't leave without at least trying to help the Jouains," he said. "Maybe here we can stem the breach."

"Mend the Circles?" said Selmana. "Can you do that?"

"Yes, to an extent," said Dernhil. "At least, in a small way. It's what the Bards did when they tried to banish Kansabur. But if the Bone Queen is hunting us, as Ceredin said, it would be a perilous thing to do. She would see us at once if we made such magery."

"Taran's had visions like our foredreams," said Cadvan. "He spoke of the Queen of the Dead riding before an army. He can only mean Kansabur… And he said the whole of Jouan was having the same dreams. It's too like what Ceredin said." Cadvan thought again over what Taran had told him. "He did say, *We've all had visits from our dead*. But that this recent disturbance is different. *Bad*, he said. But I thought he was only speaking of dreams."

"It wouldn't be surprising, if the village is beset by nightmares, that some would think the dead call them up," said Nelac. "But even so, they shape my own fears. Even if the dead only walk the byways of sleep now, I am afraid they will not stay there."

"I don't want to be part of any magery," Selmana said with unexpected violence. "I don't want to see the dead. And if Kansabur finds me, what will I do?" She paused, twisting her hands, and then spoke in a rush. "I've been so … full of dread since Ceredin spoke to me. Kansabur is hunting Bards like me, Bards with the Sight. I'd never even heard of the Sight before I met Larla, and now it's all I'm hearing about. I wish I didn't have it, whatever it is. I don't even know what it is. And if she does find me, she'll just gobble me up like a big cat, and if that's all she needs to bind herself here, she'll bring all her power into our world and everything will be over…"

Dernhil took her hand and pressed it. "Selmana," he said gently. "We understand you have a special peril in this, and a particular Knowing. And we have decided nothing as yet."

Selmana gulped and looked down, feeling abashed. "I'm not very brave," she said shakily. "When I saw Kansabur, after I listened for the Shika – that is the worst thing that has ever happened to me. I never want to see her again. I never want her to see me. It's disgusting and horrible. I think if she found me, all of me would fall to ash…"

"Don't be ashamed of being frightened," said Cadvan. "We are all afraid."

"Selmana is correct that she has the most to fear," said Nelac. "And her Knowing isn't to be discounted. Yet I am also thinking: the most potent weapon the Dark has at present is fear. And powerful though she is, Kansabur still isn't in her full strength. I'm wondering whether we misjudge the peril: perhaps now is the time not to flee before her. Perhaps now we should bring the attack. If we turn and face her, we may win some time. And we need time."

"Only if we prevail," said Dernhil.

"Then we must prevail."

"If it goes wrong, what will happen here?" said Dernhil.

"Which risk is greater?" said Nelac. "We weigh the unknown against the unknown. Perhaps Jouan is a gate through which the armies of the dead might lead their assault on the living."

"And perhaps it is simply an accidental rip in the fabric

of the World, too unimportant for Kansabur's notice," said
Cadvan. "I wonder how many others there are? They might be
all over Annar. I fear that we may draw attention where none
would otherwise be. But remember what Ceredin said. I think
the dead are gathering here. Why else would their voices be
clear even to those who have no magery? We should close the
breach before it's too late."

Jonalan brought in their dinner, roast ham and turnips and
winter spinach. It was plain fare, but well cooked. Selmana's
mouth filled with water and in her hunger she almost forgot
her fears: it seemed years, not a mere week, since she had eaten
a hot meal around a table. Dernhil glanced at her in amusement.

"The Bone Queen may be gathering her forces, but a good
roast is always a good roast," he said. "Sometimes I wonder if
we Bards think too much about our vittles."

Selmana blushed at his teasing. "It smells so good," she said.

"The Dark dismisses such pleasures as trivial, mere enslave-
ments of the flesh," said Nelac. "And yet: a meal made with
care for others, that nourishes the body and the soul ... how is
that not the heart of the Light?"

"So the greatest minds in Annar justify their appetite,"
said Cadvan gravely. "I shall serve, of course, since my plate
requires special attention."

"But courtesy demands that you serve others first," said
Dernhil.

Cadvan bowed his head mockingly. "I defer then to your
greater courtesy," he said. "You should serve. I was forced to
refuse a dish of unparalleled magnificence at Taran's, and that
went hard."

Selmana smiled, her heart suddenly lighter, and concentrated on her meal. Cadvan was telling Dernhil about his goat,
Stubborn, who in his absence had become the scourge of the

village. "No garden is safe, apparently," he said. "If she is tethered, she unties the rope. They are saying she has magical powers that mean she can loose herself even from a chain. She is certainly not a magical goat, but she is a creature of rare intelligence. It seems I'm obliged to give her a stern warning." Dernhil laughed, and served him more turnips. Anyone casually watching those two young men jesting would never guess that anything was wrong. It was one of the things Selmana liked best about them, a kind of courage.

As she ate, she wondered whether she was as afraid as she had told the others. Yes. Yes, she was. But did that mean she was right to listen only to fear? It was true – lamentably true, she thought – that a good meal made her feel stronger. And even her brief meetings made her understand something of Cadvan's respect for the Jouains. They reminded her of her father's people: stoic, private, stubborn and honest.

After dinner, the Bards resumed their earlier discussion. Cadvan was of the opinion that if they were to act, it ought to be that night. Dernhil demurred, suggesting they'd be stronger after a night's rest. Selmana listened without partaking in the conversation; for the moment she was content merely to sit, enjoying the warmth of the fire and the wellbeing of a good meal among friends. It would pass soon enough.

She could hear Jonalan in the kitchen near by talking to his wife, and unconsciously sharpened her hearing to eavesdrop.

"They're not too high and mighty to listen," Jonalan was saying. "Perhaps they will help us."

"Maybe they can't help us, for all their fine manners," said Dana. She was silent for a time, amid a clattering of dishes. "Can they really put the dead to rest, Jona?" she asked, her voice breaking. "Can anyone? I can't bear much more of it."

"Hey, lass. We'll get through. We always do," said Jonalan, his voice muffled. Selmana thought he must be embracing his wife. Suddenly uncomfortably aware that she was listening to a private conversation, she started and closed her hearing. She realized that over the past hour she had changed her mind. Cadvan was right: they couldn't abandon these people to deal with the Bone Queen on their own. Perhaps she was braver than she thought. She was, after all, a Bard of Lirigon...

"I suppose the obvious thing," she said, abruptly interrupting the other Bards, "is to use me as bait to trap the Bone Queen."

The other Bards turned towards her, politely covering their surprise.

"It's one obvious thing," said Nelac, frowning. "But putting you at such risk isn't necessary. What we do depends whether we seek to ambush Kansabur, in whatever form she is able to take, or whether we simply seek to close the breach in the Circles. I think we shouldn't be too ambitious..."

Selmana lifted her chin. "Why not?" she said. Her pulse quickened at her own recklessness. "Also, the longer we wait, the stronger she'll be."

After a long argument about what they should do, they decided to act that night. It was near midnight when they walked away from the village, up the rise that led to the minehead, their hands linked. Selmana was in the middle, between Nelac and Dernhil. They moved like scouts, slowly and cautiously, their listening alert, questing for the centre of the rupture. There was no sign of life: the entire landscape seemed sterile of presence, as if every beast and bird had simply vanished from the face of the earth.

As the night deepened, it grew colder. There was no wind to drive away the rising mists, and they pooled and swirled about the Bards' feet, making ghostly eddies in the pale magelights. Selmana could see no sign of the mountains, which were hidden completely in the haze. A half-moon, haloed in icy blue light, stood low on the horizon, but it cast little illumination. All around them stretched a wide silence. Even their footsteps, damped by the mist, made little sound. It was as if they waded through a vast, shallow, edgeless sea.

They were cloaked and muffled against the cold, and were heavily shielded, invisible to any casual eye. Nelac, Dernhil and Cadvan were poised on the very threshold of the Shadowplains, which meant that their vision was uncertain, a doubled pattern of light and shadow from both realities. Selmana, the only one of them able to see clearly, had to act as guide so they didn't stumble.

Staying at the midpoint between the Circles without falling one way or the other was difficult. Dernhil, who had never journeyed to the Shadowplains before, already had drops of sweat rolling down his brow. He had no desire to enter them; even at the threshold, the Shadowplains felt malign and deadly. The double vision meant the Bards could see into both Circles, if imperfectly, and had the lesser chance of being ambushed by the Bone Queen; and it also meant that they could find the rupture that was afflicting Jouan. Walking on the edge of things, they could feel it near by, an anguish in the fabric of the World.

The others, especially Cadvan, had argued fiercely with Selmana about her proposition that she should act as a bait. But her panic had solidified into defiance; she was driven by a smouldering anger that burned out her fear. How dare this revenant rise and seek to destroy everything she loved? How dare the Bone Queen hunt her cousin through the long plains of death? How dare the Dark try to destroy the School that had given meaning to her life?

A cold voice inside her recognized that this confrontation might be in vain, that they might be courting their own destruction. It seemed worth the gamble. She was tired of being frightened. When she hadn't been afraid in the past weeks, she had just been exhausted. Now she felt neither exhausted nor afraid: fury ran silver through her, a bright energy that lightened her limbs. It tasted good.

They halted about half a mile out of Jouan. Selmana could see the mine winch not far away, silhouetted on the bare rise, and a lone star prickling through the haze behind it. "Here," said Cadvan. There was a flinching in his voice, something nearer disgust than fear. Nelac and Dernhil nodded. Selmana couldn't see how this place, a little way off the path to the mine, was different from anywhere else.

The four Bards arranged themselves in a ring, their hands still locked together, and Nelac spoke into Selmana's mind.

We'll start the mending, he said. *Are you ready?*

Selmana swallowed. She hoped she was. *Yes,* she said.

Whatever happens, don't break the ring, said Nelac. *You will be outside the mindmeld, but we will be aware of you. You are our watchman and our guard. The instant you sense Kansabur, do not hesitate: call us.*

Selmana nodded. She still felt no sign of life as far as her senses could quest, and it made her uneasy. She thought with a shiver that perhaps, as they stepped out of the warm lamplight of the tavern, the Bone Queen had devoured every living thing for miles. Perhaps she was hidden right next to her, listening to her thoughts, and Selmana's mind was naked before her, all their plans exposed, despite the veils of magery that sought to conceal them. For an instant, Selmana's resolve wavered. With an effort, she pushed her fears aside.

The other Bards bent their minds to weaving, and for an endless moment Selmana forgot everything else. This was a charm unlike any she had encountered before, and she was awed by its power. Weaving magery was like making music, if music were forged out of steel and light: its melodies and notes were the fabric of reality itself, softened and made fluid in the voices of the Bards. She saw that each Bard possessed a subtly different magery from the others; Nelac glowed with a rich gold light that made her think of sunset, while Dernhil was like the rays of the spring sun through new foliage, and Cadvan was a pure silver, the quality of starlight. The mageries met and flowed together, making a complex, ever-changing harmony, like the mingled melodies of a river, but shaped with conscious purpose and form.

She saw how the Bards stood in the impossible place between the Circles, weaving a fabric of light over the breach that opened between them. The gap was horribly visible now, even to her: she wondered that she hadn't seen it before. It was huge, a rent that bled a deathly vapour of darkness, its spectral edges flapping in unseen winds. She flinched, as from a terrible wound. It was a violence against the World, a wrong. There was a will behind this act, she perceived that clearly. It was a will that saw the obscene damage it would create and was indifferent, that coldly enjoyed the suffering it caused as a confirmation of its power, a will that accounted only itself as the measure of value, that sought to possess and command but never to understand. She gagged, wondering how the other Bards could bear it. She had learned to fear the Dark in the past few weeks, but now she felt more than fear or horror: she shuddered with revulsion and contempt.

She drew a deep breath, suddenly aware of her cold hands grasping Nelac and Dernhil's glowing fingers, and wrenched herself out of the vortex of magery. She was supposed to be keeping watch... She sent out the web of her perceptions, her listening and that other awareness, the between sense that Larla had called the Sight. Around her stretched that strange, unnatural silence, as if all sound had been swallowed in the vast, chilly dome of the sky. If anything, the quiet was deeper now: even her blood seemed stilled in her veins. But was there a feeling of watchfulness, of waiting? Was there something there?

The back of her neck prickled. She turned her head slowly, dreading what she might see. Behind her stood a child, perhaps ten years old. He was staring at her, his face blank but hungry, his hands stretching out towards her. And then, out of nowhere, behind him was an old woman, her dull eyes staring out of her hollow face. A young girl. Three men, all with the heavy shoulders of miners, who looked like brothers. The more she looked, the more there were, as if looking summoned them into view, dozens and then hundreds of people. They seemed as corporeal as the mages beside her, but something told her they were apparitions only. She knew they were dead, but somehow she wasn't frightened; instead, she was pierced with a sharp, intolerable sorrow. They all seemed so lost. She had seen something of that forlornness in Ceredin's face.

She took a deep breath, feeling the icy air knife into her lungs with relief: at least cold was just an ordinary thing. Her neck began to ache from looking over her shoulder and she turned back, facing inside the ring of Bards. The dead were all around them, stretching into the darkness as far as she could see, more than she could possibly count, all of them motionless, their eyes fixed on her, as if they were mutely pleading. She was tempted to interrupt the other Bards, but they had agreed that the signal was to be given if she saw Kansabur, or was in any way imperilled. The dead were uncanny and sorrowful, but she felt no threat from them. She looked for Ceredin, wondering if she were among these sad ranks, but saw no sign of her. She shifted uncomfortably, and blinked, and the dead vanished. Now the darkness was empty again.

It was strange, being part of a ring of Bards, but not part of their mindmeld. She could see the power building between the other three, but she was outside it. She heard their mingled voices at the margins of her mind, patiently weaving the gaping edges of the rent Circles together, but within that singing she was silent. She felt terribly alone, even though they were hand-linked. The power of magery rippled out of their circle, a beacon in the darkness. Every creature of the Dark for leagues would be aware of them now. And yet she felt no trace of sorcery, nor of the suffocating pall of malice that she associated with the Bone Queen. She would never forget that sense, which was more than physical: it afflicted the mind as the stench of a rotting corpse might affect the body.

She reminded herself that the other Bards would know if Kansabur walked in the Shadowplains; they would recognize that presence just as she did. Her absence troubled Selmana; for the first time since they had left Jonalan's tavern, she began to be fearful. *She is so close,* Ceredin had said. *So close...* But where was she? Was she hiding herself? Did she tense to strike them down, even now?

Selmana didn't need to look to know that the charm of mending was almost complete. The power of the three Bards almost made her feel dizzy; they were drawing on deep magery, funnelling the hidden powers of the world through their bodies as they wove the shimmering tapestry that would close the gaping rent between the Circles.

Perhaps Ceredin was wrong, she thought. Perhaps the Bone Queen is not here. Perhaps it is simply that this break makes everything seem close, when it is not, because it twists and distorts the matter of the Circles. Time and space are not the same in the Shadowplains as they are here. She could feel the inexorable weight that the torn place exerted, like a whirlpool that stretches and distorts the water around it. It was getting hard to judge where she was, it was hard to know who she was.

I am Selmana, Bard of Lirigon, she said fiercely to herself, I walk on this earth as myself, I am no other thing. But the force was bearing down on her: as the mingled light of magery wound itself around the gap, the vortex became more violent. She felt herself leaning towards the whirling centre, helplessly drawn, as if she were a branch trembling at the edge of a waterfall, held from tipping over the brink only by a crumbling bank, by some chance of the raging torrent that had swirled her to a boiling flood of darkness that fell down and down and down, endlessly beneath her. What held her? Was it a hand, or was it stone? She couldn't tell any more. It was slipping, her hand was slipping, she scrabbled desperately, blind with panic. And then she fell.

XXX

CADVAN could patch a broken kettle or a worn boot with a word when he was seven years old. Patching was the least of mageries, as easy as making illusions. It was sometimes a useful skill, but the result was never as good as crafting: after a few days the charm would evaporate, usually leaving the object more tattered than before. A mending charm required a more profound magery, and was beyond the untaught skill of a child, however talented: the aim was to make the object whole, as if it had never been broken.

The first time Cadvan had used that charm, it was to mend an old jug that belonged to Ceredin. It was fine glassware from Lanorial, a gift from Ceredin's mother. He had knocked it over one night, gesticulating too wildly during one of the gatherings they sometimes had, when the young Bards would drink wine and argue about everything under the sun, from music to herblore, the proper way to make cheese, the greatest poet of the Light, the best composition for inks... Cadvan was remorseful at his carelessness and had offered to mend it. Even with a simple object, the charm was much more difficult than he had imagined.

The next time had been to close the rift between the Abyss and the World that the Bards themselves had opened, when they sought to banish Kansabur back to the Abyss. It was essentially the same charm, but amplified through the power of six Bards and many times more complex. Making the magery while attempting to keep Kansabur chained was a torment.

Cadvan remembered the hunt and defeat of the Bone Queen as pure anguish; he had lain ill for days afterwards. And for all the anguish, they had failed.

At the time, although he said nothing, Cadvan had thought there was something of sorcery in the spells used to open the rift. Even in the mending charm, which undid the earlier charm that opened the Circles, there were rhymes and echoes that reminded him of spells he had encountered with Likod. Now, weaving the charm with Nelac and Dernhil, he felt these echoes again, and more strongly. This time the magery was different: the wound between the Circles hadn't been cut by Bards, who worked with the precision of surgeons, seeking to make as little disturbance as possible. This rift had been torn open crudely, wreaking damage widely around it. No wonder the Jouains were suffering from bad dreams; it was such a serious breach that Cadvan thought it likely that the rumours of the dead walking at night were more than the imaginings of frightened villagers.

As the mindmelded Bards felt gingerly about the torn edges, which furled vaporously through the threshold between the Shadowplains and the World, Cadvan fought against an overwhelming feeling of revulsion. He had hoped, despite Ceredin's warning, that this flaw between the Circles was a natural distortion, which might as naturally close over. The cosmos was full of ruptures: it was well known that in certain places there were fault lines. The Pilanel had told him that the shamans in the icy vastnesses of the far north called such places fountains of truth, thinking of them as akin to the hot springs that burst through rock with healing waters. They tended these places, using secret charms to keep them open for their visions and prophecies. But this rift was a wanton, deliberate violence.

He nodded to Selmana, who stood pale in front of him on the opposite side of their ring, and began to concentrate on weaving the charm. He kept part of his mind watchful and separate, letting the weight of the magery fall on Nelac and Dernhil. He had argued most forcefully against Selmana's proposal that she stand out to lure Kansabur, and although they had taken every precaution they could imagine, he was still worried. He remembered Kansabur's strength: even if she were diminished, they didn't know how weakened she was. What if she took Selmana, despite everything they had done? If Selmana held the secret to Kansabur regaining her full power, wasn't it the deepest folly even to consider what they were planning to do now? He was surprised that Nelac even considered it; he was astonished that he supported Selmana. In the end Cadvan had given way with great reluctance, insisting that they should set the strongest shields they could make.

It was always impossible to track the passage of time while making a powerful charm: what could seem like the work of hours could take only a few moments. Cadvan kept his eye on the moon; by the time they had almost completed the weaving, it had scarcely moved in its journey across the sky. Together the Bards traced the rent edges, outlining them with light, drawing them together, closer and closer. The smaller the rupture became, the more difficult it was to hold. Their magery blazed into the night, but there was no sign of Kansabur, neither in the Shadowplains nor in the World.

Cadvan saw Selmana turn her head and look behind her, staring fascinatedly at the empty darkness, and almost stepped out of the charm to ask her what she saw; but she made no move to alert them. It was hard to keep all these double awarenesses in balance: Cadvan was poised on the edge of the Shadowplains and the World, both inside the mindmeld and apart from it. He began to feel the strain as the charm intensified, and clenched his jaw, fighting to keep everything in focus.

Then, with a jolt of disbelief, he saw Selmana in the

mindmeld, where she shouldn't be: where, by now, she couldn't be. Nelac and Dernhil were deep in the charm, preparing to set the key that would lock it whole, and betrayed no sign that they had seen her. She was somehow part of the mending, a shining form woven into the magery. Then she seemed to twist herself out of the charm and he fleetingly saw two of her, as if in a mirror: one in the World, the other in the Shadowplains.

Stop! Cadvan cried out into their minds. *Ware Selmana!* The other two Bards instantly paused, teetering agonisedly on the very edge of the culmination of the mending. A blade of sorcery came out of nowhere, cleaving the charm in two. Nelac and Dernhil swayed with the shock of it, even under the shields they had made against this chance, and turned towards Selmana, clutching her hands as if she were being swept away by a mighty wind, although the night was absolutely still: and then the ring of Bards broke and the mindmeld shattered. Selmana vanished before their eyes. In her place, towering over the three Bards, stood Kansabur, the Bone Queen.

They saw her as the Iron Tyrant of Lir, the revenant Cadvan had summoned to the Inkadh Grove. She was helmed and armoured in black, and the metal gleamed smooth, like the wing casing of a beetle. The skull sigil of her reign blazed crimson on her breastplate, and a black broadsword swung in her hands. Red flames licked its length, streaming into the night. Cadvan knew that blade: it was Thuruk, forged of sorcery in Dagra, some said by the Nameless One himself. It was the weapon that had killed Ceredin.

There was no time even to think. Dernhil and Nelac, reeling from the breaking of the charm, stood momentarily stunned. As Kansabur swung her blade to shatter their mageshield, Cadvan loosed a bolt of white fire at her chest, exposed by her sweeping blow. It was driven by all his rage and despair and grief, everything he had suffered since the Dark had riven his life. The white fire drove home: Kansabur stumbled back at the force of it, and the black blade shivered, and silver fire flickered among the red.

It gave Nelac and Dernhil a crucial moment to recover and to draw back their magery from the mending charm. The mageshield shimmered, briefly visible as a veil of light around them as power flowed into it, and Cadvan felt the mindmeld snap open again, Dernhil and Nelac's strength flowing into his. Kansabur leapt forward into the space between them, directing a brutal slash at Cadvan. He stepped back, and Thuruk whipped past his face. He briefly met Kansabur's eyes, which burned behind the slits in her visor. It was as if a beam of hatred lanced into his soul. His own hatred surged forward to meet it in a blast of magery, with a sudden vicious gladness. He needed no sword. Kansabur could not hate him more than he hated her.

She sprang back to avoid his blow, only to find she was trapped. The mageshield no longer protected the Bards: now it enclosed Kansabur in a net of white fire, stronger than steel, colder than the stars. She stood up straight, very still, and then she leant on her sword and laughed at them.

Treacherous scum, she said, in the Black Speech. *Do you really think your pathetic chains can hold me? Oh, how I will enjoy your torment, when the mighty dungeons of Lir are rebuilt…*

She flung up her hand and spoke a summons, and as the words fell from her mouth, it seemed to the Bards that a stream of smoke also issued forth, winding out in a cloud that seeped through the mageshield, toxic and foul. And the night was no longer empty. Behind and before him Cadvan saw the shadowy dead, pouring in all their endless legions through the breach between the Circles, and dread shook his heart.

Now, said Nelac to Cadvan. *Now. She's right that we cannot hold her.*

And out of his hatred, Cadvan spoke the Curse of Harm, one of the bitterest spells he had learned from Likod. It gathered strength as he spoke, foul and disgusting on his tongue, but given life and force by the fury that roiled through his whole being. The summoning died on Kansabur's lips and the dead legions faded and vanished. The Bone Queen shrank back, writhing against the agony of the spell. The more Kansabur twisted in pain, the more merciless Cadvan's power: here was his revenge, for every wound the Dark had dealt him, for each loss, for each grief. Kansabur began to lose her human form: her outline blurred as if smudged by smoke, and then suddenly, as if she inwardly collapsed, all that was inside the cage of magefire was a mess of darkness, pulsing and squirming against itself like the many larvae of some obscene insect.

Released from the spell, Cadvan stumbled forward and fell onto his knees, sobbing with exhaustion. Nelac and Dernhil now struck, winding the magefire inwards, ever smaller. The shadow within fought desperately, resisting them with every vestige of its power, and even as they drew the net tight, a blast of sorcery tore it open and a boiling plume of shadow burst out, briefly obscuring the sky above them. And then it was gone, and the night was clean and silent.

Dernhil and Nelac slumped against each other, breathing hard.

"Selmana," said Dernhil. "Where is she? What happened?"

"I wish I knew," said Nelac. He shook his head to clear his thoughts. "That was a hard thing." He knelt beside Cadvan, and embraced him. "My friend, be glad. If we didn't destroy Kansabur, she is surely diminished."

Cadvan met his eyes, and Nelac flinched at the bitterness he saw there. Then Cadvan blinked, angrily brushing away the sweat and tears that ran down his face. "Aye," he whispered. "I would be a fearsome Hull. The Light did well to banish me."

Nelac kissed his brow. "You are a child of the Light," he said. "I have no doubt in you."

"I was glad to speak that curse," said Cadvan. "Think about that." He rose and staggered a short distance, and then fell onto his knees again and retched. The other Bards watched him in silence. At last he turned back.

"What now?" he said. "Should we remake the mending, or should we seek Selmana first?"

Dernhil hesitated. "We must make the charm."

"But what if it locks her out?"

"Selmana can step between this plane and that without need for a gateway," said Dernhil. "Last time, she came back without our seeking her."

"It was Ceredin who sent her back, remember."

Nelac put up his hand to silence them and shut his eyes, questing for Selmana's presence. Cadvan cried out in protest, but Dernhil stopped him with a look. They watched anxiously until Nelac opened his eyes again, only a short time later. He swayed and almost fell.

"She is not in the Shadowplains. Nor is Kansabur. They are utterly empty," he said. "I think we cannot find her. I would wager my life that she is hidden from Kansabur." He sighed and knuckled his eyes like a little boy. "By the Light, I am weary to death, and my whole body feels like a bruise. But let's do the task before us first."

The descent seemed endless. As she tumbled over the lip of the World, Selmana thought her body dissolved, as if she became part of everything that was falling. She shut her eyes against the terror of the speed of it, but it made no difference at all. Perhaps she no longer had eyes or eyelids, perhaps all that was left of her was this awareness, this depth that yawned above and beneath her, an impossible gulf in which the only direction was down, in which time no longer existed.

And yet, there was even an end to this. So gradually that she at first didn't notice, the speed gentled: she was no longer plunging like a stone, but like a leaf or a feather twirling in a current, and then at last she was still. There was no ground to hold her, no sense of above or beneath: she was suspended. And she realized that it wasn't water or wind that had rushed her along, but a torrent of stars. She stared, awestruck: she had never seen anything so beautiful. She had thought the stars were white, but they burned with colours that she had never seen before, gathering in spirals and clouds of intricate fire, infinitely various, infinitely complex. There was no limit to her sight: the more she looked, the more she could see. She thought she could stay for ever, looking into the vastness; she would never tire of the boundless beauty that now burned around her. And she was part of this beauty, one flame among these countless fires, so tiny that the least of these mighty orbs could destroy her in less than a moment. Yet, strangely, the thought didn't daunt her: at the same time as she recognized her insignificance, she knew that she was as complex and intricate as the dance she saw unfolding before her, that she was forged of the same fires.

And then it seemed to her that the stars shifted their dance, and began to arrange themselves into a pattern, a form outlined in light. It reminded her of the star maps that she had sometimes studied in the library in Lirigon, which named the constellations, but here there were no lines to join the stars into a figure of an archer or a bear: the stars themselves made the form. She saw before her a woman crowned with emerald and ruby stars, clad in a silver robe that pulsed and flickered, her long golden hair streaming into the void.

Dearest one, said a voice, impossibly. *You have come too far. Come. It is time to go home.*

Selmana stared at her in wonder. *Who are you?* she asked.

The woman laughed, and reached out a giant hand. *I have many names,* she said. *I have forgotten most of them.* And she clasped Selmana's hand. A cold thrill went through Selmana's being, a clear pulse of joy. And the woman was no longer a vast, dazzling queen of the heavens, but a girl like Selmana, clad in a white dress, wearing a coronet of leaves and red flowers, and her hand was warm and alive.

Come, she said again. *You must go home.*

I want to go home with you, said Selmana.

My home is not yours, said the girl. *In time you may come there. But now is not your time.*

She began to run, pulling Selmana, and gladness leapt in Selmana's breast and she ran with her. The further they ran, the faster they raced, until the stars were streaming past them in cascades of white fire. And then it seemed to Selmana that they were running along a white beach with the sea sobbing beside them, and in the distance on a cliff she saw high gates shining, before a lofty castle with banners of silver and blue that fluttered in a keen wind. Selmana knew that she wanted to enter those gates, more than anything she had desired in her life, and she pulled on the girl's hand to change their direction, picking up their pace yet again. But the gates never came any closer.

No, dear one, this is not your time, said the girl.

Is that your home? said Selmana. She wasn't out of breath at all, although they were running with such speed that the ground rolled beneath them in a blur and her hair streamed straight behind her.

I have many homes, said the girl. And now they were no longer beside the sea, but on dark plains, and the gates and the castle had vanished, and to their right the white peaks of mountains shone like knives in the starlight.

No! cried Selmana, tugging the girl's hand. *Let's go back!* But the girl said nothing, and pulled her along through the rushing night. They were slowing now, and Selmana began to feel the weight of her body dragging her down. She saw a track winding through tangled grasslands, and the outlines of houses, and she recognized the place. And then she tripped over a grassy tussock and there was the shock of earth under her feet, and they stopped. They were just outside Jouan.

The girl turned to face her, still holding her hand, and Selmana saw that her eyes were not human eyes, but slotted, like a cat's.

You are home now, she said. *You must do what you must do.*

Please don't go, said Selmana. *Take me with you. Please.*

I cannot, said the girl. *Even if I could, I would not. Now is not the time. Come, don't be sad. We will meet again.*

She smiled and leant forward and kissed Selmana's cheek, and it felt like ice and fire at once. And then Selmana's hand was empty, and the girl was gone. The night was just the night. The fierce joy that had winged Selmana's body flickered and died, leaving her ashen. She thought her heart would break with loss.

She stood for a long time, listening to the ordinary night noises. A wind sprang up, and she saw that the sky was clouding over. The half-moon sailed in the west, letting fall a dim light. She smelled rain. It was deep night, but she didn't know which night it was. Was it the same night she had left behind her, an aeon ago? With an effort, she wrenched her mind from the desolation that overwhelmed her, remembering what had happened before she met the wild girl.

Kansabur. Where was Kansabur? Where were the other Bards? She had forgotten all about them. She brushed her hair out of her eyes, and realized her cheeks were wet with tears. Dully, almost without thought, she walked to the tavern. The door was shut, but a yellow light lined the edges of the window shutters. She raised her hand and knocked.

Almost at once, Cadvan opened the door. They stared at each other without speaking. Then Cadvan smiled.

"I suppose you had better come in," he said.

XXXI

WHEN Selmana turned up at the tavern, Dernhil, Cadvan and Nelac were debating the risks of searching for her through the Circles. They had returned to the tavern scarcely an hour before, in despair and exhaustion: the rupture between the Circles was now closed, but they had found no sign of Selmana anywhere, and none of them had any notion of where to begin searching for her. Beyond telling them that she had taken no harm, Selmana didn't want to speak about what had happened. When Cadvan impatiently questioned her, she turned her shoulder against him.

In truth, as Dernhil said in the silence that followed, they were all too tired to talk. They each retired to their tiny chambers, and none of them was seen until the sun was high in the sky the following day. Cadvan was up first. He felt too sick to break his fast and instead went in search of Taran. Taran was down the mine with his brothers, but Hal was waiting for him, and invited him to her healing house.

"I dreamed of you last night," she said shyly, as she prepared him a tea. "I saw you fighting with a man in black armour, and I thought he was going to strike you down and kill you, but instead you killed him."

"It was the Bone Queen," said Cadvan absently. "You shouldn't have any more trouble here."

"The Bone Queen?" Hal's brow wrinkled. "Who is she?"

Cadvan took the mug she offered and looked about Hal's kitchen. She had made this house her own; besides the herbs and salves that lined the shelves, she had arranged her precious things about the room: a carving of a wooden cat that had belonged to her mother, the mortar and pestle that Cadvan had given her when he left, a length of bright red cloth that she had laid on the table. Everything was meticulously clean. He looked back at Hal and smiled, wondering how to answer her question.

"The Bone Queen is a terrible spirit who tore open the World, and called the dead into Jouan," he said. "We mended the hole, and I think those dreams won't trouble the village again."

"That's good," said Hal, and wriggled in her chair like a little girl, flashing him a look that spoke of everything she found difficult to say. When she had brought Cadvan into the house, she had been a gracious hostess, anxious that he be pleased with what he saw, but now it was as if she suddenly relaxed.

"I like your house," said Cadvan, and her face lit up.

"Do you?" she said. "Oh, Cadvan, there's so much that I don't know. I haven't done anything wrong yet, I remembered what you said about being honest about what I can do, but people come to me almost every day. Mostly I can help them, even if it's just a little bit, but sometimes I can't at all. I wish I knew more."

"I've never had a better or more eager pupil than you, Hal," Cadvan said.

Her face reddened with pleasure, and she began to tell him of some of the cases she had dealt with, questioning Cadvan about her decisions, and listening seriously to his answers. They fell easily into their old relationship of teacher and student, but Hal pushed him further, willing now to challenge his judgements or jumping ahead of him. Cadvan wondered again whether he had missed the Gift in her: she was so quick and intuitive, and her memory was formidable. But, no, she showed no signs of magery.

At last, remembering the time with a start, Cadvan took his leave, asking Hal to tell Taran that they had dealt with the problem as well as they could. She looked down, her face shadowed. "I almost forgot you don't live here any more," she said. "I've missed you so much."

Cadvan smiled painfully. "I don't think I'll live here again," he said. "And I haven't finished the task that took me away. But my promise still stands. I'll return when I can."

"And not die."

"And not die." He stood up and Hal, suddenly formal again, showed him to the door, wishing him blessings for his journey. He took her hand in farewell, studying her face.

"You are doing so well on your own," he said. "I'm proud of you, Hal. You do me great credit."

Tears started in her eyes, and she threw her arms around his neck and hugged him. Then she stood back, swallowing hard and trying to smile, and shut the door.

Cadvan walked back to the tavern, hunching his cloak against a heavy fall of rain that had swept over from the mountains. The nausea that had made him want to gag since he uttered the curse the night before had lifted. Although he remembered all the spells that Likod had shown him, this was only the second time he had attempted sorcery. He remembered, with shame, the awful joy he had felt in using that power. He hoped that he never had to use it again. But it had worked: as he had conjectured, Kansabur had been unprepared for sorcery. He thought of the unshadowed light in Hal's serious eyes when she spoke about healing. He had, at least, protected that. But there was no justification that could make him forgive the malice he saw in himself.

Back at the tavern, Dernhil and Nelac were spooning up bowls of oaten porridge well laced with honey. Dernhil looked up when Cadvan entered, studying him coolly.

"I like this tavern," he said. "I never was fond of porridge, but this is delicious. Back in Gent, they make it with salt."

"Traders have to journey far to come here, so Jonalan pays attention to his fare," said Cadvan, joining them. "He has a reputation to keep up."

"He might as easily serve pig slop, since there is no one else," said Dernhil.

"Well, I'm grateful he does not."

There was no sign of Selmana. They didn't talk about the events of the night before until she came down the stairs an hour later. Then all four Bards talked for a long time, as the increasing rain beat against the windows. This time Selmana told them of what had happened when she had vanished from the World, and the other three listened in astonishment.

"I've never heard of anything like that," said Cadvan. "I wonder who this woman is. A creature of the stars?"

"She must have been an Elemental," said Dernhil. "Think you, Nelac? I have read a little about them. It's said that they can take any form they like, but always their eyes are slotted."

"She was so beautiful," said Selmana quietly. It still hurt to speak of the wild girl. "I've never been so happy... I didn't want to come back."

"If she was an Elidhu, then you have stepped with perilous beings," said Nelac. "They are not as we are, and follow different laws."

"She helped me," said Selmana fiercely. "She found me and brought me back here. Yes, she was different from us. But not that different..."

"Good and evil don't look to them as they do to us," said Nelac. "They cannot die, and they do not know the sorrow of mortals. Remember, the Elidhu allied with the Dark... I wonder what their part in this might be."

"That they have a part seems certain," said Cadvan. "I think we ought to be encouraged rather than daunted."

"But it is a power that is not to be trusted." Nelac studied Selmana doubtfully.

Selmana opened her mouth to argue, and then shut it. There seemed no point: if they thought the wild girl was an Elidhu, and perhaps she was, then she foresaw all their objections. Bards saw Elementals as traitors: if they were not the Dark itself, they were as lawless, following their own ends. It was in all the songs: the treachery of the Elidhu had brought down the Great Silence, permitting the Dark to rule over Annar. Yet the woman she had seen among the stars had nothing to do with the Dark. Whoever she was, Selmana had loved her at once, as if she had known her all her life. The desire to see her again still ached inside her; she thought that the memory of that blazing freedom would never leave her. She hadn't told the others that the girl had said that they would meet again; that was her own secret. And yet she didn't even know her name. Perhaps she had bewitched her, but even as the thought occurred to her, Selmana realized she didn't care. All love was a form of bewitchment: did that make it evil?

She listened to what had happened after she had vanished, but to her surprise, it seemed of no great moment to her. She was glad for the villagers of Jouan, and she was glad that the obscene rip in the fabric of the World had been mended. More than in their words, she saw the tale of the struggle in the grey faces of the Bards before her, still gaunt with exhaustion. But somehow this struggle, which had been so pressing, now seemed only of passing importance.

"Well," she said at last, growing tired of the conversation. "I suppose we should just move on to Pellinor."

"But not at once," said Cadvan, casting her a glance of amusement. "I think we have bought ourselves some time. Unless you want to rush out into this rainstorm." She caught

his eye, and wondered if he had guessed what she was thinking. Cadvan seemed different today, somehow freer, but she
couldn't think what had changed.

"Tomorrow will do," she said.

V

XXXII

"THERE!" said Dernhil, pointing down the valley. They had emerged quite suddenly from a pine wood over the lip of a stony ridge. A thin wind drove ragged clouds south from the mountains that loomed over the horizon, their grim buttresses jutting through the first heavy snows. Selmana shivered against the chill, looking to where Dernhil pointed, and caught her breath. Pellinor nestled like a jewel in the breast of the valley, its white walls already lit against the darkening day. A single finger of light broke through the clouds and struck the great copper dome of the Singing Hall, which glowed green, like a living thing.

It was six days since they had left Jouan, and they had travelled hard, using healcharms to hasten their way. As before, it had been a boring, cold and punishing journey, darkened always by a fear of pursuit. After the battle in Jouan, they couldn't hope that the Dark hadn't guessed where they planned to go, and they travelled shielded, alert for any sign of its presence. Aside from an increasing sense of foreboding, they saw nothing.

There had been one reprieve from watchfulness, on the third night, when they had camped in a Bardhome, a dingle circled by a stand of ash trees. There were a number of these in northern Annar, planted by Bards centuries before and ringed with a virtue of protection, and Bards used them when travelling through the wilderness for respite and refuge. They set no watch, and it seemed to Selmana that when they arose the following day, her three companions were healed of more than tiredness: for the first time since Jouan, their faces were unshadowed.

That night, Selmana had dreamt of the wild girl. A tree had stepped down from the edge of the dingle and bent towards her, and when she looked up she saw the girl curled in a forked branch, smiling mischievously. A pale sun filtered through the leaves and haloed her in a green light.

Selmana cried out and leapt to her feet, as delight surged through her. *What's your name?* she said. *Tell me your name, at least!*

You do not need my name, dear one, said the girl. *You know me already. I am with you always, in your Making and your Knowing.*

But what will I call you?

Are words so important? It seemed then that the branches of the tree bent down to the ground, as if the ash tenderly placed her before Selmana. The girl stepped up to her, her feet naked on the grass, and took her hand. *You do not need words.*

I need you! Selmana didn't think she said it out loud, but she knew the girl heard her, *What am I to call you?*

The girl looked at her, smiling. *You need a name so much?* she said. *Well then. I have so many names... Which would you like? I was once called the Moonchild, which is "Anghar" in one of the tongues of the north.*

Anghar, said Selmana, trying it on her tongue, like a charm. *Anghar.* She looked into the girl's slotted eyes, and felt her strangeness. *Who are you? Why did you rescue me when I was lost?*

So many questions! Anghar laughed, and Selmana felt it like a shower of silver rain through her soul, cleansing and vital. *I had forgotten the curiosity of humans... Dear one, you are fleet and supple, and step between dimensions as one of my kin. And so the Bitter Queen seeks you. I do not choose that she should find you.*

The Bitter Queen?

The laughter vanished from Anghar's eyes, and she was

suddenly solemn. *The lifehaters,* she said. *They steal our life from us, taking what is most precious. But even the Bitter Queen is not as mighty as the great Lifehater, who burned with envy in years long past and stole the song of our hearts. I name them enemy. I will not permit them to take you also.*

Selmana felt an unquestioning faith that the Bone Queen couldn't find her if Anghar didn't let her, and she realized that, for the first time in weeks, she felt completely safe. Other questions bubbled up inside her, but in the enchantment of the moment she forgot them all. Nothing mattered except Anghar's loveliness, the cool touch of her hand.

I wish I could stay with you for ever, Selmana said.

You cannot. But be glad, said the girl. *I am with you now. In time I will leave, as I must. But all leaving is brief...*

The sunlight through the branches brightened until Selmana blinked in dazzlement, and then Anghar was gone. But somehow Selmana wasn't so bereft this time, and when she woke up the next day, the burden of loss she had borne since Jouan was less heavy. Travelling was not so hard after that. She didn't tell the other Bards of her dream. She felt, fiercely, that it was for her alone, and she didn't want them picking over the secret joy in her heart.

Now they had at last reached the Fesse of Pellinor, an older desire quickened in Selmana's breast: her passion for Making. Here lived the lore she loved.

The valley was beautiful, even in the sombre dress of approaching winter, with its fields ploughed in and the orchards raising bare branches. Selmana realized, with a jolt of surprise, that what she felt was very similar to the yearning that had possessed her when she saw the castle from the white beach, when she ran with Anghar through the stars. She puzzled over this as they trotted down into the valley, cursing that she hadn't thought to ask Anghar the name of the citadel. Anghar had all but promised that one day she would go there.

The Fesse was sheltered from the worst of the weather that swept down from the Osidh Elanor by the rocky shoulders of the ridges that rose around the valley, and they passed through many villages on the broad road. Selmana had an odd feeling of familiarity, as if she knew this place well, although she had never seen it before. Of course, she had read of Pellinor, and had seen pictures in books, and Calis had spoken often about it. But that didn't explain why she felt as if she were coming home.

Although they had travelled fast, the Bards feared that news from Lirigon may have come before them, and they were cautious. Cadvan was again disguised by the Pilanel charm, and the others rode heavily cloaked. When they reached the School, Nelac would not give their names. The Bard at the gate was taken aback, since this was a basic courtesy, but something in the urgency of these travel-stained visitors struck him and he didn't argue. Nelac asked to see Milana at once, sending in the Ring of Silur as a token, and they were told to wait by the gate until they had word.

Word didn't take long to come back, and clearly the instructions were that they were to be treated with honour. A Bard, who obviously recognized Nelac but was too polite to say so, was sent to be their guide. In a surprisingly short time they had led their weary horses to the stables and seen them settled with warm mashes in thick beds of straw. Nelac insisted they speak to Milana before they did anything else, and they were escorted to her Bardhouse in the Inner Circle.

As they wound their way through the streets, Selmana began to understand why people spoke of the beauty of Pellinor. For centuries it had attracted the greatest Makers in Annar, and their art was to be seen everywhere: in the many-coloured tessellated pavements that led to shady gardens of evergreen shrubs, or the carved lintels of the stone houses, or the bright enamelled tiles

that framed the doorways and windows. She glimpsed a courtyard where a white statue of a woman poured water endlessly
from a stone ewer into a fountain, and a garden through a gateway that was filled with red flowers that stood out against the
dark earth. Almost every house had a window of stained glass,
and as lights bloomed in the dusk, they shone like jewels: she
saw a winged horse, and a man robed in crimson, crowned with
white lilies, and a green-leaved tree with a circlet of golden blossoms. The Bard lamps that lit the stone streets were shaped like
lilies, opening gracefully from stems of black iron. She dawdled
behind the other Bards, looking about her in wonder, and had to
hurry to catch up lest she become lost.

She could have wandered these streets for hours, but in all
too short a time they reached Milana's chambers. They thanked
the Bard who had escorted them, and he nodded and retired,
closing the door behind him. Milana was alone in the room,
and she stood as they entered, a short, slender woman with
very white skin and raven-black hair that fell loosely about her
shoulders almost to her waist.

"*Samandalamë*, Nelac, Dernhil," she said gravely, welcoming
them in the Speech. "I do not know these other two?"

Cadvan bowed, undoing the disguising charm, and to
Selmana's surprise Milana laughed. "Ah, Cadvan," she said. "I
might have known. So you have mastered Pilanel magic? Not
many Bards of Annar can do that. I salute you."

"The Pilanel own a complex lore, my lady. But I suspect it's
more that many Bards of Annar do not care to master it."

"I think you are right," said Milana. "But even I, who have
no such incuriosity, have never got my tongue around that
charm, although I have the best and dearest of teachers."

Selmana remembered then that Milana's consort was
a Pilanel Bard, a man called Dorn who had arrived from the
north many years ago. But now Milana was turning to greet her.

Selmana felt clumsy as she took the First Bard's delicate hand: she towered over her. She felt Milana's power as soon as she touched her, an electric thrill that ran up her arm and made the hairs stand up on her neck.

"Selmana of Lirigon, my lady," she said. "I am but a student..."

"A Maker, I think?"

Selmana nodded, suddenly shy. "Yes," she said. "I've long wanted to come to Pellinor, to learn from you."

Milana's eyes were a profound blue, and they seemed to look deep into Selmana's being. She shifted uncomfortably under that clear gaze, feeling exposed. "A Maker of rare talent, I see. Welcome to Pellinor! But sadly, I think that is not why you are here, although I hope you may study with me hereafter. Come, sit down. Nelac, you have news, though I fear it isn't good. We will be private as long as you need."

Nelac met Milana's eyes. "Have you had word from Lirigon, my lady?"

"Yes," said Milana. "I know something of what has passed there. Bird news is swift, if partial. I am told that Cadvan, formerly of Lirigon, Nelac of Lirigon and Dernhil of Gent are abjured as traitors to the Light, accused of the murder of the First Bard." She glanced again at Selmana. "I have heard nothing of Selmana, Minor Bard, and I am the more curious..."

A heavy silence fell. "Bashar is dead, then?" said Nelac, his voice harsh.

"Alas, it is so. Did you not know? It is a heavy loss. Though I don't believe that any of you could be responsible for it, nor that our friend Cadvan of Lirigon is any kind of servant of the Dark. It's clearly absurd."

Selmana felt a rush of relief at Milana's brusque dismissal of the accusations of treachery. She glanced at Cadvan: she saw the same relief reflected there, and something else, something more complex. Milana had given him his proper title, as a Bard of Lirigon, and it had clearly taken him by surprise. For a moment, before he hid his feeling, his face was open and it seemed that he might weep. Looking away swiftly, Selmana thought she might begin to understand why Ceredin loved him. She had thought it was because Cadvan was handsome and gifted and charismatic, one of the great Bards of his generation, but it wasn't that at all...

Nelac told Milana of what had happened in Lirigon and Jouan, speaking swiftly and clearly. She listened intently, without interrupting. When he talked about how Kansabur had hunted Selmana, she shot the young Bard a speculative look and nodded.

"You know that Enkir is here," she said, when Nelac had finished speaking. "We should tell him this: he should permit himself to be scried, if there is any peril that he too houses a fragment of Kansabur, as you two did. But for now, you are my guests. You should bathe and eat and rest: come here in an hour and dine with me, when I have had a chance to think over this." She rose and smiled. "Have no fear in Pellinor: you need not be hidden among my folk. Lirigon holds no authority over us, and will not, so long as it remains so misled."

Selmana knew that outside Annar – in the Seven Kingdoms, or in the Suderain, where the ancient city of Turbansk was raised long before the Great Silence – Schools followed their own design. But in Annar, every School had been built on the same principle: it was a wheel of eleven concentric circles, linked by straight roads. These all led to the wide hub of the Inner Circle, an open space that was flanked by the library, the Singing Hall and the Bardhouses of the First Circle.

Pellinor, with its slate roofs and white stone halls, its verdigrised copper domes and coloured pavements, was very different from the red tiles and grey granite of Lirigon, but Selmana had no trouble finding her way to the common bathing rooms, which were exactly where she expected them to be. To her discomfiture, when she entered she discovered that the bath was communal. It was a large room, tiled in many colours to the ceiling, and in the centre was a steaming rectangular pool. There was a ledge inside the pool where half a dozen people already sat, up to their necks in water, gossiping idly.

This was very different from Lirigon, where bathing was a private business. Selmana turned to leave, stricken with embarrassment, but an attendant stepped up and greeted her courteously, handing her a silver basin of hot water, a cake of soap and a drying cloth of soft wool. Selmana thanked her awkwardly, and looked around covertly at the others there to see what she should do with them. It seemed she had to clean herself before she went into the bath. Around the walls were open cubicles with wooden benches where people scrubbed themselves and washed their hair, before walking naked to the pool, in full view of everyone else. Selmana walked to an empty cubicle, doing her best to look unconcerned. She could feel herself blushing with self-consciousness, although no one took any notice of her as she hurried to the pool and lowered herself quickly into the steaming, fragrant water, choosing the corner furthest from the other bathers.

But the water was so delicious! Its healing warmth leached into her sore muscles. She sighed and leaned her head back, shutting her eyes, letting her legs float up, weightless and free. Then it occurred to her that her three companions would want to bathe too. The thought dragged her out of the pool much more quickly than she would have liked and sent her scurrying back to her chamber. She didn't feel able to confront Nelac and Cadvan and Dernhil naked, even after a fortnight of travelling together: it would be altogether too awkward.

Back in her room, Selmana thought that the familiarities of Pellinor were as disconcerting as the differences. They made her think she knew her way about, only to find herself tripped up by strangeness. She dressed herself in the clean clothes laid out for her, and then sank back on her bed with a sigh. It was a truism that every School differed from the others. Far to the south, in the Suderain, Turbansk was a city of red towers and brazen halls, where scholars studied the stars; Il Arunedh was famed for its vineyards and terraced flower gardens, which stretched their perfumed lengths down the side of the mountain that embraced the School; Gent in the forested kingdom of Ileadh was a city of singers, and Dernhil was only one of many poets who came from there. But she had somehow thought, even so, that Pellinor would simply be a more beautiful version of Lirigon.

It was good to be alone. Since they had left Jouan, she had had little time to think: she had been too cold, or too tired, or too sad. She let her mind wander, remembering, as she did in all her idle moments, the girl who had brought her back from the stars. She thought of how Milana had nodded when Nelac told her of Selmana's Gift of Sight, and of how Kansabur was hunting her. Did Milana know something that Nelac didn't? Perhaps she could tell Milana what had happened: perhaps Milana might understand, as the other Bards did not, her certainty that Anghar intended her no ill. Perhaps she might understand how it was she loved her. Did she dare to confess to her? Even as she thought it, she discarded the idea. It would hurt to see the shadows of mistrust on Milana's face...

Her musings were interrupted by a knock on the door, and she started, realizing that she had almost fallen asleep. Cadvan waited outside, as he had promised; they had planned to meet Nelac and Dernhil, and to walk together to Milana's Bardhouse for dinner. She blinked: Cadvan was dressed as a Bard, in a tunic and leggings of fine blue wool, a cloak of dark crimson pinned at his shoulder with a silver brooch in the shape of a four-pointed star: the sign of Lirigon. She hadn't seen him in Bard raiment for a long time, and she had forgotten how handsome he was.

"I didn't see you at the baths, Selmana," said Cadvan, as they walked to Milana's chambers. "But you look very clean."

She blushed and glanced sideways at him, suspecting that he was teasing her. "I am very efficient at my ablutions," she said primly.

"It occurred to me that I should have warned you," said Cadvan. "In Lirigon it is different, no? Here bathing is a social thing."

Selmana laughed. "It was a bit of a shock," she said. "But I suppose, if ever I am to live here, I will have to get used to seeing Bards with no clothes on."

She saw a mischievous sparkle in Cadvan's eye and suspected he was about to say something outrageous, but to her relief he thought better of it. "You get used to it quickly," he said. "But if you want the baths all to yourself, just before noon is a very quiet time."

"I feel very ... untravelled," she said. "Everything is stranger than I expected, somehow. But as soon as I saw Pellinor, I felt it was my home... Maybe that's the strangest thing. I was never here before."

"It is the greatest School of Making in Annar," said Cadvan. "You feel a tug of kinship, perhaps. Home is more than a birthplace. And sometimes a birthplace cannot be a home."

"But where you're born is always home," she said. "Maybe you can have different kinds of home."

"And maybe you can have none," he said. Selmana didn't know how to answer the bleakness she saw suddenly in his eyes. But now they had met the others, and walked together across the Inner Circle, chatting idly. Selmana braced herself for the ordeal of dining with the First Bard. She was very nervous; there would be important Bards there, she was sure, and she would probably knock over some exquisite glassware, or spill a plate on the floor, or say something stupid in her embarrassment. Dernhil caught her eye and smiled reassuringly as they entered Milana's dining room, where the Bards already seated at the table rose to greet them.

Selmana caught her breath at the beauty of the room. In the centre was a circular table of a wood so dark it was almost black, inlaid with curving patterns in mother of pearl, which she recognized as charms for good appetite and fellowship. The walls were hung with plain hangings of gold, and above them on the ceiling was a painting of fruits and flowers. Bard lamps shaped like lilies filled the room with a warm light.

Selmana thought that Milana's face was drawn, as if she concealed a deep weariness, and she wondered briefly what had happened in the last hour to carve the shadows under her eyes. To her relief, there were only two other Bards present: Dorn of Pellinor and Enkir of Il Arunedh. Dorn was tall and black-haired, with the dark skin and eyes of the Pilanel people, and wore a neatly trimmed beard. Selmana studied him curiously as she was introduced, although she tried not to stare. Nelac had told her a little of Dorn's history during one of their long, rambling conversations.

There were rules all Minor Bards learned as children, which were taught by rote as unbending rules of the Light. Selmana had chanted the Twelve Codes in the classroom from her first day in Lirigon. They were listed in the *Paur Libridha*, written by Maninaë when he founded the Schools of Annar to defend the Light against the return of the Great Silence. The First Code was that all who wished to learn must be taught. Some restricted this law to include only Bards, but Nelac had told

Selmana that it meant anybody, whether they had the Speech or not: the knowledge of the Schools was for everyone, not just for the few. Some Bards, Nelac had said, sought to restrict this law even further, claiming that only Annaren Bards should be taught Annaren lore. He had then told her of the debate that had broken out when the young Dorn had knocked proudly on the gates of Pellinor, demanding as a *Dhillarearën* that he be taught the lore of the Bards.

Dorn still spoke with an accent, and occasionally formed his sentences oddly, but when he arrived at Pellinor two decades before he had scarcely any Annaren, and was forced to use the Speech in every communication with other Bards. Inghalt, who taught the ways of the Speech to the Minor Bards in Lirigon, had been in Pellinor at that time, and he and some others had protested at his admission, even after Dorn demonstrated his mastery of several Bardic charms.

"Inghalt said that even if Dorn had the Speech, it was corrupted by the primitive magic of the Pilanel," Nelac had told her. "He argued that only those of correct Speech should be admitted into the secrets of Barding. But Milana laughed at Inghalt, and told him that no Barding ought to be secret. She asked him how he knew which Speech was correct and which was not, and he had no answer. So Dorn was admitted into the School. And he has become a formidable scholar of the Reading, and is a member of the First Circle. Inghalt left Pellinor, swearing never to return, and he still bears no fondness for Milana, the more so as Dorn became more distinguished. When she and Dorn declared their troth, he said the First Bard was a slut who had permitted lust to overcome her love for the Light."

The story had shocked Selmana, not least because of the disrespect towards a First Bard. "But why would he hate Dorn, just because he is from a different people?" she had asked.

Nelac shrugged. "Perhaps he fears him," he said. "Many

Bards distrust the Pilanel people, for no good reason that I can understand. The Speech, alas, is no guarantee of wisdom. Bards can have power, and be respected for that, and yet have little insight."

Selmana frowned. "I suppose that's why he's such a boring teacher," she said. "I have fallen asleep in his classes. *Twice*."

"He is certainly a disappointed man," said Nelac dryly. "And yet, like so many, he is the major architect of his own unhappiness. Those who have no generosity in their hearts seldom perceive it in others."

Dorn greeted Selmana kindly, as an equal, and she immediately warmed to him. She wasn't so sure of Enkir of Il Arunedh, who was placed opposite her. She could feel Enkir's power from across the table, stern and austere. He was old, as old as Nelac, thin as straw and tall, his long white hair sweeping back from a broad forehead. She felt abashed as his gaze swept indifferently across her, as if she were of no importance, and settled on Cadvan. A deep disdain flooded through Enkir's features.

"I had hoped our paths would never cross again," he said to Cadvan.

"Sometimes fate is unkind," Cadvan answered, his voice as cold as Enkir's. "For which all of us are sorry."

"Shall we put our personal differences aside?" Milana's voice, sharp and authoritative, cut across the table. "I know you two share little love, but to be frank, that is beside the point. I value both of you, and we need the Knowing that each of you can offer in this present pass."

Enkir inclined his head to Milana, acknowledging her rebuke. "My apologies for any impoliteness. But this young man brings with him some bad memories." Enkir's eyes were a very pale blue, and as he turned to answer Milana, Selmana thought they were curiously empty. "And if I am not mistaken, these memories are not the finished story that we thought they were, but only the beginning of a struggle that, thanks to this young man's carelessness and arrogance, we may yet lose." He turned back to Cadvan. "I do you the courtesy of disbelieving that you serve the Dark," he said. "But I do not, either, believe that you are worthy of the Light."

Cadvan didn't answer, although Selmana saw how his lips tightened. She thought he would leave the table, but Nelac clasped his shoulder, staying him.

"I remember being told that I was not worthy of the Light," Dorn said, breaking the silence. "It is a hard thing. By my reckoning, whatever wrongs Cadvan of Lirigon has committed are accounted by his penitence, and his service since to the Light. Who is to say that Kansabur returned only by his agency? Do you believe the Dark wouldn't have found a way? Cadvan is unfortunate in being the means. You cannot tell me that the Hull Likod would not have found another, if Cadvan had not served. And who is to say they might have acted differently, had they been in Cadvan's place? The wiles and stratagems of the Dark can be too obscure even for the wise to perceive."

Enkir snorted audibly, but made no reply. "I thank you, Dorn, for those fair words," said Nelac. "And now the courtesies are done, perhaps I can avail myself of this excellent wine?"

Milana smiled and filled Nelac's glass. The housemaster, a Bard called Ilien, brought in several covered serving plates and opened them with a flourish, and a cloud of steam floated up to the ceiling. Selmana's mouth filled with water: she hadn't eaten since their brief stop at noon, hours before, and she was ravenous. She recognized few of the dishes, and Dorn named them as he passed them to her. There was mountain trout baked in almond and rose sauce, and mashed neats' tongues in verjuice and butter and wine, and pork in a sauce of pomegranate and herbs, and spinach with sweet spices. They seemed very exotic to Selmana, used to the less highly flavoured cooking of Lirhan, but she thought they were delicious. She concentrated on eating, while the other Bards talked generally around her.

When the sweetmeats were brought in, Dorn poured out a light wine, as golden as summer, which he said was a specialty of the vineyards of Pellinor. By now, after the frosty beginning, the Bards had relaxed. Enkir had smiled once or twice and had even deigned to notice Selmana, although he still addressed Cadvan only with the iciest civility.

"Now, my friends, we have matters to discuss," said Milana, leaning back in her chair. "Firstly, Enkir, I want you to hear Nelac out on the question of scrying…"

Enkir's nostrils pinched white, and the genial effects of the meal seemed to evaporate instantly. "To force me to be scried is a monstrous impertinence, at best," he said. "There is absolutely no question of my allegiance to the Light. None. You know it, Milana."

"No one is suggesting that you be forced," said Milana. "For my part, I have myself been scried, in this past hour. I wouldn't ask anything of you that I wouldn't demand of myself."

"I do not question your allegiance any more than I do mine," said Nelac. "I question none here. And yet even I was forced to dig this thing out of me, and I did not know it was there. I am almost certain that Bashar was similarly afflicted, and that this is why the Dark could destroy her. How can we risk such a breach in our protection?"

Enkir began to say something, and then seemed to think better of it. "Some are stronger than others," he said. "I sense no diminution in my Knowing, as you described. I feel no blurring of my power. I see absolutely no need for scrying. After all, Calis escaped this blight, yes? And I assume that you did, Milana?" Milana nodded. "It seems that only the weaker among us were afflicted."

"It had nothing to do with weakness," said Cadvan, his eyes

kindling with anger. "It occurs to me that those who suffered this were closest to the centre of the mending. Me, and Nelac, and Bashar. And, as I recall, you…"

Again Enkir snorted. Selmana, watching, thought that she disliked him very much. She wondered why the other Bards treated him with such respect. He was certainly a powerful mage, but she decided, looking covertly between Nelac and Enkir, that Nelac was the stronger. Where Enkir crackled with magery, Nelac's power sat within him, a glow that had no need to show itself. She reminded herself that good people were not always nice.

"No one here is saying that you should be forced into a scrying," Milana was saying. "We are not the Dark. But I wish you would consider it, Enkir. It would be wise to do it, rather than to be sorry later."

"I am offended that you trust my self-knowledge so little," said Enkir. "As I told you, I feel no sense of unease in any of my powers, such as others here have described. I would tell you if I did, and if it were so, I would submit to be scried, however distasteful I find the idea."

"There is no need for offence," said Dorn quietly. "And none is intended."

There was a short silence, and then Milana said, "I would rather be certain. But I will defer to your judgement on this, Enkir. You have earned our trust, and I don't doubt your Knowing is as you say."

Enkir nodded, mollified. The discussion was dropped, and instead turned to Selmana. She had had little part in the conversation over dinner, partly from shyness and partly from hunger.

"Selmana, Minor Bard," said Milana. "You are a puzzle indeed. What is your part in all this?"

The gaze of the Bards turned thoughtfully on her. Selmana stared back, refusing to drop her eyes. She wasn't some kind of curious object, to be prodded and examined.

"I don't know," she said. "Things just started happening to me. I didn't ask for it to happen."

"But why would the Dark be interested in you?" said Enkir. She felt the flash of his perception needling her mind and shifted uncomfortably in her chair. "You have no especial Gift, it seems to me."

"That's where you're wrong," said Dorn. "She is clearly a Maker of great promise. But she also has the Sight. That may be dismissed by the Bards of Annar, but among the *Dhillarearën* of my people, those who have the Sight are honoured."

Enkir leaned back in his chair, his hands clasped. "My understanding is that it's little more than a primitive intuition, cruder by far than the perceptions of Barding," he said. "It's a virtue, is it not, of village witches?"

Selmana thought of Larla, whom Enkir would think of no account, and bit back a retort. "Ceredin had the Sight too," she said. "And she said the Bone Queen needed our blood to come fully into this World."

"Selmana indeed has unique abilities," said Nelac. "My understanding is that the Speech and the Sight seldom co-exist in the same person, and yet they do in Selmana and, it seems, they did in Ceredin. You are also forgetting Selmana's ability to step bodily between the Circles. I never heard of anyone who could do such a thing."

"The Elidhu are said to be able to do this," said Enkir, his eyebrows bristling. "I'll be frank: the tale of this young Bard's dealings with an Elidhu disturbs me greatly. Long have we feared the return of the Elidhu to Annar. It seems to me another deep stratagem of the Dark."

"Whoever she was, she had nothing to do with the Dark, and she wasn't treacherous," said Selmana. "She rescued me." She sounded sulky, even to her own ears, like a child being rebuked by her elders, impotent against their more articulate judgements.

Enkir was wrong, wrong. She thought, with a pang of guilt, that perhaps she ought to tell the Bards about her dream on the road to Pellinor, but again she rebelled at the thought. She would not expose Anghar to the cold eyes of Enkir.

"Do not be injured by our questioning," said Milana gently. "I realize it must be painful. We have to look hard at what we know, in order to think what to do." She smiled, her eyes full of understanding, and Selmana swallowed and nodded, a little comforted. She felt hot and ungracious in the gaze of all these sober Bards.

Enkir was still frowning. "There is too much that is not of the Light for my liking," he said. "Too much is unknown. We do not know what agencies these powers effect. The Elidhu are lawless and untamed, and they do not love the Light."

"Perhaps there is reason for that," said Dorn. "That doesn't make the Elidhu the servants of evil. Perhaps we need to widen our thought, and think again about what we assume. There is no ban against the Elidhu in the *Paur Libridha*."

"It is foolish to believe that the Light holds the sum of all knowledge," said Dernhil. "There are many kinds of Knowing."

"The Light is the highest Knowing, taking the best of knowledge and sifting out that which misleads us into shadows," said Enkir sharply. "That is beyond argument. It is what we were bound to, when we were all instated as Bards." Nelac glanced at him, as if he would take issue, but said nothing. "In any case, perhaps we take too much notice of the fancy of one who, after all, is little more than a child."

"It wasn't a fancy!" said Selmana hotly. She almost added, *And I'm not a child!* but it sounded petty. To someone of Enkir's age, two centuries or more, she could be nothing else. Yet Nelac, who was at least as old as Enkir, had never scorned her because she was young.

"If it were a mere fancy," said Nelac mildly, "it doesn't

explain how Selmana vanished, nor how she was momently woven into the charm of mending, nor how she could be seen in both the Shadowplains and the World at once, before she disappeared."

There was a short silence, and then Milana spoke. "It seems clear to me that Enkir is correct in this, that there are other wills at work here, besides the Dark and the Light," she said. "And we know that the Bone Queen's reign wounded many more than just Bards. Perhaps, Enkir, she is remembered and feared by others, who might aid us against her. I agree with Dernhil: we dismiss other Knowings at our peril."

"If that is so, how should we best use her?" Enkir studied Selmana speculatively, and she suddenly felt cold. "I am reluctant to employ such powers in crisis, not knowing what they are."

"We do not *use* anyone in our struggles," said Milana, an edge to her voice. "That is not our way."

"Kansabur, even diminished, is a formidable foe," said Enkir. "And what of Likod? I do not doubt that he is a Hull. Surely it is clear that this is part of a much larger plan? It's true we need help wherever we can find it. Even, it seems, if it must be stolen from the Dark itself. If Cadvan hadn't known the spell that Likod was bringing down on Lirigon, even now it would be in ruins, laid waste by the Shika. And it was sorcery that struck down Kansabur in Jouan."

"I cannot think that is good," said Cadvan, leaning forward, his face troubled.

To Selmana's surprise, Enkir laughed. "The Dark, worsted by its own tools!" he said. "If the thought burdens you, Cadvan, then you are rightly punished. Those who deal with the Dark will bear the scar always. Each spell you have spoken will have stained your magery. This is why the doom is exile. I think it is a just doom."

"Perhaps it is," said Cadvan. "And perhaps I am simply a

sacrifice on the altar of your purity."

"Mercy is not the aim of the Light," said Enkir.

"What is, then?" said Nelac softly.

"Justice."

"Yet wisdom is the meeting of justice and compassion," said Nelac. "Be not so quick to dismiss the claims of mercy."

Enkir met Nelac's gaze, and it seemed to Selmana that they wrestled in thought, although neither of them moved or spoke. At last Enkir put up his hands and looked away. "I have no desire to quarrel with you, Nelac. Of course all judgements of the Light are complex. That isn't my point. I respect Milana's decision to welcome Cadvan, and even see her reasons, although I disagree. For all that, we are no clearer about what we should do next."

"What's clear to me is that we must banish the Bone Queen," said Milana. "And now, rather than later."

"Easily said," said Cadvan. "But not so easily done. We have already failed once."

XXXIII

MILANA climbed the stone stairway that wound inside the walls of the Singing Hall and stepped out onto the arched walkway that ran beneath its vast copper dome. She huddled her cloak close against the cold and took a deep breath. She often came here when her thoughts were restless. From this height she could look over the Pellinor valley as it stretched back to the embrace of the mountains, which loomed black and shrouded on the horizon. She could see the yellow trembling lights of villages and farms, small and isolated on the valley flanks and gathering in clusters along the dim grey ribbon of the River Pel. Silently she named each village: Pilan, Sher, Westban, Ashkin...

She had walked the paths of this valley all her long life. She had been to every village, to visit friends, or to learn some new detail of crafting; to teach children their letters, or to heal sickness, or to arbitrate disputes. She had made the spring blessing of increase, when Bards sang the Tree of Light into the dawn sky, lifting its white branches so they swelled with golden blossoms that opened and let fall their glowing petals onto the dark earth of the fields and woods. She had danced the funeral rites in every village square, to comfort the lost soul and set its feet on its journey across the Long Path of Stars to the Gates. She had broken bread in these houses, and shared their joys and sorrows. She was Pellinor's First Bard and that was her duty and her love. No one in this valley went hungry, and no one needing succour or seeking knowledge was turned away. That was the Way of the Light, as Milana had known and lived it all her life.

Tonight she was deeply troubled. The arrival of the Bards hadn't surprised her; after the news from Lirigon, she had expected that they might seek refuge in Pellinor. But she felt it as an echo of doom, as one step closer towards the dark end that Dorn had seen in his dreams. She couldn't shake the sorrow this loosened in her breast; even if they staved back the evil now, even if they succeeded in banishing the Bone Queen utterly from the bright margins of the World, Pellinor would fall and all its beauty would be lost for ever. It seemed to Milana that the decision she made now spelled out the first words of that sorrowful tale. And yet, no matter how deeply she searched her conscience, she could see no other choice. To turn her face away from a darkening of the Light out of a cowardly fear for her own skin would be a greater wrong still.

Night deepened over Pellinor. One by one, the lights in the valley went out. From where she stood, her listening open, Milana could hear a rising wind rustling through the meadows, the cough of a fox, a plover calling. The cold, clear skies of the past two days closed in, and a heavy cloud rolled down into the valley, blotting out the stars. She watched, her brow creasing. Were there deeper shadows there than the pure darkness of night? The cloud muffled sound as it flowed towards the School, blurring her listening, but she thought she heard a faint howl that belonged to no creature that she knew. She stood for a long time, alert and wary, but she heard nothing more, and at last she shivered, feeling the cold seep through her cloak, and made her way to her bedchamber.

Cadvan of Lirigon. Cadvan woke and lay a while in bed, studying the ceiling of his room, which was painted with a pattern of birds in flight. All of them were birds that lived in the Fesse of

Pellinor: ducks, ospreys, eagles and hawks, pigeons and owls, warblers and blackbirds and finches, and many others. He idly identified the different species, reflecting that the Bard who had painted this room had clearly been a passionate observer as well as a painter of rare skill: each kind was meticulously depicted in every detail. He could name almost all of them.

He thought then of his own name. *Cadvan of Lirigon.* When Milana had spoken his Bard name the day before, Cadvan's heart had jolted in his breast: he had never thought to hear himself addressed in that way ever again. For the past few years he had been *Cadvan, formerly of Lirigon,* or merely Cadvan, of Nowhere: a disgraced exile, marred by the Dark. But Milana had broken the ban of the First Circle of Lirigon, first by welcoming him into her School as a Bard, and then by giving him back his title. She had spoken clearly and deliberately, and there had been a magery in her words, as if she uttered his Truename. All Bards understood the power of naming, but Cadvan had never felt it so intimately. With those words, Milana had restored him as a Bard of the Light.

And here he lay, in a comfortable bed with sheets of finely woven linen, in a room made beautiful by some gifted artist of Pellinor, as if he had never been banished, as if he were not outlawed. Milana had coolly undone that shame. He knew that she did so because of Nelac's trust in him, but he was fiercely grateful. It had helped him to bear Enkir's needling the evening before, and stilled his tongue when he would have taken foolish exception. He and Enkir had never liked each other. Cadvan couldn't help but respect him, as a deep scholar and a mage of rare power. He wondered if it was impossible that Kansabur had hidden something of herself in Enkir. Nothing was impossible, if even Nelac had taken that hurt … and yet, thinking over it as fairly as he could, Cadvan thought it was very unlikely.

When Enkir had challenged Milana the night before, claiming that his allegiance to the Light was beyond question, Cadvan had felt no doubt that he was speaking the truth. Enkir's magery had blazed with a fierce flame in the mindmeld when they had worked together to banish Kansabur, pure as diamond. No shadow could find a home there, surely. Part of Cadvan – an unworthy voice, he acknowledged to himself – wished that Enkir had been tainted. To have the Dark clinging inside his soul would humble him, and if ever a Bard needed humbling, it was Enkir.

But, for all his faults, Cadvan didn't doubt Enkir's honesty: he was severe, pitilessly so, but no one had ever known him to be less than utterly truthful. If he said he sensed no diminution in his Knowing, it must be the case. The man was swift-tempered, and he wielded his power with an inflexible will, but no one could be less apt to the wiles of the Dark. If there was little kindliness in his judgements, they were also untempered by self-interest or malice, and the stern passion of his long devotion to the Light was written on his face. Nelac had once said, after a stinging session with the First Circle of Lirigon during which Enkir had told Cadvan exactly what he thought of him, that if Enkir judged others harshly, he reserved the sternest judgements for himself. Nelac had also said, with an ironic glance, that perhaps they disliked each other because they were too alike.

Cadvan sighed and dragged himself out of his warm bed, thinking that if Enkir was a vision of his future as an old Bard, he should probably travel back to Jouan and learn mining. He dressed slowly, enjoying the thick carpet beneath his toes, the whisper of silk underclothes against his skin, the warm air of the heated chamber. Milana certainly ensured the comfort of her guests... He was reluctant to leave: while he was alone in his room, he could indulge the fantasy that he was merely visiting, a Bard like any other Bard. But that's what it was: an indulgence. He squared his shoulders and made his way downstairs.

He found Dernhil in the dining room, where he was piling a plate with green salad and white cheese and freshly baked rye bread, dark and soft as earth. "You'd better hurry, if you want to eat," Dernhil said. "I have a rare appetite this morning."

"It's the mountain air," said Cadvan, taking a plate and doing the same. "That, and days of short vittles and hard ground."

"I've had more than my share of that these past months," Dernhil answered. "When all this is over, I'm planning to retire to Gent, where I'll not stir from my rooms except for meals."

"It wouldn't be unpleasant to stay here," said Cadvan, through a mouthful of bread. "The ceiling of my bedchamber is some sort of masterpiece."

"It is Pellinor," said Dernhil. "It's to be expected."

They finished their meal, and then, as neither Nelac nor Selmana were to be seen, they decided to go for a stroll. Outside the door, Dernhil stopped and looked across the Inner Circle. A pale winter sunshine lent the paved stone a fugitive gold, and glanced off a fine statue in the middle. It was of Maninaë, when he had returned from his journey beyond the Gates, to the Empyrean: he was on one knee, his face raised to the heavens, his long hair falling down his back in graceful curves of stone. One hand touched the ground, and the other was stretched before him, empty, and on his face was an expression that was at once calm and filled with unassuageable yearning.

"I've always loved that carving," said Dernhil. "It seems right to me that Ilborc chose to depict Maninaë at that moment: not in his triumph, striking down the Nameless One, but instead with the sorrow of knowledge and acceptance, understanding his mortality at last…"

Cadvan glanced at him. "Ilborc understood human sadness,"

he said. "Few have surpassed him in the art of sculpture."

"Aye. His work is one reason why I love coming to this School." They began to walk across the Circle. "Cadvan, I was thinking about our discussion last night. It troubles me that we reached no firm decision."

"It was very inconclusive. But at least Enkir has been brought to Milana's way of thinking."

"Most unwillingly, it must be said. Do you believe we can trust him? You know him better than I do."

"I will never enjoy his company," Cadvan said. "But, yes, I believe we can trust him. And he is a formidable ally in the struggle with the Dark."

"I don't doubt that." Dernhil walked a few paces, frowning. "But still… Something in my heart misgives me. Why did he so object to being scried?"

"No Bard is willingly scried," said Cadvan. "It's a hard thing."

"As we both know." Dernhil smiled briefly at Cadvan and then shook his head. "Ah, it's of no matter. I dislike his arrogance. It's likely nothing more than that." He walked on restlessly. "I'm wondering if we did right to come to Pellinor."

"None of us can return to Lirigon," said Cadvan. "Where else could we go?"

"I know. But I feel at a loss again. It was good, in Jouan, knowing what to do and who to fight. Now I just feel like we're back poking sticks at fog."

"Do you not feel the Dark gathering?" said Cadvan. "I do, all the time. It's like a pressure in my mind. It went away for a couple of days after Jouan, and it was such a relief. But now it's coming back, like a storm under the horizon. And it's looking for us. The Dark will want revenge."

Dernhil turned his face away and was silent for a time. "I sense it, but vaguely," he said. "A distant threat. Perhaps it's simply what I wish were the case. I don't doubt your Knowing,

Cadvan. Not for a moment."

They walked on without speaking for a while.

"Do you think the Dark seeks us here?" asked Dernhil.

Cadvan shrugged. "It wouldn't be hard to guess where we were heading, after Jouan. I don't doubt Likod is looking for us. Word will be out soon that we are in Pellinor, in any case. Milana scorns to hide from Lirigon: she is making her disavowal of the Circle's judgement very plain. Which is why it's encouraging that Enkir sides with us, whatever his disapproval."

"He did say that he didn't believe that you were a servant of the Dark," said Dernhil. "Which, coming from him, is some concession. It will force the Circle to think again."

"Aye. I'm worse than that: a failed servant of the Light." Cadvan laughed, but there was a bitterness in it. "Sadly, he is right in that."

"That's where I differ with Enkir," said Dernhil. "In fact, I think he is completely wrong. I saw what you did in Jouan."

"Yes, I struck down the Bone Queen, and saved us from what might have been a terrible death," said Cadvan. "But employing the Black Arts is hardly an argument for my being a Bard of the Light."

"No," said Dernhil, and now he was smiling. "I wasn't thinking of that, although you know very well you made that sorcery for good reason, and you can't tell me that it didn't cost you more than you will admit. I was thinking of young Hal, and how you helped the villagers there. Jonalan told us what you did after the explosion in the mine. They love you for good reason, Cadvan. And that can only be the work of the Light."

Again a silence fell between them, and they made their way back, both wrapped in thought. On the threshold of the guesthouse, Dernhil looked up at the sky. "I think our little bit of sunshine will soon pass," he said. "I smell a cold rain on the wind."

Cadvan clasped his shoulder. "Thank you, Dernhil," he said.

Dernhil's eyes lit up. "What did I do?"

"For what you said before. It comforts me."

"Good." Dernhil opened the door, bowing Cadvan before him. "You are very awkward to comfort. I've been trying ever since I decided that I liked you after all."

Cadvan smiled. "I warned you I was made of spikes."

On their return, the housemaster told Cadvan and Dernhil that Milana awaited them in the music room. This was a large, comfortable chamber on the ground floor. On one wall was a mural of a wintry landscape, where a dozen wolves with white pelts played beneath a copse of bare trees. The wide windows were hung with curtains of blue Thoroldian silk, and looked out over the Inner Circle, where the first drops of rain were beginning to patter down.

Everywhere was evidence of the room's use. In one corner there was an elaborately carved wooden harp, of the style that were played in the far north of Annar, and many other instruments, hand drums and zithers, flutes and rebecs, were placed on a shelf on the far wall. Cadvan felt an itch in his fingers and thought of his own lyre. How long since he had taken it from its case? He had packed it, as he always did, even when he went to Jouan, but it was so long since he had played that he wondered if he had forgotten the skill.

Milana and Nelac were seated on a couch, deep in conversation, and the two turned when Cadvan and Dernhil entered. "Selmana is still abed, I'm told," said Milana. "I'm loath to disturb her; I know how it feels to return to a warm bed after a hard journey! She is yet young and needs her sleep. But in any case, I wanted to speak privately to you three."

"About Selmana?" asked Dernhil, sitting down beside her.

"Yes," said Milana. "Nelac knows her best, but you all have

spent time in her company. Do you think she has been completely frank with you about this meeting with the Elidhu?"

Cadvan looked surprised. "I've no reason to think that she has hidden anything," he said. "What should she conceal? She didn't even know she spoke to an Elidhu."

"I've no doubt that she did speak to one," said Milana. "Enkir is right: we know so little of these folk, and although they have sometimes intervened in human affairs, they have not been seen in Annar for a long age. Do you think her bewitched?"

Nelac shook his head. "Not bewitched," he said. "But I think something has changed in her since her vision in Jouan. She is like a burning glass: through her, I could see the presence of shadows I couldn't otherwise perceive. But now, it's as if that glass is filled with a blinding light." He paused. "I will say that I sense no trace of the Dark in her."

"I see none either, but I confess I am troubled," said Milana. "In any case, whether it portends harm or no, I think this vision of hers must remain secret, or else other Bards will come to distrust her."

"She seems to me like a young girl in love for the first time," Dernhil said slowly. "Perhaps that is a kind of bewitchment."

"In love, you think?" Nelac leaned back on the couch and stared at the ceiling.

"I only said, *seems*," said Dernhil. "But that light, I have perceived it too, and it is tremulous and joyous and unafraid. It is a beautiful thing."

"If she has indeed fallen in love with an Elidhu, then she is imperilled," said Nelac.

"How do you know that it means peril?"

"Dernhil, don't be obtuse. She might as well have fallen in love with a wildfire, or a storm. Even if it intends her no harm, it might destroy her. Immortals do not understand death."

"Who among us knows what immortals understand?"

Dernhil stood up and walked restlessly to the window. The rain had now swept in and was beating on the panes, and the trees of the Inner Circle thrashed in the wind. "Why must we always fear what we don't know?"

"It is well to be cautious, rather than to be sorry later," said Milana. "But you speak as if you understand something of this girl. Tell me what you perceive."

"In Selmana?" Dernhil turned around and leaned against the wall. "I see what all of us do, I think. A Bard who has the passion of Making in her. She is young, but she is wise beyond her years, beyond even her own understanding of herself. She is stronger than she knows."

Milana met his eyes. "Dorn says much the same thing," she said. "He thinks she is key to this crisis, although his Knowing will not tell him why. The Pilanel do not distrust the Elidhu as Bards do, although they fear their power." She hesitated. "It is true, is it not, that Selmana and Ceredin are cousins?" Nelac nodded. "Dorn also told me that the Pilanel say that those with the Sight carry the blood of the Elidhu."

Nelac's eyebrows rose. "That is not something I have heard before," he said. "But it wouldn't be unlikely."

"Both of them were born with strong Gifts," said Dernhil. "And both had the Sight."

"Neither are from a Barding family," Nelac said. "A long line of smiths and cheesemakers, if I recall rightly. Few of us know our lineages, and almost no one can trace back through the Great Silence."

"It's said that there are people of Elidhu blood in the north," said Milana. "The minstrels of Pellinor Fesse have many songs about women and men who disappeared into the mountains, lured by the beauty of an Elidhu, and who returned many years later leading a child by the hand…"

"No Bard songs?" said Dernhil.

"Bards wouldn't sing of such things, even if they were true," said Milana. "Such stories became too shameful, after the Great Silence. But Dorn has made a study of the Elementals."

Dernhil cast a speculative glance at Milana. "Has Dorn any thought on who Selmana's Elidhu might be? She would give no name."

"Names don't matter to the Elidhu in the same way they matter to us. They simply are, and need not call themselves anything," said Milana. "My guess is that she is the Moonchild, who is spoken of as one of the Elidhu who came to Afinil. But there are countless Elidhu who had nothing to do with Bards, and are not spoken of in the records. It could be any one of them."

"The Moonchild?" said Cadvan. "That one we call Ardina?"

Milana nodded. Cadvan thought she seemed reluctant to speak further about the Elementals. She turned the question. "I don't know what the castle was, that Selmana spoke of," she said. "I know of no such place in any tale. But it seems to me that Selmana saw the Gates of the Empyrean."

Again the Bards were silent. "These are deep waters," said Nelac. "They go beyond the knowledge of Light and Dark."

"Aye," said Milana. "There is much at stake here, and it is vital we move rightly. But I feel clearer now, after speaking to you. Selmana must be part of what we do. Enkir speaks strongly against it, but I think he is mistaken. If she has caught the notice of an Elidhu, then we must include her."

"And what are we to do?"

"I fear an attack, and soon," said Milana. "My first thought is to defend Pellinor, but we must also seek to destroy or banish the Bone Queen. This is the other thing I wished to discuss with you." Milana fixed her eyes on Nelac. "I want to be very clear about what it is we face. If Kansabur is divided, each part is weaker, as we all know. And it seems to me that some of these divisions are large, and some are small: they are not equal parts. At least one has been destroyed completely, after the scrying of Cadvan and Nelac. And at least one is powerful enough to appear to you in Jouan. We don't know if she has gathered all of herself together, or if she remains divided."

The others nodded.

"The longer we wait, the more she can re-collect herself and arm against us. So to strike sooner rather than later is our aim. The Dark must know already that you three are in Pellinor and even now I feel it gathers against us. I have set Bards to watch through the valley, and they will alert us if there is any sign, even the most trivial."

"You are ahead of me, then," said Cadvan. "I was going to urge you to do just that."

"I must look to my people. I hope they will take no harm from this, but they must be warned so they may prepare themselves for any conflict." She paused, and Cadvan fleetingly saw a deep sadness in her face.

"You must take special care, I think," said Nelac. "Likod would especially seek to destroy you. And if he could break even Bashar…"

Milana met his eyes, her mouth set in a stern line. "I have taken thought of that. I may venture myself in this desperate game without conscience, I think. I am not so certain about drawing the malice of the Dark upon others, but I see no choice." She was silent a moment. "Before even you came here, I sent a rebuke to Coglint of Lirigon, taking issue with the judgements of the First Circle. I have sent bird news this morning of your arrival here, and of my intention to recognize each of you as Bards of the Light, in no way complicit in the murder of Bashar. They will hear of that even as we speak. I am hoping that Pellinor's defiance means that the enmity of the Dark is turned from Lirigon towards us."

Dernhil, watching her from across the room, drew in a sharp breath. "I see your gamble, my lady," he said. "And I salute you."

"It is a gamble," Milana said. "I hope with all my heart I make the right throw." She swept her gaze across the three Bards. "Is there anything in what I have said with which you disagree? Or anything you would like to add?"

"No," said Cadvan. "I have felt the will of the Dark, as a constant and growing oppression, since we left Jouan. And I wonder, since wards did not serve in Lirigon, how to protect Pellinor against an incursion like that we suffered there. Likod can step past any wards we place, and we can't trace how he did it."

"It seems to me that he stepped between the Circles," said Nelac. "Perhaps even as Selmana does."

"Then we need eyes in the Shadowplains as much as we need them in Pellinor," said Milana.

"You are forgetting the Abyss," said Dernhil.

"But the Abyss is locked."

"I think it may not be." Dernhil looked down at his hands. "I am no great scholar of the Circles, and I certainly know less than any of you. But why do you say the Abyss is locked? Didn't Ceredin say that all the Circles were bleeding, each into the others?"

"Yes," said Milana. "But the Abyss isn't as the Shadowplains. It is of a different nature, and closes in upon itself with a great weight. When the Shika are summoned forth, they may only remain for a short time before they are drawn back inside it. Kansabur could emerge from the Abyss only because she is also of the World."

Nelac was frowning. "That is true, but what if the force of the Abyss were reversed? What if the weight that spins it closed should suddenly force it open? Isn't that what sorcery itself does, in a very small way?" He glanced enquiringly at Cadvan.

"I suppose that would be possible," Cadvan answered. "It is indeed the basic principle of sorcery. But I can't imagine how the forces of the Abyss could be wholly reversed. And if it should happen, it would rip apart everything we know, both Light and Dark, down to the smallest particle, and send us all howling into emptiness. Even the Dark couldn't desire that."

"But perhaps a powerful Hull, say, Likod, could pull on those forces sufficiently to step bodily in and out of the Abyss, without destroying himself?"

Cadvan's gaze turned inward. "Perhaps," he said at last. "I can't say it would be impossible. But I know of no spell that would do such a thing. Admittedly, my knowledge is limited."

"Then we can't dismiss the chance. And how would we guard against it?"

"I don't know." Cadvan raised his hands in a gesture of frustration. "I feel like Enkir. There is too much that is imponderable."

"We must work with what we do know," said Milana calmly. "If we can't have any warning of Likod appearing among us, even if we watch the Shadowplains, we must be prepared for the chance that he will. That is all. And perhaps we can make a trap for him, as you trapped the Bone Queen."

Cadvan flinched. "I have no desire to use more sorcery," he said.

"The Light can make traps as ingenious as any of the Dark. We are dangerous too." Milana rose to leave, smoothing down her robes. She now seemed brisk and decided. "I'll take my leave of you. I've called the Circle of Pellinor to meet in the hour before noon, and we'll speak of all these things. I wish to consult with my colleagues before we speak again."

Nelac rose and bowed. "We are, of course, at your disposal," he said. "And we are deeply grateful for your help."

"It isn't only my decision. Pellinor has been behind me in

every choice I have made, and especially in revoking your out-lawing and the ban of Lirigon on Cadvan," said Milana. "It is no small thing for a School to undo the ruling of another, but that is the measure of our disquiet. And we don't seek only to help Lirigon. I fear for Pellinor."

Dernhil looked searchingly at the First Bard. "If you fear for this School, then I am sure there is good reason," he said.

Milana hesitated, and then met Dernhil's gaze, her anxiety open. "Dorn has had foredreams," she said. "It is not gener-ally known, although I have told Nelac. I believe that we will be struck soon, and hard. But I trust our wisdom and strength. If Pellinor cannot challenge the might of the Dark, no one can. And even if Pellinor should fall, it is better to fight than to cower and meanly crumble."

She nodded and left the room. Cadvan turned to Nelac, smiling wryly. "Milana of Pellinor is one of the most redoubt-able Bards I have ever met," he said.

"If the measure of courage is how much fear you must overcome, then hers is great indeed," said Dernhil.

"That is the measure," said Nelac soberly. "I hope I can match it. I will not hide from you two that I am very afraid."

Cadvan walked to the window and gazed out over the Inner Circle. The shower had now passed, violent but swift, and a vagrant sunshine briefly gleamed silver on the wet stone before the sun slid again behind cloud. The sky was steel-grey, with more rain sweeping in from the north. Then his vision seemed to slip: for the blink of an eye, it seemed that he looked out on a ruin, the paving stones blackened as if with flame, weeds creeping across their broken faces, Ilborc's great statue shat-tered and abandoned, strangled with wild ivy. He had barely registered what he saw, when everything was as it had been before. Cadvan clutched the curtain, dizzy and afraid, and looked again. The sunlight was fragile and unreal, a veil over an uncertain world. Pellinor seemed like one of its own paintings seen in some dark future, its colours leached by age, which might at any moment crumble into dust.

XXXIV

S NUG in the blankets of sleep, Selmana thought she was in her mother's house. She had slept for hours and hours, and it felt late. It must be a rest day because no one had woken her, and she had been left to lie abed, warm as a rabbit in its burrow, listening to the friendly sound of rain hammering on the roof. She curled up under the coverlet, enjoying her laziness. Perhaps there would be pancakes for breakfast, hot off the griddle and served with fresh butter and honey. The thought made her realize that she was very hungry and she blinked open her eyes. For an instant she thought she must have dozed off in a meadow, for all she could see were butterflies, clouds of them circling above her in an azure sky that paled to pink at its edges. But, no, they didn't move, they weren't real butterflies. She wasn't in a meadow nor in her mother's house. She was in Pellinor.

She sat up, rubbing her eyes, and snapped on a magelight: her body told her that it must be near noon, but the shutters were still closed and the room was dark. If no one had called her, she reasoned, then she was not needed. And she was glad of the long sleep. She washed briefly, using the jug and basin that waited for her use, and dressed in the warm woollen robes that were folded in a chest by her bed, admiring their fineness. Then she wandered idly over to her window and pulled open the shutters to see the colour of the day.

There was no day outside. There was no night. She knew at once that she was overlooking the endless twilight of the

Shadowplains. She went cold, as if the blood had stilled in her body, and then she slammed the shutters and latched them tight and turned around, leaning against them, breathing hard. Not this, please not this…

She looked around her bedchamber, fighting down her panic. Every other Bard could decide when they wished to step through the Circles. They willed it, and it was so. Why wasn't it so with her? Was there some hidden part of her that worked beyond her conscious thought, or was she at the whim of some other mind, which pulled her this way and that?

She stared blankly at the wall, attempting to think. Whenever she had found herself in the Shadowplains, one thing was constant: it meant that Kansabur was close. Maybe it was some kind of unconscious reflex, like putting out her hands to break a fall. Or maybe someone was protecting her, pulling her through the Circles so that Kansabur couldn't reach her. Was this how Anghar kept her hidden from the Bone Queen? The thought made her less afraid. But even so, being subject to something so utterly beyond her control and will was horrible.

She undid the latch again, her hands trembling, and slowly opened the shutters. The Shadowplains were gone: ordinary daylight streamed through the window. Below her was a courtyard, its paving dark with rain. A stray beam of sunshine slipped through the heavy clouds and fell on the branches of an almond tree, striking the raindrops suspended from its naked fingers so they shone like a string of precious gems. She stared, caught by its beauty, wanting to cry with relief.

She was afraid to turn her back on the window: what if Pellinor vanished again? But she knew she had to find Nelac. She was no longer frightened for herself: instead, she felt a terrible fear mounting inside her for everyone else, for Pellinor, for her friends. At last she braced her shoulders and tore herself away from the window and ran downstairs to the entrance hall, calling for Nelac. To her relief he burst into the corridor almost at once, followed by Cadvan and Dernhil. When he saw her face, he ran up to her and took her hands.

"Kansabur," she said breathlessly. "She's here. She's in Pellinor."

Cadvan was unsettled and wary. He wondered if there was any significance in the strange vision he had seen from the window: it had vanished so swiftly that he thought he must have imagined it. But when he told Nelac and Dernhil, they looked grave.

"Perhaps it begins already," said Nelac.

"But what begins?" said Dernhil impatiently. "What?"

"Something is poised on the lip of disaster," said Cadvan. He shivered. "The past, the future, this world… Maybe we see our end here."

"Perhaps. Or perhaps a beginning," said Nelac.

"I can't tell." Cadvan sat down morosely, his arms crossed, and stared at the wall as if he suspected that it might dissolve into mist before his eyes. "Everything seems very thin, as if we walk on a knife edge, blindly…"

"Milana meets with her Bards," said Nelac. "I wonder how long she will take."

"We just have to wait." Dernhil was pacing the room restlessly. "I don't like waiting."

But they waited, having nothing else to do, until they heard Selmana calling on the stairs. Cadvan felt his pulse thumping in his throat. *It begins…* He ran out after Nelac, who moved even more swiftly than he did. Selmana was standing in the hallway, her face white, her words tumbling over each other as she told Nelac what she had seen from the window of her chamber.

"It must mean that Kansabur is here," she said. "That's what it meant last time, she's there every time it happens, and then

I just step into the Shadowplains. It's like the first time, when I saw the Shadowplains in Lirigon, and I'm so frightened Nelac, I don't want that to happen…"

"Hush now," said Nelac. "We are all four here."

"I wish Anghar were here too," said Selmana. "Where is she? She could make it all go away."

"You mean the Elidhu?" said Dernhil, looking at her oddly.

Selmana realized she had said Anghar's name, and bit her lip. She had hardly known what she was saying. All the fear that had been staved off since Jouan seemed to have rushed back at once, doubled and tripled. "Something has slipped," she said.

The front door opened and all the Bards jumped and turned, each half expecting to see that the Inner Circle had vanished: perhaps the dim slopes of the Shadowplains, or a glimpse of ruins, or a blaze of unseeable light from another dimension beyond imagining. But it was a red-headed Bard, who introduced herself as Kenran, her hand still resting lightly on the door handle, the darkening sky behind her.

"Milana says you had better come now," she said. "It has begun."

As they hurried after Kenran to the Singing Hall, a thin, vicious sleet tore at their cloaks. The weather was coming in fast, and the light retreated in every moment: although it was just past noon, it was already so dark that lamps were lit in the Singing Hall. Its high arched windows blazed ruby and emerald and gold, still and calm in the midst of the rising wind. Cadvan cocked his head; on the edge of his hearing he thought he heard a cry or a wail from some evil throat. He had no sense of Likod at all, or of Kansabur, but all around was the presence of the Dark. There was no focus point: it was a miasma that seemed to be in the very air they breathed, a pressure like despair.

The domed Singing Hall seemed full of people. There were tables set inside, as if for a feast, but they were scattered with scrolls and different kinds of equipment, jugs of water and medhyl. Cadvan blinked: the Hall blazed with the light of magery, which dimmed even the Bard lamps. He saw a ring of forty or so Bards, their faces still with concentration. He almost staggered back with the force of the charm they were weaving: it was a gigantic ward. He realized with astonishment, as he felt around its edges, that it was intended to be set not only about the walls of the School, but the whole valley.

Milana stepped out of a knot of Bards to greet them. "They strike, even as I expected," she said. "But sooner than I hoped. I thought perhaps we had until sunset."

Nelac nodded. "There is a stormbringer among them," he said. "In Lirigon, we wondered if it was brought by an Elemental. But what is the news?"

"A band of wers has attacked the Fesse. I am told by three of the Bards I sent across the valley. But that's not the worst..."

"Wers?" said Cadvan. "Surely they have no real power in daylight?"

"Do you think it will be daylight for long?" Milana gestured towards the windows. "That is no natural storm. There are twenty Bards in the Fesse and they each report to me by mind-touch. In the north it is already dark as midnight, and there are deaths. A woman in Pilan, a child in Labranem..."

Even as she spoke, the keyword of the ward was sung into place, and the pressure of darkness on Cadvan's mind lifted. He breathed out with relief, although the strange sense that Pellinor wasn't quite solid now flooded back, as if the weight of the Dark had concealed its fragility. Ilean, Milana's housemaster, stepped up to her, the light of magery still flickering about him.

"It is done, my lady," he said, in the Speech.

"Good." Her face went blank, as if she were listening to

some inner conversation, and her eyes flew to Ilean. "Ranstum at Pilan tells me the ward has driven back the wers. But he says the darkness is increasing every moment, and there is hail as big as goose eggs."

Ilean nodded soberly. "What should we do next?" he asked.

"We cannot give more help to those out in the Fesse," said Milana. "I pray they are prepared as I told them. Now I wish you all to be vigilant, and to protect the ward. If I am right, the real battle will be fought here." She turned to Nelac. "The storm is on our heads," she said. "But as you see, we are not unprepared. Come."

"Wards may keep back wers," said Cadvan, as they walked quickly towards the Bards gathered in the centre of the hall. "But they will be little protection against what assails us."

"But still, I must give thought to Pellinor," said Milana. "I will not have these people slaughtered by the base servants of the Dark."

"Selmana said something had slipped," said Nelac. "She thinks Kansabur is close."

Milana turned, her face pale. "That's what Dorn said, before he…" Her voice faltered. "Not all of us felt it, but Enkir did," she said. "I do not know what has happened to Dorn. I am hoping you can tell me."

Dorn was with Enkir and some other Bards. He was seated straight and rigid, and Cadvan saw that his eyes were turned up so only the whites showed under his half-closed lids. Then he realized that Dorn's lips were moving, and he was speaking or chanting, his voice barely audible.

"I cannot bring him back," said Enkir, looking up as the others joined the group. He looked pale and shaken. "He is not in the Shadowplains, as far as I can see. And I can't make out what he is saying."

Nelac touched Dorn. His skin was cold and slick, like clay.

"This looks like some kind of haunting," he said. "Did it occur in the Shadowplains?"

"Aye. Though we stayed on the threshold, looking both in and out, as Milana asked us. And then there was a great quake, or so it seemed to me, and a crack opened beneath our feet, and I was thrust out, back into the World, despite all my striving." He met Nelac's eyes. "I do not know what force could treat me with such violence, without any warning," he said.

"And Dorn?" said Cadvan.

"I do not know what happened to him. By the time I recalled myself, he was as you see."

Cadvan leant close to Dorn, putting his ear to his lips. He was muttering fast, in a thin, keening whisper, what sounded like nonsense words, with a strange singsong rhythm. His lips seemed somehow independent of the rest of his face, and the more Cadvan listened, the more he was filled with dread.

"It's some kind of spell, I'm certain," he said, straightening. He put his hands over Dorn's mouth, trying to cease his speaking, but Dorn's lips kept moving against his hand. "We have to stop him."

"I've been trying for some time," said Enkir. "Perhaps, with your superior knowledge of the Dark, you understand how to do this without actually killing him?"

Cadvan took no notice of the edge to Enkir's voice. "I might," he said, "if I knew the spell. But I don't. It's not even in the Black Speech."

"Perhaps it's some Pilanel nonsense," said Enkir.

Cadvan shook his head. "Nay," he said. "It's not Pilanel. I don't recognize the language, but it is a language. Should we gag him, perhaps?"

"We tried that," said another Bard, a thickset blond man called Malgorn. "He kept speaking even though he couldn't move his mouth." He paused. "It was too strange and we took it off."

"Perhaps it isn't a spell," said another. "No magery moves in him."

It was true: if Dorn was weaving a spell, there was no sense of its power. And yet Cadvan felt sure that these were words of power. "Perhaps his magery moves elsewhere," said Cadvan uncertainly. "Not here…"

Selmana was staring at Dorn, her eyes wide. "I don't like it," she said, her voice high. "It's not right. He's not here properly. He's not there, either. He's stuck somewhere between."

Dorn's head snapped round to face Selmana, as if his sightless eyes could see her, and she jumped. His lips still moved, the hoarse whisper tumbling from his mouth. Cadvan heard strange repetitions that wound back on themselves and tangled and then began again. He now was speaking faster.

"Stop him," said Selmana. She couldn't take her eyes from his face, as if something compelled her. "You have to stop him."

Milana had been watching them, her expression veiled. Then her head went up as if she were listening, and Cadvan's eyes turned to her. "Elbaran speaks from Hess," she said, loudly so all the in the Hall could hear her. "She says…" She frowned, listening. "She says the ward is broken there. No, not broken…" She listened again. "Frayed, she says. The ward … dissolves. She says there are many wers, hundreds. They are not attacking the villages. They are running towards Pellinor under the stormcover. They are shaped like lizards, with wings."

She looked about the Hall, her face white. "All of you, except the First Circle: go to the walls and help the Thane's watchers. Keep the ward strong where it is attacked. Wers can die on cold steel, but they bring fear with them. They could win their way into the School without a stroke in its defence, if terror makes our defenders flee…"

The Hall seemed to empty almost at once, in a flurry of Bards reaching for cloaks and swords and setting mageshields.

When the great doors opened, the sound of the storm swept loudly across the Hall, the pounding rain amplified by its high walls. Outside was black, as if it were night, and the Bards were swallowed at once in the darkness. There were only a dozen people left in the centre of the Singing Hall, their faces wan in the edgeless light of the lamps. The doors swung shut on the rain and it seemed suddenly very quiet. The only sound was Dorn's strange chant.

Milana, her stern face suddenly breaking, threw her arms about his neck. "Dorn," she said. "Dorn. Please."

He made no sign that he heard. Now the strange circular chant echoed around the dome and it began to sound as if came from many throats. All the watching Bards shielded themselves. Milana let Dorn go and turned to hide her face. The chant was reaching a climax, but still none of them felt any prickle of sorcery.

"Selmana," said Dernhil. "What do you see?"

"I don't know," she said. Her eyes were still fixed on Dorn's face, as if she were unable to turn away. "You have to stop him."

As she spoke, Dorn's chant rose to a sudden scream, and then ceased. He slumped in his chair and would have fallen to the ground if Nelac had not grasped him. Then he stirred and groaned, and Milana started towards him. He raised his eyes to her face and fainted.

Selmana, released from his sightless gaze, looked about her fearfully. At first everything seemed as it was before. Then she thought the lamps were flickering at the edge of her sight, although when she looked straight at them they were steady, and the floor beneath her feet felt soft and spongy. She thought she might be sick.

"He's not dead," said Milana, crouched beside Dorn, her fingers on his wrist. "But what has happened to him?" She looked at Nelac, her mouth wavering. "I'm afraid, Nelac."

"Indeed, you should be afraid," said a voice behind them. "You have good reason."

Cadvan whirled around so fast he almost fell over. In front of the great doors of the Singing Hall stood Likod. He was dressed as a Bard, in tunic and cloak, but he was in black from head to foot and wore no sign.

"Ah, Cadvan. Of Lirigon, I believe, although this seems uncertain of late." Likod laughed and walked easily towards the Bards. At once every Bard present attacked him with white fire. Such an assault should have destroyed him at once, but the white fire gathered about his head, surrounding him in a blinding halo. Likod didn't even break the rhythm of his steps. His eyes were fixed on Cadvan, who hadn't moved a muscle.

"You can't touch me," said Likod. "I don't doubt you believe that you crushed us in Lirigon. That you thought you found the means to destroy our Queen. How wrong you are. You haven't seen a single finger of our strength." His head thrust forward on his shoulders, like a snake's. "And now you will suffer, Bard," he hissed. "*Traitor*. Thrice traitor."

Cadvan's hand went to his hip, as if it searched for a sword hilt; but he hadn't carried a sword since he was exiled from Lirigon. The Pellinor Bards were still attacking Likod, and the air was hot and bright with the crackle of magery, but still Likod walked towards them, smiling. Selmana stepped behind Dernhil, hoping that she wouldn't catch the Hull's eye. She felt dull with terror, as if she were watching everything that happened through thick glass. She heard, in the back of her mind, Milana's silent command to her Bards: *Stop. Wait. Watch. He is not shielded.* Their arms fell, all together, and they stood silently, warily.

"He isn't here," someone said flatly. Selmana thought it was Kenran. "That's just a seeming."

"Yes," said Likod. "And, no. Your friend Dorn has opened a little place where I might stand. He has been very helpful." He sent out a sudden deafening blast of sorcery that made the Bards, all heavily shielded, sway where they stood. "I can hurt you," he said. "But you cannot injure me."

Malgorn jumped forward with a yell and thrust a deadly stroke at the Hull. Silver flames flickered on his sword. Likod made no move to evade or defend himself, and the blow should have hewn him in two; but it was as if the blade passed through water. When it touched Likod, the white fire died on Malgorn's weapon and he cried out. It fell from his grasp, and Malgorn wrung his hands, bending over in agony. Two other Bards, who had followed Malgorn, halted and stared in sudden doubt.

Likod had almost reached the group. He stopped in front of them, and made a swift gesture. All the Bards who were holding swords dropped them, a cold clatter of metal on the flagstones.

"Begone, foul slave of the Dark." Milana's voice rang coldly about the Hall, and with it a silver web of fire leapt from the floor, surrounding Likod. It burned with an intensity that made the Bards step back hastily. "You have no place here." The web brightened, throwing sharp shadows on the walls, distorted and bloated. Selmana knew at once that it was woven by both Milana and Enkir, and hope sparked in her breast. One by one, she heard other Bards entering the mindmeld, and the web grew so dazzling that she couldn't look at it. Its power made her gasp. Slowly, inch by inch, it forced Likod back, away from the group of Bards, and the web began to shrink inwards, as she had seen Dernhil and Cadvan use it against the shapeless shadow of Kansabur. Her hands clenched so hard her nails made red crescents in her palm.

Then Likod spoke and the bright web vanished, like a tiny flame stamped out by a boot. The Bards in the mindmeld reeled with the shock. A plume of darkness coiled out of Likod's mouth, splitting into tendrils that wound themselves about each Bard with a rapidity that defeated the eye.

"I told you that you couldn't injure me," said Likod. "You Bards, you should listen! But that was ever the weakness of the Light, in your arrogance, making your little Schools and prating of love and justice. You were ever deaf." He laughed softly, watching the horror of the Bards as they realized they couldn't move a finger: even through their mageshields, Likod had frozen them where they stood. "Have you run through all your tricks now? It's time you saw mine."

He crooked a finger, and as if he were a puppet, Dorn shakily stood, his eyes turned up, his head lolling. "Tell them, Dorn, great Bard of the Pilanel."

"There is no power but the Dark," said Dorn. He spoke thickly, as if his tongue wouldn't move properly in his mouth, and his voice was so hoarse it wasn't recognizable as his. "There is only the Dark in all the World. There is only the Dark in all the Circles. There is no other law."

"Well said," said Likod. "This is the new order, which all of you will obey."

Milana twisted, as if she struggled against strong cables that bound her, and then she spat on the floor. "*That* for your new order," she said, her eyes glittering. "It is no law of mine."

"It is now," said Likod. His eyes blazed with a sudden red light, and Milana's body jerked. "Do not think I couldn't throttle you from where I stand."

Cadvan felt the spell wrapped around his bones, a command that stilled his muscles and made his breath catch in his chest. He struggled against it until the sweat ran into his eyes, but it made no difference. His thoughts were slow and thick. The power that held them now was outside his Knowing: it slid around his will, and he could find no fulcrum from which to push back, no way of resisting it.

A hot despair rose in his chest. How was it possible that Likod held them so, a dozen Bards, all in their full power? He saw the same bafflement in Enkir, who stood before him, frozen like the rest of them, impotent against the gloating Hull. Enkir stared at Likod, his face frozen with contempt and loathing. He didn't seem at all afraid, but his eyes were cold with an icy hatred.

Likod lounged casually against a table. "Now, my friends," he said. "We come to the nub of it. I expect you will all enjoy helping me. Your magery has its uses, even in this new realm... And it will take all your power." He laughed again. "Mind you, I don't need to teach Cadvan this one. He can lead you."

Likod made a swift pass with his hands, and all the Bards turned to face him, even Dorn, whose head still rolled loosely on his shoulders. Slowly, like automatons, they lifted their arms, and then, as if in a stupor, against the will of their minds and bodies, they began to chant in chorus.

Cadvan felt the bitter, metallic taste of sorcery on his tongue. He tried to clamp shut his jaws until his resistance cramped his muscles in an intolerable agony, but still he kept speaking, the foul invocation issuing out of his mouth like vomit. His body would no longer obey him. He felt an awful shame, a humiliation that was deeper and more painful than any he had ever known: how could his magery, his most intimate power, be so forced?

Word by word, the spell wove itself in front of his eyes. A vortex of darkness began to open above the Bards, a whirlpool of energy that spun faster and faster as the chant continued. Inside it a shadow began to thicken and take shape, bit by bit coalescing into a form that Cadvan knew all too well. He couldn't stop it. None of them could stop it. Instead they poured their own power into it, giving it strength and vitality, feeling its pulse quicken in the shudder of their own blood, feeling its living structure knit together and flow into bone and sinew, finding a mortal shape for its immortal flesh. And then the whirlpool stilled and Kansabur stepped out under the great dome of the Singing Hall, suspended high in the air as if she trod solid ground. The sound of steel on steel rang cold and heavy in the silent Hall as she drew her black blade from its scabbard and thrust it high. And the Bone Queen threw back her head and howled with triumph.

XXXV

SELMANA was so frightened that her muscles didn't seem to belong to her; she thought at first that Likod had bewitched her as well. She watched helplessly as the Bards were turned to puppets before her eyes. She stood at the back of the group, hidden from Likod's direct gaze, her knees shaking, tears running unnoticed down her face. She knew what Likod planned to do; she could feel his intent in his every gesture.

She only understood that Likod's spell hadn't touched her when the other Bards began to mouth the summoning. She saw how they resisted, how their faces writhed against the will that drove them, how they gagged against the sorcery that filled their mouths. She wriggled her fingers and they obeyed her. She now dared not move in case Likod saw that she was outside his bewitchment. She wondered that he didn't sense her, outside the black meld that held the other Bards in its intolerable prison.

She knew that they were summoning Kansabur. She could smell her presence, toxic and alien, even before her shadow began to clot and grow in the vortex of sorcery. I could escape, she thought to herself. If she steps here, I could step elsewhere, and I would be safe…

Then she looked at Dernhil in front of her, his hands clenched at his sides, and she realized that even if she could, she wouldn't choose to escape. If Kansabur came, Pellinor would be laid waste. And then Annar would fall before the tyranny of the Dark. Where would she escape to? And yet how could she, all on her own, outface Likod and Kansabur?

Desperately she tried to gather her thoughts. Anghar. Surely, if she could step between the stars as a queen of the sky, the Elidhu had a power greater than Likod, stronger than the Bone Queen? Selmana shut her eyes and called, sending out all her desire, all her love, all her despair. But no answer came back, no slender girl with the power of stars in her hands. The spell droned on, gathering and weaving itself, until her ears were buzzing with the force of it. Selmana wanted to weep with anger. She was abandoned, alone before the might and malice of the Dark. She felt the Bone Queen's presence thickening in the room and her terror almost choked her. She would be seen. She would be taken.

When the Bone Queen stepped out above the Bards, it seemed to Selmana that the stone walls wavered, and her sight blurred as if everything solid had become swift currents of water, a tide that sought to drag her away. The anger in Selmana turned to fury: so Anghar thought only to rescue her, when she should be here, beside her, fighting to save Pellinor. She set her jaw, clutching the edge of a table until her knuckles were white and her nails broke against the wood, bracing every fibre of her being against the surge that broke around her. To her amazement, it worked: the Singing Hall focused again in her vision, as if a pool struck into ripples became gradually still and then clear. The force ebbed away. She could see Kansabur. But Kansabur had not seen her.

The Bone Queen stood impossibly on air, her black armour glinting in the Bard lamps, smooth and polished, like the armour of an ant or a beetle, spiked at shoulder and hip. Perhaps it wasn't iron or steel at all, but some metal Selmana knew nothing of. The helmed head turned slowly, surveying the Singing Hall, and then Kansabur slashed down with her sword, rending the air with a sound that tore through Selmana's ears. Somehow Selmana knew that the blade's keen edge cut through more than she could see, shearing through the invisible boundaries between the Circles. She felt it in the nerves of her teeth, in the void that opened in her stomach. The lamps in the Hall flickered and went out completely, leaving the chamber in dim shadow. The only light came from Likod and the Bone Queen, a pitiless radiance that streamed out of their bodies, but which illuminated nothing.

Gradually the light of sorcery died away, leaving its sour, metallic aftertaste staining the air. All that was left was a dreary, damaged reality, the beginning of the end of Pellinor. The Bards would be slaughtered, Selmana among them. The Singing Hall would be taken apart, stone by stone. The beauty of Pellinor would die, never to be seen again. Selmana saw it all in the arrogance of the Bone Queen, in that sweeping triumphal glance about the Hall, in the malice and unchallengeable power of her stance, and she wept silently, ignored and insignificant among the ensorcelled Bards.

The Bone Queen took off her knived helm, holding it lightly in her fingers as if it were a mere trinket, and turned her terrible gaze on Likod. For the first time, Selmana saw Kansabur's face. She almost cried out, but managed to stifle herself in time, biting her lip so it bled. Bones held no horrors for Selmana: she had seen human skulls, white and polished in the anatomy rooms of the healing house in Lirigon. They were simply the remains of someone who had once lived, and now was dead. She had sometimes admired the strange mineral beauty of skulls, the intricate curves and pits where skin and sinew had grown, and had wondered what thoughts and memories and desires they had once housed.

This was different. All that was left of Kansabur's face was a skull, but it was a living skull, with a yellow parchment of skin stretched over its bones. Thin strands of red hair were looped and knotted over her cranium in an elaborate fashion Selmana had seen in portraits from centuries before. Around the twisted sinews of her throat was a torc of polished white metal, set with a huge ruby that burned in the dim light. The worst was her eyes: they opened on an abyss that seemed to suck all light into it. They devoured everything they saw.

"Well done, slave," said Kansabur. It was the Speech, but not as Selmana knew it: she could understand the words, but they stabbed her, the light and truth of them extinguished, their power inverted. In their hour of triumph, the Hulls had released the sorcery that shielded them. The strange unreality of their flesh, that sense of them being both here and not here, had gone: they had both stepped wholly into the World, out of the place between the Circles that had protected them from the magery of some of the greatest Bards of Annar.

Likod brought his arms up in a gesture of supplication. "Welcome at last, my queen," he said. He seemed much smaller now, his stature diminished against the Bone Queen. Selmana thought she saw fear in his eyes. "This is merely the first of the offerings I make on your altar." He swept his arms out to indicate the Bards and snickered. "How easily they fell in the end, after all the vanities of their defiance. But perhaps you should show mercy: all of them lent their voices to your summoning."

"Mercy?" Kansabur laughed. "Yes, they shall be shown mercy. They deserve death, each one of them, but perhaps I will not give them what they deserve. They shall be shown how life may be an endless torment. They will be shown the shape of their pitiful souls."

"But first, they must set the seal and confirm this spell. Where is the young Bard of the Sight?" Likod crooked his finger and Milana tottered forward out of the group of Bards and stood before him. "I think you can tell us, lady of Pellinor. You will fetch her from where you have hidden her, and then you will draw your sword and spill her blood. Yours alone is the honour. And you will know, for the rest of your miserable life, that it was your hands that made the final binding and blessed the endless reign of the Black Queen."

Selmana realized, with a thrill of terror, that Likod had no idea that she was in the Singing Hall. How could he not know? She saw Milana's hands twitch. Her body was shaking in its chains of sorcery, as she struggled in vain against the spell that held her in thrall. Selmana looked at the other Bards, all of them, from Dernhil to Cadvan to Enkir, helpless and shamed in their ensorcelment, and the rage that lay underneath her fear erupted to the surface. Everything was already lost: she had nothing further to lose. She had no hope left, but perhaps she could injure the Hulls before she was killed. She drew in a harsh sob of breath, bracing herself, and loosed a bolt of magery at Kansabur, aiming at her terrible eyes. Then, so quickly that it was almost simultaneous, she set another at Likod.

They weren't very powerful attacks, but they took the Hulls wholly by surprise. Likod was knocked sideways, and the Bone Queen cried out and fell in a great sweep out of the air, landing heavily on the floor. Her sword, Thuruk, clattered onto the stones and skidded away from her hand. Selmana saw that this time the white fire had burned Likod: the side of his face was charred and white flame fastened on his clothes. The stink of burning hair floated through the hall.

Selmana's unexpected assault broke the ensorcellment: Nelac and Dernhil burst out of their bonds, letting fly a sheet of magefire that billowed from their arms and hit the Hulls and then the wall behind them, setting the hangings there in flames. Kansabur scrambled to her feet, screaming defiance, and threw out her left arm. An invisible force lifted six Pellinor Bards, including Dorn, and threw them with a sickening thump against the wall. Likod rose shakily to his feet, stunned. He stared at the Bards, his mouth open, all his arrogance shattered. Malgorn picked up his sword from the ground and ran towards him, murder in his eyes. Likod staggered aside as Malgorn swept down his weapon, and in his fury the Bard missed him. He leaped around to deal another stroke and halted in bafflement. Likod had vanished, stepping out of the Singing Hall as swiftly as he had stepped into it.

Cadvan ran to where the black blade of Thuruk had fallen and hefted it up. It was so heavy that he could scarcely lift it, but he brought it up high, his shoulders shaking with the effort, and back down like a club on Kansabur's unhelmed head, and split her skull.

There was no blood: instead, a transparent ichor spilled smoking across the flagstones. Impossibly, as Cadvan struggled to lift Thuruk again, Kansabur stood up, swaying. One of her eyes was knocked out of her skull and hung down over her cheekbone, and her mouth was torn and dribbling the clear fluid, but she screamed in the Black Speech, a bubbling shriek of rage. Cadvan slashed the heavy sword around again, using it like a scythe against her legs, and knocked her to the floor. Then, with the last of his strength, he swung it down on her neck. There was a loud crack, like the breaking of stone, and her head rolled away from her body. The scream was cut off, but its echo rang horribly about the Hall as if it had its own life, before it trailed into silence.

Cadvan leaned on the black sword, his face wet with sweat and the foul ichor of the Bone Queen, panting. "So you wished for a body," he said. "And this is what your body is. A shape for your death." He wiped his face and spat on the corpse and then flinched back in sudden alarm. It seemed to him that the headless ruin changed shape, and for a moment he feared that he had not killed Kansabur after all, that she would rise again in some new and terrible form. And then he saw that the Bone Queen's body, its ensorcellment of immortality broken by her own black blade, was crumbling into dust.

XXXVI

AFTER the defeat of the Bone Queen, Selmana's memories were a whirl of fragments. She remembered the wreckage of the Singing Hall, curls of smoke drifting in the air, tables broken and charred, a burning tapestry, and someone hauling open the door to let in the good daylight. She remembered the rain trickling down her neck as she walked to the guesthouse, her knees trembling so badly she had to be supported, although she couldn't remember who led her. She remembered people talking and shouting, a confusion of activity. She didn't remember lying down on her bed, although she woke later, undressed and warm between clean sheets, and cried all alone in her chamber for the mercy of a safe, comfortable bed.

Kansabur was dead. She could never be recalled: the spells she had woven into what remained of her human body, the sorcery of the Nameless One that granted her the deathlessness of a Hull, or the less ponderable power of the Shika, had been shattered. Nothing could call her back. A day later, or perhaps it was the day after that, Selmana ate privately with Nelac and Cadvan and Dernhil, and they spoke of what had happened. The first snows were falling over Pellinor, and Selmana looked out of the window and watched the flakes spiralling down, covering the hurts of the School with a silent, white blanket.

Few had escaped unscathed. Cadvan's face was burned where the Bone Queen's ichor had splattered onto his skin, and Nelac looked ill and old. Dernhil had a wound above his eye,

where a flying piece of glass from a broken window had cut
him. She knew she should be glad, for they had survived. Two
Bards had died in the Singing Hall, their necks broken when
Kansabur had flung them against the wall; Dorn was abed with
a sickness that Milana thought was driven into his blood by the
unknown spell that had brought Likod past the strongest wards
into the Singing Hall and protected him against the white fire of
the Bards of Pellinor. In the Fesse, five people had been killed
by wers, and three Bards, fighting their assault on the walls of
Pellinor, had suffered grievous wounds.

Yet it could have been so much worse. The other Bards
praised Selmana for her courage and wondered what had made
her immune to the dark spell that had defeated all the other
Bards. Dernhil joked that she must be some new kind of mage.
Nelac told her that when they returned to Lirigon, she would
no longer be a Minor Bard, that she would be instated into her
Name. Selmana smiled, but she felt nothing beyond relief that
at last the ordeal was over. They were gentle with her, seeing
her shock. Dernhil insisted that she eat, and she took some
morsels to please him, and tried to smile.

More than anything, she wanted to be alone. The weather
didn't permit her to walk about the streets of Pellinor, and so
she retreated to her bedchamber and sat by her window, looking out on to the courtyard. The snow swirled down outside,
growing heavier as the day darkened; she could barely see the
almond tree as it stretched up its bare arms. She felt heavy with
sadness. Why had Anghar not come in her need? Never had she
been in such need. There had been a promise, and the promise
was broken. The other Bards were right: she was mistaken to
love an Elidhu. They were not to be trusted.

Yet she had believed, in the first moment that she had seen
the wild girl, that she could trust her. She had felt this in every
part of her being. How could she have been so wrong? She had

thought that Anghar would help her, that she would save them all from the devouring eyes of Kansabur. But when Selmana had called, there had been no answer. Anghar had left her to face the might of Kansabur on her own. And yet, despite the bitterness of that betrayal, Selmana still longed to see her. She hated herself for her weakness.

Foolish. Did I not say I was with you?

Selmana jumped. The voice was as clear as if someone spoke by her shoulder, but there was no one in the room. It was Anghar. Her heart leaped with sudden unreasoning gladness.

"Is it you?" she said.

You should remember what I tell you, said the wild girl.

"Where are you?" Selmana looked about wildly. "Stay, please…"

I was with you, as I said.

A light bloomed in the almond tree, shining through the dim veils of snow as if the moon rested in its branches: and suddenly Selmana saw her, slim and supple among the naked branches, swinging her foot like a girl playing in midsummer. Snowflakes lodged in her hair like blossoms. Selmana gazed into Anghar's eyes and thought she understood at last why the Hull's spell hadn't touched her. She leaned her forehead against the cold glass.

"Did you save me after all?" she asked.

No, said the girl. *You saved yourself. You could have chosen otherwise and hidden in the desolate plains. That was always up to you. You chose to stay with those you love.*

"But I love you," said Selmana, her heart constricting painfully.

You chose those you love, said Anghar. *I salute your courage, dear one. I come to say farewell.*

"Don't leave me!" said Selmana. "Take me with you!"

You have a life that you must live, said the girl. *Your time will*

*come. Be joyful! This ill is broken, although others will rise. But they
are not your task.*

Anghar smiled and stretched out her hands, and then the
wind lifted a flurry of snow that hid the tree, and when it had
passed, the wild girl was gone. And Selmana hid her face in her
hands and wept again, but now there was no bitterness in her
sorrow.

The night after he killed the Bone Queen, Cadvan sat with
Dernhil in his chamber in the guesthouse, as Dernhil insisted
on tending his wounds. The ichor that had splashed on his face
burned like acid, but otherwise he had taken no major hurt. The
spell that had bound them to Likod's will had left them with
a shivering sickness, a nausea that Nelac assured them would
pass. Medhyl stayed it a little, and Iaradhel helped even more.

"What will you do, Cadvan?" asked Dernhil, as he carefully
dabbed a salve over the marks on Cadvan's face. "Surely now
no one will argue for your exile."

"I wouldn't be so sure," said Cadvan, screwing up his face
against the sting of the ointment. "There were some who were
glad to see me banished, whether I was guilty or no."

"Yet I expect Milana's judgement will prevail, even in
Lirigon." Dernhil sat back. "I think that will do," he said, examining his handiwork. "I doubt you'll scar."

"Handsome as ever, then." Cadvan grinned. "I'm not sure
what I will do. My heart longs for home. But…"

"But what?"

"Things will not be as they were. They can't be. And even if
Kansabur is utterly vanquished, the wrongs that she caused are
not undone. I have much to atone. I am not sure I have a home
any more."

Dernhil frowned and looked away. "I don't know how you
can say that," he said. "Beware of punishing yourself, Cadvan.

It does no good, and may do harm."

"I'm past punishing myself. I think that is just the truth." He glanced at Dernhil. "What will you do?"

"I am homesick. I miss Gent. I miss my chambers and my books. I can feel poetry whispering in me again. It's been a long time, and it reproaches me for my neglect." He smiled, and took Cadvan's hand. "I hope you will come and stay in Gent. You have never been there, no? Of all the Schools in Annar, even Pellinor, I think it is the most beautiful. Though I admit I am partial."

"I will," said Cadvan, smiling. "But for now, I feel a weariness heavy as any I have felt, and I am going to sleep until the sun is high in the sky. Or maybe longer than that. Rest well, my friend."

After Dernhil left, Cadvan prepared for bed. Despite his crushing exhaustion, he still felt wakeful. He dimmed the Bard lamp and lay on his back, studying the birds painted on the ceiling. It wasn't merely that the artist had been accurate in every detail, he thought; each bird had in its form a sense of motion, so they seemed vividly alive, as if they might at any moment fly off the ceiling and perch on his bedstead. He must ask Milana the name of the Maker who had painted the murals in the guesthouse. All of them were extraordinary…

He had almost dropped off to sleep when he heard someone say his name. He sat up, blinking; he had heard no one step into his room, and yet it sounded close.

Cadvan. His heart lurched: it was Ceredin. She stood by the bed, looking down on him, and in that instant it seemed that she was alive again, warm and solid beside him.

"Ceredin," he said. He reached out his arms to embrace her, but she stepped back. And then he saw that she was not quite substantial, that he could see the other side of the room dimly through her form.

Nay, my love, you cannot touch me. Her form blurred, and

Cadvan thought she would vanish, but it was tears filling his eyes. All the things he had wished he could say to Ceredin rushed into his mind at once, tangled together, and silenced him. He didn't know what to say.

I miss you so much, he said at last. *Every hour of every day I wish…*

Ceredin looked at him gravely. *You need say nothing,* she said. *There is nothing you have thought or said that I do not know. At last I can find the Gates, and I can leave. The World is mended. Do not be sad, my love. I am not sad.*

Cadvan stared at her, all his yearning naked in his face. *I avenged your death,* he said. *I'll spend my life trying to mend what I did. But I would give everything if only I could have you back.*

I will never come back, she said softly. *The river flows only one way, and I am almost at the sea. Farewell, my love. Remember me without bitterness. Remember how we loved. Be all the things that I could never be.*

Her form began to fade. Cadvan cried out Ceredin's name, bidding her stay, but even as he spoke she vanished. His chamber was empty, and he was alone with all the choices that had formed his life. And he saw, with an anguish that he couldn't contain, everything that would never happen: the futures that had died with Ceredin, the children they would never hold, the laughter and sorrow they would never share. And his love burned inside him, a pain beyond bearing, a living thing.

The four Bards stayed in Pellinor the whole winter, helping to heal the hurts in the School and the Fesse. Selmana slowly began to enter the life of Pellinor. She felt that she would never be whole again, but when she looked back, she remembered that winter as a time of great joy. There were long nights in the Singing Hall, which she loved for their laughter and fellowship, even though she had no ear for music, and there were new friends. She began her studies with Milana, and Nelac, who said that he was taking a well-earned holiday, helped her ransack the Pellinor library.

She knew she had changed over that dark autumn. She never spoke of Anghar to anyone, but she remembered her promise: *Your time will come.* She rediscovered her passion for Making, and put all her longing and desire into the things she created. Then the seasons turned, and the valley was loud with meltwater, and the orchards showed their fresh green.

All winter there had been embassies between Lirigon and Pellinor. Despite some opposition in Lirigon, Cadvan's exile was lifted, in recognition of his part in the struggle against the Bone Queen. Dernhil and Nelac were no longer outlawed; the Bards of Lirigon now seemed, if anything, embarrassed by their hasty judgement. And as the days lengthened, Dernhil, Cadvan and Nelac left Pellinor at last. Selmana stayed on, as she was midway through some studies. She would travel back to Lirigon in the summer for her Instatement. She missed her mother sorely, but she knew now that her home was Pellinor.

This time they took the Bard roads, and their travelling was easier. They were welcomed back to Lirigon as heroes, even Cadvan, although some Bards muttered against the lifting of the ban, and some would distrust him all his life. Dernhil stayed a few days and then rode on to Gent, extracting a promise from Cadvan that he would travel there before the year was over. Nelac returned to his chambers and pulled out the book he had been writing before Dernhil had arrived in Lirigon the previous spring. He had almost forgotten what it was about, and now he read it again, he thought he would be better to begin another book.

Despite the revocation of his exile, Cadvan found he was no longer at ease in Lirigon. He went to visit his father and found that he was ill, refusing all treatment. Nartan still looked askance at Cadvan, although he was now treated as a hero in the village.

"I don't think he will ever forgive me," Cadvan said to Juna, after a particularly difficult conversation.

She smiled sadly. "He is a proud man, and his pride in you was broken," she said. "And he is old, and set in his ways. I think he will never forgive you for being a Bard."

"There's nothing I can do about that," said Cadvan. He tended his father through his illness, despite his silences and rough ingratitude. Even on his deathbed, Nartan had no kind words for Cadvan. After Nartan's death, on Midsummer's Day, Cadvan took on the mantle of a Bard and said the rites, as his brothers and sisters had asked. When the funeral was over, the five siblings stood together on the edge of his grave in silence.

"He was a difficult father," said Ilios. He had come home with Ardur when he heard that Nartan was ill. "And not only to you, Cadvan."

"I know." Cadvan smiled at Ilios, the quick, brilliant smile that illuminated his face. "And I was a difficult son."

"And brother," said Ardur.

"Perhaps we're past all that now," said Tera. Her smile was like Cadvan's. "I can't but mourn him. He was a good man despite it all. But perhaps we can bury our bitterness with him."

Cadvan looked at the fresh grave, with the mild summer breeze blowing the flowers back and forth, and wondered if that was true. He felt that a black wind was howling across a desert inside him. He had longed for his father to forgive him, and now he never would. But he was grateful for the company of his siblings.

The next day he rode out of the Fesse, heading north. Two weeks later he came to Jouan. It was a windy day, with white clouds chasing each other across a pale blue sky, and the hawthorn flowers dropping their white petals to the ground. He passed a wagon trundling out of the village, loaded with shining black coal, and waved at the Jouains who recognized him as he rode between their houses. He took lodgement with Jonalan, stabling his horse, and walked on to the edge of the village.

When he reached Hal's house, she was pegging out her washing. He halted and watched as the sheets billowed out in the heavy gusts, waiting for her to finish her task. She stood back, propping the empty basket on her hip, and nodded to herself, as at a job well done. And then she turned around and saw him, and she dropped her basket and ran towards him, her face shining. Cadvan stretched out his arms, and she threw herself at him. He staggered back against her embrace.

He kissed her tangled hair and then held her at arm's length, studying her. "You've grown again," he said.

"You didn't die!" she said. "I'm so happy!"

Cadvan looked at the neatly scrubbed house with its beds of flowering herbs, the linen sheets dancing in the keen wind, the carved sign above the door that announced the presence of a healer. Hal had been busy since last he had been in Jouan. A dragonfly was darting among the flowers, its iridescent wings catching the light, and he caught his breath, struck by how beautiful Hal's home was, with the pale sunshine glowing on its roof.

No, he thought, I didn't die. Not yet. He realized, with surprise, that he was happy. Happiness wasn't what he had thought it was: it was like the dragonfly, a fragile, winged thing that arrived, unsought and unexpected, and graced the work of living. You couldn't hunt it down, you couldn't hold it. But sometimes, in a blessed moment, it was there.

It was good to be alive.

READ OTHER BOOKS BY

ALISON CROGGON

"This is a tale with passion, inspiring characters, an enchanting protagonist and vividly described landscapes … a great series of fantasy novels that will delight fans of Garth Nix and G P Taylor."

The Bookseller

THE SECOND BOOK OF
≍ PELLINOR ≍

The Gift

Maerad is an orphaned slave in a harsh settlement,
unaware that she possesses a powerful Gift: one that
marks her as a member of the School of Pellinor.
When she is rescued by Cadvan, a Bard of Lirigon,
her destiny begins to unfold. But before Maerad
can attain her true heritage, she and Cadvan must
embark on a treacherous journey and confront dark
forces of the most terrifying kind.

"Croggon's world is rich and passionate, brimming with archetypal motifs but freshly splendorous in its own right. Supremely satisfying."
Kirkus Reviews (starred review)

THE THIRD BOOK OF
⤐ P E L L I N O R ⤏

The
Riddle

Despite her tragic and bitter past, Maerad's powers
grow stronger by the day. Pursued by both the
Light and the Dark, she and her mentor, Cadvan
of Lirigon, seek the Riddle of the Treesong – the key
to restoring peace to their kingdom. As they travel
across the ravaged landscape, Maerad is drawn ever
closer to the Winterking, the author of her sorrows
and the strongest ally of the Nameless One –
the greatest tyrant of all.

"The action never flags in this compellingly readable fantasy tale. Riveting and intense, it is a spellbinding addition to a stellar fantasy series."
VOYA

THE FOURTH BOOK OF

≻ P E L L I N O R ≺

The Crow

The forces of the Nameless One grow ever stronger,
and in the frozen wastelands of the north Maerad
seeks to unravel the mysteries of the Treesong,
which may hold the key to peace. Meanwhile her
troubled and unhappy brother, Hem, is sent south
to Turbansk. But evil forces threaten to destroy the
city, and it becomes clear that Hem's own destiny is
linked to the Treesong more closely than he knows.
Aided by his pet crow, Irc, Hem spies on the child
armies of the Dark … with perilous consequences.

"Fans of the series will enjoy seeing the final stage of Maerad's transformation from a slave to her world's savior, and they will once again be drawn into this complex and gripping tale."

School Library Journal

THE FIFTH BOOK OF
✄ P E L L I N O R ✄

The · Singing

In a desperate fight against the Dark, Maerad
must solve the final Riddle of the Treesong in order
to defeat the Nameless One and restore peace to the
Seven Kingdoms. But Maerad only holds the key to
half the riddle; her long-lost brother, Hem, has the
other. As the Dark grows more powerful, Maerad
and her mentor, Cadvan of Lirigon, must find
Hem before it is too late. But will brother
and sister be reunited in time?

"Atmospheric throughout, and gripping till the end,
with a tension that never abates, *Black Spring*
is a lyrical masterpiece."
ArtsHub

BLACK SPRING

In the grim Northern Plateau, where vendetta holds sway and wizards enforce the code of blood and vengeance, corruption of minds and of nature go hand in hand. Lina has witch's powers but they cannot guard her against the enigmatic, brooding force of Damek, with whom she is besotted.

A wild, passionate story of possessive desire and destructive longing, inspired by the timeless classic *Wuthering Heights*.

"This is a lyrical and rewarding story... It raises complex issues about the rights of Indigenous peoples, environmental degradation and the impact of Western society in ways that are engaging and thought-provoking."
Books+Publishing

The
RIVER
and the
BOOK

Simbala is a Keeper, the latest in a long line of
women who can read the Book to find answers
to people's questions.

When developers begin to poison the River on
which Simbala's village relies, the Book predicts
change. But this does not come in the form they
expect; it is the sympathetic foreigner who comes
to stay who inflicts the greatest damage of all.